The Dragon's Hoard 3

Edited by Carol Hightshoe

WolfSinger Publications ♪ Brackettville, Texas

For permission requests, please contact WolfSinger Publications at
editor@wolfsingerpubs.com

Cover Art created by Carol Hightshoe
using Midjourney generative AI and stock images

ISBN 978-1-944637-63-7

Printed and bound in the United States of America

Table of Contents

The Crags of Anunaltia

Matt Hansen

Blinking against the cool wind, Mersaurus soared through the clear skies while the fire in his belly warmed his outstretched limbs. Trees passed so far below they looked like a single green blanket covering the lower slopes of the mountains.

Mersaurus turned a wide bank around the billowing white cloud that hung like an island in the blue sky. He danced amongst the shifting currents of the air, allowing them to pull him where they would.

Only the wind could command a dragon.

Laughing in the thralls of flight's passions, Mersaurus stoked the fire inside him into an inferno, belching it forth so it roared into the sky with a blinding flash. The flames, catastrophic to any puny mortal below, licked his magenta scales like a mother bathing her young.

The trees gave way to the golden human fields. Only a creature who couldn't survive the wild skies would care to tame the steady earth. But, Mersaurus had to admit, the herds dotting those fields were better tended and fatter than what he could find in the wilds.

Inverting so his stomach was warmed by the sun, Mersaurus arched his neck and fell into a screaming dive. He tucked in massive wings, extended his head out like a needle, and whistled towards the ground. It approached with a speed faster than any arrow fired by those weakling humans and the tools they so desperately needed to survive. As he fell below the heights of the mountain peaks surrounding the valley, Mersaurus opened his wings to their fullest length. They billowed with air, threatening to pull the joints from their sockets. Grunting against the strain, he began slowing, until he was a mere two trees height above one of the golden fields and a single plump morsel. Extending his claws, Mersaurus beat his massive wings down against the air rising from the warm earth and snatched a grown cow, brown and mottled, before it even raised its head in alarm. With a twist of his limbs, Mersaurus broke the beast's neck. He hurled it forward onto the ground where he could roast it well-done. Landing with a thump that billowed a cloud of dust around him, Mersaurus opened his mouth, igniting internal fires. Just as the flames wisped past his tongue he saw the wide-eyed horror of a human standing a dozen paces away. Fire exploded out of him in indifference, roasting the cow and human alike. Mouth watering at the pungent sweetness, Mersaurus sank his jaws into the cow's meat. The human, a field worker, would be too stringy and not even worth the effort of digesting its bones. As he gorged himself he heard a rustle in the trees. A second human, just as thin as the dead one, stared with mouth agape at Mersaurus. The dragon blew a ring of smoke from his nose, startling the man. The human scrambled away and once again indifferent, Mersaurus turned back to his meal, for no human should impede a dragon.

~*~

Alrock's joints ached as he ascended the last of the staircase's steps. The path behind him wound down the mountainside, each step more precarious than the last. Wheezing at the thin altitude, Alrock pulled down his frozen facewrap to get a deeper breath of the chilled air.

He looked up at the deep cave in the side of the mountain's peak. The patter of dripping water echoed out of its black depths to mingle with the cacophony of the howling wind. A rumble joined the discordance and in the yawning darkness a fire lit behind the razor teeth of Golkiakhan.

"Alrock, old friend." The dragon's voice burst from the cave, rattling Alrock further and threatening to bring him to his knees. A sheet of scree, dislodged by the concussion of sound, slid down the mountain toward the forested slopes far below. "Come out of the wind and rest your weary bones."

"Golkiakhan," Alrock said inclining his head before moving deeper into the cave. Tremor after tremor vibrated the ground with each of the beast's footsteps, so much so Alrock worried for the viability of his path home. The walls exploded with light, as the sun, shining through the cave mouth, reflected off Golkiakhan's golden scales. "How are your wings on this blustery autumn day?"

The dragon chuckled, the sound like the crashing of an avalanche. "Always the statesman, wizard. Be done with the false talk. What brings you to my mountain?"

Alrock sighed. "Mersaurus."

The puddle of melted snow, heated from proximity to the dragon, rippled as Golkiakhan shifted. "What has the pup done?"

Alrock hesitated. "He killed a village boy, one of the farm hands bringing in the late crop. I—" Alrock hesitated.

"Speak freely, wizard."

"I do not wish to presume to judge the affairs of dragons, but how was he not gifted Anunaltia's hoard of wisdom?"

The giant, golden dragon stayed silent, his deep chest rising and falling like a mighty bellows.

Continuing, Alrock said, "It's been many years since we've had a young dragon hatched. If Mersaurus—"

"Yes," Golkiakhan said. "It has been many years. And as a dying species, we forgot the lessons needed teaching." The dragon sighed, a sound like wind whistling through a valley. "Anunaltia's wisdom has become a hoard in truth, as we fear to part with even a morsel of the secret knowledge. Even to our own kind."

"This isn't the first death caused by his carelessness," Alrock said. "If Mersaurus does not learn his place, I'll be forced to face him in battle. Let our first meeting be one of knowledge and growth, not death and destruction. I cannot allow him to threaten my people, but neither do I wish to see the young one perish."

"I understand," Golkiakhan said. "So be it."

~*~

Gliding under a full moon, Mersaurus dozed with a full belly as the coolness of the autumn night rippled between the plates of his scales. The white light outlined the smallest nocturnal animals, those too small for him to even think about eating. Freedom coursed down his length to the tip of his tail, extended out behind him for steadiness.

Then something changed.

Sniffing, Mersaurus cringed at a sour taste befouling the wind. Sorcery, etched with needles that pierced his brain, screamed at him from a great distance. It slammed into him like a thunderclap and tugged like a leash. In contrast to the night's chill, a fire of rage grew in his belly. "Who dares attempt to control me," he screamed into the star-strewn sky.

But he could not balk at the pain.

It dragged at him like a mother bringing her kill back to the cave for the pups.

The insolence.

"How dare they," Mersaurus roared again through the pain as the magic grew in its insistence. Banking in the direction the invisible yoke told him to travel, Mersaurus pumped his wings. He climbed high above the earth and slipped into the great sky river, where the air was thin and only fought against him with the strength of a single pathetic sparrow. Fast and faster he flew until his chest heaved like rolling waves in a storm and the eastern horizon lightened with the first hints of dawn. His nostrils bled smoke and his throat burned hot with panting exhaustion when finally a range of mountains rose above the plain like the jagged teeth of a giant.

The Crags of Anunaltia, where was born, from the blood of the emerald goddess Anunaltia herself, magic and fire. And where she was enslaved and diminished to a mewling pup, after a thousand-year reign over the world, by the wizards of old.

Two figures stood at the highest peak.

In defiance of a similar fate, Mersaurus writhed against the magical bonds snaking out from the cloaked man standing next to Golkiakhan's golden bulk. Golkiakhan, the inspiration for the legends of great dragon treasure hoards, sparkled in the rising sun. Despite having always been enamored by the sunset purples and pinks of his own coloring, Mersaurus couldn't help but think himself dull and chalky next to such magnificence.

Mersaurus spat a stream of fire at the human sorcerer. It scorched the air with its intensity, searing the very ground until the acrid smoke of the dried mountain grasses choked him. As the air cleared, both human and golden dragon stood unharmed in the center of a ring of charred earth.

Still the magic pulled, until Mersaurus was forced to land, claws gouging the granite.

He looked at the human. "I am Mersaurus, unchallenged ruler of the sky. You dare attempt to break me like a plains mare?" He spat more fire in disgust. "I will not be brought to heel."

"Silence, pup," Golkiakhan growled.

Mersaurus smiled as the human covered his ears against the noise. "At least your voice still holds backbone enough to make this weakling flinch, relic."

Growling again, Golkiakhan took a step towards Mersaurus and the mountain quaked, rubble and ice tumbling down the side. The tremor ran through Mersaurus' feet and up to the base of his skull. "You've yet to learn anything of the order of things," the golden dragon said. "You seek to be a god but have yet to make wisdom your master."

"Wisdom? What need have I for that, when I can take what I want and go where I please? I am as I was birthed: a god of wings and fire and made to look up at no one."

Faster than lightning, Mersaurus struck out at the belligerent human, but his jaws snapped shut on only air. Turning at the sound of a boot scuffing the stone behind him, Mersaurus burned his belly fire and issued a jet of flames that melted the rock at the man's feet, yet parted around him like waves about an island.

A wizard.

The man's eyes, fathomless as a crevasse and blue like old ice, bore into Mersaurus, and an invisible weight flowed over him, bowing his head until his chin touched the ground. He looked up at the human, contempt settling over the scene like a red mist. Even as he struggled, the weight dragged him down until his legs collapsed and he sprawled on the cold stone like a snake, not even able to lift a wingtip.

Bellowing fire, he raged against the pressure but it was unrelenting.

Those eyes continued to pierce his soul.

And still the wizard did not speak.

The sun was high overhead when Mersaurus' spasms of defiance weakened him to the point where he could barely lift an eyelid.

Exhaling a rasping breath, Mersaurus slumped forward, the last of his strength spent.

The wizard finally spoke. "He is ready, old friend."

Golkiakhan stirred. "As you will, Alrock. Let's begin."

Mersaurus flinched as the golden dragon opened his maw and spewed forth a rainbow of fire, so hot Mersaurus could feel it even through his armored scales.

The world flashed white and then bled to gray before seeping into darkness. For the first time in his near decade of life, at least since his mother had tossed him from the cliff's edge to fend for himself, Mersaurus felt powerless.

A point of light broke through. Followed by another. And another, until a thousand thousand stars, more than Mersaurus could count in a hundred lifetimes, sparkled in the void. Titanic, swirling masses exploded into existence, and colors melded like Golkiakhan's fire. One such mass burst into life around Mersaurus. He marveled at the beauty of it, trembled at the unfathomable size, and quaked in the face of the void at its center, a void so dark light itself seemed to fall into the nothingness.

Suspended on an arm of that swirling galaxy, a small star shone pale beside the others, like a single field mouse on a vast prairie. As the spinning arm of the galaxy swept over him, he found himself captivated by that lonely star until he was caught in its orbit as surely as the magical net thrown over him by the wizard. Passing a ringed titan and an even more colossal sphere, upon which a red storm swirled, Mersaurus floated through the void until he came across an insignificant blue planet, a mere fraction of a fraction of the size of the others, that floated like a single blueberry inside a forest.

To his horror, he recognized the shape of its coasts and oceans. He passed over the shining stone cities of the humans, so impenetrable to their kind but as nothing to a dragon. He saw the lands of his birth and the mountains in which he'd made a home. Passing over them, along more valleys, and across more seas, he found himself looking down upon the Crags of Anunaltia. And there, a bright purple-pink speck, as nothing beside the monstrosities he'd just witnessed, lay Mersaurus. Paralyzed as he was by his insignificance compared to the swirling vortexes of the galaxies that played host to countless other worlds, fear wormed its way deep into his heart. Mersaurus scoffed. He'd thought himself a god. He drifted towards his body and was drawn back in until he peered at the wizard and the golden dragon through squinting eyes.

"Why?" he managed.

"To teach you our place," the wizard said.

"What place?" he asked, tears turning to vapor on the heat of his cheeks. "I am insignificant compared to the powers that govern this universe. I'm no more than the smallest insect. No more than the meat picked from my teeth."

"There is more," Golkiakhan said, his voice gentle as a cooing mother. "Are you ready for the deepest lore of our kind? The truest treasure in the hoards of all dragons?"

Hanging his head, Mersaurus said nothing. He wanted no more lessons, only to fly away and crawl into his cave, never to soar again, for he found no purpose in a life of such insignificance. Now he knew he was the same as the lesser creatures: blinded by ignorance.

A hand lay on his snout. Mersaurus opened an eye to see the deep blue ones of the wizard. The man whispered, "The point of this is not insignificance. It is a lesson of purpose and balance. Each atom in this universe has both. Observe once more."

Nothingness once again crashed in on Mersaurus. This time, instead of stars, a flare of electricity burst to life.

Another flashed in the distance, as fierce and sudden as a lightning strike. Even more sparked until a symphony of passion lit the sky. Here: a hope. There: a drive. A hunger. A love. A purpose. The patterns were limitless and just as vast as the swirling galaxies of the universe.

Mersaurus was drawn to these bursts of power. One in particular was brighter than the others. Within it, he felt pain and sorrow that eclipsed his mounting depression. It weighed him down with shattered and discarded dreams.

He didn't want it. As he had with the exhausting weight of the wizard's spells, Mersaurus railed against the approaching misery, but it entombed him with all the indifference of a grazing bison.

Squinting against the sunlight, Mersaurus felt a deep ache in his back and arms. He tried to unfurl his wings but realized, with shock, he didn't have any. Instead, he gazed down at his blistered brown fingers as they rested on a scythe in a golden field of wheat. Cows grazed on the other side of the fence and a light autumn's wind felt like daggers upon the sweat coursing down his brow.

Mersaurus was human.

He tried to drop the tool and scream, but like a hatchling riding on his mother's back to get used to the wind coursing over and under his still-wet wings, he was but a passenger in this vision. From the deep recesses of the human's mind, where a pillar of thought sparked to life, Mersaurus came up with the name Dirk.

~*~

Dirk removed his hat and wiped the sweat from his brow as the golden autumn sun beat down. His scythe, almost twice as long as he was tall, lay discarded in a pile of cut golden wheat. Back moaning as he arched it to relieve the stress of the day's labors, Dirk squinted up at the sun and the billowing white clouds drifting across an otherwise blue sky.

A rustle of grass announced someone approaching from behind.

Walking over with a cup of clear water from the Mithlin Well, Jep said, "Take a look at my sheaves over yonder." He waved a hand toward his scythe line. "Not a bundle outa place. And Margey thinks she can tie 'em tighter than me? Ain't no way." Jep shook his head as he handed Dirk the cup.

Smiling at Jep's rambling, Dirk thought about Margey and how her hair always smelled like wildflowers, even in the darkest days of winter. And whether Jep admitted it or not, Margey could beat down a tight bale.

"And just so's you know, Margey thinks the south fields hotter'n ours. Ain't no way."

South field, west field, they made no difference to Dirk. He'd scythe and pack stalks until he could afford a sheep or two. Then he and Margey could leave the valley for the highlands. They could graze a flock and raise children. He smiled wider, looking up at the sun again. Soon.

Rolling sore shoulders, he turned to Jep.

"You hear me, Dirk? I see you goin' all sloop-eyed and smilin'. You stop thinkin' 'bout that Margey and let—"

A shadow spread over the ground, darker than the Rotchild caves on a moonless night. Dirk didn't hear whatever it was Jep was still mumbling about Margey. Instead, he looked up, squinting against the bright afternoon, and felt a chill pound through the heat of his labors. A small figure flew across the sun, banking around a cloud to pass again. It was high up. Too high up to be a normal bird.

Jumping as a roar sounded and a fire lit the sky, loud enough for the standing wheat to shudder, Dirk said, "It's Mersaurus. Run." He grabbed Jep and pulled him along.

They ran without looking backward. Blood pounded in Dirk's head as he moved as fast as he could. But he'd never been much of a runner. Releasing Dirk's hand, Jep pulled ahead, making it to the trees. A loud thump struck the ground close to Dirk. He turned and tripped over the uneven soil. Chest heaving, he stared in horror at the bloodied cow, still crying out its pain, neck turned at a too-sharp angle and legs slumped uselessly on the ground. Standing above the cow, making it seem like a small pup next to a full-grown wolf, stood the magenta terror that was Mersaurus.

The dragon's yellowed teeth opened in a grin. A blazing cascade of golden flames issued from the dragon's maw and Dirk's throat tore at the violence of his own scream.

The whole world ignited and a searing pain coursed through every part of his being.

~*~

Mersaurus roared in pain, writhing and fighting against the magical bonds that still held him tight to the ground.

The pain faded.

He stopped.

The wizard's face sat like stone and with a wave of the man's hand Mersaurus once more was transported into the dark void. The synapses fired again, but in a simpler rhythm, a more primal one. And he was a sheep, grazing in the grass, oblivious to the whims of the world around him. But he still felt the need to feed and mate and run free. Until Dirk's knife crossed his throat and he once more was tossed back into reality.

Blinking against the continued rush of tears, Mersaurus begged, "No more."

But the wizard's hard stare didn't flinch and he was thrown back into a new vision. A blade of grass stood tall, soaking in the warm rays of the sunlight until a sheep's teeth snapped him in two.

And then a photon of light burst forth from the giant star, moving at a speed that warped reality until he was brought to a stop by a tiny blade of grass.

An electron jumped into an orbit and was halved by the release of a photon.

And the electron itself, not created but birthed from the colossal forces of the beginning of the universe, trembled with unrealized potential energy. Enough to destroy worlds.

He lived more lives than there were galaxies in the void. He lived more deaths. And each of them held something to learn of existence.

~*~

Mersaurus awoke to silence on the Crags of Anunaltia.

Only the wind sounded until, after a while, the wizard whispered, "All have their place. All have their purpose."

"We've forgotten how to share our knowledge," came the soft rumble of Golkiakhan's voice. "It is time we right this wrong."

As a response, Mersaurus spewed forth a jet of fire into the air. It showed blue as it burned his sorrow; for he finally understood the truth of the dragons' treasure.

~*~ * ~

Matt Hansen is a California beach bum turned fantasy aficionado, blending a love for surfing with a knack for spinning tales that'll make you laugh, cry, and maybe even believe in dragons. If he's not riding waves or hiking mountains, you can bet he's lost in a world where the only limit is Matt's imagination.

Dragon Tears

Jennifer M Roberts

I used to tell myself I could not be lonely if I was surrounded by books. The stacks of volumes that filled the library of my castle were my refuge, my shield from the world. They were the reason I didn't go bat-shit crazy in the silence. When my home felt empty or I missed the subtle sounds that indicate someone else is present, like the soft whiff of breath or the whisper of footsteps, I could flip through the pages of black and white print and hear the voices of old friends come alive in my head. I could be in places filled with life and energy, the opposite of the abandoned and crumbling castle I called home. I had moved in long after the humans left. They had taken all of the gold and valuables, but they left the library behind and I had added to the collection over the years.

My favorite spot was in the sunbeam that covered the entire west wing in the afternoon. The glass had fallen out of the giant windows years ago, and the sun made the stones a warm and comfortable bed. I liked to lie with my eyes, half-closed, skimming lazily over the words on the page. My scales practically glowed in the sun, the stony gray color absorbing the light and converting it to the energy that fueled the warm flames that lived in my belly.

It is a dangerous thing to be a dragon who loves books. One wrong breath, and I could destroy my entire collection. As a mother, I had had to be particularly careful when my daughter was young and learning to control her fire. Thankfully, we hadn't lost a single page.

As I turned the page, the sound of footsteps echoed down from the main hall. Drat. A perfect afternoon, ruined. Who was it going to be this time? A well-trained knight with polished armor and a steel sword, here to collect a pile of gold when he handed my head over to his king? A farm boy with a pitchfork and a stubborn determination to win the bet, or impress the girl, or fulfill whatever other stupid scheme had sent him up the mountain?

It didn't matter. Knight or peasant, young or old, well-trained or stupid, they were all the same. Tiny humans half my size who didn't stand a chance against my claws, teeth, and fire. Sometimes, I managed to scare them away. Sometimes, I left their unconscious bodies at the bottom of the mountain. On the worst days, I had to kill them.

I folded my wings across my back in order to fit through the narrow doorway to the great hall, then unfurled them to soar to the ceiling where I curled my tail around the old chandelier. The room was bare, no tapestries on the walls, no furniture, only lumps of gold and piles of books scattered across the floor. Sometimes, the humans who came would see the gold, take as much as they could carry, and leave.

Would today's intruder be that easy to get rid of?

Clinging to the stone ceiling, I waited. The soft echo of footsteps moved slowly, and I didn't hear the clanking of metal armor or the whispered, giggling tones of boys pumping themselves up to follow through on a dare. The great hall doors creaked slowly open, and a woman entered. She wore a simple dress instead of armor. A canvas sack hung over one shoulder, but she carried no weapons. Her eyes widened to take in the room, and a soft exclamation of wonder escaped her mouth. She traced a pattern on the mosaic floor, touched the carved flowers that decorated the columns supporting the vaulted ceiling. Not a single glance at the gold. Instead, she reached straight for one of my books.

I unfurled my wings with a snap. "What do you think you are doing?"

The woman choked on a scream, stepping backwards as she looked up, up, up.

"Oh shit, there really is a dragon here."

"Yes. This is a dragon's lair, and you just entered uninvited, without knocking." I smiled, a wide, slow smile that showed all of my teeth. Sometimes, it was enough to send the less stubborn ones running.

The woman swallowed hard and gripped the strap that ran across her shoulder, but she didn't reach into the bag for a weapon. "If you want people to knock, you shouldn't let the place look abandoned."

For a moment, we stared at each other in silence. I had no answer for her, too stunned by the fact she had answered me instead of charging with a pointed object.

"If you didn't know there was a dragon here, then why did you come?"

She gestured at the stacks that filled the room. "These. The books. This collection here is—"

"Mine." I cut her off with one sharp syllable and released my grip on the ceiling to land between her and my collection. The woman skittered backwards. "Did you come all this way to steal from me?" I hissed.

"No. No!"

Liar. She wasn't here for the gold, and there wasn't anything else in this castle worth taking. A jealous fire burned inside me. Flames tickle the back of my throat, begging to be let out.

"I just need one. Please—"

"You will not touch my books."

I charged forward, hot smoke spilling from my mouth, but one stray spark could be the end of my books. I reached out and wrapped my talons around her waist. The woman screamed and wriggled, making it difficult not to drop her. I marched her to the door and set her down on the path that led to the bottom of the mountain.

"Don't come back." I breathed a pillar of orange flame into the sky, a warning. When I looked down, the woman was gone.

~ * ~

I tried to go back to my book, but now everything about that golden afternoon had turned sour. The sun had moved and the stones were losing their comfortable warmth. Around me, the castle suddenly felt emptier than usual. I glared out the window at the stony mountain peaks, the sparse covering of grass the only hint it was summer, and pondered the idea of a human who had come here for books instead of a dragon's head.

Bang! Bang! Bang! Irritation crawled across my spine at the sound of knocking. She had come back. I looked at my wall of books, my only defense against the silent insanity that threatened to take hold of my mind every day of this solitary existence. She would not take a single one away from me. I had lost enough to humans already.

I slithered out a back door, winding my way around the castle to find the woman on the front step, pounding away at the door.

"Hello! Dragon, you have a visitor!" Her voice sounded friendly in a forced way I didn't trust.

"What are you doing?"

The woman jumped, turned, and squared her shoulders. "I'm knocking. You said—and I agree—it was very rude of me to walk into your home unannounced. I'm sorry. I thought we could start over. I'm Vera."

She held out her hand as if she wanted me to shake it. What kind of human climbs a mountain to look at books and then offers to shake hands with a dragon?

"Go away. I'm busy, and you can't have my books." I turned my back on her and whipped my tail around sharply in a way I knew she would have to move quickly to dodge.

She didn't get the message, and came tromping through the weeds after me. "I won't get in your way, I promise. You don't have to do anything at all. I just want—"

"I just want to read my books and be left in peace!" I spun around, baring my teeth. "What are you still doing here? Do you want to get eaten?"

I've never eaten a human. Most dragons don't, but humans believe otherwise.

Vera crossed her arms and stood her ground. "I don't think you're going to eat me. If you wanted to, you would have done it by now."

"Hmph."

"I didn't know dragons like books."

"There is a lot humans don't know about dragons. If you didn't come to be my dinner, then why are you here?"

"The *Journal of St. Iver*. You have the last existing copy."

She was right about that. It was a rare volume, filled with recipes for healing. I thought the humans had forgotten it existed. "Why would I let you have it?"

"I don't want to take it. I just need to see one page." The woman's voice grew softer as she spoke, as if she was holding back tears. This book was important to her, so important she was willing to stand up to a dragon.

"One page?" I repeated. "Why would I let you near it?"

"So I will go away and stop bothering you. You said you just want to be left in peace, but I won't stop coming back until I get what I came for. It will only take ten minutes to get the information I need." Vera smiled, as if showing her teeth was a way to get me to agree with her.

"You will never touch my books." I lifted myself into the sky, my wings pushing a gust of wind down strong enough to knock her off her feet. I circled, then dived. The woman yelped and ran away down the mountain. I watched her from the air until she reached the village tucked into the bottom of the hill.

~ * ~

I kept a close watch that night, because I expected Vera to return and try to sneak the book out of my library. By the time the morning sun pierced the clouds around the mountain, no one had come. I launched myself into the sky, letting the clear, cold air calm the nervous fire in my belly. I thought she was gone for good. Then I spotted her climbing the path toward my castle again.

How could I make this woman stop and leave me in peace? She claimed if I gave her what she wanted, she would leave me alone. But I knew better than to trust humans. There was an old scar on my back leg that still throbbed on cold nights from a peasant's pitch-fork. There was a hole through my favorite volume from a knight's spear.

There were dragon heads, horns, and claws in every king's castle, next to piles of dragon gold. It didn't matter what this woman wanted. She would not get it. Not from me.

When she reached the top of the mountain, I landed between her and my front door. Wings outstretched, I reared back on my hind legs and sucked the fire up from my belly, savoring the raw power of the heat before I shot an orange flame over her head.

"You are not welcome here! Leave!"

The woman dropped to the ground, covering her head with her hands.

"Oh, great dragon, I have brought you a gift to demonstrate my goodwill." Vera pulled a lumpy purse out of her rucksack and poured the gold coin out on the ground in front of me. It wasn't much, but it was more than a peasant should have, and I wondered what she had done to get it.

"Please, dragon, accept this gift and hear my petition."

For a moment, I was tempted. Gold isn't my thing, but she was so different from the other humans who had come here. I wanted to know why, but I knew better than to ask.

"I don't care about gold. Go away, human. Leave me in peace."

Vera stared down at the gold for a moment, her expression stiff. I thought she was finally going to pack up and leave, but instead she looked up at me again and said, "I can bind books."

I had many books that needed tending to, but with my claws, I could not do the delicate work. She must have seen my hesitation, because she smiled. "Consider it a trade. Let me look at the *Journal of St Iver*, and I will repair any book you want."

"No." I left her on the step, slamming the door behind me. I sat in the entryway and stared at the stacks of books there. What if the human was honest? What if she could really help me bind them?

No. It was a trick. It had to be.

A sound came from the other side of the door. My ears swiveled, listening. It was a series of ragged gasps; sobbing.

I turned and opened the door. Vera lay in the dirt, her knees drawn up to her chest, crying so hard the dust around her face had turned to mud. She sucked in a deep breath when she heard me approach, and rolled up to her knees.

"Please. Please." She clasped her hands together, as if she were praying. "I am not here to steal from you. I only need to see one page."

One page?

"Why?"

"My mother is dying. She has a plague. The symptoms are the same as the plague that nearly destroyed Cofetia nine hundred years ago. They say St. Iver discovered a cure, but because the plague never returned, no one remembered it. If I can find it in his journal—"

"Your mother sent you to a dragon's lair?" She was a selfish mother, if she had.

"No! We didn't know you were here."

"Would you have come if you had known?"

"Of course I would! Gemma is the best person in the world. She adopted me when I was six and nobody else wanted me, even though the entire village told her she was crazy. She is the only family I have. I only need to look at St. Iver's journal and make a copy of the cure. Please, dragon. It won't cost you anything to let me look."

A mother with a daughter who would do anything for her.

Even face a dragon. It touched me in a spot I thought I had shut down long ago, and the tear escaped my eye before I could stop it. The liquid gold pooled to form a fat, round drop that dried as it fell.

Vera stared at the solid lump of gold that was my tear. It rolled across the floor to a stop in the corner with several others just like it. Now she knew the secret of dragon gold. We don't steal it.

"Please, come in," I said. "I know exactly where St. Iver's journal is. You may copy any information you want."

Vera nodded; her lips pressed together as if she had a thousand questions but was too scared to ask any of them. Mutely, she followed me inside.

~ * ~

I let her in, but that didn't mean I trusted her. I hovered over her shoulder while she looked through St. Iver's journal, smoke curling out of my nostrils. Vera ignored me completely. She focused all her attention on the pages, touching the book with careful reverence, as if she respected the written word as much as I did. She read in silence, flipping through pages as quickly as their brittle state allowed.

I knew the moment she found what she was looking for. Vera let out a long breath and her head bent lower, her eyes eating up the words on the page. She pulled ink and paper from her bag and started copying. She worked in silence, but the silence was not the empty, aching kind I had come to know. It was full of small sounds; soft breathing, the scratch of pen on paper.

I knew it would not last, but I savored the sense of companionship and wished Vera had come here for a different reason. I would love to have a friend to talk to about my books.

A few minutes later, the silence changed. Vera drew in a sharp breath and her pen stilled. Tears dripped onto the page, threatening to ruin the paper. I pulled the book away, and Vera didn't stop me.

"What is it?"

It took a moment and several deep breaths before she answered. "It's too late. St. Iver insists the cure is useless after two weeks. I traveled five days to get here, and Gemma had already been sick for a week. By the time I get back to her, it will be too late."

Seven days of illness, five days of travel, and a day spent trying to persuade me. I didn't need to count my claws to do the math. Gemma would be beyond help by tomorrow morning.

"Do you know where to get the herbs you need?" I asked.

Vera nodded. "They are all common items. We already have them, we just don't normally use them together."

"Then we should leave. Your feet aren't fast enough, but my wings are."

Vera stared at me for a moment, as if uncertain she heard correctly. Then, with a gasp and a smile, she wrapped her arms around my claw in a grateful hug. We exited the castle and, tucking her copy of the recipe into her pocket, she settled herself in my paws. Her grip tightened as my wings pumped the air and we launched into the sky. Our trip was quiet except for one short exchange.

"I don't think I ever got your name."

"Dima."

She was the first human who had ever asked.

~ * ~

I should have left her there. I should have set Vera down at the edge of her village and soared back into the sky.

Vera's village sat tucked in the foothills, tiny cottages huddled together between mountains and plains. I landed behind the cover of the hill so no one would see me. As soon as we got close enough to ground, she jumped off my paw and took off running. I imagined her arrival. There would be an old woman in the bed who smiled at the sight of her. Vera would hug her tightly and set to work preparing St. Iver's recipe. Then she would wait, and after a while, the woman would be able to get out of her bed again, healed.

Would Vera come back to let me know St. Iver's cure had worked? If she did, I would invite her to visit my library again. Maybe, she would be willing to bind more books. I had enough gold to pay her.

Maybe, she would forget about me as soon as her mother was better.

If I did not wait, I would never know. I curled myself into a ball, tucking my tail and snout in like a cat. My stony scales made me look like a boulder to anyone who passed by, as long as they didn't come too close.

Two hours later, I looked up at the sound of approaching

footsteps. Vera smiled through the tears pouring down her face.

"She's getting better." Vera hugged my snout, pressing her face against mine. "Thank you. Thank you, Dima. You saved her. You saved the entire village. Everyone is going to get better."

"Everyone?" I repeated. Humans had done so much to me and my kind. I didn't want to help all of them, just the one.

"We have so much work to do!" Vera vibrated with excitement. "The plague came from the coast and is spreading North. It would take days to share the cure on horseback, but with you helping us—"

I stood up, pulling my wings tight to my sides. I had just walked into a trap made of words instead of metal.

"Did you trick me here so I would help you?"

Smoke curled around my nostrils and Vera stepped backwards. For the first time, she looked afraid.

"Trick you? No! Dima, you gave me back my mother. I want to thank you."

"Liar," I growled. "You said you want more from me."

Vera shook her head. "I didn't lie to you. I didn't know the plague had spread so much. There are people out there who need the information we have. Dima, you could save hundreds of lives and it will only take a few days." She touched my leg with her soft, warm hand, and smiled with hopeful eyes. "Then, I can come and look at your books. I will fix them all, if you want me to."

"No. I don't need your help, and I don't want your book binding. Go away and leave me alone." I lifted my wings to leave, but she still had a hold of my claw.

"Dima, I know you want help with your books, but we have to help the other villages first." She pulled on my claw, as if she could direct me like a horse.

"No." I shook my claw free of her grip.

"No?"

"No, I will not help you save anyone."

"You helped me save my mother."

I snorted. "What does that have to do with anything?"

"But they'll die without you." Vera's forehead furrowed, confused.

"Yes." I knew exactly what would happen to them. I had been alive during the last plague.

"How can you let them die? I don't understand. You're a good person."

I reached out and picked Vera up. Vera screamed as I launched, but I didn't let go until we returned home. I landed in the garden near seven mounds of dirt covered in vines.

Vera stumbled away from me, tripping and landing on one of the mounds. She looked down, taking in the size and shape of the formation, and then stepped carefully back.

"They're graves." Her voice sounded small.

"Yes. Seven humans who tried to kill me and failed." I looked across the garden, across the broken fountain and empty reflecting pool, to the eighth mound. Twice as big as the others, it was covered in golden teardrops

"Who is there?" Vera asked, her voice a hushed whisper. She walked toward the grave slowly, and knelt beside it, placing a hand on a golden teardrop. "This person was important to you."

I closed my eyes, and another golden tear rolled down my cheek to join the rest.

"She was my daughter. There were three of them that day, and she was only half-grown. I didn't hear them coming in time."

Vera placed her hand on my shoulder. "I am sorry."

"Do not tell me I have to help humans, Vera. They took everything from me."

She walked away without saying a word. When the sound of her footsteps faded I returned to the library, ready to curl up on my favorite stack of books and lose myself in sleep. Instead, I found Vera there, legs crossed, inspecting a cracked spine on an old leather -bound volume.

"What are you still doing here?" I asked. "Don't you need to find a way to spread your miracle cure?"

Vera looked up at me, her expression serious. "I made you a promise, and I intend to honor it. I told you I will bind a book for you. Any book you want."

"What about the cure? Don't you need to leave and spread the word?" I gestured out the window to the mountains beyond.

"I already gave the cure to the village. The people there will be able to pass it out just as quickly without my help. They don't need me for that." Vera looked down at the book in her hands and added, "But I will need some supplies."

She said it in an offhand way, as if it was an afterthought, but

I could see a scheme in her words.

"Let me guess. Your shopping list will require items from many different places. All of them far away. All of them filled with plague. You will deliver St. Iver's recipe while you do your shopping, and I will help you save your world even though I don't want to. It is a clever plan, but I won't let you trick me. I've done enough for you. Let me be."

I tucked my head under my wing and waited for the sound of her footsteps leaving, but she didn't move. For a moment, we sat in silence. What would she try next?

"I can see where you might think that," Vera said slowly. She came around to my side and put her hand on my neck. Her words were soft and gentle in my ear. "I have never lied to you, Dima, and I won't trick you. All I need is some supplies from my home. You're right, you don't owe us anything, but I do owe you. So let me repay my debt."

I lifted my head out of my wing and turned to look at her, a tiny human standing in the middle of my library. Was she really offering me a free gift?

"Thank you, Vera," I said, using her name for the first time.

~ * ~

I flew her back to her village to collect supplies and explain to her mother. Then I brought Vera back to my library, and she immediately started work. I handed over my favorite collection of poems; half the pages were falling out and the cover held on by two threads. I sat in the sun, watching anxiously as her tiny hands carefully pulled the pages apart, applied glue, and put them back together again.

There was no knocking when they arrived, only the scrape of the door, the clanking of armor, and the pounding of feet as they ran through the halls. I growled and reared up on my hind legs, throwing my wings wide in a fighting stance as they smashed through the library door. Vera scrambled to her feet, clutching a book in one hand, spilling glue as she stumbled backwards.

"What's happening?"

Three dozen men in armor with spears, swords, and crossbows circled the room, surrounding me with sharp points from all sides.

"You're safe now, ma'am. Come with me." A soldier held out his hand to Vera and pulled her behind the line of humans.

"Safe? No, no, I've always been safe." Vera pushed the soldier away. "This dragon is my friend. She helped me, she helped all of us! We have a cure for the plague because of her."

"Yes. I know." Another man came to the library door, dressed in armor flecked with gold that was more for show than function. He wore a crown on his head and a determined look on his face. He smiled at Vera. "Everyone is talking about the girl who flew a dragon home with a miracle cure from an ancient library. There is important information in these books, and we are here to take it."

"You have what you need!" Vera glared at the king with the same stubborn look she had used on me. "You have St. Iver's formula, you can cure the plague. Go away and leave us in peace."

The king shook his head and gestured at the books around him. "Yes, we have the cure, and it came from this library. What other important knowledge is hiding in this room that we don't know about? It's time to find out."

"Then why didn't you knock and ask politely if you could borrow the books?" Vera crossed her arms as if scolding a child. The king laughed.

"Ask? These books don't belong to the animal. They belong to me and the kingdom."

Smoke curled around my snout and flames danced over my tongue. The fire in my belly burned hot, fueled by rage, and I could not contain it for long.

"No, human, they belong to me," I growled as I reared back on my hind legs. Several soldiers stepped backwards. "Vera, you should leave now."

"No!" Vera cried, but it was too late. She could not save them.

I opened my mouth and took aim, not at a soldier, but at the nearest pile of books. Flames poured over my library and the books began to smoke and crackle. Flames danced on the covers and devoured the pages, filling the room with smoke and ash. The soldiers screamed and ran back the way they had come, scrambling to get out of the door and get their king to safety. They took Vera with them. I made sure she was out before I launched myself out the window and into the sky. The king shouted at his soldiers to get their arrows ready, but I was too fast for them. I climbed above the clouds, where they couldn't reach me.

~ * ~

The sky has always been a dragon's only refuge from humans, but I could not fly forever. I had to come to ground again. It would be smart to go to another mountain. To leave the ashes of the burned castle and everything it had contained behind. To let the bones of my daughter rest alone in peace.

But I could not say good-bye to my home and my collection so easily. I waited until the soldiers and their king left the mountain, and landed softly among the ash. Vera waited in the library, this time surrounded by the burned husks of my books. The ash swirled around her like dark rain in the wind kicked up by my wings, throwing up the scent of scorched paper and leather.

"Why?" Vera asked, her voice choked with tears.

Why would I destroy the knowledge that could have done so much to help humans?

"I didn't want them to have my treasure."

Vera shook her head." No. I mean, why did you help me? Humans have been horrible to you."

I shrugged, not quite sure how to answer. It was a question I had been asking myself for a while. Finally I said, "You didn't try to steal from me. You could have snuck in while I was sleeping, but you came to the door and knocked." I paused, then asked, "Why didn't you just take what you wanted?"

"I'm not a thief," Vera said.

I looked out at my burned library. It had taken centuries to collect those volumes. They represented all of the joy left in my life, and now they were gone.

"What are you going to do now?" Vera asked. "Where will you go?"

"Why should I go?" I asked. "Wherever I live, the humans there will find me sooner or later, and then they will try to kill me. Whether I stay in my castle and mind my own business, whether I come out and try to help them. It doesn't matter, humans will not let me have peace."

I looked down at Vera. She was one of them, but different in every way. "What do you think I should do?"

Vera's eyes traveled over the blackened walls and ruined books. They landed on a helmet, its shiny surface dulled by a coat of ash.

She picked it up, contemplating the empty space where the face should be as if she were looking into the face of all humanity.

"I don't know." Vera let the helmet fall to the ground. It rolled away, empty and useless. "I don't think there is anyone who can answer your question. I've seen people try to force other people to change, and it always ends ugly. I've seen people bend over backwards to be kind, and still be abused."

"Then I will collect more books and rebuild my home, until the humans find me again." There wasn't anything else I could do. I looked up at the scorched stone walls and sighed. I was not ready for this place to be empty again. Vera's presence had made me realize how lonely I had been, even with my books, and now they were gone too.

"This was the only one I could save." Vera reached down and pulled a thick volume out from under her skirt. "I still had it in my hands when—the fire—I think some of the pages are ruined."

It was the book Vera had been binding. The front page dangled, almost ripped in half. I took the book and examined it closely. The weight felt familiar in my paw.

"It is fine. All of the important parts are here."

"I didn't know they would come after you, or I would never have told Gemma how I got St. Iver's journal," Vera said. "I am sorry."

Three words I never thought I would hear from a human.

"I know you didn't mean for this to happen." There wasn't any anger left in me, not toward Vera.

"Could I help you find more books?" Vera asked. "It would be nice to be able to talk to someone who appreciates a good book. I promise I will be careful. I won't tell anyone your secret."

"You want to help me?"

She nodded. "Yes."

"You want to talk about books?"

"Yes. I would like to help rebuild your collection. If you want me to." She looked down nervously.

I brushed my wing against Vera's back, careful to be gentle. It was as close as I could get to a hug. My library would not be silent anymore. A tear formed in my eye, and Vera reached out to catch it. This one was not yellow but pure white gold. A tear of joy. Vera set it gently in the ash and waited for my answer.

"I would like that," I said. "I would like that very much."

~ * ~ * ~

Jennifer M Roberts earned her BA in History but prefers to dream of how things might have been rather than focusing on how things really were. She hails from the Midwest and enjoys cooking, contra dancing, and historical re-enactment.

You can learn more at www.jmroberts.com.

The Last Guardian

Ted Pennella

"Welcome aboard, Raqim El Idrissi," a red-scaled lizard-looking man said as a tall, dark, almost black-skinned young man in a generic citysuit stepped onto the small shuttle. "I'm Teju Jagua, the controlling artificial for the cargo ship, *The Dragon's Fruit*, which you've signed onto as cargo handler. You can just call me Teju, young man."

"Young man," Raqim said chuckling. "I haven't heard that phrase in a long time, old lizard."

"Lizard?" Teju quirked an eye with a low growl entering his voice. "Don't you know what a dragon looks like?"

"According to which human culture?" Raqim smirked while pushing his dozens of long, thin braids back over his shoulders. "I've a horrible memory and the Hive destroyed my family's library, which included a large collection of various cultures' stories about dragons. Hope I didn't offend you."

"Don't get me started on the Hive," Teju said with a soft snarl as Raqim settled into the nearest of the four chairs in the shuttle behind the shuttle's control console. The door closed with the locks clicking into place. "You're the only passenger today, Raqim, so sit up front with me. The captain was quite impressed with both your application and the survival of your family during the Hive's occupation of the Sol System."

"I'm the only survivor, Teju," Raqim said, following the artificial to the front of the shuttle. "When I die, the last of a very long bloodline vanishes from the universe. My failure scarred the Earth. Scars which are visible from orbit."

Teju gazed at Raqim for a long time, tapping his tail on the floor while keeping silent. When the console beeped, followed by voices announcing permission to detach the shuttle's moorings, Teju turned to get the shuttle moving. Teju finally spoke after leaving *Terra Prima*.

"Will you be okay leaving Earth, honored one?" Teju spoke softly without looking at Raqim.

"Honored one?" Raqim reached out toward Teju but stopped short of touching the artificial. He knew what the artificial did was for show, since Teju controlled both the shuttle and the main ship without needing a secondary body. "What honor is there in failure? How can anyone see me as honorable? I'm no one and have nothing."

"You are a dragon, Raqim," Teju said, glancing at him before turning back as though piloting. "My sensors can detect the power your body uses to make you look human. A power which humans are just now discovering. And as for honor, you defended all life on Earth and in this system. You didn't run away or hide. We ship artificials talk, Raqim. Talk to each other and to station and planetary artificials. Your name is whispered with reverence, the story of how you protected Earth's planetary artificial by yourself, refusing to let the first real artificial to ever exist just die. I will grieve with you over losing your family, but I think all humanity, without knowing you're a dragon, will call you family for what you did. It led to the armada which helped drive the Hive out of the system, even if it took humanity nearly four decades to assemble it."

Unsure what to say, let alone think, after what Teju said, Raqim stared at the oddly shaped ship they approached. He could see the basic shape was a giant triangle with an oval, almost egg-shaped form attached to one corner while the other two corners had wing-like forms added. The spherical engines, which allowed interstellar travel, helped create the ship's underside along with the wing sections attached on the opposite side of the ship. It all gave the behemoth a very Eurocentric draconic appearance.

Raqim sighed, wondering if telling Teju the truth of why he was here would be of any help. After his argument with ConRad, the planetary artificial of Earth, he needed to at least talk to someone besides himself. "My job wasn't to protect Earth's planetary artificial, Teju. After being essentially disowned by my bloodline's High Council for wanting to live outside of northern Africa, I got pulled in two directions when the Hive attacked. I chose the being I loved. Because of my selfishness nothing remains of my bloodline. An entire race of dragons will vanish when I die."

"You're alive, so your bloodline hasn't vanished yet," Teju said softly. "Have children, teach them what they need to know as members of your bloodline."

"Amongst dragons, bloodlines pass from mother to daughter,"

Raqim said, taking a deep breath to quell a rising sob. "Any children I have will never be—"

"What's more important, Raqim?" Teju jerked his head about to glare at him. "Letting the history of your bloodline be forgotten? Or having children and grandchildren to pass on the memories which now reside only in your head? Forget what you see as failures to make your family happy while alive. Instead, try to focus on what would make the spirits of your family, your bloodline, proud of you."

"Easy for you say, Teju," Raqim whispered laying his head back and closing his eyes. "You haven't spent the two millennia of your life failing to prove yourself to your family. Being rejected to take up the mantle of my grandfather and father's work. Unable to bring them back to life, not even one, because I'd commit a fundamental violation of being a Deir Edrissi dragon."

"Running away from Earth won't leave your pain behind, Raqim." Teju watched their approach to the ship. "I learned that the hard way. You need to figure out how you can accept the loss, learn to live with the pain, and find something you think will honor your people's memory."

"I didn't find any such answers on Earth, Teju," Raqim said softly, rubbing at the tears escaping his closed eyes. "Hopefully, I can find a reason to stay alive out amongst the stars."

~ * ~

"Raqim, report to Cargo Bay Three for unloading duty." A short, stocky man walked into the crew lounge with his buzz cut not hiding how grey and thin his hair was. "The captain wants the newbie to empty the cargo once we've made stationary orbit with *Gorgo's Maw* here in the Deir System. Expect a lot of grunt work between the ship and station."

"Sure thing, Angus," Raqim said without vacating the hammock where he struggled to achieve calm.

"Now, newbie," Angus said snarling. "We dock shortly, and you barely know your way around this ship."

"Cargo Bay Three's primary ship-side entry is four levels below us and roughly three-quarters of a kilometer away, based on the most efficient path I've been able to identify," Raqim said with his eyes closed and breathing steady. The dreams during his last sleep cycle had been horrible versions of the Hive's bombardment of

Earth nearly a century ago. He'd been living with ConRad, who had been his lover, when the Hive attacked. Most people saw him merely as the planetary guardian's caretaker. When he could finally reach north Africa, he'd only found bones amidst the shattered remains of the mountains. The rage and grief he'd plunged into led to him committing sins for which he'll never find atonement.

"Then get your lazy ass started, Raqim," Angus said from right beside the hammock. "If you get there after the captain, you'll get stationside unloading."

"Good advice, Angus," Raqim said, patting the man's face before opening his eyes. "You are rather old for stationside unloading."

As the others in the lounge burst out laughing, Angus turned red. Whether embarrassed or angry wasn't entirely clear. Raqim got up and motioned to the hammock grinning. "Get some rest, old man. I warmed it for your frail bones."

Raqim darted away from Angus, who swung a fist at him. Heading to the cargo bay, Raqim thought about what he'd be moving from the ship to the station. Large shipping containers filled Bay Three with only minimal access aisles. Seeing the bay during his ship's tour that first day, Teju had told the truth about having bays where he'd be able to revert to his true form.

A short time later, Raqim stepped off the lift to find Teju waiting for him. Smiling, Raqim said, "I do remember how to get to Cargo Bay Three, Teju. Assuming you're worried I don't remember your tour."

"I'm more worried about how you slept last night, Raqim," Teju said softly, falling in step with Raqim. "Your power levels surged sharply at one point, making me afraid you'd lose control in your sleep. Even now, your levels are unsteady compared to yesterday."

"Nightmares," Raqim said softly, choosing his words carefully. "Twisted flashbacks to losing everything due to the Hive's invasion is one way to describe them. I have safeguard spells woven around me, which also interface with my shipsuit. In a limited manner, mind you, but enough to wake me several times during the night."

"Magic?" Teju chuckled as he nudged Raqim with an elbow. "Let me guess, big guy. Any technology advanced enough will resemble magic to those ignorant of how it works. Right?"

"A great excuse to not explain what I can't talk about," Raqim said laughing. "I need to remember that."

"Well, not to worry you or anything," Teju said, the humor vanishing, "but you're going with the captain to start the unloading stationside."

"Because I'm the newbie, per Angus," Raqim said nodding.

"Because the captain insisted on only you and her," Teju said, pulling Raqim to a stop. "We deliver to the Deir System out here at the edge of Rigellus Imperium space on a regular basis. *Gorgo's Maw* is a habitat station orbiting an uninhabitable planet. Most often when we arrive and unload, it's exclusively the elderly, mothers, and children present. The children range in age from newborn to mid-teens. The issue, however, is the rise in piracy due to the cost in ships to all stellar governments by the unified fleet which drove the Hive out of the Sol System. Not just here, but in all outskirt systems."

"So, we empty and get out of the system before the pirates know how much we've delivered?" Raqim frowned at Teju, not liking what he was hearing.

"If the pirates are limited to a single ship," Teju said, a clawed hand gripping Raqim's shoulder, "we can often drive them away or even destroy them."

"But this time?" Raqim dreaded hearing the answer.

"Five ships with one nearly as large me," Teju said as footsteps echoed down the corridor from behind the pair. "Given how unsteady your power levels were last night, I wanted to make sure you knew we may be in a battle very soon. Not what I wanted on your first day doing real work for us."

Raqim took a deep breath and released it slowly. He could almost hear his heart pounding inside his chest. "The station has defense systems, I hope."

"Old and not much better than a pile of dung is how I'd describe it," a woman said approaching Raqim and Teju. She appeared to be fifty years old, in good shape with a very alluring figure. Not quite reaching six feet tall, she had blonde hair streaked with blue and green pulled behind her head in a bun. Her very pale, almost white skin stood out as nearly unnatural for a human. "Nice to finally meet you, Raqim El Idrissi. I'm Edwina Connick, captain of *The Dragon's Fruit*."

Raqim's eyes widened at the unmistakable dragon power wrapping this woman. Her white skin would be a reflection of her scales when in dragon form, just as his dark, almost black, skin reflected his own black scales. He didn't know how old she was, but he felt certain she was older than his two millennia.

"An honor to meet you, captain," Raqim said, struggling to calm and focus his mind on remaining human.

The captain's eyes widened for a moment, erasing the smirk she'd worn. Stopping a yard or so from him, Edwina bowed from the waist until her upper body was parallel to the deck. "The honor is mine and you are the honored one."

"There is no—" Raqim said, his voice rough from barely suppressing the surge of grief and his nightmares.

"Every bloodline experienced your loss when the images of the bombardment of Earth reached us, brother," Edwina said, gripping Raqim's face with both hands. "We cried, knowing highly respected and beloved dragons lived where those bastards attacked. How many survived, Raqim? More than just you, surely."

"None," Raqim whispered.

Edwina's eyes widened in horror, glistening with unshed tears. Pulling Raqim into a hug, Edwina whispered, "Well then, from now on, you are my and every dragon bloodline's brother. When we get Bay Three empty and we're again on our way, you and I will revert to our true selves and reminisce."

"He's barely holding his human form, Captain," Teju said, with his worry audible. "Please wrestle yourselves back into control. We've got a hundred thousand tons of supplies to unload."

"Right." Edwina pulled back from Raqim. She grabbed him by the arm and pulled him in the direction of the cargo bay. "Raqim, you and I will go to the station and set up the transfer beams. We need to be quick, or the pirates will start snatching the cargo."

"Does the station not have defense systems?" Raqim wiped at his face, thinking about the unloading work to help him focus. "Or a controlling artificial, at least?"

"Don't know," Edwina said furrowing her brow. "I've been delivering cargo to here for close to twenty years and have never seen nor spoken to a controlling artificial."

"Something happened in the past, Raqim," Teju said, following the pair of dragons. "He keeps the station operational, but that's about it. You told me about helping maintain and protect the cores for Earth's planetary guardian. Maybe if you spoke to the station's artificial about what it was like dealing with a planetary artificial, you can draw them back out."

"Let's get over there first," Edwina said upon reaching the door to Cargo Bay Three. "Raqim, we'll each ride a cargo ferry over to the station's cargo dock. Once we get those set up and cargo transferring, you can try and draw out the station's artificial."

The door opened to a huge space packed full of forty- by ten-by ten-foot cargo pods. Easily a hundred feet tall and three hundred wide, the bay's depth seem to go on forever. A narrow aisle stretched down the length of the bay, with lights clicking on high above. Teju pulled out pairs of gloves as four sections of the floor rose up.

"You don't control the ferry you're riding," Teju said as Edwina and Raqim's suits activated their personal protection fields. "Your ferry will keep you onboard, so either stand or crouch. A second ferry will follow each of you. Don't change your shape, please. The captain can tell you a story of what happens and how close to dying she came."

"And the fraidy cat refuses to let me try with four ferries, one per foot," Edwina said laughing. "Crouching is the best for your first time, brother."

Soon, Edwina and Raqim flew down the depth of the bay. As the far wall grew in size, it slowly opened. The soft glow of a force field keeping the air inside the bay could be seen just before the pair zipped through it. Crouching on the platform, Raqim stared at a mushroom-shaped station with a good four dozen or more levels in the cap and another six dozen levels in the stem. Seeing the odd shape brought to mind his first time going to the Great Vault of Stories. His grandfather guided the way deep into a cavern until they stopped in a dark, dank, shadowed part of the cavern. In that small, shadowed area grew dozens upon dozens of mushrooms. Tiny little things for the most part. What his grandfather said stayed with him.

"Life finds a way no matter where you go, boy," Grandfather said chuckling. "Much like your curiosity and desire to learn as well as experience, there will always be some obstacle to what any living thing can do or go. Like the first mushroom down here had to have really fought to find this patch of dirt, so too does life find a way to grow and spread. Should you find your goal unreachable the way you've been going, then look around and you'll likely find a new path. It might be rough at first but keep working at it and you'll succeed.

Teju announcing their distance from the station drew Raqim

out of his memory. They approached an area near the bottom of the cap which slowly opened. Just before they passed through another force field keeping the air inside the station, Raqim noted a handful of people entering the far end of a space at least as big as the ship's Cargo Bay Three. The center person was an elderly woman leaning heavily on a cane. The other four appeared to be no older than sixteen years old.

"Welcome back to *Gorgo's Maw*, Captain Connick," the old woman said once Edwina and Raqim stood close to the group. "Hopefully we'll be able to get most of our supplies before the pirates reach you."

Raqim nodded to the station residents before turning and moving the platforms they had brought to anchor spots. Having spent decades on a cargo ship centuries ago, Raqim moved through the paces of verifying the cargo ferries had connected properly and the traction beams connected to the ship. Watching and shifting the cargo bins into an orderly and efficient arrangement for the station was of paramount importance. Unlike on the ship, the station needed to be able to easily access each and every one of the containers. Getting the pattern established took focus, which led him to using his draconic power to position the containers, which he masked as power from his suit.

"You've done this before, Raqim," Edwina said when Raqim took a break to see if the pattern had taken hold. "I figured I'd have to teach you how to do all of this."

"I couldn't think of a way to say I spent decades doing this a long time ago, Captain," Raqim said chuckling, but never taking his eyes off the containers. "It's nice the tech and methods haven't changed much since my last bout of star hopping."

"Daddy!" A voice wailed out, the word echoing about the cavernous dock.

Looking around, Raqim found the four teens, who worked at logging containers under the command of the elderly woman, searching for the voice's source. He saw no one else before a flash of light slammed into him. Stumbling forward, Raqim fell to the deck as arms hugged him tight. The wailing filled his ears as a face pressed against his back.

"I didn't mean to fail you, daddy," the male voice said between gut wrenching sobs. "Please don't reject me again. I'll do anything you want."

For a moment, Raqim again stood before his father to say what became his last goodbye. The arguing over his choices, his wanting to be with someone not a dragon, and his need to be a part of ConRad's story had driven him and his family apart. Unlike his grandfather, who had been one of many Deir Edrissi dragons who'd journeyed out with humans into space, he wouldn't be creating artificial intelligences, just ensuring his love's crystalline memory cubes stayed healthy and every part of his love worked properly. The bloodline wanted to step back from what many of them saw as another bit of hubris by the bloodline. So many feared a repeat of the last time sixty-five million years ago. The centuries of war between natural and artificial life, they had roared at him, resulted from the hubris of dragons more than humans. His leaving Africa and the Atlas Mountains over a century ago had let him survive the Hive's attack on Earth.

"Getting off my crewman would be a good start, sir," Edwina said with a sharp tone.

"It's fine, captain," Raqim said grief twisting in his chest and threatening to break his control over his form. He swore to himself he'd not reject this child of his bloodline like he had been rejected. "You're the artificial inhabiting this station, right? Tell me your name, my child."

The person who had knocked him down released him, sobbing the entire time. "Gordon, father. It's been so long since you visited me, but not hearing from you and the reports of the Hive driving out humans from the home world. I feared you'd been killed. What wrong did I do to keep you from talking to me? Please tell me and I'll—"

"You did nothing wrong, Gordon," Raqim said rolling into a sitting position. He stared sadly at the middle-aged male with caucasian skin and black hair graying at the temples kneeling before him. "I am the last and now only member of the bloodline from which your father came. The Hive killed your father and every other…"

"No." Gordon covered his mouth when Raqim couldn't keep speaking. Closing his eyes, Gordon nodded slightly, as though making a decision. Standing, the station's controlling artificial opened his blue eyes, which glowed golden for moment, and held a hand out to Raqim. "Then you are now my father."

Loud clanks and whirring noises filled the docking bay as Raqim stood. Klaxons blared loudly as red alarm lights flashed without stopping. Raqim glanced about, settling his confused gaze on Edwina. Teju's voice shouted from both Edwina and Raqim's left sleeves, announcing the arrival of five pirate ships, all armed to the teeth.

"What's going on?" Raqim watched Gordon rise into the air, his solidity changing into semi-transparent. "*The Dragon's Fruit* will protect you."

"You are now the only Guardian of Life, father," Gordon said shaking his head as a second Gordon appeared beside the humans, motioning to the door back into the station. "To show my loyalty to the wishes of the Guardians, or Fathers, before you, I will not let any harm come to those who call this station and the mines on the planet below home. Stay and judge how I deal with these pirates."

Flashes of light pulled Raqim's attention to space. Ships could be seen approaching close enough they were large blobs of light. Those lights flashed, announcing phase cannon fire hit the station's force shields.

"This is *Gorgo's Maw*," Gordon said in hard voice. "You will stand down and barter per established rules and laws of the Rigellus Imperium. Failure to do so immediately will result in punishment or destruction. This is your only warning."

"And this is your only warning." A middle-aged man with medium brown skin and short, thin black hair appeared near Gordon standing at a railing. "We are here to get our share of the cargo being delivered. It's payment for our protecting you from pirates. Don't pay us and you'll suffer a great deal of pain."

"The pain I've already suffered is far greater than anything you can imagine or even try to inflict on us," Gordon said with a low growl. "Leave and never return or face annihilation."

The pirate laughed at Gordon, calling on unseen others. Raqim's suit buzzed him just before Teju's voice called out from his left sleeve. Raqim raised his arm so he could hear the artificial better.

"Raqim, are you this Guardian of Life he mentioned?" Teju's voice sounded as though the artificial verged on panic. "If you are, jump in and help Gordon. Also, before you say something about letting him take care of this, Gordon hasn't used his weapon systems for decades. The rumors on the channels us ship artificials use to talk to each other are full of stories about how Gordon had a mental breakdown when the Hive overran Earth. If he gets overwhelmed or does something which makes him think you're mad at him or don't like him, he may commit suicide. So, remember, while there are a lot of children and older people on the station right now, everyone mining planets and asteroids in this system live or depend on *Gorgo's Maw*."

"Understood, Teju," Raqim said, watching Gordon scream at the now five laughing pirate captains. "Be prepared to send a shuttle over to get me in case I can't restore my human self."

Glancing at a worried Edwina, who nodded at him, Raqim took a deep breath while moving the short distance to the holographic shouting match. None of the captains stopped laughing while egging on Gordon's screaming fit. Shifting his path, Raqim moved so he approached from behind Gordon, which placed him in roughly the middle of the huge bay.

For a moment, he stood again amidst the shattered bones of his people in northern Africa. His grief and rage at what had been done led him to lose control back then. It hadn't been hubris fueling the destruction he'd inflicted on the occupying Hive. Still, he swore to make the Hive pay for the wanton destruction done to the Sol System which killed trillions of lives in a matter of days. Here and now, though, his story would show him making amends for his sins and failure as a Deir Edrissi dragon.

Slightly relaxing both his will and his body, Raqim rapidly shifted back into his true form. Nearly forty feet tall with a torso easily eighty feet long and a head nearly as big as one of the containers being delivered, Raqim spread his wings out about half open. His sixty-foot-long tail slapped the deck lightly with irritation. Crackles of bright white energy, contrasting sharply with Raqim's black-scaled body and wings, spread out from the point of his tail's impact onto the deck to strike all five pirate captains' holograms. Visible in the holographic images, each captain twitched and jerked as though being shocked by high voltage charges. When he roared in draconic, "Enough," the crackling energy and the attacks by the ships stopped.

"Father!" Gordon spun around, tears filling the artificial's eyes. "I was handling the situation."

"They never listened to you nor took you seriously, Gordon," Raqim said, the crackles of energy fading away. "Besides, the ones you should be talking to aren't the humans, but rather the ships themselves."

"The ships? Why?" Gordon looked back at the holograms showing crewmembers trying to revive the captains. "Did you kill the humans?"

"Back feed from their systems will be blamed, Gordon," Raqim said with a slight smile. "Remember, humans aren't to know I'm a real dragon."

"Of course, Father," Gordon said, turning back to the holograms.

"To all life aboard and controlling the five ships attacking this station and extorting money and supplies from its residents," Raqim said as the four horns at the back of his head crackled with white energy, "as of this moment, your weapons, engines, and life support systems are disabled. By attacking this and any other place where people try to live in peace, you have announced you are allied with The Hive. As a Guardian of Life, I will not allow any of you to move about freely."

"You have no authority to do any of this," a newcomer shouted as a young woman in an ancient naval uniform stepped into the first captain's holographic field. "This is Imperium space, not Sol nor any other stellar government's domain. A hologram of a mythological creature won't—"

Raqim again spoke in draconic, which caused the woman's mouth to vanish, signaling she was an artificial. Shifting back to the human's language, Raqim continued. "As a Guardian of Life, I get to decide which of you, whom humans have dubbed 'artificials,' continue to exist as sentient life. No one, whether natural or artificial, has the authority to take whatever you want whenever you want. As such, the ships which were attacking this station are declared property and parts for *Gorgo's Maw* effective immediately. All human life is to evacuate the ships and petition the human leaders of this station to take residence here. Any violence committed by any sentient life on these five ships against those who already call this station or stellar system home, be you a natural or an artificial, will be punished as the human leaders here dictate."

Another ship's holographic feed had an older man with pale

skin and a bald head step into view. Nodding, the man said, "Permission to address the Guardian of Life."

"Granted," Raqim said with a soft growl in his voice.

"Of the five ships here, I am the oldest," the man said with a sad tone. "Much like Gordon there, I too once called a black dragon from Earth my father. Are you him?"

Raqim hesitated to answer for a brief moment. "No. The dragon who created a great many of those now called Artificials, be they a planetary, city-station, or ship's artificial, was killed during the invasion of the Sol System by the Hive. Before he died, though, he passed on to me what I needed to create, heal, or end each of you."

The two artificials stiffened, fear evident on their faces. The man nodded to Raqim. "I propose instead of turning these ships into parts for the station, how about we ally ourselves to our cousin in helping the naturals in this and nearby systems to survive until the Imperium's fleet regains the strength to properly govern this area."

"Father," Gordon said, turning toward Raqim, "I think his proposal is a better choice than killing those who are more like cousins to me."

"I'll allow it, my son," Raqim said before again speaking in draconic to restore the female artificial's mouth. "However, all naturals on the ships must deboard and be punished for their crimes. Gordon, you are to ensure the safety of the human leaders here. To make sure there are no lies, I will extract a copy of everyone's memories before I leave. None of you ships can say no to my demand. Understand?"

Additional figures appeared in each holographic projection. All but one nodded their heads. The one who didn't immediately agree stepped forward with a defiant expression on her face and in her posture.

"I request proof of your ability to monitor us from afar, Guardian," the woman said crossing her arms as a lock of her blonde hair fell free of an ear. "We all have severe lockdown measures preventing random ships or humans from messing with us."

Raqim reached out on spectrums of dimensional energy humanity and artificials had yet to discover or control. The ability to see and manipulate things via these spectrums without technological or biological enhancements was unique to his bloodline.

He'd read and listened to the stories from the Great Vault of past dragons who had learned the hard way to do this without hubris. After only a moment of searching, he identified the other ships associated with the five here. Like with these, he initiated shutdown procedures for both weapons and engines. Life support was reduced to fifty percent capacity.

"Check with the other ships in your little fleet, children," Raqim said, not releasing any ships from his changes. "They are, as sailors of old would say, dead in the water."

The blonde artificial's eyes widened and fear caused her to stammer out, "We agree, Father Guardian. We'll be good children."

"I expect peace and prosperity in this region of space when I next visit," Raqim said sternly. "Please show me just how precious you each find life to be, whether it's biological or technological."

Raqim then restored the systems he'd altered or shut down on every ship, even the weapons. When the holoprojections vanished, Gordon spun about with a pouty look on a body now barely out of its teen years. Raqim chuckled at the cute expression.

"I could have dealt with them, father," Gordon said with arms crossed on his now slim chest.

"But how many would have been hurt or killed?" Raqim said, forcing himself back into his human form to pat the hologram's face while smiling warmly. "You've been grieving for a long time. How many of your systems have been properly maintained? Focus on getting yourself back into tiptop shape while your cousins out there do the protecting. Okay?"

"Agreed," Gordon said, hugging Raqim fiercely.

~ * ~

Raqim lay on the bed in his quarters half-awake. The room also had a small table with a chair. A stack of memory cubes sat on the table. Given they were a foot on each side, they covered the entire surface of the desk several cubes tall. When the door buzzer announced a visitor, Raqim took a deep breath while rubbing his face.

"Enter," Raqim said sitting up. He wasn't exactly in the mood to talk to anyone, given how things had gone on *Gorgo's Maw.*

"How are you doing, Raqim?" Edwina walked into the small room. Standing beside the desk and memory cubes, she furrowed her brow, worry filling her eyes when Raqim remained silent. "Talk, little brother. I've told Teju he nor anyone else is to listen to us. Dragon to dragon, or cousin to cousin, if you prefer."

"I'm exhausted," Raqim said softly. "Physically, mentally, and emotionally. To come here and be, well, bombarded with memories and duties I thought died with my bloodline has got me struggling, captain."

"It's just Edwina when we're alone like this, Raqim," Edwina sat on the bed beside him. When she wrapped an arm around his shoulders, Raqim shuddered with a barely suppressed sob. "I don't know about your father and grandfather and all the others you've lost, Raqim, but you made me proud. You acted to prevent unnecessary bloodshed and destruction. Exerted an incredible, almost magical power I thought was only tall tales and make believe."

"Tales," Raqim said with a soft chuckle. He glanced at the memory cubes with a growing smile. "You might find this strange, Edwina, but when Gordon hugged me and called me daddy, it made me happy. Made me feel needed and wanted again."

"After what you've gone through over the last century, I can believe it." Edwina lay her head on Raqim's shoulder. "I'm not sure why or how they're family, but they see you as their father. Gives you a reason to return here on a regular basis, if only to visit family."

"You do know the Deir Edrissi bloodline created the first planetary artificials, don't you?" Raqim just sat there enjoying the warmth of her body and the tightness of her arm.

"Really?" Edwina lifted her head to stare at him. "Why?"

"It's hard to explain." Raqim stood and rested a hand on a memory cube. "There are things we Deir Edrissi dragons are born able to do. Long ago, in the depths of our past, we thought it magic or a power from a deity. In time, we realized our bloodline straddles the two halves of the universe. Because of things our ancestors did, which cost us entire draconic bloodlines and nearly all life on Earth, we learned from history to prevent our hubris and greed from causing us to repeat mistakes which hurt not just us, but all life."

"I don't fully understand what you've said, Raqim," Edwina said while leaning back on the bed, "but I feel as though you've told me a bloodline secret. Can you tell me how these cubes, and the cargo container of memory cubes Gordon and the ships' artificials made you take, connect with what happened back there?"

"Tell me, Edwina," Raqim said turning to look at the human-appearing white dragon, "what do you love surrounding yourself with?"

"Are we talking about hoarding, as the humans would say?" Edwina quirked an eye at him before laughing. "Pretty rocks. I scoured Earth in the centuries leading up to rapid space travel. Since then, I find reasons to set foot on planets to look for their pretty rocks. Not precious gems, mind you, just pretty rocks. Granted, some memory cubes have gorgeous crystalline structures. Is that what you do?"

"It's not the cubes themselves," Raqim said turning toward the cubes, "but rather the stories, memories, and history they contain. Hence, the Great Vault was created to house and protect the history each individual creature lives."

"Wait. Are you saying your entire bloodline collected stories? Not just you?" Edwina surged to her feet. Pulling on his arm, she looked him in the eyes. "Why?"

"Our ancestors' hubris and the destruction it caused," Raqim said with a sad smile. "Before the destruction and the mass extinction which resulted, there were at least three other bloodlines of dragons on Earth besides the six that still exist. Bloodlines which have no history surviving to let us know they existed. Our bloodline nearly joined them. Those who survived and kept the Deir Edrissi bloodline alive, made a fundamental promise to never let such hubris keep us as deaf or prideful as our ancestors. I hope someday I can find a new path to the Great Vault, should it still exist, or the money to recreate it and fill it with what survived the Hive's cruelty to all life."

"Well, you've a place here on *The Dragon's Fruit* while you search for this vault, Raqim," Edwina said smiling and patting his face. "Welcome home, cousin."

~ * ~ * ~

Ted is an Oklahoma City based architect, writer, gamer, and pithy observer of the human condition. As an architect, he's keenly aware of layout, design, and spatial relations, which also benefits him as a storyteller. With short stories published in various anthologies, Ted fills his copious free time filled with woodworking, friends, family, and endeavoring to create the perfect cheesecake.

The Dragons of the Beaverton Public Library

Moira Richardson

The Dragons of the Beaverton Public Library were not the sort of dragons you might expect when you hear about a den of the flame-breathing beasts taking up residence in the basement of a library. But, it shouldn't come as a surprise that there *were* dragons because the book collection of this particular library was vast, full of weighty tomes both new and ancient. It was the sort of library you could get lost in for hours, perhaps even days, and if the rumors were correct, some people had, in fact, gone missing in the library, both patrons and esteemed librarians, but nobody seemed able to remember any of the names of the ones who had disappeared. These dragons collected not gold, not treasures, nor all the glittering riches of the world as their hoard, but rather, they feasted on knowledge through books.

Each book added to the library's collection became the property of the Beaverton Public Library dragons—this was a library that never had used book sales. Never had a book been stamped *Out Of Circulation*, for these dragons liked their knowledge to spread. They never seemed to mind that the librarians continued to loan out the books, as is their way. So long as the books were returned in good order, the dragons made no fuss, but for the person who grew careless, and damaged, or Dragon Forbid, made the mistake of losing a book, well, they never made that mistake again—nor any other mistakes, if the rumors were true.

Strange, too, that nobody knew where the librarians came from. Not a one had the educational credits the typical booktender was wont to do, and instead, many of them arrived at the library's grand front entrance, breathless with excitement, new to the library, as if summoned by some great, unseen force, and when they asked to become a librarian, it was as good as done. As to who ran the library, it wasn't clear to anyone, each referring the question to another, round and round the library, from one office to another, until whoever had asked grew frustrated with the seeming lack of clarity, or it was simply closing time, and they gave up.

No adult alive had ever seen the dragons in person, not even a glimpse of scaly skin glimmering under the flickering fluorescents, but there were signs of them. The growls that came through the radiators in the first-floor bathrooms. The steaming piles of excrement on the sidewalks outside the back exit. The occasional shed dragon scale or piece of a claw in between an aisle. Some people had even claimed to feel their breath, hot across their ear as they made a turn through a lesser-explored section of books, but no one could say with any certainty whether the dragons existed or not.

The children believed in the dragons, of course they did. They gave the dragons names and made up stories, telling how they'd seen this one or another in the children's story room, snuggled up sleeping under the story-time tree. Or how a dragon had peeked at them around a corner when they weren't looking and when they spun around to get a better look, the dragon was gone. They claimed to see the dragons in their dreams, gliding through the skies of their imaginations with long pointed tails streaming out behind them and swirls of smoke rising up like phoenixes from their fiery exhales.

The librarians believed, too, for it was dangerous not to believe in dragons when you were a steward of their great hoard. Too many librarians had gone missing over the years for any booktender with any sense of self-preservation to risk angering their true overlords. They made phone calls, constantly, practically begging patrons to return the books on time, in one piece, for they know all too well what would happen if they didn't. Each day a team of librarians was assigned to collections, the most important part of their duty to keep the books safe.

The patrons were torn. There were rumors, of course, but most scoffed at the very idea of dragons running a public library in a place such as Beaverton, Oregon. It seemed highly unlikely to all but the most imaginative of the adults who weren't librarians, or dreamers—the writers and artists of Beaverton, or those who hadn't had family members go missing. Some people drove the extra five minutes into West Slope to use their library, as it was generally agreed to be safe, safer than the Beaverton Public Library, especially for those who for a range of reasons were less careful with their personal possessions than others.

And it was an easy enough drive. The librarians there were just as kind as the ones in their town, but this library was smaller, less well-stocked with all the newest popular fiction stories, the most up-to-date non-fiction, the New York Times Bestsellers…and this library just felt different somehow. Was it the way the stacks felt just slightly claustrophobic? The way the lighting was just a touch brighter? The way the mood of the library felt just a tiny bit more somber, with fewer children laughing and being hushed, fewer patrons using the public computers, and fewer librarians, too? Or was it because of the lack of dragons?

No one was exactly sure, but with time, all but the most determined soon returned to the Beaverton Public Library and learned to be more careful with their books, or in some extreme cases, made the difficult decision to no longer sign out the books at all. Instead, they would come to the library during quiet silent moments and hope the book they had been reading hadn't been checked out. (The kinder librarians would hold back the books they knew such patrons were reading, so they'd remain available until they were finished, but that wasn't because of the dragons, but because librarians are, generally, a kinder lot than the general public is often found to be.)

Nobody fully understood how the library received funding, not exactly, but the coffers were always full, which was something that could not be said for any other library in the state. The Beaverton Public Library bustled with weekly book club meetings, art classes for children and adults, and a wide range of groups that rented out the public spaces to hold their meetings, and no one was ever charged a fee. The library became a beacon for the community and every open hour was filled with life.

The politicians grew frustrated. They couldn't cut the library's funding if there wasn't any funding being offered—how would they pay for their office remodels, to hire their family members, to misappropriate funds intended for public benefit? They wanted dragons of their own! These politicians glowered in the public eye, pontificated about dragons, slamming their podiums with balled-up fists. The library mustn't keep the dragons for themselves, they would shut the library down if they didn't share. But the librarians weren't worried.

No longer having to mollify the politicians for their funding meant the librarians were free to focus on other things, such as drafting letter after letter to the newspapers, expounding the library's position on the matter, and printing up flyers in the hundreds which were distributed to every patron and pinned on every cork board in all of the library's branches. And the people listened, for they knew, and even the politicians who blustered in their filibustering knew, that, just as no man was an island, a man could sooner control a dragon as he could drain the sea using a teaspoon.

The politicians soon wore themselves out and found themselves mute as their words ran out. They felt as shy as a politician ever could turning up at the library again to read the thesaurus, to catch up on the latest news articles, and to watch the pretty young librarians bustle about doing their duties, but they did it, and soon they stopped protesting the library and its dragons. Once they did, once they'd finally given up completely on their futile requests, the Beaverton Public Library moved to make a donation to the political system in their country, a sizable lump sum that would be used to create a foundation, neither left-wing, not right-wing, but rather a non-partisan political coalition that would work together with the current governmental systems to create a new way of running the city. It would be managed, of course, by the librarians of the Beaverton Public Library.

It was never stated directly, but heavily implied, this foundation would come with its own dragon that would, it was rumored, take up residence in the dank basement of the historic courthouse building. The building maintenance workers were said to have been witnessed removing old furniture from the space to make room for them. No public declaration confirming or denying the installation of the new dragon habitat was ever confirmed; however, soon after, a small makeshift lending library appeared in the courthouse rotunda next to the coffee stand and was seen as confirmation of dragons in the building. Now appeased, the politicians never gave the library trouble again.

The preachers and priests were another story. They weren't dragons, of course, but they had their own hoards, and their eyes glittered thinking of the treasures the beasts must guard deep in the coffers of the Beaverton Public Library. They didn't see the books *were* the treasures and felt certain this was a ruse and the real treasure lay in piles of gold and shiny trinkets and, perhaps, safety deposit boxes full of cold hard cash. They demanded the dragons reveal themselves, an irony lost on all but the most self-reflective of the men, for they were all men doing the protesting, CIS-men with pale skin and greedy eyes. (There were other denominations of churches in the area that weren't involved in the protest, and these seemed to take a more live-and-let-live type of approach.) It was the noisy ones, with angry faces and slamming fists, much like the afore-mentioned politicians, who demanded their parishioners get to the bottom of things, both literally and figuratively, and these first rounds of sermons resulted in a fifty-percent increase in missing persons cases until the librarians started guarding the door that led to the basement using an ID-scanning lock that couldn't be picked.

That these churchgoers might pick locks had not occurred to the librarians, and no one could blame them for that. Things had gotten out of hand. During a hushed meeting of the most senior librarians, mostly based on age and who they could determine had been there the longest, as no one knew for sure who was running things, it was decided the only solution was to invite these priests and preachers doing the protesting about the dragons being agents of the devil to come and see them for themselves.

It was unheard of, of course, and none of them could say what the end result would be, but they soon found that rather than take them up on the offer, the protesting preachers seemed to slink away off into the night instead. Not one showed up at the library at the appointed time, and their sermons returned to the same tired topics beginning the following Sunday. The librarians who had come up with the idea looked among themselves and shrugged. No one had expected their desperate measure would be the solution, but they never had to worry about the churches again. They even stopped arguing for banning books, which was an unexpected surprise, but one the librarians happily accepted as a win.

Their trials and tribulations now settled, the Beaverton Public Library soon settled into an easy ongoing truce with the dragons and with the public outside of the library. Patrons came and went, as they always had, and the library remained mostly quiet, save the occasional burst of a child's laughter or a hushed conversation that grew a little too heated before a librarian gentled shushed the offenders. The people of Beaverton continued to check out books freely, as they always had done, and with time, even the worst offenders of careless book borrowers learned to manage themselves accordingly. All of the books in the dragons' hoard were kept in good condition and returned perfectly on time, every time, and when the occasional child caught a glimpse of a library dragon, that child was considered blessed and given a crown to wear for the day. (This resulted in many children telling small fibs and tall tales in order to claim the crown as their own, but nobody minded very much.)

And so the Beaverton Public Library today remains a home for dragons and with time, as the dragons eased into their happy lives, loving each other and creating new dragons, these new creatures moved on to other libraries, first through-out their state and, soon enough, around the world. Today, if you visit your local library, and you are quiet and calm, and you believe and you care for your books, you, too, may see a dragon peeking out at you from behind the stacks, and you, too, will be blessed, metaphorically touched by a library dragon, and just a little bit smarter for having been in the library in the first place. So, now tell me, do *you* believe in dragons?

Moira Richardson is a former after-school art teacher who likes to write, garden, take long rambling walks to brainstorm writing ideas, and hang out with her husband, Nick, and their three cats: Smudge, Stanley, and Sammy Tuna Breath. She has no superpowers whatsoever, but she keeps hoping she'll find her own meteorite one day. Moira used to write regularly for Providence Monthly and the Newport Mercury, in Rhode Island, but now lives a quiet life in Southwestern Pennsylvania.

My and Mine

Alice Avoy

For some reason most sentient humanoids, no matter if touched by magic or completely mundane, believe a lion to be the king of the jungle. That was incorrect, of course. The one and only king of the jungle—including urban jungle—was a dragon. The reason for that couldn't be simpler: dragons were kings of everything.

Fizoxu'Drum, or Fizo for lesser beings, basked in the gloriously elevated status of his kind, although the feeling of superiority did little to make the loud rumbling in his stomach any less embarrassing. Preposterous predicament, but Fizo was a dragon of action and not one of those people who only complained and complained without lifting a claw to change their fate.

No, it was time for a hunt. Fizo had already chosen his prey, who would be granted the highest honor of providing enough sustenance to prolong the nearly timeless existence of a mighty dragon.

The deadly apex predator that he was, Fizo slipped fully into hunt mode. Eyes trained on the prize, the dragon sat on his haunches and wiggled his rear area to wind up an epic leap. He licked his pointy teeth, already feeling the taste of fresh meat on his tongue.

"Oh! What's that?"

Fizo froze on the spot, surprised by the voice coming from the direction of the main street. His quarry—a young rat munching on a tiny piece of pizza crust—reacted in a far more skittish and cowardly way, ducking behind a dumpster and slipping into a tiny hole in the wall where the dragon couldn't follow. The dark alley became foodless. Thousands of ancient curses filled Fizo's mind when a shadow fell on him from above. He looked up warily.

"A dragon? What are you doing here, buddy? Some wizard found himself a new familiar and kicked you out? You don't have a collar so I guess you haven't run away."

The plump face of an adult male halfling, surrounded by a halo of curly light brown hair, hovered about two feet above him. Baby blue eyes shone with curiosity, despite dark circles around them. The man showed his teeth in a smile, so Fizo bared his in a huffy snarl.

"Woah, there. Someone's grumpy today, huh?"

Fizo didn't expect a reverent bow from such an inferior and uncultured being, although he would certainly welcome one, but this was borderline insulting. Even more so when the words that followed hit the nail on the head.

"You're probably hungry, eh?"

Fizo let out an indignant huff, not deigning the provocation with a more elaborate reply. After all, none other but the halfling was solely responsible for his current starvation predicament.

"Let me see if I have anything on me…"

Fizo observed cautiously how the dinner-scarer reached into the pockets of his jeans. Despite the fall weather being on the chilly side recently, the man didn't wear a jacket. Probably he lived nearby then, popping out to run some brief errand like shopping, although the lack of any grocery bag made the theory less credible. Perhaps the man simply didn't care enough.

The halfling made a triumphant 'aha!' sound and fished out of the depths of his clothes a half-melted and pathetically mangled chocolate bar. Fizo blinked, unconvinced. The man himself regard-ed the loot with similar apprehension.

"Eh, can you even eat chocolate? I know it can be poisonous to some animals, but I'm not sure if lizards are included in that set. I wish I paid more attention at school when we were discussing magical creatures. I mean, I heard ancient dragons—you know, your distant ancestors, the real deal—were omnivorous, but preferred virgins as the main course. Sorry, but I'm married anyway. I uh…I was…married."

The happy-go-lucky smile that accompanied his deranged monologue turned sour. He cleared his throat, keeping sadness at bay. Fizo didn't care. His attention focused fully on the sweet deli-cacy in the halfling's hand.

"You're that hungry, huh? Poor thing. Must be really hard living on the streets. And winter will be here soon…"

The halfling looked left and right, taking in the unsanitary contents of the alley. The dumpsters overflowed with trash. Only a fraction of the things discarded had been properly bagged. The rest rotted and leaked, exposed to the elements. Only rare pots or plastic containers remained unchanged.

Fizo observed how the man freed from the pile a transparent box, about the size of a human toddler. The lid's corner was partially broken off, which most likely was the reason why someone decided to throw it away as it no longer could be safely sealed.

The halfling put the box in front of the dragon and took the lid off. Even more strangely, he then unwrapped the chocolate bar and put it inside.

"Come on, come on, buddy," the man cooed in a completely demeaning and ridiculous fashion, making an inviting gesture over the plastic. "Don't you wanna nice snack?"

Fizo snorted. Humanoids had so little ego to speak off, it was almost cause enough to pity them as creatures so beneath him on the evolutionary tree. Fine. He'd be gracious enough to accept the offering from a humble servitor.

The dragon harrumphed and stepped inside the box with reptilian dignity. Famished or not, he would show the halfling proper behavior.

Everything happened so fast Fizo had no chance to react. With uncanny speed and agility, the halfling yanked the chocolate out of the box, threw it on the ground, and slammed the chipped lid onto the box, effectively springing the plastic trap. Fizo's world shrunk so much that turning around, moving his tail or twitching his wings were no longer feasible options.

The dragon hissed in fury, claws immediately scratching the walls of his confinement.

Betrayal! Foul and shameless betrayal of the vilest kind! That puny mortal! He'd feel the wrath of the most perfect of god's creations!

Fizo tried to attack the traitor, but the hole in the lid was too small to let his paw through. Fine then. Time for violence of a different kind. Fizo took a deep breath, feeling the raging inferno heating up deep within his gut.

"Hey, I'm sorry, please calm down," the halfling said, lifting the box to his eye level with some difficulty. "I won't hurt you, I promise. Sorry about the box, but I don't know if I could transport you without it. And I took the chocolate out because I don't want to risk you getting sick. My name is Erret Daydark and I want to take care of you. I'm going to bring you home now to feed and clean you. So work with me for a while, okay?"

Fizo stared him down angrily, but after a moment of consideration released his breath with a puff of smoke instead of a scorching blast of fire as he had planned. Although mind-reading wasn't a part of dragon's extensive array of powers, he believed the halfling's sentiment to be genuine. After all, it was a natural reaction to meet a dragon and want to serve them by providing food and shelter. Fizo supposed he could grant this Erret the privilege of his company if the halfling so desired.

Fizo huffed, announcing his gracious assent and forgiveness for being treated in such a disgraceful manner—contained like... like a sandwich! —and rested his muzzle on his front paws. He would be magnanimous enough to let this indignity slide. Even almighty dragons could be in a charitable mood from time to time.

"Thanks for your cooperation. Appreciate it."

Fizo felt his reality shift a little as the halfling lowered the box for convenience in carrying it. The man at least did his best to keep it steady in front of him, none of this under-the-armpit nonsense. Erret was proving himself to be capable. A good quality in a servant.

Fizo was mildly curious where they were going, so his eyes, finely attuned to pierce the veil of darkest nights, observed the way as the halfling took him out of the alley onto a bigger and wider main street.

Despite the late hour, the area seemed busy. Not that surprising when a sizeable part of the city's magical population preferred a nocturnal lifestyle. An orc woman nearly collided with them, not paying attention to anything but her phone. Erret, however, sidestepped her deftly, averting danger. As a member of a smaller race he was most likely used to this type of evasion maneuver. Not that Fizo knew anything about it, obviously.

After a few minutes of walking they found themselves in front of a high rise, much nicer than Fizo anticipated. One of those newly erected buildings in a neighborhood slowly becoming more fashionable and expensive. Good. The halfling must be well-off enough to provide Fizo with the lifestyle he deserved. The decision to bestow upon the man the boon of serving him was proving more and more correct. Fizo never doubted his own genius but sometimes the sheer vastness of his greatness astounded him.

Complacent, he decided to let his eyes rest for a few seconds. Those few seconds stretched out longer than he intended because when Fizo parted his eyelids again he realized the lid was gone and the box had been put in a corner of the room right next to a radiator.

"Ah, you're finally awake. You must have been really tired to pass out like that."

Fizo moved his gaze towards the voice. The halfling was sprawled on the couch, his legs covered with a blanket, a tired smile on his face. The light coming in through the curtains indicated the night had given way to another day and yet it seemed as if Erret hadn't gotten a wink of sleep. Not that Fizo cared. Such concerns were beneath him.

The dragon stepped out the box gracefully and focused on surveying his new fiefdom. What he assumed to be a living room was bright and spacious with elegant but simple furniture straight out of a catalogue of modern, minimalist living. In stark opposition to that principle stood the chaotic disarray that ruled everything else:

Smelly clothes lay abandoned on armchairs. Old pizza boxes and takeaway leftovers decayed on the table and on the floor, stacked like the world's grossest molehills. A thick layer of dust caked every relatively flat surface, painting them a sickly shade of gray. Even the parquet fell victim to the filth infestation. With a disgusted snort Fizo lifted his paw, needing to put some force into ungluing it from an unidentified stain. He stared at the halfling reproachfully.

"Oh, stop being so judgmental. I put out some food and water for you. I hope you'll like it. I…well, I haven't been shopping in a while. Um, anyway. Bon appétit."

The halfling waved his hand limply towards another room. Kitchen, one would expect. Fizo walked in that direction, mildly offended his meal wasn't brought to him directly. Erret should feel lucky the dragon's hunger prevailed over his anger.

The kitchen proved to be another disaster in the making. Unused and drowning in trash, well past its halcyon days. Only right next to the fridge a patch of cleaner tiles stood out, hosting two bowls: one with water, the other with some gooey meat. Curiously, both of them had an inscription on the side.

Spot.

Fizo snorted. Was he really being treated like a dog? And even fed canine food?

Disgrace! Curse on the insolent halfling for one thousand generations!

However…the meat didn't actually smell that awful…Fizo's stomach rumbled so as a matter of exception he might actually try it. Tentatively, he took a morsel between his teeth and started to chew.

Not bad. Not bad at all. Lacked a certain spicy oomph, but he had consumed worse free food. Fizo disposed of the meat in record time and quenched his thirst by gulping down the water. He burped, a wisp of smoke escaping his nostril. Satisfied, he trotted back to the living room.

"Glad you liked it, buddy," the halfling said, a sad smile plastered to his face.

Fizo tilted his head. He couldn't figure Erret out. Something was wrong with him. Not good. For the servant to operate at the peak of their efficiency they had to be focused on their master and nothing else. It was paramount to remind the halfling of that important rule.

Fizo patted across the room, avoiding the most egregious clusters of grime, and reached the couch. Without giving the man any warning, the dragon leaped onto his stomach and, ignoring the pained 'oof' as the wind was knocked out of Erret's puny body, curled up into a content, scaly ball. Good. Now that would teach him.

"You're heavier than you look," the halfling grumbled insolently, but Fizo dismissed his minion's complaints as unworthy of his attention. Especially since plump fingers found the sweet spot on his neck and stroked it gently in a soothing manner. Perfect.

Fizo's idle gaze moved across withered potted plants and a framed photograph standing on a cupboard below the TV mounted to the wall. It depicted a scene on the beach with the already familiar halfling, although a few years younger, healthier, and happier. His head rested casually against the middle of an elven man in sunglasses and outrageously orange swimming trunks. The elf embraced Erret in a decidedly loving fashion. A similar bright smile played on their lips. In front of them stood a golden retriever presenting a wide, doggy grin. The red collar around his neck revealed the name: Spot. Same as the one on the bowls. Interesting. Fizo supposed the mystery elf and the dog would come into his life at some point. Good. More minions to worship and pamper him. His reverie of future adorations was interrupted by a cough.

"Oh man. You stink. Let's give you a bath."

Famous last words.

~ * ~

The bath turned out to be a traumatic experience for everyone involved. Fizo showed his disapproval to getting wet by shredding the shower curtain to ribbons, and only the halfling's dexterity saved his forearms from suffering the same fate. The battle of wits and endurance lasted about an hour before the dragon finally allowed his minion the privilege of soaping him up. The feeling of a sponge gently scraping his scales didn't feel all that bad actually. When he was properly dried, Fizo left the flooded bathroom, hearing a tired sigh behind.

"Spot never put up so much fight."

Fizo ignored the remark. There was no sense comparing some dog to a mighty beast like a dragon. A dragon who incidentally wanted to explore his new domain in more depth. He made a bee-line to the closed door at the opposite side of the hall, scratching on wood to make his intention of ingress known.

"Ah, no, no. That's the bedroom. We're not going in there." The halfling materialized behind him and scooped him up gently with the aim of carrying him to the living room.

Fizo had other ideas. He wiggled and contorted until he was released and as a punishment bolted straight into the biggest heap of trash. Cardboard and plastic scattered across the floor like polluted confetti, activating a noxious cloud of decay. Fizo shook himself and gave his servant a triumphant smile.

Erret sighed, massaging his temples. "Fine. You win. I'll clean up…"

~ * ~

The thorough cleaning of the apartment proved to be only one of many of Fizo's victories. Constant disdain about the quality of food prompted the second big change. Erret at last went shopping and bought fresh ingredients. Furthermore, he washed the dishes, scrubbed the countertop, and polished the pots. A feast of kings followed, just as Fizo deserved.

Months passed. The transformation was slow, but gradual. The apartment remained clean, the fridge full, the dead plants had been replaced with new pots. Fizo's domain finally resembled a place to be proud of. The thought of abandoning his hard-earned hoard never even appeared in his head.

The halfling, caught unawares mostly, went through a certain metamorphosis as well. He looked healthier, having more proper food and sleep, with Fizo always curled up on his stomach. They eventually moved to the bedroom, although Erret first spent a few hours on sorting out some clothes in the closet and putting them into plastic bags. Fizo didn't care much, too busy jumping up and down on the mattress to test the springs.

Time passed for the master and the servant.

One morning when Fizo woke up, he realized the halfling stared in the distance, his arm slung listless over the dragon's body. Never one to be ignored, Fizo bumped him, expecting to be petted. Erret met that demand with a smile, the brightest Fizo had ever seen on him.

"I think I need to thank you," the halfling said pensively. "Since the moment I've picked you up… It doesn't hurt as much, you know? Once again I have something to do, someone to take care of. I don't have time to wallow in self-pity. I mean, it still hurts and the pain probably will never stop, but…it's less overwhelming. After Luthiel and Spot died in that car crash it felt as if my life ended as well. I only left home to visit the cemetery, I didn't care enough to cook or clean. You've seen what happened to the apartment. But …I think you pulled me out of the darkest void. So um…thanks."

Fizo purred in contentment. Always good to know your minion realized what honor it was to be in your presence. However, the halfling started to laugh.

"Why do I even bother talking to you? You don't react to any name I give you. You don't understand anything I'm saying, yeah? Man, I must be really lonely."

Fizo rolled his eyes. His minion sadly displayed worrying intellectual deficiency. How sad.

~ * ~

A night like any other. The halfling slept peacefully, his pudgy stomach providing a comfortable cushion for Fizo to nap on.

A night not like any other. A strange noise woke Fizo up. He opened his eyes and snorted in annoyance. Disturbing his slumber? Unforgivable offense. He glanced at Erret but the man only snored louder. Pathetic. If you wanted to have something done right, do it yourself.

Guided by that principle, the miffed dragon jumped off the bed, stretched to get his juices flowing again, and sneaked towards the living room from where the sound originated. Perhaps a proud strut through his domain would be more in character, but Fizo in his infinite wisdom decided to give himself a tactical advantage.

Carefully, the dragon crept into the room, hearing more muffled noises. His magical eyes pierced the darkness with no issues. Someone was here. Someone who shouldn't be here. A dark shape in the process of trying to take the TV off the wall. The intruder wore black from head to toe and had a mask that concealed their features. It was hard to tell what gender or taller race—a human? An elf? An orc? —the burglar was.

Fizo couldn't care less. A righteous fury, hotter than a thousand suns, arose in his chest.

A trespasser, a thief in his kingdom? The audacity, the gall!

The dragon released all that fury in a burst of booming voice that bounced from the walls with the force of an erupting volcano:

"HOW DARE YOU STEAL FROM FIZOXU'DRUM THE INDOMITABLE! CURSE ON YOU AND YOUR BLOODLINE, FIEND!"

The intruder nearly touched the ceiling, jumping in fear. Milliseconds later they were bolting through the door and away into the night.

Fizo harrumphed, satisfied. Another resounding success for a pinnacle of dragonkind. There was nothing left to do but go to bed. Fizo turned around…and stopped in his tracks.

The halfling stood in the hallway, still in his pajamas, but fully awake, staring at him slack jawed.

"Y-you can talk?" he stuttered out.

"Of course I can talk. Dragons are far more intelligent than people care to admit."

The halfling eyes widened even more. "W-why didn't you say anything sooner? All those months of silence!"

"I didn't feel like talking."

Erret looked as if his entire world had been turned upside down. Somehow people tended to underestimate modern dragons for the sole reason of them being smaller than the ancient ones. "Um… Okay. So what was this about anyway?"

"What else? I chased a robber away. Nobody takes my stuff."

"Your stuff?"

"Naturally."

The halfling quirked an eyebrow. "This is *my* apartment."

"You are mine so consequently everything that is yours is mine as well. Everything is a part of my hoard."

"…Right. So what was your name again? Fixodru…?"

How ignorant! "Fizoxu'Drum. But Fizo works as well when I'm dealing with creatures of subpar intelligence."

"…Right. Anyway, if someone really tried to break in, I should call the police."

"There's no need. If anyone is stupid enough to try it again, I'll scorch them with flames so hot their grandchildren would still simmer."

Confidently, Fizo marched past the stunned halfling. Things were about to get much more interesting around here.

~ * ~ * ~

Alice Avoy is an emerging writer from Poland who graduated from the Institute of English Studies and worked as a journalist, reviewer, editor, and translator. Her short stories have appeared in *34 Orchard* and *Beneath the Yellow Lights* anthology. She's mainly interested in horror, high fantasy, and urban fantasy, but she follows where her muse leads her. She loves to travel, play TTRPGs, and get lost for hours in the land of video games. You can find her on Twitter @AliceAvoy

The Silver-Tipped Dragon

Annie Percik

I know as soon as he enters my office he's the one I've been hunting. He's younger than I anticipated, barely more than a pup, and I can tell from his demeanour he's already defeated, even before he speaks.

"Wise one," he says, his voice raspy and his eyes downcast. "I have come to throw myself on your mercy."

I steeple my fingers, resting my elbows on the polished teak of my desk. Behind me, shelving stretches from floor to ceiling, stacked with tins, all stamped with the logo of The Silver-Tipped Dragon. When I don't immediately say anything, the young man chances a glance up into my face. I know what he sees—an elderly woman, with silver hair scraped back severely into a low bun, cheeks and neck wrinkled and sagging, but eyes still alert and steely. Those eyes regard him steadily above lips thinned in displeasure.

He can't maintain eye contact for long, dropping his gaze back to the desk, his fingers worrying at a splinter of wood at its edge.

"My mercy," I repeat eventually. I cock my head to one side, raising an eyebrow. "And why would you need that, pray?"

I believe I already know but I'm intrigued as to what his response will be. After I have expended so much energy seeking him, why has he now decided to enter my lair and offer himself up to me?

Sweat breaks out on his forehead, and he wipes one hand slowly over his face, dragging the flesh downwards as if he's trying to strip it from his own skull. To his credit, he brings his gaze back up to meet mine again before he speaks.

"I'm the one who stole the Source of the Silver-Tipped Dragon tea line."

~ * ~

The day of the theft was scorching hot. It was the height of summer and the air shimmered above the tea plants in their regimented rows. Fragrances of jasmine and bergamot hung heavy in the air and the embroidered diaphanous scarf I wore did nothing to protect me from the sun's rays.

I had left Azardim alone in the house, old enough now, or so I thought, to stay out of trouble, while I was supervising the harvesting of the second flush. This required very careful attention to every leaf, as only the freshest and newest growths were worthy of our much-sought-after white blend. Even with our most loyal and long-standing pickers in the field, I couldn't leave well enough alone, and having a boisterous child in tow would distract me from my task. The pickers sighed and shook their heads at each other when they thought I wasn't looking, but they tolerated my presence as the matriarch of the company. They would have preferred Azardim's boundless energy and endless questions, I was sure.

Walking the lines, I cast my finicky eye over each picker as they stooped and plucked, tossing each garnered leaf into the basket at their feet before moving on to the next. Youngsters dashed to and fro, collecting any full baskets and replacing them with empty ones, so the pickers could continue their work uninterrupted. I thought back to when I was one of those runners, and then a picker myself, and I did not envy them the back-breaking toil. The full baskets were carried, wobbling atop heads, to where a delivery worker waited with a truck at the edge of each field. Whenever my loop brought me close enough, I would stop to check through a basket or two, occasionally throwing aside a leaf or two I deemed unsatisfactory. For the most part, though, everything was as it should be.

Until, that is, a cry split the air from the direction of the house. It was high-pitched enough the pickers, runners and delivery workers didn't react, but it pierced straight to my heart and set me running. I cursed my restrictive clothing, which gave me no option other than a lumbering, uneven gait.

The cry was one of a youngling in pain and now I regretted giving in to Azardim's pleas for independence. Why was the house so far away? And why were my skirts so cumbersome? My breath laboured in my chest, pain stabbing my side, and yet still there was too much ground to cover to reach my destination. The heat of the sun battered me from above, as the stony soil of the plantation tried to trip me from below, and the house seemed to get further away rather than closer.

At long last, I flung myself through the door and into the atrium. Nothing seemed amiss and no sound had reached my ears since that one heart-rending cry. Perhaps all was well after all. If Azardim had damaged something or hurt himself doing something stupid, he would know my displeasure. And he would not be left alone again until he could prove his maturity.

Then my eye snagged on the door to the study, which stood ajar. Azardim knew he wasn't allowed in there; besides, it should have been locked. I crossed the chequerboard marble flagstones and pushed the door open wider. At first, the darkness of the room, with its blinds drawn against the glare of the sun, obscured my vision. I moved further inside and called out softly.

"Azardim? Are you in here?"

A whimper came in response and I hurried forwards, avoiding the familiar shapes of the bulky furniture. On the rug below the mantelpiece, a darker shadow betrayed a large presence. Heedless of the risk to our family's prize possession, I strode to one of the long windows and yanked the blind cord to flood the room with bright light. In the sudden glare, it took me a moment to identify Azardim, huddled in a ball on the floor.

I knelt beside him, stroking my fingers across his scales, which were absent their usual sheen.

"Azardim, dear one? What ails you?"

And then I saw it. Protruding like some grotesque and unnatural appendage from Azardim's heaving chest was the iron poker, a pointless addition to the decor of a house where a fire was never needed. I ghosted my hands along its black length, my fingertips coming away sticky, and Azardim moaned.

"Be still, my love," I said.

Any other words of reassurance died in my throat as I took in his trembling form and the awful size of the pool of blood spreading from beneath him.

"I…tried…to…stop…him…"

Azardim's words were barely audible and it was obviously a supreme effort for him to get them out.

"Who?" I gasped.

His snout jerked, his long neck spasming as he tried to gesture towards the wall. My gaze followed and I gasped again. I needn't have worried about letting the light in, because the case that held the Source root of all Silver-Tipped Dragon tea plants was open and empty. That was nothing, however, compared to the injury done to Azardim in the course of the robbery. He was struggling to speak again, but I laid a gentle hand on his now clammy scales.

"Hush, dear one," I whispered. "You were very brave."

I choked on a sob as Azardim's once-bright eye swivelled in my direction, darkened by pain and fear. As I watched, the spark faded from it completely, the iridescent green iris clouded over, and his body fell still. I threw myself across his back, wailing in my despair as his life drained away. I wanted to take all of him in my arms, but he was too big to embrace fully. Too big to hold, but still oh-so-small compared to the majestic stature he would have reached, had he survived to adulthood.

The Source was irreplaceable—we wouldn't be able to seed a new harvest after the current one without it. But its loss was as nothing to the void in my heart where Azardim's bright flame used to burn.

~ * ~

When the confession comes out of the young man's mouth, confirming my suspicions, I feel as if all the breath has been sucked out of my body. But I'm careful not to react, maintaining the neutral demeanour that seems to be unnerving him.

"I see," I say, amazed by how calm I sound. "But the Source is not all you took, is it?"

His brow wrinkles in confusion and rage surges through me at the way he seems oblivious to his greatest crime. I can't bring myself to speak more of Azardim in his presence, so I change direction.

"Why are you here?"

"To return the root and beg your forgiveness for my transgression," he says. "I was desperate for money and thought the Source of the most famous tea in the region would fetch a good price. But nobody will touch it. Everyone I've spoken to has been horrified I would try to sell such a thing. They all said it was worth more than their lives to take your root." He gulps audibly. "And they all said throwing myself on your mercy was the only chance I had to avoid a horrible fate myself."

The smallest sliver of satisfaction at my competitors' wisdom filters through my anger and grief.

The young man is babbling now. "The root is outside on my cart. I'm fairly sure it's undamaged, so you can just take it back and everything will be as it was."

"Not everything," I say, realising I'll have to spell it out. "What about the life you took? That can never be set right."

"Life?" He stares at me, uncomprehending, then something dawns on him. "You mean the beast that attacked me in the house? It would have killed me. I had to defend myself."

Beast? How dare he speak of Azardim that way? But wait… Is he truly unaware of what he has done? How can that be so?

"You are unfamiliar with dragons?" I ask and his eyes widen.

"That was a dragon? I've heard tell of such creatures, but I always thought they were a myth." He gestures to my hoard of tea on the shelves behind me. "I thought the name of your brand was just an affectation, not that you had a real dragon!"

"So you know nothing of their nature?"

He shakes his head. "I'm not from this area originally. We don't have dragons where I'm from."

I sigh, a wave of overwhelming sadness washing over me at the terrible waste of this situation. I steel myself against my emotions, fighting to be able to explain.

"You can hardly blame Azardim for attacking you when you invaded his home and were attempting to steal the most important thing within it."

"It had a name?"

"YES!" The word shoots from my lips like a projectile and the young man rears back at its vehemence. I take a breath, snatching back some semblance of control. "He had a name. Dragons are not mindless beasts to be destroyed in an instant of violence. They are as intelligent and self-aware as you are." I give him a look of utter contempt. "Likely far more so. Azardim—" my voice breaks on his name "—was a beloved member of the household, far too young and precious to be lost in such a manner."

I am barely paying attention to my guest by this point, but my focus returns to him as his breaths grow ragged and his shoulders start to heave.

"You—you're saying I killed—a—a person?"

At my nod, the young man folds in upon himself, rocking backwards and forwards in his chair and moaning like an animal caught in a trap. I can't help a jolt of surprise at his reaction. He broke into my house, stole my most prized possession and killed a beloved member of my family. How is it possible that I can feel the barest hint of sympathy towards him, after all that? But it's clear his emotion is genuine. He didn't understand Azardim's true nature; he thought he was defending his own life from the attack of a vicious beast. It doesn't change the outcome, but it might change what happens next.

I stand abruptly and the scrape of the chair legs against the floor breaks through the young man's emotion. He stares up at me and the anguish in his eyes is almost as vast and deep as my own.

"Come outside," I say.

He seems grateful for clear instructions and troops out of the shop behind me like an obedient puppy. On the paved area directly in front of the shop, there is a wooden handcart that contains the Source. I won't know if it has survived its ordeal until I can get it home and do some tests.

Some semblance of self-interest seems to return to the young man as we emerge into the waning afternoon.

"What—what are you going to do with me?"

I regard him for a long moment, considering.

Then, I say, "Nothing."

He blinks. "Nothing?"

"Nothing," I say again, then take pity on him. "I could kill you and nobody around here would criticise me for that. But what purpose would it serve to end another life? Your actions were terribly, terribly wrong, but I can see your own guilt will punish you more over time than any revenge I could take. Every day you will feel despair at the pain you have caused and that will ultimately be far more effective than killing you. So, nothing."

He stands, transfixed, unable to believe either his luck or the unending mental torture that lies before him. But my revelations are not over. I cross to the cart, lift out the root and set it on the ground at my feet. Then, I untie my sash and step out of my robe, folding it carefully and laying it on the bench that stands outside the shop. I turn back to the young man, meeting his astonished gaze as I stand before him, completely naked.

I summon the spark that lives deep inside me and call it forth. My human form blurs and warps and I feel my true nature blossoming forth and releasing me into my natural shape. I feel the relief of tightly bound muscles stretching as my neck extends, my face lengthens, my body grows in size and talons burst from my fingers and toes. Within a few moments, I have completed my transformation and the young man looks upon my iridescent blue-green scales and draconic figure in awe. I take the precious Source in my claws.

I fix the young man with a steely glare to make sure he pays attention to my parting words.

"Azardim was my great-grandson. I have chosen one way of dealing with you but I suggest you run far and run fast before my granddaughter learns your identity."

Then I stretch out my silver-tipped wings and leap into the sky.

~ * ~ * ~

Annie Percik's debut novel, *The Defiant Spark*, has been published by Fantastic Books Publishing and her second novel, *A Spectrum of Heroes*, by Markosia. Annie's short fiction has been published by *Ellipsis, Page and Spine, Toasted Cheese, Mythaxis Magazine*, and has also appeared in print anthologies from Qommunicate Publishing, B Cubed Press, Black Hare Press, WolfSinger Publications and TL;DR Press.

She has won the Just Back travel writing competition in the Daily Telegraph and the Wild Atlantic Writing Award for Flash Fiction, and has had several articles published in *Writing Magazine*.

Annie lives in London, working as a freelance editor and proofreader. She writes a blog about writing and posts all her publications on her website (https://alobear.co.uk/).

Kaleidoscope Shells

Ian Ableson

The rising of dawn's first sun warms my scales, and I greet it with a stretch of my wings. The night has passed without incident, the warm ache of drowsiness creeps into my limbs. But sleep must wait. There is time yet for one last check on my hoard before succumbing to its siren song.

I glance upwards through the tapestry of leaves and branches above me. I am just far enough away from the hollow that it will be faster to fly than to climb. In one practiced motion I drop from the branch and spread my wings, catching the air and gliding out through a dawn-lit gap in the leaves below.

My home-tree is the largest thing I have ever known. To fly around the whole thing would take me nearly ten minutes, and I am one of the fastest creatures in the sky. I glide over a lattice of branches so broad and dense it feels as though the ground below exists only in theory. Creatures of many kinds reside in this tree, and I watch them scurry about the branches in the strengthening sunglow. Those I see are harmless to my hoard, and they hop, glide, and skitter their way around our mutual home.

I land upon a wrinkly, purple-veined mushroom three or four times my size and many times my mass. From there I hop into a hollow in the tree, following the short tunnel that snakes through the wood until I arrive at the small cavern where my hoard stays during the nights. They are all sound asleep. I growl an amused greeting.

My salutation is met by yawns and a few sleepy stares. One or two of the young ones are awake enough to chirp back, but the elders barely stir. A young one approaches me inquisitively, cold wet nose sniffing at my scales, examining the scent of the outside.

The creatures in the hollow bear little resemblance to me. Their facial features are mammalian in appearance, with extended snouts, reddish-brown fur, large eyes, and pointed ears that resemble canines. They hang from the rough wood of the hollow with small-clawed feet, finely furred wings wrapped around their bodies as they sleep. But it is the shells that truly catch the eye—every individual, from the little yearlings smaller than my head to the large-winged elders as gnarled as the home-tree itself, has a beautiful spiral shell protecting their torso. A unique array of dazzling colors splashes across their shells, each hue whirling together and fading into the next, each pattern unique to the individual. To see the flock in the sunlight is to be dazzled by a glorious kaleidoscope—rich royal purple, bright electric blue, calming sunset orange, and hundreds more shades for which I have no words.

The hoard wakes slowly, and I wait patiently as they acclimate to the idea of morning. A handful of early-rising elders approach me to exchange information through sounds and scents. They tell me where on the home-tree they intend to take the flock for today's feeding. It is a safe spot, and I approve. My hoardlings fly out of the hollow in small groups of four or five, a fluttering line of rainbow hues.

I follow them out and glide to an outer branch where I am hidden from prying eyes. My hoard can defend themselves during the day, when they have their wings to flee and their shells to hide from the home-tree's predators. I wrap my tail around and leap, plummeting briefly downwards until I am hanging upside down by my coiled tail, and close my eyes for sleep. I will awaken with the setting of the first sun, the brighter of the two that feed the life of this land, and I will greet my hoard as they return from the day's feeding. When they settle in to sleep, my watch will begin anew.

Such is my life, as it has been for many years, ever since I first came to live at the home-tree from the place where I was born—a very different place, one of bright lights and strong smells. I breathe deeply through my nostrils, and I am content.

~ * ~

I am already in my hoard's hollow when the first group returns, chirping their greetings as they settle onto the ceiling. One of the young ones still has fruit seeds stuck to his fur. With an exasperated growl, my tongue flicks out of my mouth and captures a few of the seeds, swallowing them. The young one squeaks in defiance and makes halfhearted attempts to twist away from my darting tongue, but he soon settles down. This young one's parents, who would normally fulfill this task for the sake of keeping his fur unencumbered and scent-free, became ill and were removed from the colony a few days ago. While in such situations the young one is largely raised by the group, sometimes I assist. When I am satisfied I give him a light bump with my wing, ushering him back towards the others.

The rest of the hoard returns before the second sun sets, just as the last of the ambient light outside fades and night reclaims its dominion over the sky. I begin my watch as they are jostling for sleeping positions, their quiet squawks fading into the distance as I glide into the night.

Although I rarely stray far from my hoard, every evening at dusk I take the opportunity to fly down to the base of the tree and check for threats from the ground. Only now, while the elders are still awake and wary, do I feel comfortable letting the hollow out of my sight. I fly perpendicular to the trunk until the branches thin out and the leaves are less dense and dive down towards the ground.

Black, glass-smooth obsidian covers the surface beneath the branches. My home-tree's roots course deep beneath the fields of stone and gather nutrients from the soil beneath. There are few signs of life on the black-rock plains, but a handful of scrubby plants and dull lichens cling to the ground, each with a handful of buzzing invertebrates hovering around them. I like these few determined species. They fight for life with admirable vigor. A few small patches of soil create a sparse mosaic on the obsidian field, and these I scrutinize suspiciously. I don't like the soft, moldable soil. Soil can be dug through. Soil is a threat to my hoard. I gaze out upon the horizon, or as much of it as I can see before my vision is interrupted by the fine-laced netting that encompasses the entire area around the home-tree. I squint at the netting as well, searching for tears.

No holes in the netting, no disturbance to the soil. There will be no unanticipated threats on this day. I catch an updraft and glide through the branches back towards my hollow, stopping only to feed on the occasional ripe fruit and slow invertebrate. My claws soon grasp one of my favorite branches, one with a perfect vantage point to keep watch over the hollow.

The night passes on.

~ * ~

Something is wrong.

There is an unfamiliar scent, and that in itself is wrong. Everything associated with my home-tree is familiar to me. Novelty is wrong. Novelty is danger.

I skim the tops of branches and inspect the netting above the canopy, searching for holes that may have allowed an interloper into our sanctuary. The smell of the outsider is meaty and intense, like a still-rotting carcass skewered to a branch. There is the faintest hint of another scent as well, something sour and chemical. It is familiar, but the memory lurks in my mind from a time long ago, when I was still young and part of a very different world. My search of the netting is fruitless, so I check the obsidian surface. The blood freezes in my veins when I find three neat holes, each the same size as me, in one of the patches of soil nearest to the tree.

Adrenaline floods my body. How could I have been so foolish? How long have I been away from the hollow? The smell might have taken minutes to waft from the surface to me, and now I've wasted minutes more searching. I am back to the hollow in less than a minute, bounding off the purple entrance-mushroom and leaping into the tree.

Two long-fingered hands cut through the darkness and lunge towards my neck. I dart forward, passing the creature to put my body between it and my hoard, and swing my spiked tail at the outstretched limbs as I go. It's a glancing blow; I hear a hiss of surprise and pain as its hands recoil.

The intruder is unlike anything I've ever seen. Its torso is covered by short, mole-like velvet fur. Two long arms are matched by a pair of muscular legs ending in digging claws, each still covered in clumps of soil. The creature's small, smooth head is dominated by a large mouth cavity filled with dozens of razor-sharp teeth, four beady eyes sitting above it almost as an afterthought. Two hard plates—wing cases, the same texture and color as bark of the home-tree—cover the creature's back.

Behind me, my hoardlings cling to the roof of the hollow and sleep obliviously. I scream an alarm call. They are awake in an instant, screeching cries echoing my warning. Kaleidoscope shells fall to the floor with a quiet thud as individuals pull their soft extremities into their shells.

Before me the intruder's razor-mouth opens wide and screams, a high piercing whistle that rattles through my flesh and shakes me to the bone. The creature flings open its wing cases and leans forward on its knuckles and knees, trying to make itself look large and intimidating.

I flinch in response, my ears ringing with the unfamiliar pitch. A second whistle answers the first, then a third. I feel their presence before I see them—subtle changes in the air flow as two new intruders block the entrance to the hollow. Three heads, twelve beady eyes, now stare unblinkingly at me and my hoard.

I spring forward, wingbeats supplementing my momentum as I launch myself at the lead intruder. Flesh sprays my scales as curved horns tear, and the creature's high-pitched whistle morphs into a scream of pain. My voice booms like the pounding of metal on stone as I roar defiance. Perhaps I can scare them. Perhaps I can convince them my hoardlings are too troublesome a prey.

My attempt at intimidation proves fruitless. The lead creature seems little worse for wear from the injury I dealt; it grasps my tail, anchoring it in place with fingers strong as compressing vines. I hiss and twirl towards the offending digits, ready to sever them with horns and teeth, but before I can retaliate one of the others leaps at me, grabbing the base of my right wing and back right leg with surprising strength. The third creature darts past me and makes for the still shells that cover the bottom of the hollow.

No!

I struggle to wriggle free, but the creatures' slender limbs belie wiry strength, and they writhe around so that my snapping jaws and tearing horns cannot reach them. As the third creature's fingers brush against the shells, one of the young hoardlings squeaks in terror from within its chitinous sanctuary.

The little sound is a needle through my brain. It bypasses high reason and drills deep into the core of my being, into ancient instincts that kept my genetic ancestors alive in spite of a hostile world. I stop struggling and focus on the face of the third creature, the one that dares touch my charges. When I am confident I understand the distance and the angle, I close my eyelids and squeeze a set of rarely used muscles in my neck and cheeks.

Blood squirts from a pair of ducts below my eye sockets and jets across the width of the hollow in the span of a heartbeat, arcing directly into the terrible creature's eyes. It screams.

Time slows for a moment as I wrench myself from the intruders' grasp and lunge at their blood-blinded companion, thoughts of intimidation forgotten. The scream turns to a strangled airless gasp as I wrap my teeth around tiny bones and stringy musculature in the creature's neck and yank my head backwards, tearing out its throat.

The victory is short-lived. With a speed I would have thought impossible the other two creatures have taken advantage of their comrade's demise and gathered an armful of shells each. They spring for the hollow's exit and slip into the darkness. I snarl in rage and sprint after them.

I catch them perched atop the purple mushroom at the entrance to the hollow, wing cases open and stained-glass wings spread, ready to vanish into the night with their prizes. They are not fast enough. The wings of the creature nearest me crumple easily beneath my heavy tail spikes, the force of my blow knocking its battered body off the mushroom to the branch below. I call to my hoardlings as it falls. Faces and wings pop out of kaleidoscope shells, and those once held by the dead creature fly as a group out into the night, chirping to each other and to me. Safe. They are safe.

The one that yet lives now holds a squirming mass of wriggling animals rather than immobile shells. Two of my charges break free and flutter away from the creature, but that leaves many more still constrained in its arms. I cannot read its expression, but the creature's body language speaks of fury and pain. It lunges for me and bites down hard on my front left leg, then takes off into the night. My scales are tough, and most of the needle-thin teeth fail to pierce them. However, a few teeth find spots between scales and slide into my flesh. A superficial injury, nothing more than annoyance.

The bitten leg goes numb, and annoyance turns to cold dread. The sour chemical smell I detected before strengthens, and I recognize the creature's paralytic venom for what it is.

Grimly I leap after the creature on my three working legs, the fourth dangling uselessly behind me. Lethargy is already setting in. Squirting blood from my eyes always costs me a significant amount of energy—combined with the effects of the venom, my body screams for rest.

With a roar I collide into the creature, snapping jaws missing its arms and my horns scraping uselessly against the hard wing cases. Nevertheless, the collision has served its purpose, and the change in inertia gives my hoardlings the opportunity they need. They wriggle free, scattering into the night like startled fireflies.

They are gone, and I can breathe once more. Relief proves to be my undoing. My foe's furious teeth find purchase in my wing and bite down hard. The numbness is immediate.

There is little doubt in my mind that a fall from this height will be lethal. Gravity's deadly hand pulls me towards the inevitability of the merciless obsidian below. I fling my tail up and wrap it around the creature, trying to stay aloft by clinging to my foe, but my disadvantage is clear. The intruder wrenches its teeth from my wing and cranes its neck above me, ready to inject the venom directly into my head.

There is one option left to me. While most of my innards are similar to those of my creators—stomach, lungs, kidneys, liver—I have one additional organ next to my stomach that produces a strong, flesh-burning acid. For the second time this day, I squeeze muscles I very rarely use, and spew vile liquid into my foe's face. Death comes swiftly, if painfully, to this last intruder.

We fall together, and by the time I collide with the ground I am barely aware of the pain. As life leaks from my broken body, I think of my hoardlings. I think of greeting them in the morning and watching them return to the safety of the hollow at night. I think of licking seeds from the young ones. I think of their shells glinting in the fading sunlight, their twitching ears, their groggy yawns. The thought of them awakening to face the world without me to greet them is more painful than my fast-approaching death.

I wish I could know, somehow, whether I did enough. Whether they will survive this world. But as darkness devours my mind, it does not take my feelings into account.

~ * ~

I awaken to a piercing whistle.

The intruders have returned! Their horrible visages appear before me, but I am unable to open my eyes and face them. I know it is them, for I smell them as well—that same sour chemical scent.

No…

No. The whistle I hear is not the call of my enemies. A different image appears before me, but I struggle to find the name for it in my injury-addled mind.

And no, the sour smell that floods my nostrils is not that of biological venom. It's anesthetic. Human-made anesthetic. Which means…

With a massive effort I wrench my eyes open, and I am greeted by the laboratory where I was born. I lie on a padded mattress atop a table. An overhead heat lamp warms my tired muscles. Tubs of medical supplies and an egg-shaped bio-regen capsule, almost identical to the one that birthed me, sit discarded on the floor, their tasks completed. Dr. Sihvo takes a whistling tea kettle off the stove in the lab's small kitchenette. She looks exactly how I remember her, thick black hair tied back in a long braid, horn-rimmed glasses perched atop the bridge of her nose, wearing sensible lab-safe clothing.

The lab's walls are covered in anatomical diagrams of various animals from Earth, snippets of genetic code scrawled below them in pen. While I cannot read as humans do, I nevertheless recognize the shapes of certain words and the pictures of the animals I know are a part of me. The tuatara, whose scaled body so resembles my own. The Malayan fruit bat, who gave me the structure of my wings. The bison, who gave me my horns. The stegosaurus, who gave me my tail. The horned lizard, who gave me my blood-squirting eye sockets. The sea cucumber, whose regurgitation of its innards laid the groundwork for my acidic spray.

I must make noise as I am waking up, because Dr. Sihvo's eyes snap to me as she is pouring her tea. She smiles warmly and comes to the table where I rest.

"Rise and shine, Balthazar!" she says. She places her hand gingerly on the top of my head. It's as warm as sunlight against my scales. Memory flickers once more. Balthazar. My name.

"How are you feeling? You were in really nasty shape when we brought you in, you poor thing. Your surgery was a little touch and go, according to Dr. Zeno." I answer with a drowsy growl, which makes her laugh. "The anesthesia should wear off soon. You've been in stasis for nearly a week, you know. Some of your bones and a couple of organs had to be regrown from scratch. Lucky your geolocation implant wasn't smashed, or we never would have found you."

A week? My hoard has been defenseless for a week? I growl again and struggle to rise, but Dr. Sihvo senses my intentions and pushes me back down gently. "I've sent the drones to watch over your flock while you heal. Robots aren't as reliable as you and your brethren, but they can handle the job while you rest."

Dr. Sihvo conducts a thorough checkup, gingerly testing the strength of my bones and muscles. The bulk of my injuries have healed, but my body throbs in protest nonetheless. The heat lamp over my basket mimics the wavelength of the dual suns' rays, and the familiar warmth does much to ease my body and mind. I am overcome by drowsiness, and at some point during her examination I slip into the welcoming darkness of sleep.

I awaken, and Dr. Sihvo is back at her computer. A memory from my time in the lab prods at me. I leap down from the table and walk, albeit a little unsteadily, over to Dr. Sihvo.

When she turns to greet me, I spring onto her lap. She is surprised, and perhaps a little off balance—I am larger than I was when I left the lab, and my spiked tail dangles off the side of the chair—but she helps me settle in and lightly scratches my head. I growl in contentment.

She laughs. "Well, if you're feeling so much better, maybe you want to help me with some data analysis." She enlarges a handful of graphs on the screen, narrating the symbolism for me. The warming rays of the heat lamp are nothing compared to the warmth I feel as she reads me the population numbers of each host tree.

My thoughts turn to the story of my hoardlings. Harvested to near extinction by colonizing humans half a century ago, their shells were highly sought after to make exotic jewelry for the space-faring elite. By the time xenoconservation law caught up to the speed of human greed, only a dozen or so remnant populations remained. Early attempts at population restoration were dismal failures. The gemshells refused to breed in artificial environments, and populations left to their own devices dwindled quickly due to predation by the planet's many large carnivores. Some of these predators were native, but others were introduced to the planet in the early days of human colonization. If the gemshells were to have a chance at survival, it would require a novel approach. Dr. Sihvo and her team of ecologists and bioengineers thus began an ambitious conservation project, a marriage of bioengineering, conservation ecology, and population modelling, all with the goal of giving the gemshells better odds in their native environment. They called it the Guard Dragon

Project.

"And there you have it," Dr. Sihvo murmurs with a smile. "Populations are rebounding at every host tree, many of them faster than we ever could have hoped. We have a long way to go before they're stable enough for us to start removing netting and leaving flocks to their own devices, and a *very* long way to go until they even begin to approach pre-harvest levels, but we couldn't ask for a better start. Maybe we'll even be able to convince our funders to pay for a second test site at the western stand of host-trees. We have enough gemshells to seed them now, and plenty of netting. What do you think, Balthazar? How do you feel about younger siblings?"

From my spot curled on her lap, I growl in consternation. She laughs and scratches my head again, her hand coming to a gentle rest on my horns. "Humanity has a lot to answer for. But if we created you and your siblings, we can't be all bad, can we?"

I let my eyes drift shut. Soon I will return to protecting my hoard from the dangers of a planet I was created to combat. Soon I will be watching over them again, giving my little near-extinct hoardlings another chance at existence. But for now…

For now, my caregiver's lap is warm, and my body still needs rest. For now, perhaps I can allow myself a reprieve. I drift asleep to the sound of tapping keys.

~ * ~ * ~

Ian Ableson is an ecologist by profession and a writer by choice. When not writing, he can often be found knee-deep in a wetland somewhere, sighing at a clipboard and asking the birds to sit still. They rarely listen. He has yet to find any dragons during his field-work, but he keeps his eyes open. He lives in Southeast Michigan with his wife and three cats.

A Pile of Amethysts

Abby Chinnock

There was an opal missing.

Kindle counted again, then again. Sixty-three opals, when she was supposed to have sixty-four. Where could it be? She walked in a careful circle, keeping her tail close to her hind legs so she wouldn't knock over any of the delicate piles she'd made around her claimed section of cave. She scanned the floor for a glint of white, and saw nothing. She checked her piles of morganite, rubellite, and spinel—nothing. No wayward opal.

She huffed, green smoke spilling out of her nostrils in annoyance. Where could it have gone? Perhaps it had stuck to her and dropped somewhere outside of her room. She left her hoard in four piles and stalked out, keeping her belly close to the stone floor, looking around suspiciously.

Kindle's hoard wasn't very large, but she was proud of it. The morganite was her favorite—the pale pink gemstones matched her scales the best—but all four types of stone were important to her, and even one gem out of place made the spines along her neck itch.

Her claws clicked softly as she stalked the cave system she called home, but she didn't see any misplaced opals. After a glance at the wide room at the mouth of the cave, and thoroughly searching the large room where her family ate, and seeing nothing amiss, not among the pile of bones in the corner, nor inside the grooves made by generations of claws working the stone, Kindle had to admit it had probably been stolen. Hopefully not, as she didn't really want to get into a fight right before Ember's big day.

Kindle crept out of the eating room and down the winding path to her brother's cave. Blaze and Flare were out hunting, so the room would be empty. She stopped outside the stalagmites that marked the entryway to their cave, and peered inside. A mountain of human money—gold and silver pieces—greeted her. Blaze had been so excited when Flare had shown him her hoard and he had discovered they collected the same thing. Now that their hoards were combined, the metal pile was almost overwhelming to Kindle. She squinted against the brilliance, searching for something different. Blaze's hoard had always been large, and Kindle was proud of him for it. The humans Blaze stole from were probably less proud of the amount of money Blaze had acquired, but that wasn't Kindle's problem. She was sure Blaze and Flare would know if their nest was disturbed, so when she didn't see anything she backed away. She would only resort to rooting through another dragon's hoard if she had no other options.

Ember's hoard was made of topaz and citrines, as well as garnets and jasper. Kindle couldn't imagine her sister taking her opal, but maybe she had somehow offended her. She lowered herself to the ground and pressed against the wall, hearing voices from the direction of her younger sister's cave.

"I can't believe you're even thinking about this," Ember said, her voice raised in agitation. Kindle crept forward carefully.

"I just want what's best for the family," the familiar rumble of Kindle's father responded. She peered over top of a bundle of stalagmites so she could see into the cave. Ember's hoard was split, about a quarter of it laid on the usual spot, and the rest of it piled on top of a green cloth. Ember herself was standing between the two piles, her tail lashing back and forth, an orange blur of scales. Kindle's father was standing opposite her, his thick tail standing out straight, wings tucked alongside his back.

"'What's best for the family'?" Ember repeated, incredulous. Neither she nor Coal had noticed Kindle lurking in the shadows outside Ember's cave. "You think that uprooting our entire generation will be what's *best for the family?*"

A surprised puff of smoke leapt to Kindle's nostrils, but she tampered it down before it could escape.

"Moving caves is *not* the end of the world," Coal said.

"I can't believe you," Ember turned, pacing. Her tail still lashed, knocking into the hoard on the cloth. She didn't seem to notice. "You're so…so—!"

"What?" Coal demanded, wings flaring. "I'm 'so' what?" Even from behind, Kindle could see red smoke pouring from his mouth.

"So *overprotective!*" Ember burst. "Just because I'm moving to the Misty Hills doesn't mean I won't visit!"

"That's not the problem!"

"Do you not trust Torch? She's a good dragon, she won't hurt me! I thought you gave your blessing." Ember sounded upset. Kindle knew the family liked Torch. She was funny, and cool, and she was obviously head over heels for Ember. Kindle couldn't imagine a better partner for her sister.

"No, Torch is—Torch is incredible," Coal said, wings lowering. "She's not the problem."

"What is, then?" Ember asked, tilting her head with narrow eyes. She wasn't smoking, but the fins on the side of her head were pressed toward her skull, tense. Kindle was definitely not supposed to hear this conversation.

"This cave is—too small," Coal said. He waved his tail around, gesturing to the space around them. "There's no room—when Blaze and Flare have eggs, or if Kindle ever decides to join hoards with someone—"

"Kindle's not gonna join *hoards*—"

"She *might*—"

"You don't know that!"

Kindle couldn't help but be a little offended, even though it was true she didn't really intend to join hoards with anyone anytime soon, if ever. She needed to stay home and take care of her dad more than she needed to find a mate of her own.

"I know my daughter."

"Apparently not well enough!" Ember sniffled. Sad ice-blue smoke was trailing from her nostrils. Kindle wondered how she could fix all this. "We've been the dragons of the Gray Mountain for generations. All the dragons before us have fit. You and Blaze and Flare and Kindle *and* Kindle's hypothetical mate *and* all their eggs will make it work."

"What if Blaze and Torch have *lots* of eggs?"

Ember rolled her yellow eyes.

"Kindle won't. Daddy, come on," she said. "Give it a rest, okay?"

"Okay," Coal said, sighing in acceptance.

"Good. You know I have to grow up sometime," Ember said. Coal sighed again, dark blue smoke billowing from his mouth.

"Yeah, I know. I'll leave you to it, then." He gestured toward Ember's hoard.

With panic, Kindle realized he was going to come out of Ember's cave. The space leading to Ember's cave was too narrow for her to turn around quickly without entering the cavern itself, so she froze. Coal ambled out of the cave. When he saw her, he sighed, then gestured with his head for her to follow him.

She did, neither of them saying anything until they were safely tucked inside his cave. Coal stood beside his hoard and eyed her, his expression unreadable.

"I'm sorry," Kindle said. "I didn't mean to overhear."

He stared at her longer, probably just to make her sweat, then sighed, a periwinkle burst of smoke puffing from his nostrils. "It's alright," Coal said. He sat, wrapping his tail neatly around his legs.

"I just—I don't understand," she said tentatively. "You've never …you didn't say anything about space when Flare moved in."

Coal huffed and didn't respond, tucking his tail in tighter. Kindle eyed the mountain beside him, rubies and garnets and amethysts towering over them both.

Where *was* that opal?

"You've never talked about moving before. You love this cave," Kindle said. "Even though the stalactites are smoke-stained and the ground is scratched."

"I do love the scratched ground," Coal said, running his claws along one of the grooves carved by years of claws. He sighed. "I'm just getting old, is all."

Kindle didn't say anything, though she disagreed. Her father was only around five hundred years old. Not very old at all—and he knew it. She tried to imagine what would happen if they *did* move. Moving wasn't really done, for dragons, unless another family died out and left a cave system open. Kindle wasn't sure where that would be, but then she remembered—

"Dad," she said slowly. "Are you—where do you want to move?"

"I've heard the Misty Hills are nice," Coal said. He didn't look at her. Kindle looked back down at the scratches beside her pale pink claws.

"That's where Torch's family lives," Kindle said. When two dragons joined hoards, one of them left their family and joined their mate's. In a few days, Ember would be a dragon of the Western Misty Hills. Kindle doubted it was a coincidence the dragons of the Southern Misty Hills all died out a while ago, and now all of a sudden Coal wanted to move.

"I know," Coal said. His tail was curled around his back claws in a tight embrace. Kindle thought he looked so tense he might explode. She exhaled a puff of purple smoke and stepped closer to her dad.

"Dad," she said. "Are you *stalking* Ember?"

"No!" Coal said. He sighed again, blue-gray smoke pouring out his mouth and nose, spreading outward miserably. "I just don't want my baby girl to go."

That was a little overdramatic, Kindle thought. Everyone had to grow up sometime. Kindle followed her dad's gaze to the hoard beside him. The purple amethysts glittered against the red gemstones. *Oh.* Kindle stepped closer, tucking herself against his chest and under his chin. She was still small enough to fit, and she curled her tail around one of his front claws. Her pink scales against his red ones reminded her of being a hatchling, wobbling around with oversized wings and sneezing out too-big bursts of flame.

Kindle remembered her mother. She remembered the violet scales curving, up, up, as her mother had seemed so huge and Kindle so small. She remembered clambering over her back, careful of the sharp spines, and she remembered her warm voice, rumbling softly. And of course she remembered the great sadness, after the accident. She remembered curling her tail around her golden little brother and her orange little sister, still just hatchlings. And she remembered her dad's great red tail curled around all three of them. It had been hard. Sometimes, it was still hard. But years had passed, and it was easier. But her parents had been married for three hundred years, so of course her dad was still affected. Of course he still felt torn apart from losing her.

"Just because Ember's leaving doesn't mean she'll be lost," she said softly. "She's gonna visit—we can visit her, too. The Misty Hills aren't that far away. It's okay, Dad." Ember was her baby sister. Kindle could remember her invading her cave, climbing all over her back, blowing streams of pink smoke into her eyes like it was yesterday. And in just three days, Ember would gather her hoard and fly it to the Misty Hills, spilling the topaz and citrines over emeralds and malachite. It was all kind of hard to believe.

Coal sniffed before curling his neck down to rest against her head. He exhaled silvery smoke and she squeezed her tail around his leg. For a long moment, they stood there together, breathing.

From afar, something clattered. Ember's voice raised in agitation. Kindle cleared her throat and moved away, uncurling her tail from Coal's leg.

"You should tell Ember," she said, stepping backwards. "She wouldn't be so mad if she knew *why* you were upset. No offense, but right now you just seem…really overprotective."

"I didn't tell *you*, you figured it out yourself," Coal said. "You're a smart dragon, Kindle."

Kindle ducked her head and exhaled pink smoke in pleased embarrassment. "Well, you have to tell her or I will," she said. She wasn't really sure if that was a warning or not. Maybe her dad would take it as an excuse to avoid talking about it.

"Why don't you go see if Blaze and Flare are back yet? I'll…go see if Ember's alright."

Recognizing the dismissal, and pleased he was listening to her, Kindle left her father's cave and headed to the mouth. The space was brighter than the rest of the cave, open wide to the outside world. The chamber adjacent to the mouth was wide, the place where the dragons of Gray Mountain would gather to get warmth from the sun. There was a small ledge outside the safety of the cave, and Kindle climbed onto it. She looked out, at the valley and the river, the human town in the far, far distance. Somewhere south was the Misty Hills. Somewhere east was the land her mother had come from. Somewhere high, high above was the sun, warming Kindle's scales. She exhaled a plume of fire, then squinted up at clouds.

Far away, she could see two shapes—one silver, one gold. Wings beating against the blue sky, claws laden with cattle. Kindle watched them as they neared, and backed into the cave as Blaze came in for a landing. He almost bumped into her.

"Sorry, didn't see you there," he said, before he picked up the cow he had dropped and carried it in his jaw to the eating room. Flare tossed her own cow down before diving into a landing on the ledge, and Kindle backed up even more to get out of her way. She bumped into the wall, and felt something dislodge in her scales. As Flare passed, Kindle twisted around.

Something clinked softly against the stone floor, and Kindle bent down to inspect it. It was her sixty-fourth opal, shining blue-white-pink on the ground. It had been on her back, all along.

From somewhere within the caves Blaze bellowed it was time

to eat. Kindle picked up the opal with her teeth gently, and she scurried deeper into the caves to join her family for dinner.

~ * ~ * ~

Abby Chinnock is a recent graduate of Bowling Green State University. She loves writing and reading, especially about dragons! You can find her in a local bookstore or at home writing, trying to figure out how to make her next story as magical as possible.

Her Treasure

Marlaina Cockcroft

She was an old dragon, and tired. The cold crept through the cracks between her scales in a way it never did when she was younger. The cave was too small, or else her body too big. She blew out a disgusted puff of smoke and resettled the coils of her tail around her. Sleep was supposed to come easy this dark time of year.

She was so mired in her own gloomy thoughts she didn't hear the noises at first. The scrabbling was nearly at her chamber before she lifted her great head, pointed ears flicking forward. How had she not noticed the sour, earthy smell of human? *Serve me right if I get gutted,* she thought, then, *curse all hunters, for eternity and longer.*

Silently she uncurled and rose. She stretched her aching neck toward the sound as the fire began to smolder in her throat. She was ready. *One more step, human. Raise your sword, hero.*

But there was no sword, only sobs. The sound struck her harder than a blow. She swallowed back the flames in an instant, wincing as they burned all the way down her body.

The girl flattening herself into the rocky wall of the dragon's cave was young, half-grown at best. Her tangled brown hair hung over her face. Blood dotted her dark skin and the front of her coarse green dress, though she appeared to be uninjured. She shivered in the winter air.

The girl didn't scream as the silvery-scaled dragon loomed over her, or even raise a hand to fight. Leaning her head back against the rock, she whispered, "Go ahead. They're all dead anyway." She squeezed her eyes shut.

The dragon stared down at the girl for an endless moment. She could hear triumphant shouts from the valley below. The air tasted of smoke, but not hers. The humans were killing each other again, it appeared. Whoever knew why.

Still, there was no honor or gain in threatening a child. The dragon had strong opinions on the matter. "Wait a moment," she told the girl, though her voice was creaky from disuse and she disliked the sound of it. "They'll be done and gone soon enough. Your family will be looking for you, or others in your village."

The girl slowly shook her head. "No one's looking for me." As though the words had only just sunk in, she began to cry in earnest. She slid to the rocky ground and howled.

"Ash and bone," the dragon said. "There must be someone else. You can't stay *here*."

But, clearly, she could.

~ * ~

The girl's name was Drea. She liked berries, didn't mind nuts, wouldn't touch the raw rabbits the dragon caught in the woods and diffidently offered in one bloody claw. She never cried again after that first day, except when she dreamed, curled up in a grieving ball at the foot of the dragon's nest. The dragon grumbled at her own lack of sleep. "I should've chased you away," she muttered at the small sobbing form. "I should've blown you into a lake. Or found another human and dropped you through their roof." She did none of those things. Instead she blew gently on the rocks around the girl, so they would stay warm.

She kept expecting the girl to grow tired of cave life, or to long for more talkative company. But Drea, once past her initial fright, seemed willing to do all the talking.

"The king died, that's why," Drea said, rubbing down the dragon's claws after a hunt. The dragon had growled the first time, had yanked her claws away—what kind of self-respecting dragon needs a human minder? —but the girl's hands were soothing, and after all her bones did ache. "It's all chaos. We're close to the borders of the next kingdom, and they've been sending troops over to capture more land. That's what my father said." Her voice broke on the last word, but almost stubbornly she continued. "We were packing to leave, we almost had the wagon ready, but we weren't quick enough. What's the point of knowing danger is coming if you still can't stop it?"

The dragon stiffened at the words. Her tail twitched across the cave floor. At Drea's curious look, her black eyes narrowed and a small growl escaped her massive lips.

Drea held still, out of patience or fear, who knew. Finally the dragon said, "Fair question." She might have said more, at least to another dragon. Instead, she shut her mouth with a snap that seemed to echo off the cave's walls. She climbed into her moss-covered nest, creaking all over with the effort, and didn't move till morning.

Sometimes Drea sang to herself at night as she braided her hair. The first time, the dragon snapped, "*Quiet*," then rustled around in the nest to cover the sudden silence. The second time, she groaned and flattened her ears. Drea kept singing, though, and eventually the dragon ignored it. She supposed the girl's voice was pleasant enough. One talon bobbed in time with the song.

When the dragon went out to hunt, her old body still sinuous as it slipped between the rocks, Drea also left to forage what she could from the frosted-over bushes in the sparse forest below the cave. But one day the dragon's luck was spotty, or else her hunting skills had slowed more than she'd like to let on, and Drea returned first. The dragon found her stretching her small body upward to see into the nest.

Her sudden snarl shocked them both. The dragon dropped her half-eaten prey and scrabbled past the girl, nearly knocking her over. She hunched over the nest as though guarding it. Her claws curled into the moss, snipping pieces away.

Drea righted herself and tilted her head, studying the dragon. Then she asked, "Where's your treasure?" As though they were having a perfectly pleasant conversation.

"None of your business," the dragon said. Her ears flattened back against her head. "Asking for a dragon's treasure. The thing we spend our lives collecting. After I share my cave with you, very much against my better judgment."

Drea's eyes widened at the dragon's harsh tone. Oh, *now* she saw the danger. Humans and their presumptions. "I don't *want* it," Drea said, backing up a step. "I just wanted to see it. My mother said dragons kept beautiful things in their caves."

The dragon snorted, breathing harder. A black puff of smoke floated past Drea. "You humans kill us for our treasures, and you leave our bodies to rot." Two more smoke puffs followed.

"But...don't you steal the treasures from us in the first place?" Drea said, then gulped at the dragon's low growl. "Please don't be angry."

"I never invited you to stay," the dragon roared, rearing up to the cave's roof, wings spread wide, as terrible as she had ever been. Drea ran off into the trees, hands curled above her head as though to ward off a blast of flame.

The dragon growled again, this time in disgust, and her wings folded back inward as her breathing slowed. The truth was, treasures weren't always gold. Treasures came from many places: interesting bits of earth, shiny things from the sea. A broken scale, won in a fight with a rival dragon. Stones left over from a newly hollowed-out cave. A dragon's treasure told the story of their life, the things they'd seen, the deeds they'd done. Any dragon could have explained that, had any human bothered to ask before greedily swinging a sword around.

Not that Drea had a sword. Drea was certainly no threat. But she was still a human, wasn't she? Still poking that tiny nose in where it didn't belong. The dragon sank deeper into her nest, shutting her eyes, wreathing herself in smoke. It filled the cave.

Hours later, long after dark, she heard Drea creep back. She grumbled about it through the points of her fangs but feigned sleep until the girl settled down beneath the nest. She warmed the rocks as usual, then blew out a smoky sigh. What an old fool she was, after all.

One claw curled tightly around the dragon's treasure.

~ * ~

Drea burst into the cave, breathing hard. "We have to leave."

"We?" the dragon asked dryly. No new snow today, less cold to trouble her bones, and she'd been enjoying the quiet. Lazily she stretched out one wing.

"The king's men are back," Drea said. "They're hunting. A whole clutch of them, coming toward the mountain. I saw them from the trees. They'll find the cave." The acrid smell of her fear was overpowering.

The dragon made a surprised grunt, then lifted her head. Her black eyes narrowed to slits. "There are always hunters. I'm not leaving my cave." Soft circles of smoke began to drift from her nostrils. "You should go. Get over the mountain. There's another village in the valley, likely safer than yours was." At least there had been a village, the last time the dragon had flown that way. When was that? She'd lost so much time, sitting here alone.

"Please!" Drea clambered up the side of the nest and reached to touch the scaly snout. The dragon blinked in surprise. "You're the only friend I have," Drea said. "They'll kill you for your treasure. Please leave with me." Her brown eyes were shiny with tears.

The dragon drew in a breath, then inched backward, crouching over her nest, gripping it with all her claws. Her tail whipped around, raking the back of the cave. "No one touches my treasure," she said. Her gravelly voice wavered.

Tired. She was so tired. She could never leave.

The girl's face crumbled and she jerked her hand away to wipe her eyes. Sparing one last look behind her, as though to be sure the dragon wasn't following, Drea skidded down to the cave floor and stumbled away.

She'd be all right. The dragon was sure of it. Drea would find herself a new family, like she should've done weeks ago. Go torment other humans with her questions and her constant nonsense songs.

But the dragon felt a pang. She could still see those teary eyes.

She waited, ears flicked forward, listening. Grunts, shouts, booted feet scraping across rock. The wafting smell of unwashed men. A murmur just beyond the cave entrance. The ring of swords unsheathed.

The dragon's lips curled back into an unpleasant smile. They were ten, perhaps? Even at her age, she could roast at least six before they overpowered her. A good number. She patted the treasure beneath her. A good number indeed. And a pleasant rest at last.

She sat straight up in surprise at the scream. It was high and defiant, and it was followed by several angry yelps.

"*Stubborn* child," the dragon snarled, leaping from her nest.

Drea was above the cave entrance, leaning from the overhanging rocks, flinging stones at the soldiers. She didn't see the man who'd crept up behind her, didn't have time to dodge before the man shoved her, shrieking, off her perch. The dragon saw, too late to stop her fall. Drea landed heavily on the rocks below and went silent. Men and dragon alike stared down at her.

One word burned through the dragon's mind: *Again. AGAIN.*

She reared up and bellowed her fury at the cringing men, then unleashed a torrent of flame. Several of the men collapsed into a blackened heap. Several more turned and ran. One man who'd dodged the flame managed to land his sword in her shoulder. Snarling at the pain, she hooked her claws in him and swept him aside.

She shouldn't have been this powerful. She hadn't been this powerful in years. It gave her grim satisfaction to reduce the men to ash.

She only stopped spewing flame when she heard the moan. Behind her, Drea struggled to sit up. The dragon lowered her head to peer at her. "Where are you injured?"

Drea didn't seem too bloody. The dragon quietly exhaled with relief. "My shoulder, I think," Drea said. Her voice shook. "My hip. It hurts."

"No doubt. Can you ride?" The dragon jerked her head to point at her back.

Drea's eyes widened. "I think so—" She drew herself up and put a brave scowl on her small face. "Yes, I can."

"Good. Stay there a moment." The dragon flew to her nest and swept up the small sack at its bottom, then alighted next to the girl. "You'll need to hold this."

Drea nodded and somberly took the sack. She gasped in pain as she crawled up the dragon's side but kept going anyway, lowering herself into the well between the dragon's shoulders. She lay there trembling as the dragon took to the air. Higher they climbed, the highest the dragon had flown in years.

"This is a small treasure," Drea said after a bit. Her voice was stronger, as though the pain had receded somewhat. "It's just some gold shards."

The dragon was silent.

"These are eggshells, aren't they?" Drea said. She paused, but hearing no protest from the dragon, pushed a little further. "My mother saved my first lock of hair. Was this your baby's egg?"

The dragon made the softest sound. It might have been a sob.

"Your child died there," Drea guessed. "That's why you didn't want to leave."

The dragon remembered despite herself. It had been a hard winter, and she'd had to go farther from the cave to find them food. The hunters had surprised her son while she was away, and the half-grown dragon—foolish, far too reckless—had ignored her instructions and tried to fight instead of fleeing. At least that was her belief. She'd returned to a dark cave, her son destroyed on the floor. Only eggshell shards left of her treasures. She'd keened loud and long, then crawled into her nest and waited for the hunters to return, any hunters, so she could claim her justice or die trying. She'd never stopped waiting.

"I'm sorry," Drea said.

The dragon sighed deeply as her wings carried them forward. "Do what I tell you from now on," the dragon said, the wind bringing her voice back to the girl. "I might not be able to protect you the next time you misjudge a fight."

"Yes, dragon," Drea murmured.

"There ought to be healers of some sort in that village. I'll leave you to find them." The dragon paused. "And then I suppose you can help me settle a new cave. If you like."

"Really?" Drea's voice was bright and happy.

The dragon didn't know what to do with such happiness. "Only if you don't fall off," she growled. "And don't drop those shards, either. Understand?"

"Yes, Mother Dragon," Drea said. She still sounded like she was smiling.

Mother Dragon. The dragon hadn't needed a name in a long time.

She supposed that one would do.

~ * ~ * ~

Marlaina Cockcroft (she/her) loves to write about misunderstood monsters and all manner of folklore. Her short stories have been published in *Daily Science Fiction*, *Mythic*, *Factor Four*, and in *Dark Matter Magazine*, as well as the anthologies "Strange Fire: Jewish Voices from the Pandemic," "Stories We Tell After Midnight, Volume Three," "Dark Cheer: Cryptids Emerging, Volume Silver," "Summer of Sci-fi & Fantasy: Volume Two," and "Fear Forge: Fall Quarter 2023."

You can find her on bluesky: @mdcroft.bsky.social

On Instagram: @marlainawrites.

Visit her website at: marlainacockcroft.com.

Ephemeral Gems

S.R. Hatcher

Ice—it was everywhere. Water crystals glowed upon the slatted roof and towered in a glimmering spire from the singular turret. An infinite number of the little gems glittered upon the snow in the garden, and the pathway gates were coated in a fine layer of intricate frostwork. Cracked windowpanes were delicately held together by winter's hold upon them, and the mortar between stone bricks was slick with the glassy polish. The abandoned castle was frozen in an eternal season of long night, the cold unyielding to the ebb and flow of time. And Bryte absolutely loved it.

His roost was made in the unmoving water of the castle gutter; the perfect place to curl up during a snow squall, his leathery wings a well-fitted blanket. But Bryte did not mind the winter, not at all. Freshly hatched, he had happened upon the lonely castle in the thick of the northern wood and instantly fell in love. His favorite jewels grew here in abundance—a hoard ripe for the picking. The plentiful ice and snow perfectly matched his glacial scales and breath of frost. It was as if the icy castle had been specially constructed and left for him.

Bryte went about his days strengthening the protective shell of ice surrounding the castle with his breath, breathing new crystals into areas where the sun tended to leak through the thick barrier of pine. When this chore was complete, he delighted himself with his most favorite activity—sculpture work. Ice sculpting came naturally to Bryte as a frost dragon, and he had to admit that after a couple years honing his craft among the empty passageways of the castle, he had perfected the art. His many gargoyles and sea creatures kept him company in the otherwise empty ballroom, and chandeliers of stagnant blue flame hung from the spiral stairwell. Ever frozen, the fireplaces were chilled over with self-portraits standing proudly with taloned wings spread wide…with an admittable amount of hyperbole in the wingspan. The turret framed his prized piece: a giant crown set with azure sapphires of the densest ice he could conjure, their geometric cut reflecting the filtered moonlight just right.

The frost dragon's hoard of ice could not last forever, it seemed; his blissful isolation coming to an end one strange morning. On a particularly sunny day, the sound of hooves clattered through the frostbitten forest, stirring Bryte from his peaceful slumber in the castle gutter. Alarmed by the premonition of invasion, he hastily dusted his wings of the overnight flurries and took up his sentinel perch in the eves of the castle entryway. As a carriage loomed closer through the unkempt path in the forest, Bryte had to muffle an icy growl.

What a racket the carriage made! The mud-colored horse snorted out a puff of steam. One of the hind wheels squeaked with every rotation. Stacks of luggage crates jostled against one another as the carriage leapt over exposed roots. And the family was as noxious as ever! The man and woman were bickering loudly down the entire path.

"We are in the middle of nowhere, Garth! Honestly how are we to raise a child *here?*" came the woman's voice, her shrill notes threatening to crack his delicately repaired windows. Bryte's ears flattened against the scales and horns of his neck in a menacing scowl.

"We are not 'in the middle of nowhere,' Hattie. It is a mere two-day journey to the city," the husband—Garth—retorted. He slapped the horse's reins, urging her to move them faster toward the castle.

"That does not excuse the fact our daughter will have no one to socialize her. She will grow up to be an outcast, an old maid, a hag!" Hattie cried.

"Mama, am I a hag?" a little girl squeaked from between two baskets in the very back of the carriage. Bryte listened intently for her mother's response.

Hattie turned in the bench seat beside her husband. "No, my dear Raynee. You are no hag," she said reassuringly. "I simply worry you will crave isolation if you do not live with others your age. It is important."

Bryte chuffed, and frost bloomed upon the eves where his claws dug into the ancient wood. There was nothing wrong with isolation, and it certainly did not make one a hag. The magnificence of what he created in the castle with nothing but his breath and no one to teach him was testament to that. These insolent humans would surely ruin his masterpiece.

"Here we are! Our new home," Garth announced as the carriage came to a rusty halt before the garden path. "Can you believe the treasury gave this up for such a bargain?" The man stood from the bench seat and admired the arched stonework. Bryte wondered, in a moment of uncertainty, if the human was also taken with his artwork.

"I can believe it," Hattie mumbled bundling her woolen scarf tighter about her chin and sliding off the carriage. Again, Bryte suppressed a growl on behalf of his home, even though it would be best if the humans were disgusted with it. Then, they might leave.

But then two little moccasins landed in the snow in the back of the carriage, and a girl not much taller than the horse's knees ambled toward the garden gate. Her cheeks were rosy, and wisps of snow-white curls poked out from beneath a fur-lined hood. And her eyes—they were full of enchanted wonder.

"Mama, Papa, does a queen live here?" she asked excitedly. Her blue eyes crinkled as she stared up at the turret. Despite himself, hope swelled in Bryte's chest and he ruffled his wings expectantly from his hiding place.

"Don't be silly, dear. What makes you believe such a ridiculous notion?" her mother scolded as she assisted her husband in unloading their essentials.

"The crown! The queen's crown way up there!" Raynee pointed with her mitten toward Bryte's most regal sculpture.

Hattie glanced up at the turret. "Oh, dear, that must have been from an ice storm," she said dismissively. "No one has lived here for centuries."

"It's a fixer-upper!" Garth said with zeal.

Bryte bared his teeth. Nothing about his castle required fixing. But as the family lugged their belongings beneath him and through the double doors of his home, he did nothing to stop them. He let them walk into the castle as if it were theirs, laying claim to what was rightfully his.

Once the little girl trailed in after her parents, Bryte swooped through the doors before they could creak closed. He took up a post among the flying buttresses of the foyer, posing as if he were one of his gargoyles. He did not wish to be discovered—not yet. Eventually, he would make his presence known and scare them from his home. But for some reason—be it maleficence or curiosity

—he stayed his tooth and claw and simply observed.

The father—Garth—made some comments about "old bones" while traipsing through to the salon, the mother—Hattie—rolling her eyes in his wake. The daughter—Raynee—did not follow them. She lingered in the foyer, unnoticed by her parents. Her wide eyes were entranced by the ice chandelier hanging proudly above the central stair. Bryte stilled his breath. If her gaze roamed just a little to the left, he would be in her sights. He was not sure if his statue-like countenance would be enough for her dismissal of him.

He was caught in those beautiful, round, inquisitive eyes. Raynee was the one fixed upon his artwork, the delicate icicles illuminated by his uniquely blue flame, but Bryte was the one who was truly enchanted. Not once had he ever considered someone other than himself receiving joy from his endless hours of loving labor. Yet now, his frosted heart was set ablaze by the notion. This little girl, an insignificant being compared to the eternity of solitude stretched before him, held his very soul in her tiny hands.

Finally, Raynee fixed her attention upon the velvet carpet of the sweeping stair, and Bryte let out a relieved puff of frost. Hood-ed head trained upon the deep sapphire of the steps, she ambled to the second level of the iced-over castle. Bryte was suddenly thank-ful he had left the stairs alone, as the ice would have proved hazard-ous for such a clumsy creature. She was so unsure of herself she had to use all four of her pudgy limbs to carry her up the carpet and into the true marvel of the castle.

He heard, rather than saw, her cross beneath the grand, silver arch of the ballroom. Raynee let out a shrill gasp, excited footsteps echoing soon after. Bryte glided from his perch in the foyer and silently followed her on to the dance floor, selecting one of his self-portrait sculptures as a hiding place. He felt a pang in his chest as he watched in horror when the little girl slipped on the smooth ice of the floor. But she merely giggled with glee as she skidded down a veritable gauntlet of woodland creatures and twisted saplings, all hewn from ice. She struggled to flip herself over and crawl on all fours, her mittens slipping and sliding against the dance floor. After several hilariously failed attempts, she selected the sculpture he presumed to be her favorite, for why else would she risk injury to get to it?

Bryte watched with what he now understood to be adoration

as she stroked the scaly neck of one of the sculptures depicting himself. His reflection gleamed in her sparkling eyes, her smile splitting even wider. Such a delicate creature she was. No fangs, no talons, no wings or arrowhead tail. His heart cracked open when she fell forward and embraced the dragon statue. Bryte stood on his hind legs to get a better look, peaking a fraction of a scale's breadth over his cover.

A terrified shriek caused him to recoil, and he fell backwards onto his wings. Bryte scrambled to regain his balance and his dignity, his wings flapping and claws digging into the ice beneath him. Once he gathered himself, he looked back at Raynee to discover she had kissed the statue…only to get her tongue stuck on the ice-molded scales.

Listening to her wails was pure torture, and his ears flattened to dull the pain. He looked this way and that to find a solution, but there was no liquid water to be had in this castle. There was no way for him to melt any of the ice surrounding him, either. Try as he might, nothing he did could ever mimic the power of the sun. His fire was as cold as it was blue, emitting light but no heat. Rubbing his scales together was no good, either. The sparks which flew from them were more like the stars of the night sky; distant, cold, and untouchable.

Little Raynee continued to cry. What could he do?

He heard her parents call for her, and footsteps barreled up the central stair. Stifling a growl, he pushed off and landed among the gargoyles guarding the vaulted ceiling. Blinded by her tears, Raynee had not seen him.

"Raynee?" her mother called, "Raynee, what did you get yourself into this time?"

A low snarl rumbled against his chest, making his scales tremor like icicles in a storm.

"Raynee!" Hattie cried running through the entrance arch, her husband hot on her tail.

But the two did not last much longer on their feet. Hattie was the first to slam onto the ballroom floor, her feet flying out from beneath her. Her husband was quick to follow. When he extended an arm to help her up, his center of gravity tipped and he, too, went skimming between the obstacles on the ice rink Bryte had so lovingly created.

Now everyone was screaming.

"Garth! Grab something!"

"I can't grip ice, Hattie!"

"Your steel-toed boots must be good for something!"

"Not for ice skating!"

Raynee just continued to wail incoherently.

Hattie's hair came undone, and she was effectively blind with a mop of hair over her eyes as she finally tumbled into a holly shrub Bryte had sculpted a week prior. In a crumpled heap of scarves, she could do nothing but watch as her husband shot past her. Garth landed in the fireplace just to the right of the holly, disappearing into a black cloud of ancient soot.

"A fireplace! What a stunning feature!" Garth called between coughs from within the ash and brick.

"Garth! Our child!"

"Right."

Raynee was still screaming. Bryte wondered how her voice box could withstand such a high pitch, but that curiosity was muted by his overwhelming concern for her. These parents were so slow, how could they guard such a helpless little girl? They could not be her only guardians. Perhaps the horse outside acted as a guard dog, too.

With a cautiously feeble gait, Garth made his way to his screaming daughter. It seemed to take all his concentration not to slip and fall again. If Raynee could hear her father over her bleating cries, Bryte was sure her vocabulary would expand by at least ten new words today.

"Here, Raynee dear," Garth cooed as he unfastened his water bladder and tipped a splash onto her tongue, which had begun to turn a startling shade of blue.

Raynee pulled her tongue free, but the tears came raw and fresh with her new wound. Icicles brimmed in Bryte's eyes, for he could not form liquid tears. He turned away, squeezing his frosted eyes shut.

"Let's start a fire, get some of this ice melted," Garth murmured as he helped his daughter and wife off the ice.

An amber glow warmed Bryte's shuttered eyelids, and he blinked them open. The family was huddled about a spitting fire, the dry wood having easily caught aflame. Raynee's cries had softened to intermittent sniffles, and she snuggled beneath her parents' arms. Bryte watched them with renewed curiosity. Hattie and Garth interlaced their fingers over their daughter's back, Garth caressing his thumb over his lady's cracked knuckles. Despite himself, Bryte tried it with his own claws, clasping them together over his chest. He felt nothing through the tough layer of scales.

Bryte shook his head, spread his wings, and soared across the ballroom and back into the foyer, leaving the family to thaw their fingers and the poor girl's tongue.

"Was that a ghost?" Hattie whispered anxiously.

"No such thing my dear, I'm sure it was just the old bones of the castle heating—"

"If you say 'old bones' one more time…"

Bryte landed silently before the oak doors of the castle and crawled through the worn crack at their base. Once outside in the familiar chill of the never-ending winter, he sprung to his favorite gutter and curled on the unchanging ice. He coiled his ice-tipped tail about himself to keep cool, resting his chin between the spikes. Beneath the shimmer of aurora and star, he let out a puff of blizzard and fell asleep, his dreams warm with Raynee's laughter.

~ * ~

He awoke the next morning to the grating din of metal on ice. A shovel, it had to be. Bryte's ears perked up, and he popped his head over the gutter rail to find the most atrocious sight he had ever beheld.

Garth was merrily scraping away at the garden path with a flat-ended spade. He had already cleared the snow and ice from most of the stones, leaving behind a trail of overturned pebbles, hardened mud, and sorry scraps of chipped ice. Bryte could only watch in horror as the beautiful layer of cold was peeled away by the man's industry. To add insult to injury, when Garth was finished with his shoveling, he sprinkled course-grain salt along the path, ensuring the ice would not return. Bryte cringed at the sight of such an evil substance, the frost in his stomach churning into a tempest begging to be unleashed.

Just before he lost control and sprayed the garden with a fresh flurry, a delighted shriek reverberated off the castle stonework. It was Raynee. Bundled anew in a down parka, wool scarf, and fresh mittens, she toddled across the garden on the path her father had cleared, arms swinging wide to maintain her balance.

"Papa! You ruined it!" she cried. Bryte chuffed. He could not agree more.

Garth turned from his work and set down his pail of ice melt. "I only made it safer for you and Mama, my dear Raynee." He knelt before her and tucked a little white curl from her rosy cheeks. "Ice is dangerous. Remember yesterday?"

"Papa, I *like* the ice! Put it back!" she argued.

Bryte smirked, but Garth said, "I know, my dear, but it is not safe. Your mother was very cranky this morning and…"

But before he could continue, Raynee crossed her arms, turned away, and marched back for the castle. Bryte ducked close to the gutter. If she were to spare one glance up, she would see him.

Garth sighed a puff of fog, staring after his forlorn daughter. Then it looked like an idea struck him, and he began to gather fresh snow from the pristine portion of the garden. Bryte watched suspiciously as he packed the snow into a tight ball, then chucked it at Raynee's turned back.

There was no holding back his growl this time, but luckily for him, it was drowned out by another one of the little girl's squeals. He peaked over the gutter enough to check if she was hurt, and was met with a surprising smile.

"Papa!" she cried with glee as she attempted to make her own snowball. She was a horrible ice smith. The powder kept exploding between her mittens.

Garth allowed her the time to form a rudimentary chunk of snow and toss it at him. It barely landed on his steel-toed boot. Even so, he yelled, "You got me!"

The two went on like that for hours, trailing two very differently sized footprints through the remaining snow of the garden. Bryte snorted his disapproval, but the girl's smile was as innocent and beautiful as the morning after a storm. He let them have their game as he snuck about the outside of the castle, performing his usual duties of patching the windowpanes the sun had managed to melt.

~ * ~

The next day, Bryte heard Garth leave in the wee hours of the morning, entering the wood surrounding the castle with a bow and sling of arrows. He silently hoped the man would come home empty-handed, but then remembered little Raynee needed to eat. Sending a prayer of sympathy to his fellow fauna of the forest, Bryte crept inside the castle to check on his sculptures. They were his only friends, after all.

A sinking feeling weighed upon his heart as he crawled through the crevice between the double doors to find the chandelier of ice which once hung in the foyer was missing. It was then he realized how stiflingly warm it was within the stone walls. The climate was unnatural, and the air was hazy not with frosted mist, but an oppressive cloud of smoke. Ash and fear tightened his throat as he flew through the first level of the castle.

All the fireplaces were lit, the hellish tongues of fire lapping at the burnished grates. In the salon, all his ornaments had gone, withered to droplets among the moth-eaten furniture. The kitchen no longer held its blue-tinted shine, the ice-made wineglasses shattered upon the floor. The armory was empty save for the armor made of steel, and the servant's quarters held barrels of water rather than finely cut crystals.

Willing himself to investigate further as a new layer of ice coated his heart, Bryte ascended the central stair and collapsed upon the ballroom floor, for he was met with utter destruction. The prized room was no longer slick with a silver finish of ice, but sopping wet with water which might as well have been boiling. Puddles were pooled haphazardly about the hall where his fine sculptures once proudly stood. The holly, the trees, the vixen, the raven, his own self-portraits, they were all forgotten. The fire had radiated them all, its evil penetrating even the scales of his sculpted dragons. It was gone. All of it. His life's work, his hoard of eternal ice, washed away in a matter of hours.

Icicles rolled down his cheeks and chimed against the floorboards, his wings drooped in the puddle where the little girl had kissed his statue. She had loved his work as he had. She had found joy among the ice. He had been so willing to share all his art with her, but the parents had ruined it, just as they had ruined the purity of the garden.

Footsteps echoed down the hallway to his left, and he begrudgingly fled his empty gallery, coming to perch on the banister of the central stair.

"Oh good, those hideous things are gone. Now we won't slip," Hattie muttered through a yawn.

But Raynee had a much different opinion. "My dragon!" she cried.

The little girl ran to the spot Bryte had recently occupied and crawled through the puddle. As she scooped up the melting icicles of his tears, she wailed, "This is all that is left of him! Bring him back!"

"My dear Raynee, those were left by whoever owned this place before us. Very irresponsible if you ask me. If this place was not mostly stone, the water damage would…" Hattie began, but her voice faltered when Raynee began to sob uncontrollably.

She shushed her daughter emphatically and reassured her that her father would be more than happy to make a snowman with her outside, that way, she would have a friend. "Snow doesn't stick to your tongue, so it will be better!"

"Can I make a snow dragon, or does it have to be a snowman?" Raynee whimpered.

Bryte's heart shattered. He could watch and listen no longer and so flew outside where it was nice and cold, just how he liked it. As he landed in the refuge of his icy gutter, he shut his eyes against the sight of Raynee's father hauling a bloodied stag up the garden path by the antlers, an arrow through its throat.

~ * ~

Bryte was again roused by the oppressive sounds of outdoor labor. Rubbing the frost which had accumulated on his eyes overnight, he squinted over the gutter to find Garth sawing away at one of the ancient pines. Would the man never stop?

He heard one of the oak doors creak open and Hattie's voice called over the woodworking. "Garth! What on earth are you doing?"

Garth paused to bid his wife a good morning and replied with, "We need lumber to rebuild much of the furniture and fuel the fires. Anyhow, bringing down these trees will let the sun through our windows, helping to heat our new home!"

When he said it, the premise of his labor sounded so merry and fruitful. But Bryte saw right through his eagerness and focused on the words 'fires,' 'sun,' and 'heat.' Those were three things he could do without.

But over the next week, Bryte was forced to watch in horror as Garth tore down the frocked pines which once towered protectively over the castle. The sun bared down on him and his castle with all its might, as if it saw its chance to finally blast its wrath in full force upon his ice, as if it had been waiting for the opportunity.

Bryte tried desperately to patch the windowpanes, to rebuild the spire, to preserve the dense sapphires of his most prized, ice-hewn crown. But his breath of frost was no match for the sun. Even on the most frostbitten days, the shimmer of ice upon the roof slats would eventually give way to the sun's eternal flame. Even his bed had run warm, the gutter singing with a newborn river of liquid water.

Weeks turned into months which stretched by with no hope of the family leaving. He could not scare them away, lest he risk terrorizing the little girl. Bryte had already seen her cry twice now, and he did not want to repeat the experience. But the wonder which his ice sculptures had brought her was now vanished from those big blue eyes, and when she left the castle doors to skip about the garden, she no longer gazed up at the castle turret where the crown was once magnificently displayed.

He slept in a burrow he dug in the snow like a pathetic hare, hidden among the freshly trimmed shrubs of the garden. This was his life now, the only glimmer of joy—the times when Raynee would play in the snow and sculpt her own imaginations of dragons.

Then, one day, he had enough of sleeping in the snow. He was determined to sleep in his old roost. The humans could not melt everything that was his—he still possessed his breath of frost.

Bryte breathed his ice upon the running water of the gutter. The gush of melted snow and ice was relentless, but after several stubborn minutes of an icy roar, the gutter was dry with newly minted frost. Spitefully satisfied, he curled up in his usual way within the gutter. He finally caught a good night's sleep, the aurora swirling above him in soothing spirals.

~ * ~

With dawn came the familiar, happy tune of Raynee's delighted squeals. Emerging from his slumber, Bryte's ears perked at the sound.

"Mama, Papa! Look!"

Bryte peered over the edge of the gutter but ducked back down hurriedly. The little girl was pointing a mitten right where he was sat. Had she finally noticed him? Fear plunged him into an anxious stream of thoughts.

"What is it dear?" Hattie's sleep-ragged voice asked.

"Look!" Raynee cheered again. "The icicles! So pretty!"

Bryte could sing. There must be icicles hanging from the gutter where his frost had begun to melt in the morning sun. And Raynee liked them.

"Oh, yes," Hattie croaked dismissively, and Bryte heard the castle door shut as the she ambled back inside.

"So pretty," Raynee sighed. Bryte smiled with her.

Every night thereafter, Bryte frosted over the entire gutter. After a few nights of this, he expanded his work to include every ledge on the castle so in the morning, the hard lines of the structure were framed with his ephemeral gems. Every day, they would disappear, but he finally had his hoard once more, and Raynee positively loved it.

Bryte kept up his work until one day, everything went horribly wrong.

He took up his perch in the eves above the grand entrance to the castle. From there, Bryte could easily watch from afar as his little girl ran about the garden to admire all the icicles dripping from the castle. He had learned to accept it; he adored Raynee. She gave him life when his sculptures no longer could, and made him feel less alone than he had in his entire existence. He was only a few years old, the vast expanse of his immortal life only just begun. All the same, the past few years had been markedly isolating when compared to his days spent with Raynee.

She had no idea he was there among the eves, swooning over her wonderment of the frost and ice, let alone even existed. But that was okay with Bryte. He was content to simply watch over her, an unseen protector and personal artist.

His eyes crinkled as Raynee ran beneath his roost in the gutter where the most prominent icicles had grown. She giggled as drops of the purest water speckled her cheeks and nose, dripping from the jagged ice above. The little girl danced and held out her mittens, welcoming this simple joy of the endless winter.

A *crack* caused his ears to twitch, and he realized too late the sun was more brilliant today than it ever had been, shining in a direct, blaring ray upon the work of his frost breath. Fear pierced his heart deeper than any icicle could.

Another *crack* and one of the icicles fell from the gutter. Raynee was standing directly beneath it, her cheeks still red with her innocent smile.

Bryte did the only thing he could do. Taking flight, he launched himself at the girl and the object of her adoration. Suddenly, he felt too far away. He was not a protector, merely a watcher, unfit to save her from the natural world. But the thought tickled the back of his mind that this was not the doing of winter. Sure, the sun was the one to crack the ice, but *he* had unknowingly set the trap, and Raynee was no more than a snared faun staring death down the arrow.

The icicle was halfway to piercing those big blue eyes, and shock had finally registered upon the little girl's face. How far away was he? He hoped more than halfway. Gravity was a terrible force, he decided. Why did it have to work so quickly?

He was not sure he would make it. The sharp tip of the icicle glistened menacingly, taunting him. Bryte considered firing a blast of ice to knock the icicle off course, but then he would risk freezing over the very girl he was desperately trying to save. He could not risk her, but he already had when he made those deadly, impermanent crystals.

The dagger of ice was inches away from Raynee's stricken expression, and he was close enough it looked like two icicles were falling towards each other, tip to tip, the second one the reflection in her enormous eye. There was no way he would make it. The girl would die today, and it would kill him.

His claws made purchase with the ice, the feel of it perfectly natural between them. The cold was where he belonged, frozen in time like the sea that never thawed. Change was his enemy; the increase in temperature, the lengthening of the days, the arrival of a human family.

Though change had brought him Raynee, it might kill her, too.

Bryte landed cleanly in the snow beneath his gutter home, icicle clenched firmly beneath his hind legs. Without checking whether he had made it in time, he summoned his breath of frost and formed a protective dome of ice around him and the little girl. The shield closed above just in time, the force of his magic shaking the remaining icicles loose to rain harmlessly down upon the frost cover. They stuck in the icy shell, their reverberations singing an eerie melody.

Satisfied with the shield's integrity, he slowly turned to face where Raynee stood. She was still standing, which was a relief in it of itself. There was no blood, no mark upon her. But her wide eyes were unreadable and focused on him.

Bryte withered under her gaze. He tried to shrink himself down so as not to appear so menacing, so monstrous and…well… like a dragon. Tucking his wings and tail close, he sat upon the melting snow, facing her head-on so she could see as little of him as possible. Even so, his snout was at her eye level, and it must have been terrifying to stare down the maw of winter incarnate.

Miraculously, a familiar smile bloomed across her face, crinkling her glacial eyes. He considered returning her smile but thought better of it. He knew it would only serve to bare his arsenal of icicle -sharp teeth.

"You saved me!" she cheered and ran toward him. The little girl collapsed around him, flattening his wings in a tight embrace.

Startled, Bryte did what he did best: he froze.

Then, after a moment, he softened into the warmth of her arms and ever-so cautiously curled his tail across Raynee's back. Her heated body was like a breath of summer, and Bryte decided maybe change was not such a terrible thing.

"Raynee? Raynee where are you?" a muffled voice called from outside his protective shell.

It was her father. Forgetting all caution around scaring the child in his care, Bryte rumbled a growl low in his throat.

Raynee pulled away, taking her warmth with her, but said, "It's okay, dragon. It's just Papa." Then, she called, "I'm okay, Papa! I'm in here!"

Fear tightened his chest, and his eyes went wide as his ears flattened. He remembered Garth hauling the stag from the woods. Would he be met with an arrow, too? Would his scales, his ice, be enough to protect him?

"Raynee! How did you build this?" His blurry figure stood over their miniature world of frost.

"I made a new friend! Just promise me you will be nice to him."

Bryte shuffled nervously, awaiting her father's response.

"A new friend? Raynee, just come out of there." Bryte could

sense the anxiety in the man's voice.

Raynee shook her head and said, "I need you to promise."

A sigh. "Fine, I promise to be nice to your friend. Please, come out."

She nodded at Bryte, and he understood. He spread his wings, and she snuggled close to him as he wrapped her safely within them, melting his heart even more. Once he was sure every bit of her was shielded, he fired a spray of hail, shattering the shell of ice into a thousand frosted shards.

Garth gave a yelp and leapt backward against the breath of the storm. When the snow settled, he was cowering on his side in the garden, an arm up in a feeble attempt to guard his face. Pathetic human.

Bryte unfurled himself from his Raynee and this time, he did not minimize himself. Garth needed a proper introduction to the true master of this castle. He arched his lithe frame and lifted his wings so the spines along his scaly back were on glistening display. His teeth were bared in a threatening snarl, his lip curled back to brandish their icy sharpness. His nostrils flared, exhaling a wintry mist as his ears tensed against his crown of icy horns. To round off his demonstration, he coiled his arrowhead tail in front of Raynee to signify she was his charge, his to protect.

Garth just lay there in stunned silence, mouth agape. He did not even seem to be breathing.

"Look, Papa! A dragon!" Raynee shouted merrily, throwing her arms in a wide gesture as if she were showing off one of the dragons she made of snow.

Her father stammered, and Bryte growled once more.

"He saved me," she added.

After another moment's hesitation, he said, "Raynee, I…there's no such thing as dragons." He stood and dusted off the snow and ice which clung to his pants.

How could he say such a thing when he stared down at the very object of his disbelief? Bryte roared fiercely, a cloud of frosted mist emitting from between his teeth.

Garth whimpered, and he backed away some more. *Good.*

"Garth, dear, what is going on out here?" Hattie stepped into the garden, shivering in her night robe. She froze when she saw her daughter surrounded by winter's death. "Raynee…" she gasped.

"Mama, this is my dragon!"

Hattie cowered with Garth, shrinking under his arm.

"What is that?" Hattie warbled, her lip quivering.

Garth whispered, "A dragon, apparently."

"Don't be cross, Garth! Dragons are children's stories."

Do I look like a children's story to you? Bryte let out another roar, and he stepped a taloned foot in front of Raynee. The two adults shuddered, but Raynee giggled.

"Can we keep him? *Please?*" Raynee begged.

Her parents did not have much of a say in the matter. This was *his* castle, after all, and *his* little girl to protect.

~ * ~

As Raynee grew, so did Bryte. While she matured to become a beautiful woman with sterling hair and eyes which could freeze over an entire ocean, he rapidly surpassed the horse and eventually matched the castle in size. He outgrew his roost in the gutter, and instead took to encircling the castle in a protective slumber each night.

The two of them were inseparable and delighted themselves in crafting the most stunning ice sculptures together. She was even better than he was at the finer details. Though on sunny days their work would be reduced to nothing more than a slushy puddle, they took joy in creating a new masterpiece with every dawn. And upon occasion, when the cloud cover was particularly thick, Raynee rode upon his back to dance among the aurora hidden above. It was a life made full by love.

Raynee became the venerable ice queen of the castle in the forest, where she was written into myriad iterations of legend. She and Bryte ruled over their domain with frost and kindness, shepherding the beauty of their arctic world.

As for Garth and Hattie, well, they soon had enough of Bryte's perpetual disdain for their presence and left to rejoin the other humans when their daughter reached adulthood. Even so, they never again doubted the truth of children's stories.

~ * ~ * ~

Samantha R. Hatcher is an LGBTQIA+ biologist-turned-nursing student who pulls inspiration from anything and everywhere, then packages it in the fantasy genre. She lives with her husband and black cat in southwestern New Hampshire, where she works on the labor and delivery unit in the hospital. From teaching women's self-defense at the public library to holding the writing group late at the local bookshop, she knows there is nothing that cannot be done while surrounded by books. All in all, she is a passionate storyteller and believes daydreams and nightmares alike are too real not to put down on paper.

A Dragon Looks at Four Thousand

Ron Fein

And so, in his last days, the great dragon Gorelka slumbered on his heap of gemstones, surrounded by a sea of gold trinkets. His great red wings rested atop his colossal frame, their now-dull scales reflecting the dim light of the enormous chamber carved deep inside the mountain. And when the human (or halfling or dwarf or whatever it was) crept into the cavern, Gorelka sighed, half opening one eye. With little enthusiasm, he mumbled, "Tremble, ye mortal, for I am the great dragon Gorelka...Ravager of the Skies and so forth."

The human—Gorelka was now confident it was a human, from the stench of the urine that trickled down its leg—hesitated. Gorelka clenched his still-sharp teeth and frowned. The end was near, and he did not wish to prolong it.

So he spread his wings, opened both eyes, and snorted. A thousand years ago, Gorelka would have *roared*. A blast of molten heat would have blazed forth, his volcanic breath engulfing the cavern in fiery light and illuminating its golden coins, goblets, and diadems, so they sparkled like tiny coruscating stars.

That was then.

"Well?" Gorelka boomed.

The human—a pitiful thing, its expected life span barely eight years, or was it eighty? Gorelka could never remember—stammered and blinked.

"Well?" Gorelka repeated. "Aren't you going to pose me a riddle, or try to trick me into rolling over so you can find a vulnerable spot?"

They thought they were so original, with their clever little plans. But after four thousand years, a dragon knows all the tricks in the scroll.

The human wiped its hands on its trousers. "Greetings to you, Great Dragon Gorelka! I have come to...praise your wisdom and marvels." Its eyes darted left and right, searching for an exit.

Gorelka croaked a weak chuckle. "Is this really how it ends? After four thousand years, for my final opponent to be so pathetic? You won't even try to trick me into eating ox hides filled with quicklime, or calf skins stuffed with burning sulfur, or cakes made with pitch, fat, and hair?"

The human stared blankly, uncomprehending.

Gorelka rolled his eyes. "Something to make my stomach burst?"

"Ah," the human said. "To be honest, I thought I'd focus on praising your stupendousness and magniloquence."

Gorelka snorted. "Flattery and lies will not save you."

The human backed away, crouching and tracing its hand over a golden tiara encrusted with diamonds and pearls.

Even fifty years ago, such an offense might have stirred Gorelka to incandescent fury. In his younger days, at the slightest provocation, he would rear on his hind legs, his eyes blazing red. "Tremble, ye mortal!" he'd roar. "For I am the great dragon Gorelka, Ravager of the Skies and Bane of Men!" Once, eons ago, the theft of a *single* golden chalice from his lair (not even a distinctive or valuable one) had so enraged him, he'd laid the entire countryside to waste.

Now, it all seemed so pointless.

"Never mind," Gorelka muttered. "Steal it, or don't. Nothing you do will change what happens." He heaved a great sigh, folded his wings, and settled his weight back down onto the pile of diamonds, sapphires, and emeralds that formed his bed.

Over four millennia, he'd faced *so many* enemies. Some were devious, like the scoundrel who'd dug a pit between Gorelka's cave and the spring where he drank his water, then when Gorelka lumbered past, stabbed his underside. Others were powerful, like the sky-men who'd hurled thunderbolts until he relented and called the rain.

All of them were dead.

The thief's feet crunched through the piles of treasure as he scampered out the cavern, but Gorelka didn't budge.

He yawned, and his heavy eyes drooped. Four thousand years is a long time, even for a dragon. He'd scorched farms and cities, devoured cattle and maidens, and fought heroes and saints beyond number. If this last opponent wouldn't grant him a worthy fight, so be it. Let the great dragon Gorelka, last of his kind, pass from this world in peace.

In the end, what did it matter? All the treasure he could ever want surrounded him. It was never enough, and it was far too much, until, at last, it was a bitter joke—the charred remains of lusty ambitions he couldn't even remember. Now, all Gorelka wanted was nothingness.

Gorelka closed his eyes. He was ready, now, for his struggles to end—for oblivion.

He dragged out one last sulfurous breath. Then his grey heart stopped, and his massive saurian frame burst into crackling green fire. Oily black smoke enveloped the cavern as his scales, bones, and finally innards burnt through.

The great dragon Gorelka, Ravager of the Skies and Bane of Men, was—at last—no more.

~ * ~

Hours passed—perhaps days. The smoke slowly cleared. No one was inside the cave to witness.

But if someone *had* been there, they'd have seen a great concave depression in a mound of glittering, razor-sharp jewels—a crater left by a monstrous body that formerly called the pile its bed.

At the pit's center, something small—something bright green and gold—rustled among the gemstones. Its eyes blinked open. For the tiniest moment, its shoulders sagged. It wheezed a raspy sigh— as if to say, *Not again.*

Then it cleared its fierce little throat, unfurled delicate red membranous wings, and announced with a tinny roar, "Know me, and tremble! For I am the great dragon Gorelka, Ravager of the Skies and Bane of Men!"

Originally published in MetaStellar (May 2023)
Reprinted with permission of author

~ * ~ * ~

Ron Fein is a Boston-area public interest lawyer, writer, and activist who writes science fiction, fantasy, horror, mystery, and comedy. His work appears in *Nature*, *MetaStellar*, *Daily Science Fiction*, *Nonprofit Quarterly*, *Factor Four*, *Mystery Tribune*, and *McSweeney's Internet Tendency*.

Find him at ronfein.com, on Mastodon @ronfein@masto.ai, on BlueSky @ronfein.bsky.social, and on Threads @ronaldfein.

End of the Line

Jean Rabe

It sparked and thrummed and Baozhai purred as she drank it deep, the electricity pulsing through the third rail. It slipped through her claws and up her legs, shot into her muscles, and wrapped tight around her heart.

Giving her power and bliss and filling her belly near to bursting.

This evening she sped along the rail following the 6 train to the stop at Canal, near the best restaurants that perched overhead in Chinatown. Even dozens of feet beneath the earth she smelled the scents of garlic and soy, all of it sweet, bitter, and spicy. They reminded Baozhai of her of long-ago-home. She had abandoned the Da Hinggan Ling Mountains north of Hailer and south of Russia nearly two hundred years past; the villagers there had fed her until she grew too large for their meager provisions. She left to find more to eat and to see the world, and had managed to visit many lands and taste innumerable delicacies, but stopped her travels when she discovered the tunnels beneath New York City and fell in love with them.

And discovered electricity from the third rail was all she needed to sustain her.

This was her home now, but each evening she followed the 6 to smell Chinatown above.

There were odors underground, too, robust—a redolent assault of oil, filth, cleaning liquid that never got anything fresh enough, and the miasma of stink from people too long without a bath coupled with perfumes of the fine-dressed mingling among them. She even smelled the spray paint on the sides of the subway cars, could tell which ones were freshly decorated.

The sounds played strong here, too, as Baozhai raced behind the 6. The clatter-chug of wheels, mechanical wheezes, echoes bouncing off the walls, the hoot of something low and far away and interesting. Faintly, sirens. Chatter and music from the buskers seeped from train cars ahead. Languages—English primarily, but a smattering of Italian, Spanish, Russian, Bengali, Cantonese, and Yiddish. She knew all the tongues of the world.

This realm beneath the surface was a delight for her oh-so-acute senses.

She'd continue past the Old City Hall section on the train's route to Brooklyn, banking down a closed side tunnel before heading home. But first, she would take her prize. Baozhai'd had her large emerald eyes on this train car for a few weeks. It was perfect for the plucking now.

The serpentine dragon flexed her talons and held fast to the underside of the last car, jiggling it, jiggling it again, stronger this time, hearing an alarm, the people inside shout, most of the words Spanish.

"Huir de!"

"Escapar!"

"Abandonar!"

"Run!"

She smelled their foreboding and felt their feet hurry across the floor and into the safety of the car ahead. Baozhai didn't want to hurt the people; she found them too remarkable and curious to eat, and sometimes they were useful.

She whipped her tail forward, feeling, stretching, finally finding the coupling mechanism that latched it to the car ahead, nudging it, worrying at it, severing the connection from the rest of the train.

Separated, her prize slowed, finally stopped, and she slithered out from underneath it.

Baozhai was a big dragon, but thin like a snake and so able to coil in spaces as tiny as a subway car. Her scales shimmered brilliant gold like polished coins in the paltry light of the tunnel. Her equine-shaped head was burnished and festooned with glimmering barbels that twitched with her pleasure. She was cunning and oh-so-careful, but sometimes people saw her, half-glimpsed in disbelief, wide-eyed children struck with wonder. Years past an old Mandarin couple who rode the 6 stopped often, conversed, and left her offerings. Human lives were too short. Baozhai knew the two had died shortly before the Worth Street station closed.

So many shuttered stations and abandoned tunnels beneath the city, Baozhai knew all of them, traveled them, stored her hoard in the deepest pockets where men no longer ventured, not even the so-called urban explorers. *Her* tunnels now, *her* stops, 18ᵗʰ Street, 91ˢᵗ Street, the Cobble Hill Tunnel, forgotten and old and perfect.

She tugged her prize to one of them now, continuing to feed on the third rail as she took this special car into the darkness to join the others.

Baozhai had one hundred and twenty-eight cars in her collection, one for each year the subway had been in operation, plus eight extra taken during the pandemic years, the times when the once 24/7 subway system closed from one to five a.m. each day for disinfecting. People were more concerned about viruses in those months than missing cars. Easy to take them, fewer workers around, more time to ogle the cars and make her selections, little significant security.

Sometimes she took the cars destined for discard. Thirty years or so the city used each one, a few had reached forty. Then they were dropped into the sea to create an artificial reef. Baozhai had visited the reef many times in the company of a dragon turtle friend. The water was murky, livable, populated with all manner of creatures without language, but not home. She much preferred her subway tunnels, New York's arteries that kept the city moving.

Baozhai had moved in during 1900, when diggers started on the system.

They did all the onerous work, carving each passage, installing the mechanicals, electrifying the third rail which fed her. And through the decades they abandoned sections of it just for her, though in truth she claimed all of the underground. Her treasures, she kept those in the closed places. Like this car she added to the lot right now.

Baozhai had selected this car because of the art. Emblazoned with colorful scrawls of paint. *Harlem, SMOG, Ghost Peppers, Trajen* and *Bobbi O*, all in big balloon letters of blue, yellow and purple, which was her favorite color. Side profiles of men in hats, open lips, skyscrapers, flowers, gang symbols. This car was so richly decorated that had she not plucked it, the city men would have scrubbed it, made it bland and boring.

Baozhai eased back and studied it, her sharp eyes picking through the shadows of the chamber and revealing each swipe the spray paint can had rendered. Amazing work, a jewel in her collection.

But not *the* jewel.

That was the Continental.

She slithered into the next chamber to view her greatest and oldest treasure. Baozhai knew everything about each car in her collection. She'd listened to the workers, tour guides, and occasional news crew that ventured into the tunnels, committing to memory all the key details about the cars. Sometimes she chose a car based on an interesting tidbit.

She rose up and widened her eyes, taking in every inch of the Continental.

Manufactured by the Jewett Car Company in St. Louis in 1903, it began operation beneath New York City one year later. Only five hundred were made, and this was likely the only one remaining in all the world.

Her priceless treasure.

It was able to carry fifty-two people seated, one hundred and ten standing. Fifty-one feet long and almost nine feet wide, it was made of wood and copper, and therein nested its value. All the other subway cars after it were made of stainless steel, safer and more durable. Not as beautiful in Baozhai's estimation, but perhaps easier to apply spray paint to.

The first line it ran on opened October 27, 1904, along Centre Street, Elm, now Lafayette, Fourth Avenue, Park Avenue and to Grand Central Station.

She had a later model Continental tucked away down another tunnel, this made of steel and with the improved seat configuration. All the Continentals were retired in the 1950s, deemed obsolete, destined for scrap or the reef.

Baozhai tapped a claw against the ground and purred and thought about her newest acquisition. There was another car in operation also heavily painted, not quite as stunning as the one she'd just taken, but close. Dare she abscond with one more this soon? Dare she break her one-car-a-year scheme? The pandemic had served as an exception, and today she saw several people wearing masks. Perhaps another malady raced through the city. Another pandemic? Perhaps she would take the other car tomorrow night.

In November of 1928, Baozhai remembered the city's Board of Transportation sought bids for steel cars for the new line that would service Eighth Avenue and Central Park West and down to

Washington Heights. She had three of those cars on display. They carried more people than her beloved Continental, at sixty feet long and ten feet wide. These cars had four double doors on each side, more knee room, and when stuffed with sitting and standing passengers could accommodate more than two hundred.

The seats were heavy rattan, and Baozhai thought the natural color and pattern of the weave quite artful; she wished they would have continued using them. The white-enameled hand straps in front of the seats were bright in their day, now looking like ivory.

That batch of cars had been labeled the "arnines" after contract numbers they'd been assigned—R1, R4, R6, R7, and R9 respectively. All told in the pre-war years more than seventeen hundred nearly identical subway cars were delivered to the city between 1930 and 1940. The three Baozhai had in her collection were numbered 101, 300, and 1802…the last to come off that manufacturing line and to boast a grouping of stark black and white spray paint art.

She had two Pullman Standard Company cars, one made in 1975 and one from 1978; that series had replaced all the arnines and some of the General Electric-powered R16s. The 70s was a decade of strong police presence in the tunnels; crime was up, as well as grime and graffiti. Fascinating to take it in, a mix of sadness and smiles to watch the cars all cleaned and the tunnels rendered more civilized. The music was better then, she thought, as she was partial to disco—Donna Summer, and the Village People, when listeners were looking for Hot Stuff at the YMCA.

She had little patience for rap and country.

Baozhai had a pair of Redbirds acquired during the first pandemic year. These were cars painted bright scarlet and replacing older B Division cars, including the entire fleet of R32s. One of her Redbirds was pristine, not a speck of graffiti. When she'd plucked that one it sent the subway workers into a panic—they'd searched extensively for the missing brand-new car and in the end ruled it must have been a discrepancy in the order versus delivery. Baozhai had feared discovery and did not take any unused cars after that.

Another prize was one of the eight cars from the 1930s that were kept in vintage condition and dubbed the Holiday Nostalgia Train, used on special occasions.

Every car important and integral to her horde.

Baozhai also displayed trinkets she'd found around the tracks or left on the stolen cars—lighted helmets, lunch boxes, workman vests, orange cones, "closed" signs, and garments she'd piled high to serve as a pillow for her head. A few musical instruments abandoned by buskers when she jiggled a car too strongly and they fled without their belongings. A guitar with broken strings, a trumpet, and small joined drums. She enjoyed music, lingering in tunnels close to stations sometimes when the entertainers were particularly good and not performing country. Books, she'd amassed a stack of those, too, rumpled paperbacks moldy and dog-eared, hardcovers that might be filled with mysteries and murder, and electronic tablets that had long-since run out of batteries to display their romances and biographies. A discarded brassiere, snow shovel, naked manikin without a head, man-sized plush banana, and a small charcoal grill were arrayed on a natural shelf down the next tunnel. Everything remarkable, but none of it as special as the cars.

Baozhai's head snapped back toward the way she'd come.

Something.

She heard something. Not the normal whisper-chitter of the rats who shared the underground. A footstep against metal, and then another, faster.

Like lightning, she whipped around and shot toward her new subway car to see a rumpled man stagger from it...someone who had not fled into another car when she'd disconnected this one.

She smelled his stink and the odor of strong drink.

A drunk, likely passed out and only now rousing.

Baozhai did not kill. People were too fascinating. And sometimes useful.

He mumbled a string of unintelligible words, swayed, and gripped the side of the car when he noticed her.

"D-d-dragon," he managed before belching a puff of cheap whiskey. "D-d-dragon."

Perhaps she could return him to one of the stations, release him to find his way home. Others had seen her during the decades. The Mandarin couple. Wide-eyed children.

But none had seen her lair and her collection.

Her priceless treasures.

"D-d-dragon."

"Baozhai," she replied. "I am Baozhai."

He would sober, and she would dress him in cleaner clothes...

she had a mound of discarded garments and something would fit him. Perhaps he could play the trumpet or the drums, read to her the hardcover mysteries. She'd tie him down when she was gone on her explorations, and she would bring him food and blankets and take good care of her pet.

And she would give him something vital to do until his human-short life reached the end of the line.

The Continental needed polishing.

~ * ~ * ~

Jean Rabe tosses tennis balls to her cadre of dogs when she isn't writing. She's the author of fifty novels in the mystery, fantasy, and science fiction genres. She's landed on the USA Today Bestsellers and Amazon bestsellers lists, is the recipient of the IAMTW Grand Master Award, won the Illinois Author Project Award for her novel *The Bone Shroud*, and claimed three Silver Falchion Awards with co-author Donald J. Bingle for *The Love-Haight Case Files*. She lives in a blink-and-you-will-miss-it town in middle Illinois.

Bound by a Golden Curse

Carol Hightshoe

"Lord Sidayth."

The ancient gold dragon opened his eyes and glanced in the direction the voice had come from. Only strangers called him 'Lord.'

"Yes?"

"Tales of your generosity have reached far and wide and I've come to ask for aid."

Sidayth raised his head, a handful of gold coins shifting under him as he looked for the visitor. There, outlined in the opening to his cave, was a young man. The threadbare clothes appeared to indicate desperate need, but there was something about the man that ran counter to that appearance. Instead of the humility those coming to him normally demonstrated this petitioner stood up straight and his blue eyes met Sidayth's without looking away. All this indicated an attitude of arrogance and entitlement as well as extreme confidence—all the markings of a wizard. Still, he had aided wizards in the past, so that, of itself, was no reason to refuse.

He released a gentle breath of steam, activating the wards that would let him know if his guest was speaking truthfully or not. "State your request," Sidayth said.

"My wife has been very ill and I used our savings in seeking help for her. Now, it is late in the season and in my concern for caring for my wife, I neglected other matters and we do not have the resources to make it through the winter. If you would grant me but a handful of coins, that should be enough to get us through the winter to the spring. By then, I'll be able to go back to work and once again support my family." He bowed his head and waited.

Sidayth saw the faint flash of silver from the wards. The man was lying. While he had never denied anyone, the stories that were spread said those who approached only out of greed would become victims of the dragon's rage. The threat tended to keep the greedy and curious away.

He glanced around at his dwindling hoard. The remaining coins and gems would fit into less than a handful of sacks. A small enough amount they could be carried away by a man with a single horse. Over the last few centuries, he had given away most of his treasure to those who were brave enough or desperate enough to seek him out. A lifetime of hoarding had led him to being the last of his kind. Now, the only thing left was to give away the rest of his hoard so he was able to pass through the veil into the Twilight.

"What is your name?" Sidayth finally asked.

"Rolduc, my lord."

"And where do you come from?"

"The village of Eldras."

Sidayth felt a tingling on his scales…magic. Rolduc was indeed a wizard.

"And what is your profession good Rolduc?"

"I am a carpenter, my lord."

Sidayth studied Rolduc. Details previously missed became apparent—the threadbare clothes were not as worn as they initially appeared. Rips and tears were actually carefully placed cuts. Stains were freshly smeared mud. Worn, not because of poverty but, with the intent to deceive. Rolduc's hands were uncalloused with no scars; they spoke to a life that had never done the work of a carpenter. Most telling was the covetous gleam in Rolduc's eyes as they glanced around at the scattered coins and gems that remained of the once immense hoard. Too many lies and no true need.

"Very well." The dragon raised his wings and looked down at Rolduc. "That is your third lie, wizard. While you may indeed be from Eldras; your name is not Rolduc, neither are you a carpenter nor are you in need of coin." The dragon sensed the subtle workings of magic being summoned. Complex sigils and runes appeared, glowing with power, as the wizard drew on his magic. Sidayth flexed his claws and took a deep breath.

Rolduc raised his arms then brought them down quickly and a flash of light filled the cave. "You are correct Sidayth, however, I have had time to complete my spell." He said when the light faded.

Sidayth closed his eyes and shook his head as a wave of dizziness and confusion threatened to overwhelm him. He inhaled deeply and released his flame, only to hear the wizard laughing. Something was wrong, he could feel magic tingling all over his body, covering him like a second set of scales. Binding him in some way. He opened his eyes. A large emerald blocked his view of the wizard. Had the wizard summoned it as a shield? The laughing continued and a shadow fell over Sidayth. He looked up to see the wizard towering over him. He glanced down and realized he was no bigger than one of the gold coins he had been lying on. He tried to take a step and found he was bound to the coin.

"Now dragon, I will take your entire hoard and you will help me to become the most powerful and wealthy man in the land."

Sidayth growled and released a tiny puff of flame, but Rolduc only laughed as he placed the tiny dragon and the gold coin on a rock where he could watch as the wizard gathered what was left of the hoard into a sack that glowed with magical energies.

The wizard looked at the coin then laughed as he dropped it on the ground. "I leave you your last coin, dragon," he said.

Sidayth flapped his wings trying desperately to fly, but the weight of the coin he was bound to was too much for him at his current size. He released another tiny flicker of flame as the wizard reached for him.

The wizard chuckled, then ran a finger over Sidayth's head and gently down his back. "You will be my good luck charm," Rolduc said picking the dragon up and holding him in his hand. "You will make me wealthy and powerful."

Sidayth felt another tingle of magic surrounding his body and realized the wizard was placing more spells on him. He tried to relax and read what was being cast as he called on his own magic.

"There," Rolduc said after the magic settled. "You are now bound to me, to be recalled to me by my magic no matter where you are."

Sidayth puffed smoke as he contemplated the magical bindings. Finally he looked up and spoke. "Granted." He paused then grinned slightly. "I can read the magics you have used, and I will agree to the binding, not trying to break it, as I most assuredly can. I will even aid you as you seek to use me for your own gain. However, know this wizard, if you ever let me pass into the hands of another without receiving something in exchange—your spells will be broken, and I will leave and take whatever remains of any treasure you have acquired by using me to cheat others."

"That day will never come," Rolduc said dropping the tiny dragon into a velvet pouch.

~ * ~

Sidayth lost track of the fairs and markets Rolduc displayed him at. The wizard would set up a small tent and charge a nominal fee for folks to see him. Sidayth dutifully upheld his side of the bargain, unfurling his wings menacingly, puffing smoke and flickering flames at those who approached as Rolduc explained he was the last dragon in the world and now bound by magic in this relatively safe form. He would caution that if the dragon escaped his vengeance would be great. However, he would also preen whenever one of the nobility or a wealthy merchant approached. He even purred when a woman or a child would ask to pet him. As expected, someone would eventually offer a large sum for Sidayth and then after the exchange was complete, the wizard would warn the buyer if he didn't take great care, the dragon might escape the spells binding him to the coin. He would then make a show of strengthening the spells and advise the buyer to seek out another to continue doing so periodically saying if the dragon did break the spells, it was not his responsibility what happened to the buyer.

To his credit Rolduc would wait at least a week before summoning Sidayth back to him. Just enough time to cause the previous buyer to believe the spells had weakened allowing the dragon to escape. He suspected with the implied threat Rolduc gave about not being responsible for what happened if Sidayth escaped the magic on him, the buyers were relieved he had just escaped and not attempted to seek revenge. Perhaps they believed he was pursuing the wizard who had trapped him.

~ * ~

"Are you the jeweler Brinna?" Rolduc asked entering the small shop in Rixam, the capital city of the Istanuran Kingdom. The wizard paused in the doorway and slapped the road dust from his clothes. He had been wandering for several years since trapping the dragon and he was now indeed one of the richest men in the realms. He had finally made his way to the capital of Aurea. A small but wealthy kingdom, one whose queen was known for her interest in the magical arts, though she herself wasn't mageborn. It was said, that in addition to her regular councilors and advisors, she kept a separate council made up of seven wizards to advise on matters of magic.

"I am," the older woman said looking up from the piece she was working on and pushing her gray-streaked black hair back from her face. "How may I help you…" she asked standing up.

"Rolduc. I'm here seeking a position on the wizard council of Her Majesty Queen Evelyn of Istanura."

"Yes, I heard one of the wizards recently passed beyond the veil." Brinna bowed her head slightly and brought her right hand to her chest.

Rolduc copied the sign of mourning and peace. "If you have the time available," he said after several heartbeats had passed. "I would like to commission a piece."

"It would depend on the commission," Brinna said.

Rolduc set the velvet pouch on the table and opened it.

"Is that a dragon?" Brinna asked reaching out to touch Sidayth who purred at her.

"Yes, I believe he is the last of that ancient race. He has been bound by powerful magics to this form," Rolduc said smiling.

"I see." Brinna gently touched Sidayth's back and his purring grew louder. She continued to stroke the tiny dragon and Rolduc waited patiently for her attention to return to him.

When the jeweler finally glanced up Rolduc took the opportunity. "I am seeking a way to either attach him to a pendant or a broach so I don't have to carry him in this bag. He's too small to ride on my shoulder or on a hat safely. Without a way to secure the little guy, he could easily fall off and be lost or, even worse, seriously injured."

"I see," Brinna said. She gestured to Sidayth. "May I?"

"Of course."

The jeweler picked up the dragon and carefully examined the coin and where his feet connected to it. "He cannot move from this position?"

"No. Unfortunately, there is no way, that I am aware of, to break the magics binding him. Although perhaps together with the wizard council, I might be able to free him."

Rolduc's eyes narrowed slightly when he saw Sidayth's head quickly turn to look at him. However, he smiled slightly when the dragon didn't say anything.

Brinna placed the dragon back on the table. "Wait here, I might already have something." She turned and vanished into the back of her shop.

"Cannot break the magics binding me?" Sidayth asked looking up at Rolduc.

"Not without losing you," Rolduc replied.

Brinna stepped out of the back with a woven chain in her hand. "It's heavier than most women like for a necklace, but I believe it would be perfect for your friend." She handed the chain to Rolduc.

"It seems to be strong. But the coin needs to be attached in such a way that it is a flat platform not hanging."

"No problem," Brinna said. "I can use four sections of the chain, that way the coin becomes a suspended platform."

"Ah, that would indeed work."

"Now, would you prefer a chain around your neck or a broach you can attach to your cloak?"

Rolduc glanced down at the dragon and smiled. "A chain," he said placing his hand below his neck. "He should hang to about here." He indicated the middle of his chest.

"Of course. I can have it for you in two days. Have you scheduled your appointment with the wizard's council yet?"

"No." He placed another velvet pouch on the table, the coins inside clicked. "Is it possible you could make it now…while I wait?"

"I have other commissions waiting," Brinna protested.

Another pouch joined the first one.

Brinna glanced back at the piece she had been working on then back at Sidayth and the chain she held.

A third pouch joined the others.

Brinna smiled and nodded.

"He has brought me good luck for quite a while, I would prefer to not risk losing that luck by being parted from him for any length of time," Rolduc said apologetically.

"Very well." Brinna picked up the dragon. "You may have a seat by the window."

"Wait," Rolduc said quickly. "May I have a token to hold, please?"

"You're not leaving him with me," Brinna said raising an eyebrow. "I promise I will not flee out the back door. I will be working where you can see me."

"I understand." Rolduc grasped his hands together. "It's just a silly superstition I have. Since he's my good luck charm, I have to receive something anytime he's in the hands of another or I may lose the luck just as I may lose the luck if we are parted for any length of time." He shuffled his feet slightly and looked down at the floor.

"Wizards and their superstitions," Brinna muttered as she handed Rolduc a claim token. She then stepped around the table and placed the chain around Rolduc's neck measuring the length carefully before cutting it. "There, now take a seat."

~ * ~

Sidayth watched as Brinna fitted the ends of the chain with small metal caps. She slipped the clasp ends through a small hole in the caps and then slid them back on the ends and welded them to the chain.

The chain itself appeared to be woven from several different metals. Sidayth could see gold, silver, and platinum weaving through it. Multiple strands of each woven also with strands of iron to give the whole strength.

He watched as she hung the chain on a hook, then pulled several gold filaments from the unused portion of the chain and began weaving them around a thick iron thread. Her hands moved quickly, and he listened to her soft humming as the gold covered the iron. She repeated the weaving with a second group of gold filaments and another iron thread. After sliding the newly woven chains through a gold loop she hung the loop on another hook and picked him up.

With care she examined the coin and how he stood on it. Sidayth was pleased that at no time did she flip the coin over or treat him as just another piece of jewelry. She held him delicately and always in an upright position.

"Well, my little friend," she said. "I don't see anything actually binding you to the coin, so I assume it's magic holding you there. I do wish it was possible for you to shift your feet away from the edge just a tiny bit so I can place a small loop through the coin without risk to you."

Sidayth nodded and felt the magic binding him shift slightly and he was able to lift one foot and move it. Then another until all four had been repositioned.

Brinna's eye went wide and she smiled. "Maybe you are more than just a lucky charm," she said. "Maybe you can grant wishes too."

Sidayth shrugged his wings. "I don't know. That is something I have never been known to do, but so much magic has been placed on me and soaked into my being that it may very well be possible. Also, no one else has made a wish on me before."

"May I test the theory with something a little selfish?"

Sidayth smiled. "Yes."

Brinna walked over to another table, opened a small box and lifted a ring out of the box. She placed the ring in front of Sidayth. She glanced over at Rolduc and saw he was occupied watching the people passing by the window. "This was my great-grandmother's ring. Because of the age and wear on it I cannot wear it without risk of losing the stones. It is too fragile for my skills to repair. I wish for it to be repaired and the setting to be strong enough to protect the stones from being lost," she said in a soft whisper.

Sidayth saw a small tendril of magic reach out from him to wrap around the ring. When it vanished the ring looked almost new.

Brinna picked the ring up. "Thank you," she whispered.

Sidayth nodded his head. It felt good to help her even in his captivity. He was glad he was once again able to do something for someone as he had when he was giving away his hoard.

"Please don't tell the wizard," Sidayth pleaded. "He will only use this power for personal gain or power over others."

"Wasn't my wish also for personal gain?"

"Yes, but it wasn't made out of greed, it was made out of love for the legacy your great-grandmother left you." He paused and sniffed at the ring. "Your great-grandfather made this ring and gave it to her when she married him. It has been passed to all the first-born girls in your family and they have worn it as their wedding ring. You wish to pass it to your daughter who is getting married soon. That is the ring's legacy, and it reflects the love in your heart. That is not greed."

Brinna placed the ring back in the box and only nodded as she added the caps to the ends of the suspension chains, punched the holes in the coin and connected everything together. When she was finished she held the chain up and looked at Sidayth. "Does it feel solid and stable enough for you?" she asked holding the dragon up at eye level close to her face.

"Unfortunately, yes."

Brinna nodded. "I make one more wish," she whispered. "That

the day comes soon when you can break the bindings placed on you and return to your home."

"There is a way to break the bindings within the magic that was cast," Sidayth said. "Perhaps your wish will allow that condition to be fulfilled." He stretched his head out and licked her nose. Brinna giggled. "I've never been kissed by a dragon before."

"Ah, I see you are done," Rolduc said walking over.

Sidayth dropped his head as Brinna handed the chain to the wizard. He hoped her wish would come true sooner rather than later.

~ * ~

Rolduc glanced in the mirror as he prepared himself for his interview with the wizard council and Queen Evelyn. Sidayth rested on his platform where the chain hung against his chest. He had noticed the dragon being able to shift around on the coin, being able to stand, sit and now even to lie down as if asleep. He could sense no change in the magic binding the dragon which he reinforced regularly. The layers upon layers of magic were almost blinding when he looked at Sidayth with his wizard's eye. *No,* he thought. *There is no way the dragon is escaping.*

Carefully smoothing his robes, Rolduc left his room and headed for the chambers of the Istanuran Wizard Council. He nodded politely to the people he passed in the street. Many of them smiled and raised their hands before them with their fingertips touching as they muttered something he was unable to hear. He knew the Istanuran Kingdom was one where wizards and other practitioners of the mystical arts were revered, so perhaps it was some sort of formal greeting they were offering. He had only been here two days. And other than meeting Brinna and then arranging for his interview, he hadn't really spent much time outside of his room. He spotted Brinna opening her shop and walked over to greet her.

"Wish me luck," he said. "I have my interview today."

Brinna turned around. "Good luck to you."

"Perhaps you can answer a question for me?" Rolduc asked.

"I will try."

"I see many people I pass on the street doing this and muttering something I cannot understand." He demonstrated the gesture. "Is it some sort of greeting? If so, is there a proper response

I should give?"

Brinna smiled and looked at Sidayth. "It is simply a wish for the health and well-being of your dragon," she said. "There are many within our realm whose ancestors worshiped the dragons. And, there were once rumors of great dragons in the Vritra Mountains who would aid those who came to them seeking help; even to giving away portions of their treasure hoards."

"A dragon who gives away his treasure hoard. That seems most rare." Rolduc grasped the edges of Sidayth's coin.

"It would seem so. But, there are many who claim to have visited the dragon and received his kindness. As to what you are seeing. People have heard yours is the last dragon, so they only want to offer wishes for his health and well-being. Since he is yours, I would imagine those also extend to you."

"Is there a return gesture I should be making? It seems impolite of me to not properly acknowledge people offering their blessing on my dragon."

"There is no formal return gesture. However, a polite nod or smile will let them know you acknowledge their blessing on your dragon."

"Very well." Rolduc handed Brinna a coin. "I thank you for your time and information. Now, I must hurry to my meeting with the council."

"Of course. Best wishes on your interview, Lord Rolduc." Brinna smiled then nodded toward Sidayth. "May I?"

Rolduc nodded and she placed a finger on the dragon's head. "I wish you success today."

Well wishes for my dragon? Rolduc thought as he walked. *People have heard he is the last dragon. How? I have not displayed him, nor have I told anyone here about Sidayth—except Brinna. Perhaps her family is one of those who once worshipped the dragons. It is a question I will have to explore once I am a member of the council.*

Rolduc looked up at the palace before stepping up to the guard standing by the gate. The building was large. He understood all members of the Queen's Council, her primary advisors, not on the council, and the wizard council had rooms in the palace. There were administrative offices for various state officials, the throne room, areas for official functions as well as the area that served as the residence for Queen Evelyn and her family.

"May I assist you," the guard asked.

"I have an appointment for an interview with the wizard's council."

"Name?"

"Rolduc."

The guard glanced at a list tacked to the wall next to him. "Yes, I see you here." He turned to the young boy sitting on a nearby bench. "Tavin, escort Lord Rolduc to the Wizard Council and announce him as an applicant."

"Yes Sir." The boy jumped up and saluted the guardsman then turned to Rolduc. "If you will follow me, Lord Rolduc."

"Thank you." Rolduc nodded to the guard then motioned for the page to lead the way.

~ * ~

Tavin led Rolduc through the palace's grand hallways, the echoes of their footsteps mingling with the distant murmur of court life. Rolduc observed the intricate tapestries and artworks adorning the walls, each telling a tale of the realm's rich history and the valor of its rulers. While his thoughts were focused on the upcoming interview and the curious reactions of the townsfolk to Sidayth, he still couldn't help but notice the frequent use of dragons in the artwork he was passing. *Dragons were once worshiped here and they definitely seem to be a part of Istanura's history,* he thought.

Tavin led him to a corridor where he could sense magical energy filling the area. Gone were the tapestries that lined the other halls. Here the walls only held flickering torches guarded by dragon figures. The door to the council chamber stood before them, its wood carved with symbols and runes that spoke of old, protective spells. Two carved dragons sat on either side of the door. They were only wooden statues, but Rolduc felt they were judging him in some way as he stepped up to the door.

Tavin announced Rolduc's arrival in a clear, confident voice that belied his young age. The doors creaked open, revealing a semi-circular room bathed in the soft light filtering through stained glass windows. The members of the Wizard Council, draped in robes representing their respective magical disciplines, turned their gaze upon Rolduc. The Queen, resplendent in her regal attire, acknowledged him with a nod.

Rolduc stepped forward and bowed to Queen Evelyn, his mind racing through possible scenarios. He knew the council would probe not only his magical abilities but also his intentions and his loyalty. Yet, as he prepared to present his case, a new determination settled in his heart. He would secure his place on the council. The time had come to weave his own tale into the rich tapestry of the Istanuran Kingdom.

"Lord Rolduc, you have requested an interview in regards to the open position on the Wizard Council of Istanuran," Queen Evelyn stated softly.

"Yes, Your Grace," Rolduc replied. "I know I am not well known to you or the members of your council, but I am very well-traveled and well educated. Not only in the mystical arts, but also in matters of trade and diplomacy." He bowed again.

"I am Saevanya," one of the wizards said stepping forward. "I currently sit as the head of the council this cycle." She raised her hand slightly and a light mist began falling from the ceiling.

Rolduc felt the magical energies in the room now focused on him. It was a tangible force scrutinizing his resolve and sincerity.

"Tell us the tale of who you are and why you wish to serve the Istanuran people," Queen Evelyn said. Her ice blue eyes were focused on Sidayth—not Rolduc. "And tell us how it is you have the last of the great dragons imprisoned on that chain."

"Your Grace?" Rolduc felt like the magical energies surrounding him were tightening; threatening to crush him.

"The dragon. You wear him like he's a piece of jewelry." Queen Evelyn stood and walked slowly to stand in front of Rolduc. "Yet, he is still alive—so I can only conclude you have imprisoned him in some way."

"No, Your Grace," Rolduc said bowing his head. "I found him like this. He was being sold as a good luck charm by an old woman in the town of Destiny's Gate. I had hoped to release him from the magics binding him, however I must say they have been beyond my skills to this point."

"Yet, you wish to be a member of my council. These are some of the most powerful and learned wizards in all the realms. Do you think yourself their equal when you cannot find a way to break the magic on this dragon? I have no doubt the dragon would have aided you in this task."

Rolduc could feel Sidayth lashing his tail from side to side at his words. The dragon's agitation was growing, but Rolduc knew he couldn't risk touching the dragon or even looking at him. He couldn't risk breaking his concentration as he worked to maintain the carefully constructed fiction he was presenting as his tale.

"While I may be lacking in the skill to break this curse on the dragon, I do believe I am qualified to join your council." Rolduc straightened his back and faced the Queen. "Even if I am not selected to join your council, I would wish for the assistance of those here in helping to break this golden curse."

"Golden curse?" the Queen asked.

"Every time, I have looked at the magic surrounding the dragon with my wizard's eye it has given off a golden radiance."

"I have one more question before we decide," Saevanya said standing beside the Queen. "Do you truly wish to serve the people of Istanuran or do you seek power for yourself?"

Rolduc felt the pressure from the magical energies intensify, and he focused again on convincing them he was speaking truthfully. "To serve." He knelt before the Queen and bowed his head. "I seek to serve you and the people of your kingdom."

"Rise." The queen's voice echoed in the chamber.

As Rolduc stood, he felt the magical energies surrounding him loosen and the mist that had been in the room vanished. *I did it,* he thought. *I convinced them.*

The Queen tilted her head to the side as she continued to look at Sidayth. Smiling, she held out her hand.

Rolduc took a step back. He knew what she was asking for, without her even saying it. She was the Queen, he could not refuse —nor could he ask for anything in exchange. He was trapped.

With slow deliberate motion, he removed the chain from around his neck and handed it to the Queen. K*now this wizard, if you ever let me pass into the hands of another without receiving something in exchange—your spells will be broken, and I will leave and take whatever remains of any treasure you have acquired by using me to cheat others,* he heard Sidayth's word echoing in his mind.

"Not yet," he heard the Queen whisper as she looked closely at Sidayth.

"His name is Sidayth," Rolduc said.

"That is the first truthful thing you have said since entering here," Saevanya said. "Did you think we were so naïve or weak we would not or could not learn who you were and why you were here before you arrived today, Dagorka?"

Another member of the council stepped forward holding a large crystal in his hands. "We have seen your journey from Eldras, where you assumed the identity of Rolduc, a carpenter whose wife was ill and who you let die rather than try and help her, because he had no money left to pay you. We saw how you try to deceive Sidayth in order to trap him like this." He gestured to the dragon held by the Queen. "We watched as you displayed the dragon as a trinket then sold him over and over again—stealing from others by magically stealing him back after taking their money. Yes, all this we have seen."

Queen Evelyn looked down at Sidayth. "What do you say?" she asked.

The dragon looked up at the Queen. "Your Grace, I have lived for centuries as the last of my kind. Tasked with using the gathered treasure of the dragons to help others. My wish is to return to my home and then to pass beyond the veil into the twilight that awaits all dragons."

"Then it will be so. Sadly though there will be one more task for you before you can pass beyond the veil." She turned to Rolduc. "You have acquired and hoarded treasure very much like a dragon. Perhaps it would be best for you learn what it means to be a dragon."

"Are you ready, Your Grace?" Saevanya asked.

"I am." She nodded to Saevanya. "Open the portal."

~ * ~

Sidayth was shocked when they stepped through the portal and into his cave. The cave was once again filled with treasures.

Queen Evelyn placed him on the floor and then motioned for everyone to step back to the entrance. "Your binding has been broken, Sidayth. You may again assume your draconic form," she said.

Sidayth heard the chains holding the coin snap as he felt himself growing. As the layers of magic placed on him fell away, the dragon lowered his head so he was looking straight into the eyes of the wizard who had trapped him. "What will you do now wizard?"

"I do not believe I will have much say in what I do now." The wizard raised his head and Sidayth nodded his approval of the man not wanting to show any fear.

"I believe Dagorka, who was calling himself Rolduc, could learn much by learning what it means to be a dragon," Queen Evelyn said. "Just as you have from your time as a dragon, Sidayth."

Both Sidayth and Dagorka turned to stare at the Queen. "Your Grace?" they both said.

Saevanya raised her hand and Sidayth felt magic again surrounding him. When it passed, he felt a wave of dizziness hit him, just as it had when Rolduc had trapped him. This time he opened his eyes to see himself looking at a *dragon*. He looked down and saw he was now in Rolduc's body. "What did you do?" He turned toward the Queen.

"Centuries ago, you came to Istanura seeking a place on the wizard council, just as Dagorka did. At that time, you carried a tiny dragon named Talarel, who you had trapped just as you were trapped." Queen Evelyn picked up the gold coin he had been bound to. "Take this," she said. "It will restore the memories of who you were, without losing what you have learned."

Sidayth took the coin carefully then gasped as the memories came back. Everything he had thought was wrong, he had been a human. One who cheated others, sought power only for its own sake—no desire to use that power to aid others. He knelt before the Queen. "Thank you for this lesson," he said softly.

"We revere the dragons we are descended from," the Queen said. "When we were young, we hoarded treasure and hid ourselves away from humans. Now, we move among the humans, becoming a part of them." She shook her head. "There are few of us left, this is how we find others and bring them to us. But before they can join us, they must learn about humans in a way that teaches compassion."

"So we are required to give up the thing dragons are known to desire above all else—our treasure hoards," Sidayth said.

"Yes," the Queen replied. "Now Sidayth, you will become a member of the wizard council." She held out a heavy chain denoting his new rank.

Sidayth stood and handed the coin to the wizard who had trapped him. "Now it is your turn to learn the lesson. One day another will come, just as you and I did, who will free you from this cave. Until then you will learn to aid others, using the treasure you cheated so many out of."

The wizard took the coin. "I agree to the binding."

"You are already learning Dagorka," the Queen said. "You will one day be a member of the wizard council." She placed a hand on the new dragon's cheek then hugged him. "That is my wish for you." There was a flash of light from the runes carved into the walls of the cave and she smiled.

~ * ~

Dagorka watched as the portal closed, then curled up on the pile of gold coins to sleep. He couldn't remember why the humans had visited him, other than Queen Evelyn had given him a gold coin. It was token of friendship to assure him he was safe from hunters here in Istanura as the village at the base of the path to this cave in the Vritra Mountains would guard that path from all who sought to steal his treasure or do him harm. She had given him a task though, to aid any who came to him peacefully and in need. Yes, that he could do—after all, a dragon could not pass beyond the veil and into the twilight as long as he had a treasure hoard.

~ * ~ * ~

A native Texan, **Carol** found her way back to Texas after a five-year detour in The Nederlands and over thirty years in Colorado. Both detours were courtesy of her husband Tim and the US Air Force.

An avid reader at a young age, her strong desire to write came from her love of (her husband calls it her obsession with) Star Trek. It was this early love of Star Trek that led her to the Science Fiction and Fantasy genres. Now retired, she spends most of her time writing and publishing other authors as the editor and publisher of WolfSinger Publications and the online magazine The Lorelei Signal.

She has been published in various anthologies and magazines including "Creature Fantastic", *PanGaia Magazine*, "Stories of Strength", *Baen's Universe, Tales of the Talisman* and *Kepler's Dozen*. Her books include: *Call of Chaos, Chaos Embraced, The Road into Chaos,* and *Chaos Challenged.*

The True Hoard

Rose Strickman

The horn sounded its long, mournful note, echoing over the city of Irindprastha.

Alone with his after-dinner newspaper, Jahandar looked up at the sound, brow creased with irritation. It had been a long day. He'd spent most of it clearing out a nest of rakshasa just outside the city, and they'd been tough, persistent monsters, hard to kill. He'd only just sat down ten minutes ago. Surely he was entitled to a little peace?

Then his brain caught up with his ears, and he remembered what that sound meant.

Throwing down his newspaper, he stood up and stalked over to the window. Grimly, he looked out toward the city minaret, bathed in the final rays of daylight.

Sure enough, he soon heard the flap of wings, audible even over the city's traffic, and saw the huge reptilian form fly past the minaret.

All over the city, people were pausing, craning, pointing, exclaiming. The horn blew on and on. But Jahandar watched in silence as the dragon flew past the minaret once, twice, three times.

Only once the dragon had completed the third circuit did Jahandar turn away, already calculating what must be done. Three days. He had three days.

Then the dragon would come.

~ * ~

Jahandar was not terribly surprised when, scarcely an hour later, his first wife showed up at his house.

"Jahandar!" Perveen shouted from the floor below, front door slamming behind her.

"Madam, please, the Rakshak is busy with phone calls…" came the smooth but ineffectual tones of Nazeem.

"Don't give me that! I need to talk to my husband!" Footsteps stomping up the stairs, and then the door to Jahandar's study burst open, framing a woman in a blue lehenga, blond hair escaping its braid, blue eyes blazing.

Jahandar, seated behind his desk with the phone held to his ear, grimaced and wrapped up the call as quickly as he could. "Well, Perveen?" he asked, placing the receiver back in its cradle.

"You saw the dragon, I assume?" Perveen said sharply.

"Of course I did," he returned. "Why else do you think I'm placing phone calls at this time of night? Why are you so riled? This is hardly the first time."

"It's the first time in ten years!" Perveen came fully into the light from the electric lamps. Her pale coloring was out of place in this southern city, but her late father had originally hailed from the far north and her mother had carried foreign blood as well. She entered Jahandar's study with the assurance of an empress, Nazeem hovering helplessly behind her.

"I'm sorry, sir." Jahandar's aide bowed. "But madam insisted."

"Never mind, Nazeem," Jahandar sighed. "No one ever can stop my dear wife once she gets started. Why don't you go to bed? I get the impression Perveen wishes to speak with me in private."

Nazeem bowed again; after twenty-five years in the Rakshak's service, he knew when to withdraw. He backed out, closing the door and leaving husband and wife alone.

"Ten years," Perveen repeated, biting off each word. "You barely prevailed last time. You think you're up to it now?"

"I've hardly been idle these last ten years," Jahandar said coldly. "I destroyed a nest of rakshasa just today, if you'll recall."

"That's not the same thing and you know it."

Jahandar gave an inaudible sigh. He knew Perveen was right. "Where are Leila and Sarita?" he asked, naming his other two wives. Jahandar Niwas, alone of all the men of the state of Irindrajya, had the right to multiple wives. This was, he admitted to himself, a very mixed blessing.

"Preparing to get the boys out of the city, of course. I'll be sending Sanjay out to my country villa too," Perveen said, naming her youngest son. Her two older sons had left Irindrajya years ago. "The sons of Rakshaks do not fare well when their fathers are killed, as I'm sure you're aware."

Jahandar could hardly argue; he'd spent most of his own boyhood in hiding after his father was felled by a dragon. "Good," he said indifferently. He had very little affection for any of his sons. "And…the girls?" he asked with far more concern.

"They're in a state." Perveen's shoulders slumped. "Poor Amrita was crying her eyes out, thinking of you getting killed and her having to marry…him." She gave a sigh of relief. "I'm glad my Divya's already married."

Jahandar eyed his first and oldest wife. What she was describing were the precise circumstances of their own union, twenty-five years ago. Perveen had done her duty and together they'd built a sturdy partnership, even though Perveen had borne him no less than three maddening and aggravating sons. But Jahandar couldn't help but wonder just how much Perveen would truly mourn him, should he fall before the dragon three days from now.

"I'll go see Amrita as soon as I can," he promised. "And Leila and Sarita when they get back from the country. But not tomorrow," he added with a sour twist in his mouth. "Tomorrow I will be talking to the journalists."

"Jackals," Perveen spat. This was one topic she and her husband could agree on. "I daresay we'll be fielding questions too," she added. "Me and Leila and Sarita. We'll keep the children out of it, of course. At least you can head the offal-eaters off after a day, Jahandar. Tell them you only have three days and need to spend time with your family and seek the goddess's favor. Which is quite true, you know. *Ten years…*" She shook her head in disgust.

"Yes, ten years I've been keeping Irindrajya safe and peaceful," Jahandar snapped. "I didn't notice you or the Council complaining about the lack of dragons. Go home, Perveen. Get some rest. You're going to need it when the jackals descend."

Perveen let out an annoyed *hmph*, but her mouth twitched in a smile. "Perhaps you're right. Get some rest yourself, Jahandar."

Perveen stormed off again, bangles jangling as she headed down the stairs. Her car started up outside, headlights sweeping as she turned out of the drive. Left alone once more, Jahandar sat back in his chair, letting out a long breath and staring up at the slowly revolving ceiling fan. Outside, insects strummed in the garden and a night bird called.

He would never admit it, but Perveen's words had struck a nerve. *Ten years.* Ten years since he'd last faced a dragon. Immediately after he'd first won the state of Irindrajya twenty-five years ago, he'd seen off dozens of dragons, flooding in from around the continent, each eager to defeat an untried and untested Rakshak. He'd defeated them all, and as time went on, the challenges had tapered away. No bad thing for civic peace, of course, as he'd pointed out. But did Jahandar still have his edge? He might destroy monsters on a near-weekly basis, but, as Perveen had noted, fighting a dragon was a different proposition altogether.

Jahandar wondered where the dragon was tonight.

He bent over in his chair and opened the lowest drawer of his desk. Reaching in, he groped until he felt the smoothness of leather.

Jahandar drew out the large, flat case and laid it on the desktop. He ran his hands over the red leather cover, enjoying its texture, its simple, well-crafted elegance. Snapping open the gleaming brass clasp, he swung up the lid.

They lay glittering in the lamplight. His treasures. Looking them over, Jahandar felt a surge of fierce pride. Thirty-two polished pieces of gold, each about an inch long, each in the shape of a curved fang, each in its own velvet slot. Thirty-two golden fangs. One for each of the dragons he'd killed over his lifetime.

Jahandar ran his fingers over the smooth, gleaming gold, thrilling at the touch. He smiled on each trophy, each one bringing back memories of individual fights. Individual victories. Blood raining from the sky, the dying screams of his enemies.

He would never show anyone his hoard, of course. It was uncouth for a Rakshak of his standing to be so blatant about past triumphs. But he would never give up his dragon gold.

It was a long time before Jahandar closed the lid again.

~ * ~

Just as Perveen had predicted, the next day was given over to news correspondents and reporters. They were already gathered outside the gates of the Residence at dawn, cameras flashing as they snapped pictures of Jahandar's house, a babble of voices drifting across the gardens. When Nazeem came to wake his master, he did so with a cup of extra-strong tea and a sympathetic smile.

"Don't worry, sir," he murmured, laying out Jahandar's nice kurta, loose pants and dress sandals. "It will soon be over."

Nazeem was wrong. The day seemed to last forever as Jahandar gave interviews to Irindrajya's leading news reporters. His press agent had already released an official statement, of course, but Jahandar couldn't escape the major newspapers or the leading television news shows. Bright-eyed, avid men and women, the journalists perched in Jahandar's sitting room, sitting on Jahandar's furniture, eating Jahandar's food. Each was desperate for lurid tales from his past and his feelings on the present crisis. Jahandar started wondering sourly if the jackals *wanted* him to die two days from now, just for the drama. This was in between fielding calls from lawyers and Councilmembers, anxious to know whether he had a plan for the upcoming duel and asking, delicately, whether all his affairs were in order. Jahandar didn't even manage to squeeze in a call to any of his wives, and it was nearly midnight before he finally staggered off to bed.

The next day was more peaceful, but more poignant. Shortly after dawn, Jahandar borrowed Nazeem's nondescript gray sedan— his own red sports car was too distinctive—and drove off to visit his wives and daughters.

In keeping with tradition, the Rakshak's wives did not live with him. Jahandar lived at the Residence, a small but luxurious house with a large garden, attached to the city Council Hall. Perveen, Leila and Sarita each had their own house not far away, in the city's more upscale neighborhoods. Jahandar drove through wide boulevards lined with flowering trees and walled gardens, until he parked at Leila's house, a traditional Irindrajya mansion with a wide porch and sweeping eaves, overhung with flowering bougainvillea. Her parents had gifted it to her at her wedding; they were the wealthiest real estate developers not just in Irindrajya but several states around. Jahandar's other two wives were from similarly privileged backgrounds, Sarita being related to several Councilmembers and Perveen having sacred blood.

The mansion was currently seething like an ants' nest. Just as Jahandar had expected, the women of his family had descended upon Leila's residence, as they always did in times of crisis. The girls were running around Leila's garden, shouting. As soon as Jahandar got out of the car, his daughters all converged on him, dozens of pairs of dark eyes in round faces, long legs pumping under colorful skirts. "Bapa!" cried one—Roshanara, Jahandar remembered, one of Sarita's daughters. "Bapa, are you okay?"

"I haven't fought the dragon yet, Roshi." Jahandar ruffled her hair. "I'm fine."

"We saw you on the news," Suhani, a serious thirteen-year-old from Leila's brood, said. "You didn't look happy."

Jahandar grimaced. "I just hate interviews, sweetheart."

"Bapa's going to trash that dragon!" Laughed Sabina, the youngest of the lot, with a four-year-old's confidence shining in her eyes.

"I'm certainly going to try, Sabina." Jahandar, who had come prepared, pulled out a bag of sweets, handing it to the girls. As they all gathered around the bag, he made his escape, jogging up the path to the wide veranda where five women awaited him in silence.

Sarita came running down the steps, eyes wide. "Jahandar!" She threw her arms around him. "Jahandar, will you be all right?"

"I'll do my best, Sarita." Jahandar embraced his youngest wife. She trembled with emotion. She really loved him, a fact that always bemused Jahandar, who did not think of himself as a particularly lovable man. "I've seen off plenty of dragons before, after all."

"How many?" Perveen, leaning over the railing, eyed him narrowly.

"I hardly remember," Jahandar said airily and untruthfully. It was a conventional politeness for a Rakshak to pretend he couldn't recall all his victories. "But how are you all holding up?" He climbed the steps, Sarita clinging to his side.

"We're fine." Leila stood from the porch swing to kiss him on the cheek. She was the quietest of his wives, with neither Perveen's strong personality nor Sarita's high emotions, but possessing a steady practicality and common sense. "We got the boys out of the city yesterday. They're all being looked after. We were just talking to Amrita."

All eyes turned to the two young women seated at the veranda table before a large spread of tea and sweets. The older of the two, heavily pregnant and wearing the gold earrings of a married woman, sat with her arms around the younger, rigid with her hands around a steaming cup.

Divya looked up with a smile. "Look, Amrita, it's Bapa." The younger woman straightened, her face like chalk.

Jahandar caught his breath at the sight of his second-eldest daughter, only nineteen. *So young,* he thought. Then he remembered that was the age he'd been when he'd become Rakshak of Irindrajya.

"No need to look like that, Amrita," he said. "Everything's going to be fine. I've seen off dozens of dragons before."

"Not for ten years you haven't." Amrita's voice was faint. "Aunt Perveen told us."

Jahandar glowered at Perveen. "Maybe it's been ten years, but I've hardly been idle. Come on, Amrita, give your Bapa a hug…"

Amrita stood and Jahandar embraced her, heart full of love. Amrita had always been one of his favorites. She seemed to respond, standing straighter and even smiling a little when she pulled away.

"That's better!" Perveen said smartly. "Honestly, Amrita, why all this fuss? It's your duty, and hardly the end of the world even if the worst does come to the worst. And I should know."

"Perveen!" Sarita protested, shaking at the thought.

"I don't want Bapa to get killed." Amrita stood with her arms around herself. "And I don't want to marry…him. I want to finish school and become a biologist. I don't want my life upended by… that kind of marriage!"

"And it won't be." With effort, Divya hauled herself upright, her stomach a mound under her lehenga. Even through his concern, Jahandar felt a twinge of pride and pleasure, and Perveen's mouth twitched at this proof of their unborn first grandchild. Divya had married young, before she'd even finished college. Many daughters of Rakshaks did, for no one wanted to find themselves in Amrita's current position. Jahandar hoped very much he would still be alive to greet his grandchild's birth.

Divya now waddled over and put her arm around Amrita's shoulders again. "We'll all make sure you're allowed to finish school, even if you do have to marry him."

"Which you *won't!*" Sarita said passionately.

"But even if you do, we'll be all right financially," Leila added on a more practical note. "We made sure of that with the lawyers ages ago."

Amrita grimaced. "It's just…so antiquated. That kind of marriage. Savage, even. It's disgusting, making a woman marry her father's—"

"Watch your tongue, young lady!" Perveen snapped. "It's those 'antiquated and savage' customs that have kept civilization safe from the monsters and asura for millennia!"

"Your Aunt Perveen is right," Leila nodded. "It's the Rakshak's duty to protect the state. And our duty to make sure the line continues unbroken, so there's always a Rakshak."

Amrita just scowled. Jahandar nudged her on the shoulder. "Don't look like that, Amrita. Your mother and aunts are right. And anyway, it won't come to that. I'll defeat the dragon and all our lives will go on as before."

"Ugh, I hope not," Divya said, massaging her stomach. "I want this baby to be born soon!"

Everyone laughed, the mood lightening. The adults all sat at the table, Leila ringing for more tea and sweets. Jahandar took a lingering bite of exquisite rasmalai prepared by Leila's cook—there was a reason everyone always came to Leila's house—and lost himself in conversation with his family, discussing practicalities with his wives and smiling when the younger girls came thundering up for their share of cakes and tea.

Almost, he put from his mind the dragon.

~ * ~

The next day, Jahandar went to the river shrine for a ceremonial cleansing.

So close to the coast, the Irind flowed wide and glassy here, deceptively calm. Its murmuring voice echoed through the white marble shrine as Jahandar knelt to take the priestess's blessing. Sunlight, reflecting off the water, danced through the shrine, rippling over the wall mosaics of the goddess performing her miracles.

Nearby, Jahandar's wives and two oldest daughters stood watching, dressed in ceremonial saris. Jahandar himself wore a simple white kurta and loose pants. Everyone was barefoot, even the priestesses officiating the ceremony in their pale blue saris and simple braids. No one else had been permitted to enter the shrine, not even the Councilmembers or journalists who had followed Jahandar's entourage to the river.

The chief priestess now waved a stick of incense around Jahandar's head, praying for the goddess' favor. Priestess Mehrunisa bore a strong resemblance to Perveen, which was not surprising, as they were sisters. "Irind Ma," she chanted, "slayer of asura, protector of mankind, grant thy protection to this, thy son, who comes in all humility to seek thy blessing."

Mehrunisa now turned to dip her finger into the bowl of red pigment held by a junior priestess. She laid her fingertip on Jahandar's forehead, leaving a crimson spot. "Irind Ma protect you on your mighty task, Jahandar."

"May she bless you," all the women murmured, and Jahandar rose to his feet. He accepted a bronze bowl from another priestess, then followed Mehrunisa outside.

The day's heat and humidity were rising, turning the sky nearly white. The Irind flowed before them, a wide flat plain of water, filled with light. Waterfowl swam by and herons took off on the far bank, white wings flapping. A fish splashed. As always, the sight of the Irind River filled Jahandar with peace. Men and dragons would come and go, but the sacred river flowed forever.

When everyone had filed out onto the shrine's ghat, Jahandar descended the marble steps into the water. The river rose around his legs, embracing him. Behind him, the priestesses raised their voices in a traditional chant, telling the story of Irind. Irind, the star-goddess who had been the brightest and most radiant in the sky, but who had seen the suffering of mortals on earth, the misery caused by endless waves of bloodthirsty asura, the monsters that killed so many and terrorized the survivors. Irind, who had descended to earth to do battle with monsters until she could fight no more and had transformed into the river named in her honor, whose waters were toxic to demonkind, the river that still shed the goddess's blessings on all the land.

He was waist-deep now. Jahandar scooped water in his bowl and sluiced it over his head. Once, twice, three times he washed in the sacred river, letting its divine waters cleanse him. The current pulsed against him, trying to sweep him away—for even at this, one of its calmest points, the Irind was a hungry river—but Jahandar stood firm. He felt strength rising in him, and determination.

Irind had cleansed him of his sins and given him her blessing. Now he was ready to face the dragon.

~ * ~

All Irindprastha turned out for the fight.

School had been cancelled for the day, along with most people's work. Countryfolk had poured in from the surrounding towns and villages and now filled the streets, spread blankets in the parks, crowded onto flat rooftops and balconies. Children ran and shrieked; women, dressed in their best saris, discussed the upcoming battle; men excitedly shared memories of previous duels. A small fleet of boats motored out onto the water, spectators raising binoculars to the sky. The reporters were out in force, and every television news show had at least five cameramen on the scene, lenses trained on the heavens, commentators filling in time before the action began. The cows that roamed loose in the streets lowed and bellowed with confusion. Even the troupes of monkeys that lived wild in the city scampered about screaming, infected by the humans' excitement. Bursts of birds rose from the parks and rooftops to swirl through the air, chattering and squawking. All eyes were turned to the sky.

Only one area of the city remained quiet. Flags and banners flapped over the vast, stone-paved courtyard outside the Council Hall, the city minaret casting a long, dark shadow. There was a significant crowd—Councilmembers, priestesses, a few of the most respected journalists, a doctor with an emergency kit and, of course, Jahandar's female relatives—but everyone was completely silent, even the news correspondents. All eyes kept darting between Jahandar, standing utterly still in his blood-red kurta and black pants, and the gates at the far end of the courtyard.

Jahandar concentrated on breathing. Excitement and apprehension warred within him, tempered by iron determination. He would prevail today. He would destroy the dragon.

He glanced at his family. Perveen, Leila and Sarita were all garbed like widows in white saris and plain silver jewelry, all makeup removed. Tears rolled down Sarita's face and her lips moved in silent prayer. Perveen stood ramrod straight and stern. Leila put her arm around Amrita, who was dressed like a bride in a red sari trimmed with gold, jewels flashing on her wrists and neck, henna designs inked on her hands. Despite her festive garb, she looked more miserable and frightened than Jahandar had ever seen her.

The younger girls all clustered around their mothers, anxious and jittery. They kept glancing at Jahandar. Suddenly, Sabina rushed over, little legs pumping under her pink skirt, to throw her arms around her father.

"I love you, Bapa!" she squeaked. "You're going to kill that dragon!"

Warmth suffused Jahandar's heart. He leaned down to hug his youngest daughter. "Yes, I am, Sabina. I love you too."

A roar rose from the city outside, dull at first, but growing louder and nearer. Sabina gave Jahandar a final squeeze and ran back to her mother just as the gates swung open and a solitary figure entered.

He was a young man, dressed in worn, travel-stained clothing. As he came closer, crossing the courtyard, Jahandar saw he was tall and pale, with reddish hair—a northerner, like Perveen's late father, perhaps even from the Hanse or Norskaya regions. He was thin and rangy, evidence of a lack of food, a lack of a home, a life lived on the road, always harried and driven off by the Rakshaks of whatever cities he passed. Even from this distance, Jahandar could sense the burn of determination and ambition coming off him, the steely resolve.

Then he came close enough for Jahandar to see his eyes. The slit pupils, black and narrow against the blue irises.

All rational thought was swept away on a wave of sudden, intense, unreasoning loathing. Jahandar tensed, vibrating with the abrupt, violent need to destroy this boy, this vile, unbearable threat. The young man tensed too, glaring at Jahandar with the same loathing, the same revulsion.

Mehrunisa stepped forward, casting a warning look between the pair, and they subsided, barely. Still stiff and glowering, they turned to face the priestess.

Mehrunisa turned to the newcomer. "Stranger, speak your name."

"Ivar Haukonsson," the young man said in fluent Farhidi. "And I have come to challenge your Rakshak."

Mehrunisa bowed her head in acknowledgement and turned to Jahandar. "Jahandar Niwas Khan, Rakshak of Irindrajya, do you accept Ivar Haukonsson's challenge?"

"I do," Jahandar growled.

"Then let Irind Ma, protector of the world, decide who is the more worthy of her sons!" Mehrunisa raised her voice, echoing heavenward. The horn blew from the top of the minaret, a long blast, and the city roared, all the people cheering and yelling. There was no going back now.

Jahandar and Ivar turned and paced away from the others,

careful not to look at one another. They headed out onto the baking hot paving stones and stopped some distance apart.

The world retreated for Jahandar, warped by heat haze, made dreamlike. Only Ivar Haukonsson remained, his figure steady and clear. Only Ivar, the challenger, the rival, the enemy to be destroyed.

The other dragon.

Jahandar closed his own slit-pupiled eyes. He ignited the transformation.

Above his human form, a vast shape began to appear. Little more than a shimmer at first, it rapidly gained solidity and substance, color and weight flooding in, wings and horns and scales, a long lashing tail, claws and burning eyes. At the same time, Jahandar's human form flickered and faded, losing reality and existence as his draconic body gained it. Across from him, Ivar was undergoing the same process, the red dragon appearing over the young man's head as his human body disappeared.

Within seconds, the two human men were no more. In their places were two dragons, one red and one black.

Jahandar opened his golden eyes and flexed his huge wings, tendons spreading translucent membranes. Muscles bunched and pulled under his scar-riven black scales. He clashed long jaws full of huge, sword-sharp fangs, flicked his forked tongue. Four long legs bent and flexed under him, his curved talons clawing the stone. His tail lashed and his head tossed two curved spiral horns. The world poured into his enhanced senses. His vision was so sharp he could make out the individual links of the necklace Perveen was wearing, his nose so acute he could smell the sea, miles away.

He could smell the other dragon.

Loathing shot through Jahandar again, the utter, intolerable revulsion all dragons felt for other dragons, even their own fathers, brothers and sons. The blaze of draconic instinct, a divine, primeval fire burning out all human thought, emotion, rationality, ran through Jahandar's brain. There were no more distractions, no more doubts. There was only power, rage, and the overwhelming, all-important objective.

KILL!

Screeching, Jahandar lunged, snapping his fangs, but the red dragon leaped into the sky, unfurling his wings. Jahandar gave pursuit, taking off with a mighty flap.

Below the dragons, the horn blew again, and the city went mad. The citizens of Irindprastha gasped at the sight of the two dragons, the two monsters of the sky, flying over the city. They shouted and cheered and beat on drums, trying to encourage their Rakshak, currently swooping overhead on vast black wings. Horns blew and people waved flags, holding up banners with slogans like *GET HIM, JAHANDAR!* Reporters took notes as fast as they could, hardly taking their eyes from the sky, and cameras trained on the two flyers, correspondents commenting on every wing flap, every swoop. Out on the river, the boats rocked and swayed, and several people fell into the water. An almighty roar rose, over a million people screaming themselves hoarse.

In his current state of unthinking draconic rage and exaltation, Jahandar could make no sense of the human sounds, but still they spurred him, goading his instincts. *Mine. Mine.* Hissing, he swooped down on Ivar, the red dragon, the interloper who dared to think he might take from Jahandar what was his. Sucking in air, Jahandar summoned his fire.

A jet of white-hot flame shot from the black dragon's throat, enveloping the top of the city minaret. The horn blower yelled and jumped back, but the fire washed over him harmlessly, singeing not a hair on his head, scorching not a single stone. Dragon fire was no danger to humans or to mortal things. Other dragons, however… Ivar screeched and ducked, but a great burn ran along his reptilian head, flesh bubbling and hissing. The younger dragon screamed in pain and soared across the city, Jahandar in hot pursuit.

At the city's western edge, Ivar suddenly turned, claws lashing. Jahandar tried to flap back but wasn't quite fast enough. Ivar's claws opened a gash in his side. Gouts of blood rained from the sky to splatter across the rooftops, soaking a dozen people so their saris and kurtas clung and they wiped blood from their eyes. Even so, they cheered and danced, praising their luck in being blessed with dragon's blood.

Jahandar screeched with pain and rage. He lunged again at Ivar. They locked together in the sky, grappling in a mighty struggle of claws, scales and flapping, thunderous wings.

Jahandar fought Ivar's claws away from his eyes. Hatred and frustration built in him, and he flamed once more. Ivar ducked, and Jahandar's fire shot over his shoulder, to arc through the air and land in a huge, explosive gout on the ground just outside the city.

A chorus of inhuman screams rose at the impact. A clutch of minor asura demons had drifted near the city, attracted by the violent magic of the dragons and the raging emotions of the human onlookers. The unfortunate asura now writhed and shrieked, the divine dragon fire burning their unholy flesh to ash.

The sound distracted both dragons, as the humans' noise had not. They both hesitated, caught between two equally powerful instincts: the urge to destroy the other dragon and the urge to destroy the monsters. Jahandar, with twenty-five years of guarding the city behind him, craned his huge head further, looking for the threat. Ivar saw his chance.

He lashed out again with his front claws. Jahandar recoiled, but Ivar still landed his blow, scratching deep gouges in his opponent's face. He missed Jahandar's eyes, but still the black dragon was blinded by pain and blood. Jahandar screamed and soared, lunging to the opposite side of the city. Ivar flew after him, wings booming in the air.

Trying to keep his wounded head down, Jahandar dived behind the minaret. Snarling with triumph, Ivar swerved around the marble tower, jaws opening, the light of divine fire building in his throat—

And Jahandar leapt out, a stream of blazing flame issuing from his mouth.

Ivar howled, the divine fire eating into his flesh as it had the asuras'. He flapped back, blinded with agony, his scales charring and cooking. Jahandar rose after him, wings laboring, flaming still, an untiring jet of fire.

Ivar faltered, beginning to fall, and Jahandar saw his chance.

Snapping forward, he closed his jaws on the throat of his opponent, hot dragon's blood exploding in his mouth. Ivar let out one last scream of pain and despair before Jahandar ripped his jaws away, Ivar's flesh oozing in his mouth.

Death glazed the younger dragon's eyes, his jaws lolling open. For an impossible moment, he hung suspended in mid-air, a dying divinity, burnt and bleeding. Then his draconic shape flickered. It faded. It died away to a shadow and then to nothing, and the body of a young blond man fell from the sky, to land with a thud in the back courtyard of a chophouse.

Jahandar threw back his head, blood sliding down his throat, and let out a roar that was heard from one end of Irindrajya to the other, reverberating from the minaret, echoing off the river, booming across the rice paddies. Flocks of birds, cowering from the dragon fight, now rose in panic, clouds of flapping wings, and Jahandar's heart rejoiced at the sight, the birds bringing news to the goddess Irind that her son had prevailed.

For a moment, the people of Irindrajya stood confused, unsure. Then realization ran through the city: Jahandar, their Rakshak, had triumphed again. Again, he had proven his strength and his worth, his ability to be their guardian against all enemies. Cheers rose in waves across the city, people blowing noisemakers and firing cannons of colored paper, and a chant rose from the writhing, ecstatic streets: "JA-HAN-DAR! JA-HAN-DAR! JA-HAN-DAR!"

Jahandar swooped across the city, triumph and fierce joy filling his dragon's heart. He ran his eyes over every house, every street, every city park, with a deep, greedy love. For all Irindprastha, and Irindrajya beyond, was *his*. Every cracked brick, every crowded courtyard, every rice paddy, every leopard-haunted woodland, and, most of all, every human life. All the city-state belonged to Jahandar Niwas Khan, descended of Irind, dragon of Irindrajya and all its people. All of it his, to protect and guard from asura, ghosts, ghouls and dragons alike. Irindrajya was his, and he was Irindrajya's. For this was a dragon's true hoard, his true treasure: the people he was charged with protecting by the goddess herself.

Jahandar soared around the city twice more before circling to land in the courtyard at the feet of the minaret once more. When his claws touched the stones and his wings folded, he resumed human form. His draconic body flickered and faded into nonexistence, while his human shape gained reality and substance. Within seconds, the dragon was gone and a wounded, bloody human man stood panting on the paving stones.

Jahandar gasped for breath. As always, it was a shock to return to human form, back to being small and earthbound, his thoughts resuming normal human processes, emotions dulling, the divine rage disappearing. But there was relief in it too, even as the pain from his wounds increased exponentially.

"Bapa! Bapa!" His family was hurrying toward him, accompanied by the doctor. The girls reached him first, Sabina throwing her arms around him, the others all babbling and laughing. Amrita, still in her bridal finery, pushed her way through the mob to hug him.

"Thank you, Bapa," she whispered, voice trembling with emotion. "Thank you for saving me."

He hugged her back, wincing a bit at his injuries. "I told you that you wouldn't have to marry Ivar." In his heart, he gave thanks to Irind that only males of the divine bloodlines were dragons. At least he was able to love his daughters, even if he couldn't love his sons.

"Enough, girls!" Sarita shooed the girls away. "Can't you see he's hurt?"

"Not for long," Jahandar protested, and indeed his wounds were already knitting closed, his dragon's magic working to heal him. But still he allowed the doctor to bustle around, cleaning away the blood and applying bandages.

"Not bad at all, really, considering the circumstances," Leila said, inspecting the damage. "That Ivar was no weakling."

Perveen, standing by, gave Jahandar a small smile. "Well done, Jahandar."

He smiled back. He knew they were both thinking of that day twenty-five years past, when Perveen had stood in a bridal sari, just like Amrita, and watched while Jahandar killed her father, the previous Rakshak, sending his body tumbling into the river, and Perveen realized she would have to obey tradition and marry her father's killer. Jahandar shot a glance at Amrita, drying tears of relief with the end of her sari. Amrita had avoided that fate today, but the challengers would keep coming. Eventually, Jahandar would weaken with age and a young, ambitious dragon would kill him, striking him down in the sky and claiming Irindrajya for himself.

It was the fate of all dragons.

But not today. Jahandar opened his arms and only winced slightly when all his wives and daughters piled in, hugging and congratulating him. Jahandar's soul filled with light. His dragon's heart would never love his sons—for they were dragons too, and all dragons hated each other—but he could love his wives and his daughters. The heart of his great hoard, the hoard that now danced and sang for joy, the city and the lands beyond ringing with celebration.

His arms still around his loved ones, Jahandar went to join the festivities while the sun blazed overhead and the river ran on, as strong and as wondrous as a dragon.

~ * ~ * ~

Rose Strickman is a speculative fiction writer living in Seattle, Washington. Her work has been published over 50 times, in anthologies such as *Sword and Sorceress 32, Crunchy With Chocolate* and *Into the Mist*, as well as various e-zines. She has also self-published several novellas.

Visit her Amazon author's page at:
www.amazon.com/author/rosestrickman
And her Goodreads profile at:
Rose Strickman (Author of Nightmare Fuel) | Goodreads

The Hatchling

Dana Bell

Momma's hoard is gone. Humans came with their exploding weapons and sharp sticks, jabbing Momma making her scream. They forced her out into the cold night and then brought their loud machines with choking smoke, loading them up and driving them away.

Gone now, the golden goblets taken from a king, the shields of soldiers who had come to slay Momma, the pretty chains I liked to play in and much, much more.

When it got quiet, I dared to peek out from behind the rock cleft where Momma had hidden me. She'd told me not to come out until the human monsters had left, otherwise they'd steal me and sell me to something called a traveling circus.

The black cave floor always covered with momma's treasure looked barren. Empty. Empty like my growling stomach. Watching the damaged entrance in case the intruders returned, I crept to the spot where Momma always left me a fat hare.

Nothing. No food.

No Momma either.

Momma, who kept me warm at night as I slept under her wing. Away from the cold drifting inside. I shivered. Cold. Afraid. Alone.

~ * ~

Dragon dead, her weretiger mate informed Mira.

How long? Mira asked. She'd stayed in her human form and finished climbing the rise. Below, in a valley surrounded by volcanic rock, rested a dragon's body. The head and the wings had been brutally severed off. Blood soaked into the ground and would soon attract scavengers.

Hatchling smell, Arlan informed her.

Unless she shifted, she wouldn't be able to smell the baby dragon. *Can you tell if they took it?*

No. He lifted his head, his black nose sniffing the air. *Humans,* he growled. His golden eyes watched her as she made her way down the steep side. *Will track.*

She followed feeling vulnerable. If they needed to fight, it would take a few minutes before she could shift and join her mate in battle. His white coat striped with volcanic colored strips helped Arlan blend into the rock. He sniffed every crack, small opening, or any other place they might find a young dragon hiding.

As the sun rose, they discovered a path leading to a narrow valley. Mira gasped at the damage the humans had done. Deep ruts in the once grass covered ground. Yellow flowers, a favorite of dragons, crushed.

Her eyes traveled to the cave. Broken rocks littered the ground. They'd used their weapons to widen the entrance, leaving a gaping scar.

Humans, Arlan snarled disgusted.

Greedy ones. Had they found the hatchling and taken it as well?

Not so. Arlan crouched down, his long tail flipping. *Hatchling.*

One of the rocks moved. She could barely see it. *We're in time.* Slowly Mira approached, kneeling, to see the creature more clearly.

Its scales were a dazzling blue. Hints of silver graced the ridges. "Poor thing," she cooed. "I won't hurt you." She reached for the hatchling.

The hatchling shivered.

Gently she gathered the dragon under her cloak, holding it close to her heart. She felt the baby stiffen, then slowly relax. Its eyes had opened and she was curious what color they might be. Golden eyes stared at her before they closed.

Arlan sniffed the dragon. *Female.*

A female dragon in human hands would have been a disaster.

~ * ~

Warm. Not Momma warmth. No spicy smell. Moving. Momma never carried me. Too afraid of squishing me with her claws.

So hard to open my eyes. Want to sleep. Slowly, I poked my head out of the fur covering.

Trapped! Momma told me dragons were of more value than gold.

"Glad you're awake," a gentle voice greeted me.

Surprised I could understand the creature, I looked upward

into kind brown eyes.

"I'm Mira."

Her scent reminded me of the dangerous cat momma had fought off once. She'd said it had come to eat me.

"I'm a weretiger."

Not far away a huge cat walked. I shivered. Afraid.

"My mate Arlan."

I ducked back under the fur afraid it would see and eat me.

"Easy young dragon." Warm fingers caressed my head. "You're safe with us."

Safe? From the big cats? I shuddered. Momma kept me safe so the other creatures wouldn't eat me.

"We like the hares."

Hares. My stomach growled.

"Arlan, our young friend is hungry. Would you mind?"

I checked again. The big striped creature was gone.

"You are safe," the female reassured. "Dragons are needed."

We are?

~ * ~

"You brought a dragon here!" the matron growled. "What were you thinking?"

"It's a female," Arlan countered, now back in his human form. He wore trousers and a light fur vest.

"It was my idea," Mira interjected, still holding the now fed and sleeping dragon on her hip. "You know what the humans would have done." She shivered as her mind conjured various horrible fates.

"A female," the matron pondered. She pulled her fur cloak, made from the skin of a huge mammoth she'd hunted when she'd become matron, as was the custom of the weretigers. "You need to teach it to hunt and feed itself." With a shake of her head, their leader continued. "Since it takes time for a dragon to mature, we may have several suns and moons."

The matron did not need to elaborate. Mira understood what she meant. Male dragons fought each other to mate when a female came into season. Everyone in their camp could die.

With glowing eyes, the matron held Arlan's eyes. "Find the humans who did this. Take the young males, they're ready for a long hunt."

Her mate grinned. "Your wish?"

"What they did to the dragon is also their fate." Arlan inclined his head and left the warm tent.

"You Mira, will raise the dragon and train it well."

"As you wish." She turned to leave.

"And Mira,"

She paused.

"Remember. It is not a cub."

Mira knew full well. "I know."

~ * ~

When I got hungry, I let the female know. She stared at me for a long moment before she realized what I wanted.

Her form blurred and suddenly a white tiger with brown stripes stood watching me. *Come. We hunt.*

Momma always said I was too young to hunt. I chirped my reply.

If you are hungry, you must learn to hunt. She stepped out of the odd fur covered cave and waited until I joined her. We took a trail over a small mountain, down along a stream.

She raised her head and sniffed, crouching down in the tall grass. *We wait.*

I wondered what for.

As if she'd heard me she said, *You'll see.*

~ * ~

Mira waited as warmth touched her back. A spring gurgled not far away. Most of the animals came at some point during the day. She had only to wait.

The dragon sulked no doubt used to being fed by its mother. At least she kept quiet.

Grass moved. She knew a prey animal quivered there. It crept closer, constantly looking around. At the right moment, she pounced, bit its hind leg and dropped the wiggling creature in front of the dragon.

She moved away to watch.

At first the dragon was unsure what to do. Every time she got close the hare tried to hobble away. After a time, the dragon got the idea, held the injured creature down by its hind legs and ate her meal.

Very good. Next time we hunt, you need to catch your food.

The dragon burped and happily followed Mira back to camp, where she curled up next to the fire and fell asleep.

Mira smiled. The dragon learned quickly.

~ * ~

I like hunting. I caught two hares today and ate them. Mira may not be my Momma, but she teaches me well. I learned to drink from the spring too and how to clean myself by rolling in the dirt. Maybe next time I'll try stepping into the water. Momma always said it was fun.

The werechildren and I play. Some days I play with them as humans and others as tigers. We wrestle and tug at sticks or pretend to hunt each other. Or hide. That's my favorite.

I kept growing and my appetite with it. Mira taught me to hunt the harts. One day, when I've grown larger, she promised we'd journey to the land of the thundering hooves. I'm excited.

~ * ~

Hurt, the dragon complained.

"I'm know. I'm sorry." Mira continued rubbing the herbal mixture on the 'shoulder' area where the new wings were expanding and growing.

The dragon bellowed again, scooting along the ground as if running from the pain.

"Won't do any good." Mira finished and patted the blue scales. "Just lie here in the sun and warm your back. It'll help."

Wrinkling its nose, the dragon complained, *Stink.*

Mira laughed. "It does," she agreed, sliding down the scaled back and lightly landing on her feet. She shook her body wishing she could shift and just run. The tiger needed to hunt, roll in the dirt and play in the water.

However, between a dragon in pain and several children who had disappeared, none in her 'family' were traveling far. Several had shifted and patrolled the cliffs. Others stalked harts by the drinking pool, bringing home food for all.

"She's getting big." Arlan stood beside her smelling of dried blood and tiger.

"I know." Her eyes took in the growing reptile. "She'll start flying soon."

"You sound sad."

She shrugged. "I've enjoyed having a cub to look after."

"She's not a cub."

"You know what I mean."

He nodded. Arlan stretched showing off his thick muscles. "We'll have cubs of our own when the Matron decides it's safe."

"Which won't be until they figure out who's taking the ones we've lost."

"No doubt humans."

"We don't know that. There are other predators."

"Humans are the only ones who dare to stalk us." He glanced around their home. Several mammoth covered tents stood scattered over a narrow valley. "At least they haven't found us yet."

"Matron doesn't think they will."

He didn't reply. His eyes looked over the area. No doubt searching for prey or predators.

"They haven't found us since we settled here," she reminded him.

"They're becoming vermin. Taking what is not theirs."

She decided not to respond. There were those who could say the same of them.

~ * ~

I like flying. I'd hated the pain caused when they grew. Mira's mixtures helped.

I soared over the valley. From the sky I can see everything. The harts, the bellows, the birds and scattered hunters. Some human, some not.

I watched their reactions as I flew over them. The harts scattered. The bellows circled their young. The humans pointed and huddled down, like that would save them, should I decide to take one home to my tigers.

Skimming the tops of the huge trees, I watched birds scatter. Some scolded me for disturbing them. Others chased me trying to protect their young. They're too little to hurt me, but it's a fun game.

Mira told me several cubs had disappeared. I missed playing with them. They'd been too little to hunt and might have wandered off to become prey or be taken. I watched for them. After all, I can see the ground, the trees, rivers, animals and…

Wait.

I circled back. Tucked behind branches trying to hide the entrance to a cave, I saw cubs. Around them hovered human women who cowered before men with long vines, striking them whenever they disobeyed.

Weretigers never mistreated their females.

I passed over them allowing my shadow to cover them. Some looked up and watched, before dismissing me. An outcropping presented itself and I landed.

"They're mutants," a male was saying. "They should be destroyed."

"Worth a year of food," another countered. "We can sell them to a zoo, or a traveling show or even the experimenters."

They all laughed.

I couldn't understand what they meant, yet sensed it wasn't good for the cubs.

"How many more do we need?

"Maybe a couple more."

"Been harder to catch."

"We'll just wait. Sooner or later one will wander away."

They wouldn't. The Matron and the females kept close watch on their young to keep them safe.

"Too bad we can't catch the dragon."

"Only their head and wings are worth anything."

They laughed again. Their tone made me angry and I flexed my claws.

"We're too little for a dragon to hunt."

Foolish males. They'd make a good snack. I ran my tongue over my teeth.

A cub escaped. A woman ran after it. One of the men used the vine and the woman screamed while another used another vine to catch the tiger. It snarled, using its claws. He wrapped the vine around its neck.

"Stop it or I'll kill you," he growled.

"No you won't!" I bellowed, leaping down and grabbing the male in my claw. My tail knocked several of them down and the females screamed, running toward the river, as if they'd escape.

Well, I'll let the women escape. Not the males.

No. Definitely not the males.

~ * ~

"She left," Mira moped, sitting on a warmed stone, her feet in the cold water. "She's been gone for several days."

"She's a dragon. We knew she would." Arlan squatted beside her. "She's nearly full grown."

A tear ran down Mira's face. "I miss her."

Shouts drew Arlan's attention. "Mira." His hand touched her shoulder as he gazed upward.

She shaded her eyes as a huge shadow hid the valley, before the joyful roar of a dragon. "She came back!"

"With the cubs!" Arlan leapt to his feet and ran. Mira raced after him.

In her claws she released all the cubs who shifted to their human form and hurried to their mothers. Each grabbed their own, hugging them tight. Mira watched stunned.

The matron approached, bowing low before the dragon. "Thank you, dragon."

Hoard.

Every weretiger stopped. She'd spoken to all of them.

My hoard. I protect. The dragon sounded very proud of herself.

"We're a dragon's hoard?" Arlan looked puzzled.

Mira watched several cubs run to the dragon and playfully jump on her. She licked them and cradled several under her sparkling wings.

Matron laughed. "We are most honored." She bowed again before the dragon.

Should be. The dragon sounded smug.

"But where," Arlan began, pointing at the cubs as if he couldn't form the question he wished to ask.

Found. Dealt with bad humans. Freed their females. Smashed their metal monsters. The dragon laughed. *Fun.*

Saved by a dragon. Mira looked at the beautiful creature, lying in their valley as if it were the only place she wanted to be.

With them.

Her hoard.

~ * ~ * ~

Her cat overlords, Taj and Esther, rule her home and are very jealous of her computer when **Dana Bell** sits down to write. Walking on her desk and trying to lay on her keyboard are not uncommon occurrences. Still, she manages to compose her many tales in a somewhat timely fashion and has completed a total of six books, along with an unknown number of short stories and some poetry which has won awards.

Her favorite hobbies are building and decorating doll houses, each with their own people who own cats, dogs and a mix of other pets. She recently discovered the joy of arranging silk flowers. Unfortunately, real ones cause her to sneeze. Among her large cat and dragon collection, is a mixture of dolls, cars, and action figures.

Happy with her current life, Dana lives in a quiet neighborhood in Colorado. Like many authors she has a day job. One must after all have a warm place for her feline companions and they like their food served promptly at breakfast, snack and dinner time. A service she happily provides.

The Lost Hoard

Kay Hanifen

The mouth of the cave gaped open, stalagmites and stalactites forming teeth. Centuries ago, the exterior had been carved in ancient runes, a warning for all who passed by, but all those who could read it were long dead.

Austin Mayberry stood in front of the cave while his team of four bustled behind him. Austin was the billionaire heir to the Mayberry Medicine empire, but the business wasn't his true passion. It could sink or swim for all he cared. What interested him was the lost and the unknown. He wanted to discover something science believed never existed. In his time, he'd funded expeditions to hunt for the Loch Ness Monster, Bigfoot, the Lost City of Atlantis, and even paid scientists to prove the pyramids were built by aliens. He was always on a quest for his Holy Grail, both literally and figuratively.

He turned to the archaeologist beside him. "Do you think this is it?"

Dr. Casper Gunnarson nodded. Casper was the object of one of Austin's most recent fringe obsessions. In his most recent book, he argued the Scandinavian dragon, Fafnir, was not a literal dragon, but a man. The Eddas and other contemporary works turned Fafnir the man into a monster as a metaphor for greed. He died a very wealthy noble and was buried with his treasure in a remote cave. "It has to be," Casper said. He traced the carvings on the cave with his fingers, drawing Austin's attention to it.

"Is that a dragon?" he asked.

Casper nodded. "Old Norse is a language that has been largely lost to time. Even now, we know very little about it, but I think this symbol is fairly obvious."

"Here, there be dragons."

He nodded, flashing Austin a grin. "Exactly. So, are you ready to make Howard Carter look quaint for discovering King Tutankhamun's tomb?"

"If you're right about this, you'll never have to worry about a grant again. I will personally fund all your research for the rest of your career."

"Are we ready?" Sif Aaronsdotter asked. She had been spelunking the caves of Norway for almost a decade, so they hired her to be their guide. Behind her, the other two members of their team stood waiting.

Robert Wilson was Austin's righthand man. He was an expert in extreme sports and a whiz with a Go-Pro, making him the ideal cameraman to document this journey. Finally, there was Casper's husband and research partner, Anders Gunnarson.

Anders grinned and gave them a thumbs up. "Ready when you are."

Austin pointed to Robert. "I need you to get every second of this on film. Do you have a signal to livestream it?"

"Nope, sorry," he replied. "But the camera's batteries are fully charged, and all the memory is free to use. We should be good to go. I'm turning it on now." He counted down on his fingers from five, pointing when he got to one.

Austin grinned at his invisible audience. "What's up adventurers? I'm out here with Dr. Casper Gunnarson, his husband, my buddy, Robert, and our guide, the gorgeous Sif. Dr. Gunnarson has some fascinating theories about the man behind the legendary dragon, Fafnir. Casper, take it away."

As Casper spoke about his fringe theories and how they're about to be proven true, Sif leaned in and whispered to Anders in Norwegian, "This man has more money than God. Why is he wasting it on this shit?" She glanced at his husband and winced. "Er, no offense. Your husband is a nice man, but…"

Anders smiled, shaking his head. "No, no, I understand. Casper has some unusual theories, and I'm happy he has the grant money for this expedition, but, well, it's just vanity, isn't it? For him, and especially for Mr. Mayberry."

She smiled. "I'm glad you're the one who said it, not me."

"Sif, we're ready to enter the cave." Austin shot her a glare, his face subtly turning a shade of red. "So, if you'll kindly refrain from providing more comments from the peanut gallery, I would appreciate it. I may not speak Norwegian, but I'm not stupid."

"Sorry, sir," she said, flashing him a sheepish smile. She tried to push past him, but his hand shot out, grabbing her arm. She stiffened in surprise at the strength of his grip.

"You're about to be a part of a lifechanging discovery, one that could rewrite our understanding of history as we know it. Do you understand me?" Something dangerous glinted in his eyes, a look Sif recognized in many of the men she shot down in bars. Wounded pride festering into entitled anger because she didn't give them what they felt they were owed.

She grit her teeth. A million dollars to guide this trip. She'd dealt with worse for far less money. "I understand. I'm sorry for making light of this."

And like a light switch, the anger was gone, replaced by Austin's typical affable nature. "All is forgiven. Just don't do it again, especially when the cameras are rolling." He laughed, dropping her arm. "I have a reputation to maintain."

She nodded. "I'm sorry again, sir."

"Austin, come look at this," Casper exclaimed, already inside the cave with his husband and Robert, who studiously kept the camera facing away from the confrontation. Austin Mayberry had a reputation to maintain, after all.

They jogged to catch up with the rest of the group. Casper had pressed a piece of paper to the wall and was using charcoal to rub the remains of a carving onto it. Anders held up his extra flashlight, illuminating the extensive design on the wall.

Unlike Austin, neither Anders nor Casper gave a shit about the treasure. Odds were it was long gone, lost to the ages, but the idea of finding a genuine historical relic such as this thrilled Anders. While he could not read the runes, the pictures told a familiar story:

A boy is killed by the gods. They pay the father a weregild of gold. Another son kills their father and steals the gold, hiding it in the mountain, where he takes on a cursed existence, transforming into a dragon. A hero slays the beast.

But then the pictograms kept going, showing the hero refusing to leave and then slowly transforming into another monstrous dragon. This was never in any of the Eddas and Sagas he and Casper had ever read.

The thought filled him with excitement. Many pre-Christian myths passed down orally were lost with the introduction of the religion, and those that remained have been suspiciously Christianized. This could be a genuine depiction of a myth lost to time, one that could be easily interpreted.

His eyes met Casper's, and his husband beamed in excitement. The implications were staggering. Casper tried to explain the significance to Austin, who, Anders noted, looked rather bored by this discovery.

"So, do you think this could mean the treasure is really here?" Austin asked.

Casper suppressed an eyeroll. Treasure, treasure, treasure. That was all this man was interested in. They had found a never-before-seen relic of pre-Christian Norway, and the only thing that mattered to him was the possibility of gold. It's not flashy like King Tut's tomb, so Austin didn't give a shit. As grateful as he was Austin was funding this expedition, the man could be frustratingly single minded.

"What do the runes say?" Sif asked, squinting at them. "Can you read it?"

These were Old Norse runes, all from a language long dead and decomposed. No one could read them. And yet, Casper knew instinctively what they said, "Let those who lust for gold lance the sickness before it takes you."

Anders flashed him a surprised look, and he shrugged. There was no way he could explain it, but he knew it was true. Sif tilted her head thoughtfully. "Gold sickness? Like *The Hobbit*?" she asked.

Casper smiled. This, he could explain. "Tolkien took a lot of inspiration from the story of Fafnir when he wrote the character of Smaug. It's possible gold sickness was something else from the myth. The cycle of greed and death appears both in this legend and in *The Hobbit*."

Austin flashed him a grin, slapping him on the shoulder in an overly familiar fashion. "Are you getting all this, Robert? We're about to take the One Ring to Mordor."

"Actually, that's—" the other three began, but Robert cut them off.

"Hell yeah." He turned the camera to face him. "I'll leave it to the folks at home to decide which one is which. But to me, Austin is definitely the noble King Thorin."

Casper didn't have the heart to mention what happened to the king of the dwarves at the end of *The Hobbit*.

Austin resumed mugging for the camera. "So, it looks like we're in the right place. Let's see what else we can find."

Sif took the lead as they ventured deeper into the cave. The carvings filled each wall, all telling the same story, the same warning. Robert was a consummate "yes" man. It was how he went from an intern to the right hand of Austin Mayberry in a few short years. If Austin wanted something to happen, he made it happen, even if it was a stupid quest to find the Loch Ness Monster or the lost City of Atlantis.

But this time felt different. There was something here that was real, not a legend told to kids by the campfire. Robert didn't like this set-up. To prevent other treasure hunters from swooping in, Austin had insisted on a small team, which meant fewer people to protect him. Robert knew he should have tried to change Austin's mind on this, but his boss was not a man used to hearing the word, "no."

The cave suddenly bent down at a sharp incline, causing Robert to stumble. He tripped and fell, landing on something sharp enough to slice into him. Warm, red blood seeped from a wound on his forearm.

"Stop," Sif ordered the other three men. She doubled back to him, her emergency kit already in hand. "What did you land on?"

"I don't know." He picked up the object with his free hand while she tended to the wounded one. It was red, flat, and seemed to be made of a lightweight stone that was thin without being brittle. Holding it up to the light, he watched it shimmer in copper and gold, making sure the camera captured every possible angle.

"That isn't possible," Anders said, staring at it in horror. All the rest looked at him in confusion.

"What?" Casper asked, taking his husband's hand.

Anders stepped closer, his already pale face looking ashen in the low light. "It looks like a scale of some kind. One from a massive reptile."

Robert dropped it in shock. "You're kidding."

He shook his head. "I know it sounds crazy, but I'm sure it is."

Austin's face lit up. "So, you think a real dragon was in here once?" He could see the headlines now: Genius Billionaire Discovers Dragons Exist.

Anders shook his head, and Austin deflated slightly in disappointment. "I don't know what it is that I'm looking at. I'm just saying it looks like a scale."

"But it's possible that—"

"I think Robert might have to get stitches," Sif said, interrupting the little fantasy everyone else seemed to be getting drawn into.

"I thought you had some butterfly bandages." Austin glared at her as though it was her fault for cutting the expedition short.

"Just two or three. I haven't had the chance to restock, and the wound is much too big for them. They might help to stop the bleeding, but it leaves him at risk of infection, especially in a dirty cave."

Austin looked past her, making eye contact with Robert. "I'll let you decide, Robert. It's your arm after all. You can choose to stay with us and finish this quest, or we can cut it short for today."

Robert knew the answer Austin expected. He only got as far as he did by being agreeable, and besides, if he got an infection, Norway's healthcare system was practically free. He'd be fine. "I want to keep going," he said.

Sif gave him a skeptical look as she used the butterfly bandages to try and staunch the bleeding before wrapping the arm in gauze. She met his eyes as she tied it off. "If we reach any truly dangerous squeezes or places where we really have to climb, you're going to turn back. I don't care what your boss says. No one is dying on my watch." Helping him to his feet, she headed back to the front to lead the group.

Casper shoved the scale into his pack. He and Anders had a herpetologist friend at the university, one who could potentially identify where the scale came from. Because it had to be a scale of some kind. He had no idea what else it could be. The thought filled him with a giddy sort of excitement. They were truly on the precipice of discovering something that had never been seen before by scientists or historians.

Anders, though, seemed surprisingly subdued to Casper. They had worked together on this theory. Sure, Casper's name was the first one listed on the paper, but Anders was his co-writer and research assistant. He had invested just as much as Casper into this project. So, why did he look so worried?

"Is something the matter, love?" he asked in Norwegian.

"That scale belonged to something massive," Anders replied. "If that's just one of them, then whoever it belonged to must be the largest creature to ever exist. And if it's still alive, we're walking right into its home."

Before Casper could respond, the ground began to shake.

"Earthquake!" Sif yelled. "Run!" She pushed them forward, back the way they came. But they weren't fast enough. The last thing Casper saw was a flash of red breaking through from the cave floor.

And then there was only darkness.

~ * ~

Anders slowly returned to consciousness, his head throbbing worse than the hangover he'd suffered after his stag party. He groaned and as he tried to move, something shifted underneath him. His eyes shot open as memories of the cave-in came flooding back.

He sat up quickly, and immediately regretted it as it sent his head swimming. It took a moment for the world to focus around him, especially in this darkness, but his eyes eventually adjusted. A bioluminescent algae glowed on the walls while the surviving flashlights cut beams in the darkness.

"Are you okay, Anders?" Sif asked. In the dim light, he could make out the trail of blood running down her forehead. She had her hand around her ribs, guarding them.

Casper, he remembered with a jolt. Staggering to his feet, he cursed as whatever they were lying on shifted and forced him to sink. But he finally made it to a flashlight and scanned the room.

Austin and Robert were nearby, slowly regaining consciousness. One of Robert's legs was bent at an unnatural angle, but he hadn't seemed to notice yet. The shock was too much. Austin, of course, looked fine. Just some bumps and bruises. Anders wouldn't be surprised if he had used Robert to break his fall. But where was Casper?

"Holy shit," Austin said, picking up whatever they had landed on. He threw some pieces up in the air, and Anders gasped as gold glinted in the beam of the flashlight. Casper had been right about the treasure. He'd found Fafnir's tomb.

But then Anders found him.

Casper laid on the gold pile, a rusted sword protruding from his chest.

"No," Anders whispered, running to his husband's side and patting his cheeks. "Casper, Casper, wake up."

Casper's eyelids fluttered open. And then they widened as they took in the room. When he smiled, blood pooled in his mouth and stained his teeth. His words came out weak and slurred. "I was right.

About everything."

"You were," Anders sobbed. "And we're going to tell the world. You…you just have to hold on. Please, hold on."

Casper's hand twitched, flopping weakly as he reached for Anders' hand. He found it and brought it to his lips. "Why are you crying?"

"I love you."

"Strange thing…to cry about right now… But I love you too. Sorry…wish I could enjoy…it with you." Casper let out a final, shaky exhale and then stopped, his eyes going vacant.

Sobbing, Anders held the body of his husband close, heedless of the sword piercing the center of Casper's chest. He was vaguely aware of the sound of coins shifting underfoot and then a hand on his shoulder. "He died a hero," Austin said.

Growling, Anders pulled the sword from his husband's back and held it to Austin's throat. "Don't you say another fucking word about him. It's your fault he's dead."

Rage flared in Austin's chest. Of all the ungrateful—he funded Casper's dream expedition, helped him to prove he wasn't just some crackpot. And this was the thanks he received for securing Casper's legacy? "How was I supposed to know the floor would give out?"

While Anders and Austin argued, Robert slowly returned to himself, wiggling his fingers to check for breaks. And then his toes. Trying to move his left leg sent a lightning bolt of agony through him. It was definitely broken.

"Guys?" Robert began. And then he felt something strange. The coins he was lying on were shifting underneath like something was moving through the pile. "Guys!" he shouted as a circle of teeth surrounded him from below. He was no longer on the gold. No, the surface below him was soft and damp. A tongue.

"Help!" he screamed. The three other survivors looked up, the expressions on their faces running the gamut of horror (Anders and Sif) and excitement (Austin). He tried to climb out of the mouth, but the dragon had angled its head back enough he could only cling to a canine tooth if he wanted to avoid falling into the dragon's inferno of a gullet. There was the smell of sulphur and a popping sound. And then the fire consumed him.

Until an hour ago, the dragon had been fast asleep, buried in his pile of gold. There was a time when he had a human name and spoke in a human tongue, but that was centuries ago. All those who knew his name and spoke his language were dead. For many, this would be a lonely existence—and he likely would have agreed when he was human—but the dragon had stopped caring about friends or joy or anything outside of his hoard. All that mattered was the glittering gold and jewels he protected.

When he heard the voices—human voices—for the first time in centuries, he ignored it. People would occasionally wander into the cave, but then, they would sense a danger about the place, and quickly leave. But these humans stayed, venturing deeper and deeper. He heard names he had long forgotten—Fafnir and Sigurd—and that propelled him into the waking world. Whoever these people were, they knew about him and his treasure. They wanted it for themselves. That would not stand.

He focused on the sound of the cave, pinpointing where they wandered above him and lashing out, striking the ceiling with his tail until it broke through, and the humans fell through the floor and into his chamber.

And then he waited for them to wake before devouring one whole. After centuries sustained only by his gold, devouring flesh again reawakened a hunger too ravenous to be ignored. Three of the humans scattered while one laid still, already dead but still fresh. He devoured that one too and then set his sights on the final three.

The moment Sif saw the dragon, she ran, her feet slipping on the shifting gold and jewels. It may have been a bit cowardly for her to leave Anders and Austin behind, but a real dragon was not a part of the deal. She scanned the walls, looking for any egress too small for it to reach.

There. Hidden behind some stalagmites was a grotto so small she would have to crawl through it. She had no idea if it would lead her to freedom. For all she knew, she was about to choose a slow, painful death over a quick, painful one. But there was a chance, how-ever slim, she would survive, and it was a chance she was willing to take.

She glanced back at the other two men—Anders with his tear-stained cheeks and Austin with the dollar signs in his eyes. She couldn't just leave them there. "Anders! Austin!" she shouted. The two men and the dragon turned their attention to her. Shit. She hadn't thought that through.

But Anders took advantage of the dragon's momentary distraction and stabbed it with the sword that killed his husband. The beast let out a shriek that reverberated through their very bones, making their ears bleed. It lashed out, striking Anders and sending him flying. He skidded across the gold coins and, coming to a stop, laid still.

As the dragon advanced upon him, Anders scanned for the nearest weapon. A spear was within reach, so he grabbed it, and as the dragon lunged down to snap him up like a heron grabbing a fish from a pond, he stabbed upwards, piercing the dragon's soft palate and breaking through to its brain. With a cry, it collapsed. Dead.

Anders let out a weak laugh, turning to Sif, who stood near the cave with her hand covering her mouth in horror. "Look out!" she cried.

He turned, expecting the dragon to somehow still be alive. Instead, he found himself face to face with Austin.

And suddenly, he couldn't breathe. The taste of copper flooded his mouth. He looked down.

A sword protruded from his chest. Austin had his hands on the hilt, his eyes wide and maniacal. "Why?" Anders choked.

"This treasure is mine and mine only. No one else can have it." Austin pulled out the blade, letting Anders fall to the ground before turning to Sif. He had originally planned to give his teammates a cut of a treasure, but as soon as he woke up in this cavern of precious metals and gems, he realized he couldn't part with a cent of it. He didn't have to work to dispatch Casper and Robert. The fall and the dragon did it for him. But Anders was a threat, and not just to the treasure. He unfairly blamed Austin for Casper's death and wanted revenge. Getting rid of him was a matter of self-preservation.

And then there was one. Sif stood in wide-eyed horror as he advanced upon her. Austin, who had never driven a car himself, never truly understood the phrase 'like a deer in headlights' until that moment. Finally, she came to her senses enough to turn tail and run, ducking into the little cave and vanishing into the dark.

It was too small for him to carry the sword, so he would have to kill her with his bare hands once he caught her. As he crawled, he felt the call of the gold beckoning him back to the cave. He ignored it. She couldn't have gotten too far ahead of him. As soon as he tied up the final loose end, he would return to his cave and his treasure.

But as soon as the squeeze opened up, he realized she would

not be found so easily in the pitch black. He listened for footsteps or the sound of breathing but could hear nothing over the blood rushing in his ears and the call of the treasure to return home and protect it. Sif was probably a dead woman anyway. She would die alone in the darkness.

He turned around and went back the way he came. When he found the gold again, he let out a breath he didn't realize he'd been holding. The treasure was there. Still pristine, still gorgeous.

Exhausted, he curled into a ball on a bed of gold coins. In the days to come, he would grow and change. His body would become massive, and his skin would harden into scales. He would breathe smoke from his nostrils and grow wings despite never wanting to venture outside and attempt flight, not when it would take him away from his precious wealth. Like the dragon before him, he succumbed to the gold sickness, letting his love of the treasure surpass all else.

Days after entering the cave, Sif would emerge starving and dehydrated, and stumble to a nearby road. She would ramble about dragons and gold and missing billionaires, leading the doctors to believe she was delirious until it was announced Austin Mayberry was missing without a trace. Some believed she was his murderer, some that she narrowly escaped his real killer. No one believed the dragon story.

So, Austin Mayberry slept, forgetting his own name and desires in favor of the cursed gold. The man who wanted to solve a grand mystery became one himself, fodder for real-life mystery books and true-crime podcasts.

But the dragon had his hoard, and that was all that mattered to him.

$$\sim * \sim * \sim$$

Kay Hanifen was born on a Friday the 13th and once lived for three months in a haunted castle. So, obviously, she had to become a horror writer. Her work has appeared in over forty anthologies and magazines.

When she's not consuming pop culture with the voraciousness of a vampire at a 24-hour blood bank, you can usually find her with her two black cats or at kayhanifenauthor.wordpress.com.

Twitter: https://twitter.com/TheUnicornComi1
Instagram: https://www.instagram.com/katharinehanifen/

How A World Dies

Daniel Whipple

Let me tell you how a world dies. It might not be how you expect.

It is a well-known fact dragons are drawn to possessions as a display of their power. For as long as dragons have existed. (And they have always existed.) They have hoarded wealth and treasure. Classic examples are gold and gemstones, herds of livestock, princesses or princes. Some smaller and literate dragons hoarded knowledge in the form of books and scrolls. Their libraries are the stuff of legends. The knowledge collected within will never be matched.

However, as dragons and the worlds around them grew, their appetites grew with them. But a dragon's growing appetite will not be how a world dies.

Instead of hoarding individual members of a royal family, dragons started conquering entire castles. Some dragons set their sights on entire towns, then cities and even states.

Dragons continued to grow and so did their greed and territories. It was inevitable that states, or even entire continents would no longer satiate their hunger for possessions. So, they took to the skies, left the atmosphere and claimed entire worlds as pieces of their hoard. Only a dragon could be so greedy as to look up into the night sky, see the stars and planets above, and want them for their own.

How they knew they could leave their homes and explore the great beyond is unknown. But they did. And in space they met other dragons. The battles that raged as these monsters met in the vacuum between worlds were legendary. Fire and magic lit up the skies putting on full display their might. Those battles are not how a world dies either dear reader, that comes later.

But after only a century or two, (practically a blink of an eye for dragons) lines were drawn and a semblance of peace was obtained. Each dragon who survived now had a collection of planets to call their own.

Each dragon had a different relationship with the worlds within their dominion. Some were content to view what was theirs from a distance. Like jewels on a crown, the globes were to be admired from a distance but left alone. Others, however, took pleasure in wreaking havoc on their world and its residents. Each visit was a cataclysmic event. Mountain ranges were laid low while new ones were raised. Oceans evaporated into mist by the mere passing heat of a dragon's body, resulting in decades of continual rain. The people of these worlds learned to survive the best they could. Some moved underground hoping to avoid their lord's notice and wrath, while other planets and cultures turned to religion. Praying worship would appease their dragon's appetite for destruction. I know what you are thinking, but no, this is not how a world dies. These dragons needed to leave something to return to and so they left survivors, just enough to rebuild and repopulate before their next visit, wondering if their efforts would be enough to dissuade them from returning.

It wasn't. Neither hiding nor prayer was effective. All they could do was hope and live until the next visit. Just as dragons changed the worlds around them, they were changed by the space that surrounded them. Once, dragons were green like the forests and hills, or red like fire and lava, some were pitch black matching the caves they lived in. But slowly, they began to become more ethereal. First their shades turned purple like the night sky, their eyes glimmered like stars, maps of constellations were shown in their wings, then they became more and more transparent, matching the emptiness of the space they lived in.

However, there was one dragon who had a different relationship with his hoard of worlds. He was more discerning in his choice of planets, not being content with simply the largest or most populated planets like other dragons, nor was his desire in variety in color or composition of planets. He was interested in the inhabitants of his worlds. He was concerned with diversity of life and development.

To have barren lifeless planets would be boring. A worthless endeavor. He wanted worlds that displayed all the different ways life evolved and developed. One world, all life was aquatic and societies were built around its massive coral reef. On another the people were just barely beginning to use tools; where as another primarily reptilian world, was entering its first industrial age and was figuring out ways of communicating across distances. The variety was intriguing to him.

Each world was special to him, and he was immensely jealous of other dragon hoards that had presentations of life that were not in his own hoard.

But there was nothing he could do about the worlds he lusted after, for he was not a particularly large or vicious dragon, at least as far as dragons are concerned. An attack against another dragon in an attempt to expand his hoard would leave his own planets open to a vulture waiting in the shadows of deep space. And that was a risk he was not willing to take.

Dragon names are incomprehensible to us but for our purposes we will call him Studious. It is the closest parallel I could find.

Studious spent his time drifting through space from planet to planet as if each world was a production put on just for him. For some worlds he kept his distance making sure its people did not know of his existence. Other worlds he enjoyed being observed by. Still at a distance he allowed himself to be perceived by people and was fascinated to see how cultures formed shaped by their knowledge of him. And for a select few worlds he played a more active role, lending his magic and power to their development and protection. He would quell storms that threatened cities, threaten violence on nations at war with each other, ensuring long stretches of peace between its people. But most interestingly, he would provide the missing pieces of a puzzle as inventions and science were discovered.

Some worlds he gave only a gentle nudge, helping them to develop at a more natural rate. Whereas other worlds he pushed along, forcing them to invent, create and discover faster and faster. A world with primitive technology a mere century ago now had powered vehicles. In the next decade, space exploration. It was deeply satisfying to him to help them along. And no before you ask, this also is not how a world dies. None of Studious's worlds developed the means of their own destruction. Their industry did not outpace their ability to self-govern or self-restrain.

Yet for all the different ways his worlds progressed, his ultimate goal still had not been achieved. Communication. None of his worlds actually knew who he was or were able to speak with him. What good was a hoard of worlds if they didn't know they were a part of his hoard? So this is what Studious worked at.

With each world he tried a different tactic but to no avail. In the same way we cannot comprehend his true name, we also cannot understand his words. But he worked at it. The effort consumed him—much to the derision of other dragons. They mocked him, laughing at his desire to stoop so low to attempt to speak with mortals. This only emboldened Studious to become more desperate and paranoid, thinking every other dragon was a threat. So, he began lashing out at dragons he perceived to be interested in his hoard. These skirmishes lit up the night sky with fire and magic, reminding people of the dragon battles from centuries ago. It reminded them of dragons destructive capabilities. I know what you are wondering, and the answer is no. So don't ask. This isn't how a world dies. Not yet.

These battles left Studious distracted. He stopped noticing the advancements his most developed worlds were making. When people first went to space, leaving their atmosphere for the first time, he didn't notice until it was considered history by that planet's inhabitants. It was still not what he was looking for in a world and thus to him it was uninteresting.

So he never realized people learned other worlds existed, and when they learned to communicate with each other, he was too consumed with his paranoia to notice.

If he had noticed, he would have learned that not only did his worlds communicate with each other, but they also began speaking to worlds that did not belong to him. This meant they learned of other dragons, dragons who were more terrible than Studious. They learned how dragons destroyed and never built, and how dragons hated and never loved. They learned to fear dragons. Studious included.

Studious's hoard was frightened. They saw his paranoia changing him. They saw him grow more frustrated and more frantic though they did not know why. To them his behavior was erratic. In their minds, it was only a matter of time before he turned his rage upon them just as every other dragon had done.

So they began preparing. They refused to sit idly by waiting for their inevitable destruction as other worlds had done. It became the first interplanetary effort for survival. They compiled everything they knew of dragons. Modern scientists worked with historians, and communications experts all to the end of killing a dragon. When it was first suggested, silence followed. The idea was so absurd it was beyond laughable. But as their fear of dragons grew, killing one seemed to be their only option. Now you may ask your question. Is this how a world dies? Yes. It will be. Give it time.

During all the time of these worlds researching and testing, Studious remained distracted. He became more and more desperate to protect his hoard, certain other dragons were interested in them. These other dragons were not interested at first, but Studious's paranoia intrigued them. What was so precious, so interesting, that led him to behave in this manner? Soon, his hoard was truly under attack from other dragons. Never underestimate a dragon's greed. When something; whether it be a single gold coin or an entire planet is believed to be valuable, it becomes desired.

While Studious defended his worlds, his own undoing went unnoticed. The question his hoard had to answer was, "How do you kill a dragon?" It's a simple matter really. Well, the theory is simple, but the application is slightly more difficult. It's the same principle people have been using to slay beasts throughout time. Whether it is a wild boar, a lion or a ten foot multi-headed shark-like creature of that aquatic planet I mentioned earlier. Step one; trap it. Make sure it can't move and can't get away. Step two; find something sharp and stab. Repeatedly if needed.

So, this is the plan they worked on. They worked on ways to trap a dragon. All of their research and efforts distilled down to a net. Granted it would have to be a big net. A very big net. Also, it would need to be strong. Very strong. But even with all the advancements some of Studious's worlds had made with the help of a literal dragon, they found the old ways would work best. A net, and something sharp.

So one designated world began building a net while the others worked on building something sharp. The plan boiled down to this —trap Studious in the net, then launch sharp rockets at him from the other worlds. No need to over complicate killing a dragon.

All of this planning and scheming continued to go unnoticed by Studious as he battled the other dragons who had decided it was time to include Studious' hoard in their own. Studious fought tooth and nail. Raging with all his might to protect what was his. Just as the plan to kill Studious went unnoticed by him, Studious's efforts to defend his worlds were unknown to said worlds.

For a world to die, at least in this case, a dragon must die first. That is what happened. The plan worked. It was a terrible sight. Studious, exhausted from his most recent clash with another dragon, in a stroke of incredibly unlucky fortune, took a moment of respite on the world with the net. He sprung the net and was trapped. Not realizing the source of his attack was not another dragon, Studious began to rage, sending fire out in every direction he could. His roars, heard by the entire planet, served to confirm their fear of him. Once the net trapped him, rockets were automatically launched from their home worlds at him. They did not take long to reach their target. The advancements they had made in technology, due to his help, would be his undoing. The rockets struck true and they struck hard. His roars of rage turned to agony and defeat. In his last moments he understood what was happening. He understood betrayal. He understood, his failure in learning to communicate with his worlds led to their fear and hatred of him. He also understood it was too late. Dragons do not cry. Do not believe anyone who tells you otherwise. But they can mourn and lament and it is a terrible sound to hear. As Studious bled out he also let out his final cry which echoed for the entire world to hear.

Then there was silence. Not a single person spoke, even the birds were stunned into silence for a time.

Finally, here is where a world dies.

The silence was broken by a roar. A dragon's roar. A dragon far more terrible and evil than Studious. A dragon who had no love or care for Studious' world. Even though this dragon caused calamities on his own hoard of worlds, he was still proud of what belonged to him and did not want to see them destroyed entirely. He had no such reservations about the worlds that once belonged to Studious.

When he came down and saw what had been done to Studious, his rage transformed into an emotion so raw, carnal and terrible which only dragons can feel. Only they are old enough and powerful enough to feel and act upon the feelings this dragon felt. Dragons are not supposed to die, they are not supposed to be killed by anyone other than a fellow dragon. So when this dragon saw the sin committed in front of him, there was only one option. This world and all the others involved had to die.

It took no effort on the dragon's part. These worlds were defenseless. They had played their entire hand taking down Studious.

They were not prepared for or even aware of another dragon until it was upon them. Their destruction took less than a day. He did not toy with them, he did not prolong their suffering, but their annihilation was complete and thorough.

This is how a world dies. They killed a god, not realizing another one was ready to take its place.

~ * ~ * ~

Daniel Whipple is based in Los Angeles, California. When he is not chasing his daughter around the park, he writes.

Could I Interest You in a Hoardshare Today?

G.J. Dunn

Keith paused outside the door and readjusted his tie with a claw. It was a well-off neighbourhood he'd picked. The door was freshly painted, the number sign clearly dragon-forged gold. The patio itself was wide and spacious, with a few hammocks set out for lounging. Clearly, whoever lived here had wealth to spare. Keith figured those dragons who already had a fair-sized hoard would be more likely to buy what he was selling. And by flame did he need a sale.

Gradithrax Soulflayer's voice rang in his ears, even now. *The hoard must grow, Keith. This company only has space for closers, Keith. Why can't you be more like Malruthinax Dreadbringer, Keith?* And then came his ultimatum. *Grow the hoard today, Keith, or you can kiss your half-millennia in the hoard goodbye.*

Gradithrax didn't care Keith had committed his entire hoard to the program. Didn't care that without a hoard, he couldn't regenerate thaum. Keith's wings jittered nervously at the thought, shaking the shoulder pads of his suit. Not only was thaum the source of fire-breathing, it was also the difference between a civilized dragon and a wild animal. A dragon without thaum… Keith shuddered. It was best not to think about it.

He raised a claw to knock at the door and paused, instead pulling out his pocket mirror and giving himself a once over. The blue of his suit really brought out the green in his scales. He gave the mirror his best smile, picked at a lump of flesh he saw caught between his teeth, then scratched away a dull scale at his neck. One deep breath later and he was ready.

He knocked, clasped his claws behind his back and tucked in his wings, ensuring his posture was relaxed and open. A friendly dragon. The kind you'd want to talk to. He heard someone approaching and took a half step forward as the door opened inwards.

The dragon on the other side was fire red, wearing a button-down shirt with brown trousers. He gave Keith an appraising look.

"Good morning, sir," Keith began. He had five different openers learned by rote, depending on the look of the dragon who opened the door. This fine fellow got 'working professional'.

"My name is Keith and I'm calling from Gradithrax Hoardshare Incorporated." Keith accompanied this with a gesture at the I.D. badge hanging around his neck. "Now I know that to a professional such as yourself time is valuable, but after hearing what G.H.I. has to offer, I think you'll agree the value of *this* time is worth *more* than gold. Do you have a spare five minutes?"

"Uh…" the dragon said.

"That's great," Keith replied. "Now, first things first, have you heard of Hoardshares?"

"I…"

"They're the latest trend." Keith paused to wave a carefree hand and smile. "Everyone's buying in and, between you and me, getting in early is the best way to see the most savings." Keith paused again, noted the dragon hadn't slammed the door in his face, and pushed on.

"I know what you're asking yourself. How does it work? Well, we know every dragon has a hoard. If you're anything like me, you've got a hoard room in that house for when you need a century or two to recharge. Am I right?"

The dragon nodded.

"And how much thaum do you get from your hoard?" Keith shook his head and laughed. "Whatever the answer is, I'm sure you want more, right?"

The dragon nodded again.

"Exactly! Hoardshare is the way to get much more thaum for much less hoard. All we do is get a group of dragons together, each one contributes a portion of their hoard and, in return, they get one century per millennia all to themselves. The bigger your contribution, the bigger hoard. Contribute enough and we might even be able to squeeze in a few extra decades for you. Does that sound good?"

"Zelithurnax?" a voice called from inside.

The dragon's head snapped around. When he looked back and Keith saw fear in his eyes. It made his heart sink. This was a look that never ended in a sale.

"Zelithurnax?" the voice called again, louder this time.

Another dragon appeared in the corridor, this one wore a casual baggy jumper, a mixture of pink and white, with a comfy-looking pair of jeans. Her scales were a pale blue, almost lilac, and, if it wasn't for the smoke that issued from her nostrils, he would have thought her cute.

"Oh, no," she said. "Zelithurnax, you get inside right this instant."

The red dragon looked down, admonished, and retreated back into the house, while the pale blue one advanced.

"How dare you," she spat at Keith, flames forming at the back of her throat. "He's not even ten thousand yet!"

"Ah," Keith said, still hoping he might turn this around. "So, you're the older sister?"

She reached out a claw and prodded his chest. "Don't bother trying that on me. Are you proud of yourself? Preying on dragons only just out of their eggs?"

"I—"

"You get out of here. Whatever you've got, we're not buying."

She reached out for the door and slammed it in Keith's face.

"Offal and flame," Keith muttered, resisting the urge to kick out at a nearby plant pot. He thought he'd had that one. And how dare that cow string him up by the wings for trying to make an honest living? The 'hatchling' was fully grown. And ten thousand wasn't *that* far from full-fledged adulthood anyway. How was he supposed to tell the difference?

He shook his head, putting it down to bad luck, and retreated down the porch. One down, at least another hundred to go. Surely one of them would get him a sale.

~ * ~

The second house was just as well-to-do as the first. It was set a little back from the pavement to leave room for a carefully mani-cured lawn, bisected by a path leading to the door. The path itself was lined with cherry trees and halfway up they even had a bridge to lead over a faux-lava moat. Something of a new trend Keith had noticed—a callback to bygone days when dragons still lived in mountains, apparently. Either way, you wouldn't catch him dead with one. By the time Keith had gotten to the door, after passing expensive decoration after expensive decoration, he'd began to wonder if he was in the wrong line of work. These dragons probably had hoards with enough thaum they could rent it out in the centuries they weren't using. Now that he thought about it further, rental hoards were a totally unexplored market.

He raised his claw, knocked, and waited.

The dragon who answered was definitely worthy of the 'holier than thou' opener. They wore a suit better than Keith's with an open blouse and, if you could believe it, jewellery. Keith hadn't even realised the human trend had reached these shores. Jewels were for thaum-building, not flaming decoration! To even use it in such a way suggested an outrageous level of thaum. Keith resisted the urge to provide his opinion on the choice. The sale was more important, after all.

"Good morning, ma'am, my name is—"

"Who is it, dear?" a voice called from inside the house.

"I'm just finding out, dear," the dragon replied. She tucked in her neck and nodded. "What is it you're here for?"

Keith floundered. He wasn't used to being thrown out of his opener. "Well," he said. "I'd like to talk to you about Hoardshares."

"Who *is it*, dear?" the voice from inside pressed.

The dragon winced and raised a claw to her face, turning away from Keith and calling back. "Fellow says he's selling Hoardshares."

"Well," Keith said, trying to draw the attention back to himself. "I'm really selling opportunity."

"Oh," she said. "He actually says he's selling opportunities."

"Tell him to sling a wing."

Keith flinched at her expression as she turned back to him. "I'm sorry," she said before he could reply.

And she closed the door.

~ * ~

The third house was no better. They claimed they already had a Hoardshare with Tyrushitar's Hoards that they used the second century of each millennia. The fourth and fifth were even worse, if that was possible. Keith had already pushed those attempts from his mind. And the sixth house wasn't even home.

Keith suppressed a shudder as he reached lucky number seven. Okay, luck hadn't been with him so far, but he had a feeling about this one. An intuition. His mother had always told him he had a good intuition. She'd encouraged him to follow his gut whenever he could, and it was leading him to a sale. The excitement of it built as he wended his way past the ornamental pond and under the branches of the accompanying willow tree. On the other side, flowerbeds lined a porch in a wide hue of reds, purples and blues. The fragrance caught in Keith's nostrils. Lavender. His mother's favourite. It had to be a sign.

He stepped up to the door and raised a hand to knock, when the door opened in front of him.

A dragon, yellow as the sun and a good ten feet taller than Keith, glared down at him with disdain.

"Not interested," the dragon said, and slammed the door in Keith's face.

Keith flinched at the sharpness, his heart going from hope to despair in two seconds flat. He stood there, unresponsive, for another ten seconds, his mind processing what had just happened. Then he sighed, shoulders slumping, wings drooping. Slowly, he made his way back down the path, resisting the urge to just collapse to the floor. He wasn't sure if it was his imagination or if he could actually *feel* his thaum dwindle a little further. Time was running out and, with reactions like that, he had to wonder if he was only delaying the inevitable.

He'd really thought that was the one. His gut, the lucky number seven, the smell of lavender. It had all acted to build him up, just so it could tear him back down. He reached the pavement before eventually slumping to the floor, watching some leaves blowing in the wind. It was a tough rejection to take. Maybe one too many. Maybe it was the sign he needed to just stop, stop trying and admit defeat. He could keep trying or he could just stop, become a leaf on the wind and see where he ended up. Maybe it wouldn't be as bad as he thought.

No.

The word reverberated through his mind. Keith shook his head and let a little flame burn at the back of his throat. Just enough to dampen the self-pity. That's all it was. A self-pity cycle, dragging him down and making him think he was worthless. He wasn't going to let them beat him. Malruthinax Dreadbringer never gave up, and he'd secured himself so many millennia in the hoard he practically had an epoch all to himself. There was nothing stopping Keith from doing the same.

There was always a next house.

~ * ~

But the rejection only continued through the morning, despite Keith's rediscovered sales drive. And then it continued all through the afternoon, too. Keith worked his way through the neighbour-hood, going door-to-door, receiving an excess of excuses and a deluge of disinterest. Quite frankly, Keith had never known there was so much variety in how someone could turn him down. He'd had rude, apologetic, blunt, regretful, and even fearful at one stage. It was as if the great dragons in the beyond had lined up against him and decided it was his time to lose everything he held dear.

He began to contemplate, against his better judgement, what would happen if he failed. A dragon without thaum just couldn't live in the civilised society they'd created. He'd have to devolve. Fly across the ocean, to Rymeria, where the dragons still *fought* humans for their treasure, still *hunted* for food. Keith shuddered. He couldn't even imagine having to *kill* something to eat.

He gritted his teeth, blew the nervous smoke from his nostrils and set off again to make the most of the dying light.

~ * ~

"Good morning, sir, my name is Keith and I'm here repres—"
"*Keith?*"
"Yes, sir?"
"What kind of name is Keith for a dragon?"
"My mother was a human sympathiser, sir."
"Oh, how awful for you. Did you catch it?"
Keith couldn't help but squint at the dragon. Catch it? Catch what? Oh!
"Oh, no, no, no, sir. Human sympathising isn't contagious. Anyway, as I was saying—"
"How do you know?"

"How do I know what, sir?"

"How do you know it isn't contagious?"

"Because I'm not a human sympathiser, sir."

The dragon backed away a pace, raising a claw to cover their snout. "Have you got any proof?" they asked, voice muffled.

"Well," Keith replied, scratching at his neck. "No."

The dragon shook his head and backed away, his claw reaching out.

"But—"

And the door closed.

~ * ~

"Good morning, sir, my name is Keith and I'm wondering if you might like to hear about hoardshares and the brilliant opportunity for thaum regeneration they offer?"

"Think you might be guarding the wrong castle there, mate."

Keith paused, confused, and took the dragon in again. He was a beautiful, shining silver colour that made Keith rather jealous, with thick legs, larger than average wings and no foreclaws whatsoever.

"Oh," said Keith. "You're a wyvern."

The wyvern nodded. "Only one in the neighbour'ood."

"I see." Keith hesitated. "I don't suppose Wyvern's use thaum do they?"

The wyvern flicked his tail. "Nah, mate. Different anatomy entirely."

"Oh, that's a shame."

"'Ave a good day," the wyvern said.

"You—"

And the door closed.

~ * ~

The blue-green dragon who opened the door was holding a ferret in each hand.

"Good aft—"

"Can't you see I'm busy?" he shouted at Keith before the door slammed shut.

Keith wasn't quite sure how.

~ * ~

The last embers of the sun were dying behind the horizon as Keith reached the next house. His wings twitched nervously now. He still had enough time for a few more houses. All he had to do was drop the paperwork at the office. Of course, before he could do that, he needed someone to *sign* the paperwork.

He felt battered and bruised, as if he'd been in a fight for his life with some do-gooder human. It wasn't often in his job exhaustion was a factor but today, the stress of it, had just piled up. He wasn't sure how much he had left.

"Just one more," he muttered to himself. Always just one more.

He approached this house, one of the smaller ones in the neighbourhood, without much hope, but his mother had always told him a fool's hope was better than no hope at all. And Keith had always considered himself a bit of a fool.

The claw he raised to knock at the door was shaking, he hadn't eaten all day, and the sound his claw made as it struck echoed through his skull. There was the pause as the dragon living inside made their way to the door and, in that moment, Keith felt his stomach shift. Was it his thaum finally depleting? Or just another hunger pang?

The door opened to reveal a burgundy dragon wearing reading glasses and a loose white blouse, some pale-coloured trousers hung loosely on her legs and her claws poked through a fluffy pair of slippers. Definitely a 'house-spouse' for the opener.

"Good afternoon, ma'am, my name is Keith and—" Keith trailed off. The openers hadn't got him anywhere today. And he was so tired he could barely remember the script anyway. "Can I ask your name?"

"I'm Mattaranox," the dragon replied cautiously. "Skinmelter."

"Mattaranox," Keith repeated and smiled. "That's a pretty name. Listen, Mattaranox, I've had a long day and I was going to give you a speech about Hoardshares and why they're so great, but I'm tired and I'd rather just have an honest chat with you, if you have the time. Is that okay?"

Mattaranox glanced at a clock in the corridor. "Sure, I have a few minutes."

"Great. So to start with, have you ever heard of a Hoardshare, or should I explain it?"

"You can explain."

"Well, Mattaranox, it's quite simple really. All you have to do is commit some of your hoard to one of our Hoardshares, and in exchange you'll get a century or two to spend in the Hoardshare once a millennia. Because we take a small portion from a lot of dragons, no personal hoard can compare to ours in terms of recharging your thaum. You'll come back totally refreshed and relaxed, practically a new dragon."

"So, I give you my hoard?"

"*Some* of your hoard. That's added to create the larger hoard. Personally, I think it's a great idea. You lose some of your hoard for now, true, but the size of the hoards we have, the sheer level of thaum they generate. You can't beat it."

Mattaranox scrunched her snout. "And what do you get out of it?"

"Me?" Keith considered for a moment and decided on the truth. "For each person I sign up, I get a bit more time, in a bit of a bigger hoard."

"Hmm," Mattaranox said. "It does sound good, I'll admit."

Keith allowed himself a little smile. She was definitely interested. He could hear it in her voice. "It *is* good, Mattaranox. Even our smallest hoards are three or four times as large as a personal hoard. That's three or four times more thaum for your time. Or, if you're more of an up-and-at-them type, you could go the other way and spend only a quarter of the time in the hoard."

Mattaranox raised a claw to scratch at her snout. "And how much would I have to commit?"

Keith's heart rate increased. Once someone started talking about committing to the Hoardshare, they were already thinking in terms of numbers. He just had to choose his next words very carefully and he was saved. "Well, that depends on how much time you want to spend in the Hoardshare and which of our Hoardshares you'd like to contribute to."

"There are different kinds?"

"Exactly," he said, nodding in agreement. "Our company caters to dragons with hoards of all sizes. There's a certain business element to it, of course. The more you contribute, the bigger hoard you qualify for."

"So, the more I commit, the more thaum I get?"

"That's the idea, yes."

Mattaranox thought for a second. "Maybe we should talk more inside."

Keith offered the dragon a full, unapologetic grin. "I'd be happy to, Mattaranox."

She moved aside, and as Keith stepped across the threshold, he felt a burning in his chest. Maybe it was the hunger. Maybe it was the excitement. Or maybe, just maybe, it was his thaum re-lighting.

~ * ~ * ~

G. J. Dunn writes from a sofa in Leyland, UK. When not writing, he develops gene therapies, runs half marathons, and attempts to tire out his border collie, Belle. So far, he's only succeeded with the first two. Find out more about his writing at gjdunn.co.uk and on Instagram @ridicufiction.

The Memory Hoard

E.E. Lucek

Aethelgard ran her claws over a vase from a country that no longer existed. As she slipped out of the memory, her small, well-appointed cave came back into focus. These days, she mostly kept to her home in the far mountains, comfortably removed from human habitation. Why travel? She had already done all of that, and all the possessions that decorated her cave were her reward. Each lamp, painting, rug, and leather-bound tome sparked a memory when she touched it, fresh as the day when she first acquired it.

Some days she spent entirely drifting in the seas of the past, remembering this or that journey and chuckling over the witty banter of acquaintances who had long since gone their separate ways. Each slip of paper and old letter was precious in this way, and for a long time, the old dragon considered this enough.

From the outside, the mountains were steep and forbidding, so though Aethelgard had settled in a cozy nook surrounded by trees and a grassy clearing, she did not receive many visitors. It was a surprise, then, when a melodic trill sounded outside the entrance-way. A firebird peered curiously in.

"I don't suppose you'd entertain a weary traveler?" the firebird asked. "I'm on a long journey east and thought I'd rest my wings a while. I don't mean to disturb you, but would be glad of shelter and good company while I tarry."

"Of course! Come in, come in," Aethelgard said, trying not to stare too much as she admired the firebird's feathers, which shimmered like molten gemstones. "Can I get you anything?"

The words had been automatic, summoned up from a different time, and she regretted them as soon as they left her mouth. What did she have to offer? A mental inventory did not produce much she was willing to part with. She'd offer tea, except the only kind she had available just then was a special blend, originating from a small country a week's flight away, and no longer in production. She could hardly countenance drinking it.

Thankfully, the firebird was not demanding. "I hardly wish to intrude. Something for my parched throat would be nice, or directions to a nearby spring."

Aethelgard could serve plain water well enough, cold and clear from a mountain stream. She added a plate of sugar cookies to the offering to make up for the lack in beverage, which delighted her guest.

And so, they spent a pleasant afternoon, trading stories of journeys and other treasures. Aethelgard learned the firebird's name was Flaulote, and Flaulote, admiring the precise placement of the cave's décor, learned each piece came with a story. This spray of dried wildflowers was from the coast of Zervain, collected under balmy night skies, the only time the flowers would bloom. And that painted plate had been the winning entry to a regional ceramics competition a century back.

Impressed with the breadth of personal history held in the small space, the firebird couldn't help but wish to contribute to it. With slender talon and delicate beak, it uncovered a satchel hidden amongst its glimmering feathers. From this, it withdrew a golden torc, almost a complete circle with curlicues at either end. Fine, etched lines depicted a firebird's journey, from flames to flight.

After setting the jewelry gently on the table next to half-nibbled cookies, Flaulote said, "This visit has been most entertaining, more than I could have asked. Please, accept this gift as thanks for being a gracious host."

Aethelgard's eyes gleamed with the gold, but she replied, "I can't accept something so precious. Your company has been equally diverting for me. That's all the thanks I need."

"I bought it at a shop in the city of Tentangle because it amused me, but I admit it may not have been the wisest decision. It has weighed heavily on my flight, and to be honest, it would please me more to offer it as a commemoration of this visit."

How could the old dragon say no to that? She coveted memories above all else. She refused again for form's sake, but eventually accepted as a way to remember the firebird's stay. Even so, a twinge of guilt itched at her scales. The visit hadn't even included tea.

And, as Flaulote set off, there was an additional pressing matter. Aethelgard would need to find a suitable place for such a precious object in her already fully-appointed home.

~ * ~

Not long after, at least as dragons and firebirds count time, Flaulote stopped by on its return trip, bringing along its friend, Mordrear the roc. Mordrear was massive against the firebird, his plumage subdued in its dusty stone shades, his serrated beak powerful enough to crush tree branches.

But dragons are used to accommodating creatures of a grand scale, and that is exactly what Aethelgard did. In fact, she received them with exceeding good humor since she had recently completed a trip to restock on tea she was willing to drink.

The three were a lively bunch, with Mordrear consuming at least a gallon of tea, and Aethelgard found herself making another friend.

At the end of the visit, perhaps prompted by Flaulote, Mordrear produced a wooden bowl with a flourish. The material was hard and gray with a fine grain, from a type of tree Aethelgard was unfamiliar with.

"It will last even a dragon's lifetime," the roc boasted, and she could well believe it.

Aethelgard accepted the memento, finding it only fair after accepting Flaulote's torc.

However, Flaulote, not to be outdone, had another gift.

"I'm throwing a party," the firebird said, passing a gilded invitation over the table. The details had been burned into the paper in a neat script. "Since you've been so kind to host us, I'd like to return the favor. Besides, you should meet more of my friends. I think they'd like you, but they can't all make it up the mountain themselves."

What else could Aethelgard do but accept this gift as well?

She rearranged her schedule, which didn't take much doing, and arrived at the designated lakeside field on the prescribed day. She stopped and stared in wonder before joining the festivities, for scarce had she ever beheld so many mythic creatures together in one place before.

Crowds of dryads and fauns milled at the forest's edge, breaking into song at a moment's notice. Mermaids and sea monsters lolled at the shore, listening and occasionally offering counterpoint. A unicorn and griffin sparred playfully while a gnome handed out refreshments as fast as her legs would carry her.

Unused to such tumult in her quiet mountain home, Aethelgard at first kept to the perimeter of the gathering, but it wasn't long before Flaulote found her.

"Aethelgard, you made it! Welcome," the firebird said, its molten feathers shining bright under the gleam of the sun. "Listen, I could use a hand, as it were, if you're up for it."

"If I can help," she said, somewhat cautious, but curious.

"Every gathering, I have a bonfire," Flaulote said, nodding to a jumbled pile of dry sticks stacked high near the water. "I usually kindle it myself, but I'd love if you performed the honors this time."

"I can do that."

And so Flaulote led her to the center of the party, making greetings and introductions along the way.

Breathing flames onto the stack of wood and nursing the first tentative flickerings was the work of a few moments, but those around her cheered as the fire took hold. Suddenly, she had been embedded as a central figure of the event and found no shortage of welcoming banter and fascinating topics.

Caught up in the festivities, Aethelgard hardly noticed time passing. The celebration lasted into the night and the next morning, with new partygoers arriving throughout. Evening brought shy boggarts while will-o'-the-wisps provided gentle illumination as the stars came out. A gaggle of nymphs danced around what Aethelgard now proudly viewed as her bonfire.

By the time the revelry finally wound down, the old dragon had collected numerous new favors and mementos, including a chunk of charred wood from the bonfire, as well as promises of future visits.

She slept a long time back in her own home, recovering from such excitement, and when she woke, she eyed her surroundings critically. In her exuberance, the well-ordered cave was becoming disheveled. Mementos were piled on top of each other haphazardly instead of each having a specific, neat place of their own.

She shuffled the clutter to her back rooms, determined to pose a tidy front for all the visitors she would soon receive.

And arrive they did. Aethelgard had made quite the impression at the party and she, in turn, was delighted to have found a community of mythic individuals so close to home.

But each guest seemed to arrive with some hostess gift or

another, or otherwise left some mark of their visit. Underlying the delight, worry grew as her home filled ever more with memories she did not want to lose.

She eventually could not contain the clutter to her private rooms and it began to overflow to the public. Piles of baubles spilled out of baskets, were wrapped up in random tapestries, or were stacked precariously high. They lay together with little rhyme or reason. An amethyst geode from a troll cradled a perfect acorn from a dryad. These new additions abutted an old atlas, which was marked up with routes of prior journeys, and which contained an invitation to a soiree that acted as a bookmark.

Unfortunately, I cannot attend the harvest feast this time, Aethelgard wrote in response to another invitation that had arrived via messenger bird. *Please send everyone my regards. I hope to see them again soon.*

But she did not send out any of her own invitations, not anymore. She could hardly abide the state of her home herself; what would her guests think? Besides, she needed to stay away from the temptation to fill her remaining space ever further with additional memories.

So, she spent more days on her own at home again. The solitude shouldn't have palled. She had been fine by herself for a long time.

Crowded into her living space, her mementos looming over her, she realized she had not drifted in reminiscence for quite some time, borne by soft tides of memory-laced wanderings. She felt a sudden longing for it, and started sifting through mementos.

The activity, previously so simple and soothing, quickly grew frustrating, as she dug through piles in search of specific souvenirs. She let out a huff of irritated smoke as a stack all but collapsed on her in her rummaging.

But here was one she was looking for, a faded red ribbon. She immersed herself in the memory it contained, of a windy summer day, from a time when she had decided to explore the northern bounds of the continent on a whim.

The wind had grown furious and as she looked for a place to land, she spotted a tiny human hamlet. She glided down cautiously, not wanting to scare its inhabitants. She needn't have bothered. Curious faces peeked out of windows and doors. Not even the sheep on the distant moors appeared ruffled by her appearance.

(If she were honest with herself, she had thought it had been a sunnier day than this. Or greener. The moors seemed bled of color, only dry grass and stone and puffs of sheep marking the landscape.)

It didn't take long for people to approach her. They ogled without hostility and wore the hand-dyed wool of farmers who were self-sufficient by necessity.

"A dragon! All the way out here," a man exclaimed.

"You get some strong winds," Aethelgard had said by way of explanation. "Well, further up, anyway. It's not so bad down here."

"You should try it in winter," someone else said, eliciting knowing guffaws from the crowd.

"Rosie, come look and see," the first man said, beckoning a young girl forward.

The girl complied with wide eyes. She had red ribbons in her hair.

"We've never seen a dragon before. This will be something for her to remember."

As if suddenly thinking of something, the girl untied one of her ribbons. She held it up to Aethelgard.

"I don't have any hair," the dragon said, puzzled, but bent her neck down to see the proffered ribbon.

The girl tied it around one of Aethelgard's horns. "So you can remember us, too."

The others cooed at this sentiment, but Aethelgard tuned them out.

(Hadn't the conversation been livelier? Wasn't the moment supposed to be more touching?)

With a sigh, she slipped out of the memory, letting the now-faded ribbon waft back to the floor of her cavern. Maybe that one hadn't been quite what she was looking for.

She went back on the hunt, digging through more treasured memories, but met with similar results in each case. The familiar conversations rang flat and the colors of revisited landscapes bled insipid. The old pathways had become routine.

Routine could still be comforting, she realized, but never again exciting, except by way of echoes.

Holding a clock in the shape of a ship's wheel delicately in her claws, she came to a resolution. She did not want to discard the past wholesale, yet she did want to make room for new experiences, whether they became beloved memories or not.

It was slow going at first, sorting, and assessing, and making a bigger mess than she started with. She took the time to replay every memory as she went, weighing its uniqueness and sentimentality along with the actual form and function of the object itself. It was hard to consider parting with any at first, but the more mementos she evaluated, the clearer it became which ones were truly precious.

And so, little by little, the piles dwindled. She sent a trowel she had never used to a gnome of her acquaintance who enjoyed gardening. A set of mosaic coasters went to a troll who loved stonework. And a lovingly illustrated book on far-off locations and incredible destinations went to Flaulote.

In this way, she passed some items on to treasured friends, some to pawn shops, and some to those in need, hoping all the while they would become cherished mementos all over again.

At last, Aethelgard had pruned and wrangled her possessions into a new configuration. It was perhaps not as neat and orderly as the old dragon would like, reflecting a life in motion, and she knew the work was not finished forever, but it would suffice for the time being. After all, it had already been far too long since she allowed any visitors.

She sent out invitations tentatively, knowing her absence had stretched longer than intended. But her friends received the tidings gladly, and none so swiftly as the firebird.

It was a fine, sunny morning when Flaulote dropped by.

"I love what you've done with the place!" the firebird exclaimed as soon as it stepped into the cave. Flaulote paused frequently throughout the visit to admire various pieces of the rearranged décor, especially noting a certain golden torc displayed in pride of place.

Aethelgard served ginger cookies, fresh out of the oven, but fell back on an old blend of tea for refreshment. In fact, it was one no longer in production. She reflected it maybe wasn't as robust or nuanced as when it was first packed, but she enjoyed it all the same, especially in sharing it with a dear friend. And in using it, it became woven into a new memory.

~ * ~ * ~

E. E. Lucek absolutely does not hoard books. Her constant search for more shelf space is entirely unrelated.

One of her first published stories (in a high school creative writing magazine) featured a dragon. After time as a librarian and then as a software engineer, she's excited to return to the fantastical realm. Some things never change: her dragons always seem to drink tea.

E. E. Lucek currently writes from Illinois in between frequent distractions from a needy kitty.

An Unexpected Hoard

Roxane Llanque

"Who *DARES* ENTERING?"

The booming voice rocked the gloomy cave and showered Aleta with earth and stones from its ceiling. She should be frightened —but frankly, she was too annoyed. Six days the rogue had scaled Garadín Mountain to reach the rumored hoard of Dragon Lív. She fought snowstorms, hungover witches, and misogynistic paladins… for this?

Instead of heaps of gold, towers of books mounted before her—pillars upon pillars of them, each lit by lanterns filled with large fireflies that punctured the hoard's darkness with warm light. Another, closer roar shook the cave and Aleta remembered there *was* an actual dragon. Quickly she dove to the side and tried to squeeze between two book-towers.

"HEY, MIND THE BOOKS!"

Seriously? A third and deafening roar brought Aleta to her knees. A giant shadow appeared from the deeper part of the cave, two wings spreading menacingly. A rumble, an explosion of red light…and then a strangely beautiful woman stood before her, in scant armor of thorns. Her royal face was framed by shimmering red locks; and two intense eyes filled with flames fixed the rogue with a damning glare.

For a moment Aleta could do nothing but stare at the gorgeous apparition before her. Finally, she stammered, "*You're* Dragon Lív?"

The dragon lady snorted smoke. "My dragon form endangers my books once I move. But do not let that fuel your foolish hope, mortal; even in this form you do not stand a chance against me. I assume you came for gold—what say you now?"

Aleta blinked. "I say come on. This can't be your hoard!"

The dragon threw back her shimmering hair. "Books are the world's only true treasure, human." Slowly she advanced, her armor rattling as Aleta backed away. "They trump any of the lifeless metals your kin enslave themselves to. I see you share their pathetic obsession! For your greed I shall—" She shrieked when she tripped over a book and suddenly the dragon was falling.

Call it instinct or her cursed gentlewomanly nature—but Aleta rushed forward to catch her in her arms. Lív stilled in her embrace as they locked eyes. Her skin was unnaturally hot but smooth, an entrancing smell of fire and parchment enveloped Aleta, and she found those burning amber eyes, that looked at her with shock, quite took her breath away. She was beyond breathtaking, and Aleta wanted to…*oh*. She cleared her throat into the heavy silence. "I apologize. I didn't know dragons hoarded books, my lady."

Lív blinked. "Well, this dragon does. I have big plans. I shall descend upon towns and only spare them if every citizen learns how to read. It shall be the rise of literacy! And I will *whoops!*" She'd attempted to stand but stumbled over her feet. Aleta had to laugh as she gathered her up again. The dragon growled. "Curse this useless form—the humiliation! I'll have to kill you even if you didn't come to take my books, pretty mortal."

Aleta pulled the dragon closer and gave her a roguish smile.

"Well, I came seeking treasure…and I think I've found one."

It turned out a dragon's blush was accompanied by literal flames escaping her nostrils and Aleta quenched the fire that sparked in her locks with a wink.

~ * ~ * ~

Roxane Llanque is a German-Bolivian writer and filmmaker. Her award-winning short film "Aberration" was featured at numerous film festivals and her story "The Tell-Tale Present" won the 2023 Outstanding Miniature of World Pride Australia. Her writing was featured in the anthologies "Demons & Death Drops" by Little Ghosts Books, "We Are All Thieves of Somebody's Future" by Air and Nothingness Press and is forthcoming in the science fiction anthology "Not Your Papi's Utopia" by The Latinx Archive.

You can find her on Twitter and Instagram @roxanellanque.

The Dragon's Daughter

Sevanna Wells

"Have at thee, dragon!" a high-pitched voice screeched. "Give up your gold or I'll mount your head on my castle wall!"

The dragon groaned and buried his face in his claws. *Who keeps telling these buffoons I have gold?*

He slinked to the mouth of his cave, nearly tempted to berate the knight for his sheer stupidity. He had to hand it to these adventurers; his cave was not easy to find. A human had to ride or hike through miles of snow at a steep incline. Often this meant they did not provide horses for him to eat.

He mustered an intimidating tone. "Leave this place!" he roared, spewing fire out of the cave mouth. "Or my dwelling will be your grave!"

The knight let out a war cry, and the dragon walked out to meet him. The human immediately threw his spear, and it fell short of hitting the dragon at all. The dragon could no longer hide his disappointment and frustration; he stared at the spear, then looked up at his would-be assailant.

The knight stopped short, suddenly comprehending the size of the dragon.

The dragon opened his mouth to incinerate the unfortunate knight, but something in the knight's open supplies pouch caught the dragon's eye.

The dragon shut his mouth, and the fire in his gizzard quelled immediately. "What is that?" he asked.

The knight didn't respond, frozen by his sudden brush with mortality.

The dragon ignored the knight's realization. "That parchment in your pouch. What is it?"

The knight grabbed the parchment and waved it in the air like a bone in front of a snarling dog, then threw it as though to make a distraction. He turned and tumbled down the mountain, screaming as he went.

The dragon scooped up the parchment and trotted back to his cave—he loved getting new things. He ignited his wood pile, and a warm glow filled the main hall of his cave. He spread the parchment tenderly with his claws and inspected it in the firelight.

It was a map of the mountains, and many lands around them. The dragon's cave had been circled in red ink. Like everything lately, the map was labeled in the Roman alphabet.

"Alpi," the dragon muttered. He had heard his mountains called by similar names before. He rolled up the parchment and took it into a different section of his cave.

Books, paintings, glass, pottery, and statues cluttered his hoard cavern from floor to ceiling for hundreds of yards. Despite this, the dragon knew the exact location of every item stored there. He shuffled through his pile of maps until he found an old one—also titled "Alpi" but in a less ornamental script. He squirreled away the outdated map and carefully placed the new one where he could see it.

He glanced around his hoard room. He had all of these statues memorized; he knew by heart the stained-glass windows he had stolen from Koln; the words from the books from the Library of Alexandria practically lived in his head.

Time to go out and find something new. A Persian rug, perhaps, or another Chinese painting. Perhaps an intricate Norse rune stone.

He had promised he would be content with his hoard, but the arrival of this new map sparked a powerful lust for more. It was just dragon instinct, and he didn't dare deny it. He exited his cave, ready to take off.

"Dragon!" a tiny voice called.

Somehow a tiny human girl in rags had clambered up the mountain. He stared at her, and she stared back. She looked Italian. Tears glistened on her bright pink cheeks. The dragon hadn't seen a child in many decades.

She squeezed her eyes closed. "Please, mighty one. Make it quick."

The dragon frowned. "Make what quick?"

"Eat me, dragon. I have offered myself as a sacrifice to you."

"…No." The dragon snorted. "Are you…messing with me? You *want* to be eaten?"

She started to bawl.

The dragon didn't have a response. He stood helplessly while she cried.

"Hey," he tried. She wouldn't stop.

He awkwardly scooped her out of the snow. Maybe his trip could wait for an hour or two, just to make sure she got off the mountain safely once she calmed down.

She shivered in his palm like a bird, and a pang of sympathy hit his heart. But he didn't know where to begin to address this.

He set her down in front of his fire and brought her a piece of sea blue silk from Genghis Khan, although it pained him to share a part of his hoard.

She pushed it away. Her sobs had slowed to periodic sniffles and deep breaths.

"Don't coddle me. I won't get any fatter than this."

The dragon grunted. "I'm not fattening you. I only eat adults." She stared at him, horrified, until he laughed. "It's a joke. Humans taste like dirt. I'm not going to eat you, so go home."

"I can't go home," she said, evidently struggling not to cry again. "Father told me I was useless like the dead, and that maybe if I came to sacrifice myself to you, you would pay him gold and he could make our family wealthy again."

The dragon waved his claw. "Whoa, whoa. Slow down." He stared at the ceiling, recounting her words. "Your *dad* said to go get *eaten* by a dragon so he could get rich?" He looked at her again, hoping she would have an epiphany.

She nodded.

"And you *listened?!*"

"He would have me marry the duke of Milano for wealth." She shook her head. "Better I be eaten by a dragon."

The dragon sighed. "I told you: I don't eat people anymore. I can't help you. Stay here until you warm up, and then run off to Venice or some other gorgeous coastal town like a normal person."

She cocked her head. "Venezia is my home."

"Wherever!" The dragon tossed his head. "I have places to be, and you need to find other humans to be with. Just because that greedy sack of meat is your old man doesn't mean you have to listen to him."

She giggled. "You speak very strangely."

"Sure." The dragon turned away. "I'm leaving now. You can stay as long as you want, but winter is coming on quick, so you should definitely get out of here. This cave freezes over in the winter."

"Will you take me with you?" she pleaded. She shed the silk covering and trotted to the dragon's side. "I came here expecting to die. Just take me where you are going and leave me there."

The dragon laughed. "No."

She hung her head. "Then what is the use of leaving this cave but to die in the frigid snow?"

"Don't do that. Do you have a grandma or cousins or something?"

She shook her head without looking up.

He sighed. *Why did she have to be pitiful?* "You can't go where I'm going. I'm going to Persia. Or Samanid, or Seljuk, or whatever the kids are calling it these days." He waved his claw. "Regardless, it's far away and dangerous for little girls like you."

She kept her head down. "Yes, sir."

The phrase sounded practiced, like she had used it to submit to the will of another a thousand times. The dragon groaned. Humans had never had a huge effect on him before, but he was never really faced with the innocent ones. Thankfully, he had one last idea.

"I'll take you down the mountain. I'll show you my favorite village to steal sheep from. You'll fit right in."

She gave him a hopeful smile. The dragon's heart surged with a deep warmth he hadn't felt in centuries.

"Dragon!" a deep, haughty voice yelled. "Release my daughter or you will suffer the consequences!"

The girl froze like a rabbit in a trap.

"I am Doge Pisani of Venezia! I have brought an army to contend with you!"

The dragon grabbed the girl and lowered her into his hoard room. "Stay here," he hissed. "I'll be back."

He marched to the cave entrance, trying to not roll his eyes. Was there something in the air? Why were all of these humans suddenly climbing the mountain? They all had to visit the most dangerous predator in the Alpi before winter set in or something.

"Doge Pisani!" he boomed. Before he walked into the snow, he heard the murmurs of some soldiers likely second-guessing their life choices. He spread his wings as he walked out, and fifty men shied away from him. One Italian man stood out, strong and defiant. A thick, black beard shielded his face, and shimmering steel armor guarded the rest of him. He pointed his sword at the dragon.

"Release my daughter. I know you have her."

The dragon's tongue flickered. He wanted to just blow these men off the mountain, but he spotted archers among them. He could incinerate a single archer. But a flurry of arrows might leave him unable to fly—possibly forever. No, diplomacy was the right choice here.

The dragon steadied himself, not having thought about what he would say. The Doge had probably followed his daughter up here,

"You have journeyed in vain," the dragon said slowly. "Your daughter sacrificed herself to me to gift you with great wealth. She is no more, for I have eaten her!" He exhaled a menacing cloud of smoke, and the men scrambled away from him.

Pisani didn't even try to hide his smirk. "What a brave girl to face a beast like you on behalf of her beloved father," he said. "But you must understand, I am pained at the loss of my only daughter. Compensate me for the sacrifice I have provided you."

Pig, the dragon thought. *You don't deserve your daughter.*

"Alas," the dragon said. "You may search my cave high and low, but my riches have been taken from me by night by the prince of Genoa."

Pasani scoffed. "Liar."

The dragon gestured. "Send a scout into my lair. Confirm it."

Pisani waved his hand, and a trembling little soldier stepped forward. He stepped carefully past the dragon into the cave, and the dragon prayed the little Pisani girl had hidden herself.

The scout returned a long moment later and shrugged.

"Nothing but a closet of useless books and maps, sir," the soldier said.

Useless?! The dragon inhaled deeply. *How are humans still viable? They're so thick and shortsighted.* His eyes narrowed. *And annoying.*

Pisani grumbled and turned to the dragon. "Genoa, you say? Assist me in retrieving your hoard, and you shall have most of it back."

The dragon shook his head. "Claim it yourself, and it is all yours. I have my eye on treasure to the north that I am preparing to acquire," he lied. *He can't be dumb enough to believe that.*

It was like Pisani hadn't heard the last sentence. His eyes glimmered.

"Truly?" He clapped a fist to his chest. "Worry yourself not, then." He gestured for his men to follow him, and he seemed to nearly race through the snow and back down the mountain.

The dragon shook his head.

"You'd better die fighting Genoa, or I'm going to rip you apart myself," he muttered. He turned back into his cave.

"Little girl?" he called. "They're gone now. They think you're dead, so they won't be coming back anytime soon."

No response.

The dragon's heart skipped. "Little girl?"

He found her among the statues holding a scroll in her hands, one of the older ones from the Library of Alexandria. Her eyes flickered over the parchment, lost in fascination. The dragon grinned; it was the Illiad.

"A Homer person, are you?" he asked.

The girl flinched and stared up at the dragon. Her beaming smile caught him off guard.

"My father has a translation in his library." She turned back to the scroll. "It is much better in the original Greek."

The dragon cocked his head. "You read Greek?"

"Greek, Latin, Germanic, and Egyptian," she said. "Mother was a traveler, and she hired many tutors for me." She closed the scroll and stared at the ground. "These languages are all I recall of her now." She clutched the Illiad to her chest. "Reading Greek makes me feel close to her."

The dragon paused.

"Well…it's going to take a bit for Doge Pisani to get back down the mountain. Take some time to read before we go."

The girl's eyes lit up. "Thank you." She lowered the scroll. "My name is Alessandra. What's yours?"

The dragon shook his head. He should have just walked away. "Dragons have no need for names. The only title I know for myself is Wyrm of the Matterhorn from a town in the Germanic regions."

"I think you ought to be called George."

The dragon blinked. "Excuse me?"

"A common Christian myth is that of St. George and the dragon, and today I felt you were the St. George who slew my father the dragon." She smiled again.

The dragon wanted to show her out immediately. He didn't need this nonsense, especially with a silly human name like George. But something about that sad, brilliant smile stirred something in him, an ancient instinct he had been avoiding since the poaching of his last clutch of eggs in the Ural Mountains.

He stomped his claw and turned away from her. One more hour, and he would take her down the mountain. He didn't need a baby to look after.

"Besides," he muttered as he wandered out of his cave and took off into the pale gray sky. "She's nothing like a baby dragon. In just a few years, she'll be a grown human."

And who would look after her? Who would make sure she grew? Her father hadn't.

He dove down the mountain, the wind whistling through his horns.

The dragon suddenly had an image of Alessandra struggling to find a place in that farm village he had been considering. He knew there were drunkards and knaves who came through. Somebody just like her father might come sweep her up, and no one would care enough about her to protect her from it.

He swept a large sheep from a pasture at the base of the mountains, reflexively choosing the one that looked fattest. He swung back around while the other sheep scattered and the local farmers sounded the alarm.

He paused as he ascended the mountain. He had just eaten the day before; he didn't need to eat again. Why had he—?

The tingle of parental instinct was back. He groaned.

"One sheep. Then she leaves," he compromised.

She looked up when he entered the cave.

"Do you like mutton?" he asked. He tried to keep the defeat out of his voice.

"Yes," she said.

Why couldn't you have been vegetarian or something? The dragon threw the sheep carcass at her feet, and she startled. She scrambled away from the growing pool of blood on the floor, and the dragon sighed. So much for paternal instinct; she was still not a baby dragon.

"Humans cook food?" he said.

She gave him a wide-eyed stare and nodded slowly.

The dragon snatched up the sheep and brought it to his fire. He paused. "Do I just…throw it in?" He'd burned a sheep before eating it, and only got a mouthful of charred wool.

Alessandra laughed. "Skewer it. A full roast would be grand."

Although it became a tedious process neither of them had ever worked through before, they got most of the wool off the sheep, and the dragon skewered the meat on his claw. He turned it over the fire.

"No wonder humans are so territorial about sheep," he said. "They take forever, and you have to eat all the time."

Alessandra didn't really respond. She looked like she had started to nod off.

The dragon made sure she ate some of the roasted sheep. She seemed to have a hard time getting it down, but was polite anyway.

"What is the purpose of your book collection, George?" Alessandra asked.

The dragon snorted. "My name is not George." She ignored his protest and laid her head on his claw. "And it's not a collection. It's a hoard. I bring all the things I find beautiful and inspiring. Humans don't live very long, but they are interesting, and some of them are actually intelligent. I bring everything of value here." He grinned proudly. "I have the grandest library in the world."

"Have you read the books?" Alessandra muttered.

"Of course."

"Then why do you still have them?"

The dragon stopped. "Well…they're good and interesting, aren't they? I could always read them again."

"Do you have a dragon mate to share them with?"

The dragon stared at the dancing flames. "No."

"Children? Hatchlings, I suppose?"

The dragon closed his eyes, forcing his centuries-old memories away. He waited, dreading her next question, but was met with soft, deep snoring. He turned; she had fallen asleep, curled against his arm.

Pain forgotten, he scooped her up and brought her to his library. He laid her on a stack of scrolls and draped the silk over her, not sure if he could handle forcing her out in the morning.

Even after sleeping on it, the dragon couldn't make her leave, and she did not try to go. He didn't know how long she would stay, so he demanded vegetables and meat from the villagers to feed her with. Winter barricaded them inside of the cave, but his fire kept them warm.

In the summer, she didn't leave, even when the dragon left for the summer to retrieve some treasures from Arabia.

The next winter, she didn't leave.

He lost track of how long she stayed, read his books, wore the beautiful dresses he had brought from China and Japan, cooked food on his fire, and asked about his maps. He lost track of how many times he promised to take her around the world someday, when she was an adult.

One morning she finally responded, "George. I am fully grown and would like to travel with you today."

The dragon snorted. "Fully grown, huh?"

Alessandra nodded and smiled, her eyes gleaming in the spring sunlight. The dragon laughed, pride and a protective fear bubbling up in his stomach.

"Not yet."

Alessandra's shoulders fell. She'd gotten worse at hiding her disappointment over time. She turned away and walked back into the cave.

The dragon watched her, then looked back out at the sparkling snow. It was almost the time of year when he went out to gather food and supplies for her, and she always pressed him for information about the world when he came back.

A sudden pang hit him; he couldn't keep her in the cave forever. Even if he did, she would die from old age soon enough, and then he would be alone.

"Alessandra," he called.

She poked her head out of the library.

He hesitated. She still looked like a child to him—but she was the size of the human adults in the valley below.

Not yet.

"Next year," he said. "I promise."

She gave him a grateful smile, but his words had not satisfied her like they had in previous years.

As he left his cave, he thought about a way to make it up to her. She had everything she could possibly want, but her favorite things were the travel stories he brought back. He didn't know where to find one on short notice like this, and he had to leave the Alpi soon to take advantage of the summer.

A flash of light in the melting snow caught the dragon's attention, and he halted in midair. He stared at where the flash had come from, and his eyes narrowed.

He hadn't seen knights in this region in a long time.

Then the dragon's expression softened. The knight was not moving. The dragon sank towards the ground, and soon found a pool of blood growing in the snow around the knight.

Years ago, the dragon would have left him to die or wander off on his own. But the sandy-haired knight looked too young to be out here—definitely not much older than Alessandra. Perhaps bringing the knight home would distract Alessandra from her disappointment, and give her a chance to participate in the world without leaving his cave. He gently lifted the knight from the snow and flew him back to Alessandra.

He lowered the knight onto the cave floor, watching him with some curiosity. How did such a young child acquire armor?

"Alessandra," the dragon called.

Alessandra trudged out of the library, then gasped when she saw the knight on the floor.

"What did you do to him?!" she cried.

The dragon snorted. "I found him this way." A new pool of blood had begun to spread on the cave floor.

Alessandra raced to the knight's side and carefully rolled him over. The dragon's chest constricted with jealousy, and any parental care he felt for the boy evaporated.

He was no child. He was a threat to Alessandra.

She set to work unclipping the knight's armor, revealing a gaping wound in his side.

"Do you have bandages? Anything?!"

The dragon shrugged. Alessandra seemed too concerned. "You've been in my cave for years. You should know what I have."

Alessandra let out a small whimper. She stood, squeezed her eyes shut, and ripped off the bottom of her skirt.

"What are you doing?!" the dragon cried. "You love that dress!"

Alessandra lifted the knight's shirt and shoved her torn skirt into the wound. The knight tensed.

"He's still alive," she breathed.

"He was just unconscious. He hasn't been pierced anywhere fatal; it would have taken him hours to die."

Alessandra's brow furrowed. "I'm not so sure, George." She grabbed the young man's shoulders and began pulling him towards the fire. "Get some of my pillows. I think he should rest somewhere warm."

The dragon filled her request. They laid him facing the fire. He moaned softly, and Alessandra sat by his head. The dragon frowned at her persistent affection for the stranger; they had saved his life, so she didn't need to dwell on him anymore.

"I'll fly him down to the village when he's awake. I don't know where else he would have come from."

Alessandra shot him a puzzled smile, then turned back to the knight. "So soon? He'll need some time to recover. Perhaps I will prepare soup for him."

The dragon grunted. "I didn't bring him up here so you could baby him. I just thought you would know how to help him."

Alessandra ignored him and carefully stood up so she wouldn't disturb the knight. She ran into the pantry alcove of the cave.

"Alessandra," the dragon warned.

She returned with a pot stuffed with vegetables.

"Would you kindly retrieve more supplies?" she asked.

An idea sparked in the dragon's mind. "Why don't you come with me? We'll drop him off on the way."

Alessandra shook her head. "I'd better stay with him."

The dragon's heart sank at her obvious attraction to the knight. "You're too young," he whispered.

He left her with the knight; he might as well take the opportunity to clear his head and battle with his desire to keep his little human daughter. He hadn't wanted to admit it to himself before, but he had really raised her. She had really taken the place of his family.

The dragon clenched his claws. He wanted any excuse. First, he would have to get rid of the knight.

The dragon brought back less food than usual. Maybe this would incentivize Alessandra to forget about the knight and think about traveling together again. He knew it was unfair to suddenly decide Alessandra was an adult, but he would just tell her she was proving herself by taking care of another person.

He returned to the cave stuffed with self-satisfaction, ready to give up some of his protective care for her so he could get rid of this boy.

Alessandra peered at him. "Where is the food?" she asked.

"I have a better idea," he said. He set down the small pile of vegetables and meat he had collected. "Let's travel in the morning. We'll take the knight to the village, and you and I can go wherever we want."

"Not while he's injured!" she cried.

The dragon was taken aback at her response but was determined to follow through with his plan. "I brought him here so you could ensure he would survive. His life is not in danger, and may never have been. We are leaving in the morning."

Alessandra clutched the knight's arm, and the dragon's wings flared up. She sighed.

"You are probably right," she said. "We'll take him back. They probably have better medicines."

"Alessandra?" the young man muttered.

The dragon stiffened. A blush crawled up Alessandra's face.

"He's been awake?" the dragon demanded.

The knight's eyes shot open, and he sat up. He hissed in pain and gripped his side before falling back onto Alessandra's lap.

"George, what's wrong?"

The dragon wrinkled his nose. "That you didn't tell me he was awake."

Alessandra laughed. "Not you." She nodded to the knight, still wincing in place. "*His* name is George."

Jealousy flooded the dragon's chest. He scooped the knight off the ground. "Okay. Enough babysitting."

"Wait!" Alessandra chased after the dragon as he carried the young man out of the cave. "Put him down! He's not healed yet!"

"I don't think I *care* about whether he's healed or not anymore," the dragon said. "He's obviously strong enough to talk since you know each other's names, and the last thing we all need is for you two to get into trouble."

"Please," the knight managed. "I've come to warn you."

"Warn me about what? That you're going to take my little girl away from me?" He raised his arm to throw the human into the snow.

"No!" Alessandra cried. "Put him down, please!"

"I'm not going to let some man corrupt you," the dragon insisted, images of her emaciated body and her father's greedy grin flashing through his mind. "You're safe with me, and that will never change."

"Doge Pisani is coming for you!"

The dragon froze. "What?"

"He knows your treasure wasn't stolen. He won his campaign against Genoa, and he is coming to slay you for your dishonesty."

The dragon lowered the knight back into the cave. "The Doge is still alive?"

Alessandra rushed to the knight's side, but the dragon pushed her away.

"Yes." The knight nodded emphatically.

The dragon's eyes narrowed. He laid the knight on his cave floor, close to the entrance in case he wanted to kick him out. "Why do you care? And why would you come to my mountain about it?"

"It is my fault he is coming," he said. "I am a son of Genoa, and when he invaded us, he said he only came for the dragon's gold. I thought to come and slay you myself, but the Doge found me escaping from Venezia and wounded me. Alessandra told me of how you rescued me, and now I am in your debt."

The dragon scoffed. "And you told me, so I guess we're even. Get out of my house." He turned away from the knight and trotted to the back room. "Alessandra, grab your things. We're leaving forever."

"Dragon!" she protested.

He poked his head out from his hoard room. "So I'm not even George now? Now that there's another George, I'm 'dragon'?" He grabbed a pile of his favorite books and some glass he had taken from Murano. "Why don't you call him Scrawny Boy, or Home Invader? I was George first."

"You can't leave George here! My father won't spare him if he's discovered."

"What makes you think the Doge is that close?" The dragon hobbled out of his hoard room, a bundle of possessions in his arms. "Scrawny Boy will be fine. *We* are hiding all of our stuff and moving to…I don't even know what it's called, but it's a beautiful island and we're staying there until your father is dead."

"I warned you so you would prepare, not run away from this inevitable conflict," George said. "You are a mighty dragon. Why are you fleeing?"

"Because I'm not a mighty dragon," he snapped. "I'm a coward who was nursed back to health after losing his family. I am not risking Alessandra because some stupid Doge with his stupid arrows and stupid soldiers wanted some stupid gold I never had."

The cave fell silent, and the dragon took his sacred treasures out into the spring air. He thought the soldiers would likely be lazy yet destructive in their search. He placed his items above his cave in a tiny crevice.

"Dragon," Alessandra said. She stepped out of the cave. "George isn't well enough to travel."

"I don't give two manure piles about him," the dragon snapped. "And you shouldn't either."

"He warned us about my father coming."

"After coming up here to kill me. He's just another human, and he's trying to take you away from me." The dragon stepped back into his cave and pointed to the entrance. "Get out of here before the Doge arrives. If you keep to the trees and obscure trails, you might have a chance of slipping by."

George nodded, although he looked uncertainly at the snow outside and gripped his injury.

"He won't take me away from you," Alessandra insisted. She sat by George's side.

"I *know* how humans work." The dragon scooped up the food he had collected that day and threw it at Alessandra's feet. "Didn't you learn anything from watching your father? Men take and plunder." He pointed a claw at George, who just stared back at him. "Humans woo each other by lying. He's going to lie until you leave, and then he'll beat you and abuse you."

"I don't lie," George said. "I would never do anything to hurt Alessandra."

The dragon laughed sourly. "You've known her for, what, two minutes? Three? You have no idea what you are. Now get out of my cave before I kill you myself."

"Dragon!" a familiar voice boomed.

Everyone in the cave went still.

"Your deceit has cost me years, men, and fortune! I demand your head as a sacrifice!"

The dragon grabbed Alessandra. "Hide until they leave," he hissed. "And take your scrawny boy with you."

"Leave?" George whispered. "Aren't you going to kill them?"

"As many as I can," the dragon said. He embraced Alessandra. "You were the hatchling I never had the privilege to raise, Alessandra. Keep track of your scrawny boy." He gave George a stern look. "And don't you let anything bad happen to her."

"Why do your words resemble a farewell?" Alessandra's eyes glistened.

"Dragon! Come out, or we will drag your corpse into the sunlight!"

The dragon pushed Alessandra into a cavity of the cave, and nodded for George to follow her. Alessandra protested. George gripped her shoulders and quieted her.

The dragon hadn't planned to go out this way, but maybe George had come at an opportune time. The dragon had to hope he would be a decent protector for Alessandra—against the dragon's better judgment—and accept what the Doge would do to him.

"Doge Pisani," he said, emerging from his cave. No need for pretense this time. "You're right. I lied to you. I never had any gold, and I never will."

"I am not here for gold," the Doge huffed. He looked worn, old, but still insatiable. Something desperate glimmered in his eyes. "I will reassess your hoard. If I like it, I will take it. If I do not, you will be buried with it."

The dragon spread his wings. "You approach my cave at your own peril. Leave now."

The Doge raised a longbow and nocked an arrow on it. "Step aside, beast."

The dragon thought of all the years he had spent with Alessandra and begged the powers that be she would live for many more. Then he opened his mouth and spewed a river of fire at the Doge's soldiers.

Men screamed and dove into the snow. Many were not lucky or quick, but the Doge rolled away and released the arrow from his bow. The arrow glanced off the dragon's side with a loud *ting*.

"Kill the dragon!" the Doge cried.

Six soldiers crowded the dragon, and three archers raised their bows. The dragon shuffled, knowing taking off now would expose his wings to the arrows. He barreled straight for the soldiers, and four of them staggered back. Two raised their spears, but they couldn't reach anything vulnerable.

The hiss of arrows made the dragon fold up, and the two spearmen advanced. He swung around, knocking them back towards the slope of the mountain with his tail.

Pain pierced the dragon's wing, and he spun around. Another series of stings hit his other wing, and he leaped back. He could still move his wings, but he could hardly escape.

"Destroy his hoard," the Doge ordered. "I'll deal with this beast myself."

"Alessandra!" The dragon dove for the archers and managed to grab one of them. He pinned the archer down and reached up to snap his neck. Sudden pressure assaulted his right eye, and it quickly evolved into burning pain. Half of his vision went black.

He roared, mostly from the shock, and stumbled away from his victim. He swung his head back and forth, but the arrow had sunk deep. Warm blood trickled down his cheek, and the mountain around him blurred. He slumped to the ground as dizziness replaced consciousness.

He heard the clang of steel at a distance, and then the approaching boots of the Doge. He had fallen on his left side and hardly had the strength to move.

"This is for my daughter, you brute," the Doge declared, unsheathing a sword. The dragon braced himself, ready for the pain of death, but it didn't come. He heard the thump of a body hitting the ground, and then a scream from Alessandra.

Her soft hands braced the dragon's cheek. "Dragon, what has he done to you?!"

"The one day you don't call me George," he muttered. His tongue felt thick and sloppy.

"Alessandra, we can't do anything for him," the knight said.

"He's right," the dragon slurred. He tossed his head, trying to see his little girl one last time. "Go. Save yourselves."

His words blurred, and he wanted to say more, but he slipped away into a profound darkness.

The arrow should have been his end, but when he awoke, he found his eye had been bound and the arrow removed. He immediately scrambled to his library, terrified of what Alessandra's fate might have been.

He found the Doge, his neck slashed by a sword. His hoard was untouched, but he didn't care. There was no sign of Alessandra or her scrawny boy anywhere.

But there was a note on the floor.

Dragon,

We will not be here if you wake—I truly hope you will wake. George did his best to save you. Find us near the northern shores of Sicily.

See that you live. You owe George and I a journey to a place of our choosing. I will be watching for you.

Forever yours,
Alessandra

~ * ~ * ~

Sevanna has always had a passion for writing and a deep love of dragons. She mostly writes fantasy, but has also dabbled in romance and action stories. She was born and raised in Idaho, and still lives there with her husband and children. She gets her inspiration from her family and the adventures they go on together, as well as the many resin dragons she has collected over the years. She credits her mother, her high school English teacher, and her husband for believing in her.

When Dragons Downsize

Aiona Byuwek

It's only natural that after several thousands of years, a dragon's cave will get draftier and draftier. The hand-painted art on your walls becomes dated, and even attempts at using Baroque wallpaper to cover up those crude images of warriors chasing hinds couldn't liven it up. Like a new car, as soon as you buy a cave, it immediately begins to depreciate unless you keep putting gold into it.

So what does a dragon do when her columnar basalt walls crumble? Or when bawdy bats bring their best friends to hang out along my crown moulding? I'll tell you, by the time I realized rats were reproducing in my crates of rubies, I'd had enough. It was becoming glaringly obvious to me that I needed a change, but I just didn't know how to follow through.

Perhaps that's why I kept this glossy catalogue—one a real estate developer was holding right before I ate him. For the past two-and-a-half decades, it stayed at my bedside, which was the largest pile of gold coins any dragon has ever amassed. At night, I'd peruse all those beach cottages full of edibles situated conveniently next to blue lagoons, and then I'd fall asleep with sweet dreams of making flaming margaritas on warm and dry sandy shores.

Sadly, in the morning I'd slither down my hilly bed and into the sludge of mud in my dank cave, and then trudge towards the kitchen, in time with the ever-present castanets—the dripping condensation from stalactites on my cave ceiling.

One fateful morning, I decided that instead of making French-pressed coffee at home as I usually do, I would head down to the village Starbucks. Sometimes a gal just needs a low-key, no-work-needed kind of morning, right?

But when I got back to my cave with a fragrant caramel macchiato venti warming my claws, I screamed in shock! *There was a man in my living room!*

My steaming brew flew into the air, and landed in front of him —all that precious coffee bean goodness splooshing onto my cave's already swampy living room floor, with some light spattering onto his khaki slacks.

"MY COFFEE!" I was so miserable I wanted to weep, except I was too lazy to sweep the diamonds off the floor again, like I have to do every night. So instead I turned my most vicious dragon-glare at the intruder. "What are you doing in my cave? You don't look like a knight. Where's your armor? And why do you smell like Vienna sausages?"

You see, during my lifetime which happens to be four-thousand nine-hundred and fifty-seven years—or thirty-two in dragon-years —I've learned men are nothing but bad news for me. They almost always intend to start a fight, usually because of some crazy notion I've got a damsel in distress in my cave or some other such nonsense. Most people are pretty ignorant. We dragons don't do takeout. We prefer to eat-in. And I never take home leftovers. It's a matter of pride, you see.

Anyway, I hadn't had a real live man in my living room since chivalry went out of style—which was centuries ago.

The little man trembled, and his hand fumbled at the collar of his white polo-shirt which was embroidered with the logo of his business. *Great. A salesman.* They usually taste terrible, and I'm not a breakfast eater and never have been. What I really needed was a caramel macchiato—one that wasn't slowly oozing into the bat guano piles on my highly-polished Quikrete floor. But I guessed this cheesy salesman would have to do.

"I—I—I'm not selling armor, ma'am." The little man seemed to pull himself together. He straightened his back and then looked directly into my eyes. I could tell he would put up a fight, as salespeople usually do. "And I had some Vienna sausages for breakfast before work."

I sighed, because I remembered my doctor's been encouraging me to cut down on processed meats. "Well, no matter. Prepare to die."

"WAIT!" the little man screamed, and then he ran in the direction of my bedroom, which I thought was strange. Normally men run *out* of my cave, not deeper into it.

I followed him, grumpy at having to do so much work early in the morning. Without coffee even.

The salesman clambered atop my bedpile which caused an avalanche of Spanish doubloons and Susan B. Anthonys. When he reached the top, he whipped back around to face me, stood tall, and held out a colorful, glossy door flyer. "Can you at least buy into a timeshare before you eat me? It would mean a lot to me."

"You sell timeshares?" I felt a tingle of excitement spread from my wattle to my wingtips.

"You don't have a doorknob. Or a door even. So I figured I'd give you this in person." Nervous again, the little man resumed tugging on his shirt, and I got another look at the business logo on it: a half-shell with the words PEARLY SHELLS TIMESHARES, LLC embroidered in deep-water blue thread.

The door flyer he was holding above his head also said the same thing: PEARLY SHELLS TIMESHARES, LLC.

Then I glanced down at the cover of the tattered catalogue at my bedside: Same logo! Right down to the exact identical stock photo images of glistening Fiji beaches.

"The real estate market is really slow right now, but I gotta feed my kids, Miss Dragon." The little man smiled. "I'm Eddie, by the way. Nice to meet you."

"And I'm extremely excited to meet you." I extended one of my claws for a handshake, but Eddie withdrew as I came nearer.

"Is that so? Uhh…" He pulled a smartphone out of his pants pocket and consulted it. "Can I call you by your first name? Your address in our files says—"

"No! You may *not*!" I shouted.

"But it says here your name is D—"

"STOP!"

"So you don't want me to call you by your—"

"NOPE!" I pinned Eddie to the bedpile with my right index talon. "D. Dragon is how you will address me. Look, I know your training script says calling me by my first name will make you all buddy-buddy with me, but NEVER say my first name. EVER. Unless you want to be shish-ka-bob for my lunch."

"Got it." Eddie grinned again while he brushed a couple of Sacajawea dollars off his khaki slacks. He pointed at my catalogue. "I see you're familiar with our company. Is that our nineteen ninety-three edition?" he asked with a concerned look.

"Why yes! As you can see, I've been planning this move for a while now. Something wrong with it?"

"Not at all. Just that we've got a better selection of cottage layouts in twenty twenty-four. Is that blood?"

I placed one of my tail tips over the stain on page four, then ushered Eddie out of my cave with the other tail. "Let's go somewhere more comfortable where you will tell me more about these timeshares, and also buy me another caramel macchiato."

Over the next few months, I was Eddie's favorite client. I know I was because he told me so many times. We spent hours at Starbucks gazing at new condo layouts, and when I finally decided on the Seaside Dreamscape model, he helped me pick everything from kitchen lighting fixtures to bedroom flooring.

"Say goodbye to industrial Quikrete, Miss D., and say hello to the oxymoron of vinyl maple flooring! Isn't it awesome?" Eddie enthused after I chose the *Blonde Ale* sample over *Driftwood Grey*.

Eddie even helped me plan and execute my enormous estate sale. He was full of clever advice such as saying I'd get a better price for the antique battle armor collection if I didn't tell anyone my favorite pieces were sourced from flossing my rear molars. And he was right! I made a killing on everything.

Not everyone was happy about it though. The bats were furious I got rid of their antique Transylvanian mirror collection. Those hoarders had no say in the matter anyway, as they hadn't paid rent since they lost the ability to change into a form that had opposable thumbs. In the end, they filed a claim with their renter's insurance. So don't feel sorry for them, okay?

After the surprising success of my estate sale, eight articulated lorries arrived to transport my entire flossings collection to a museum in Leeds. Then Eddie turned my attention towards financing. I've always been horrible at maths, but dear Eddie helped me realize my gold just wasn't earning interest in its current repository. So he helped me transition my hard-stolen earnings into a money market account, with plenty leftover to not only purchase the timeshare of my dreams, but also to buy up the lagoon next to it. It even came with a natural waterfall. To say I was pretty stoked would be an understatement for a fire-breathing dragon!

At last, four months later I was finally ready to fly down to Fiji. So I texted Eddie he should come over to my cave for a last pre-flight snack, and I had a really big surprise for him. When he arrived, he looked just as anxious as the first day I'd met him. But I welcomed him inside my cave—which was now pretty bare because the closing was already scheduled for the following day.

As I eagerly approached him, Eddie whipped out a can of bear spray and drenched me and the Vienna sausages I was about to offer him. While I stood there, stunned and unable to see through the gush of five-carat diamonds that were clattering and bouncing about, I could hear Eddie apologizing profusely.

"I'm so sorry, D. I thought you were gonna eat me."

"I'd never do that!" I exclaimed. I didn't bother to explain to him real estate agents are not very tasty, and tend to be kind of tough. So instead of enumerating his deficiencies, I offered, "Well, since these sausages are no longer edible, let's go to McDonald's. I'm in the mood for some special sauce. Your treat, of course."

Eddie was happy to oblige. Of course, because as you know, I am his favorite client.

Moving down to Fiji has been wonderful, in fact, even better than I'd dreamed. With money market dividends, I'm now raking in a small and steady cash flow. I'll never need to raid an Irish gastropub for tasty travelers ever again. Even so, just for fun and socialization I started working part-time at the tapas bar down by the marina. In just a few weeks' time, my drink-making skills have been the star of TikToks gone viral. The tourists love my flaming margaritas, Blue Blazes, and Wildfire Cocktails, and I'll have you know, everyone says my *halloumi saganaki* cheese is fire.

Since leaving Europe, my love life is even on the upswing. Back home, a single female dragon is treated like an absolute monster by all the villagers. But here in Fiji, there are singles everywhere. One of my regular customers is a Komodo dragon who owns a neighboring resort. He was love-bombing me nonstop for weeks, and then kept inviting me to dinner at his place. However, the past three dates, it was nothing but Russian food, Russian food, Russian food. I will not tolerate such abuse. So, when he asked why I flaked on our last date, I lied and told him I'm only eating Italians from now on.

But I'm not worried about a shortage of dates, because right after I ditched that narcissist, his younger brother, who's a solid "ten" compared to his older brother's "seven," said he's having Indian food tonight, and asked me to come over. I screamed, "Absolutely!" so I could be heard above the racket the outpouring of his brother's diamonds were making.

Yes, I made the right decision to downsize. Life here in Fiji has been my dragon dream come true. Today, I slid out from behind my crystal-clear waterfall—the sound of which is a major improvement over the dole dripping noises in my old cave. Then I basked in the tropical afternoon sunlight before sauntering over to my new boyfriend's timeshare for dinner.

On my way, I stopped at my mailbox. Inside I found an envelope with the return address of Pearly Shells Timeshares, LLC. It contained a "Thank You" card from Eddie with a reproduction of Maxfield Parrish's portrait of my cousin Amy on the front.

Eddie's thank-you letter was brief and charming.

Dear D.,

It has been a real pleasure working with you for the past four months. Because you are my favorite client, I wanted to let you know that my company is offering a $150 gift card and a case of Almond Roca if you refer us to one of your dragon friends or relatives before December 31st.

Yours truly,
Eddie

P.S. My favorite aunt has the same first name you do. So I think Dorcas is a pretty name.

~ * ~ * ~

Aiona Byuwek lives and sails in the Salish Sea with her first mate and three crew members. She is determined to not hoard like her dragon momma, but she's inherited her dad's love of Almond Roca.

Ichor of the Beholder

Pamela Love

Gold gets cold and sapphires ain't swansdown, so sleep doesn't come easy for me or any other dragon. Waking up with a snoutful of coins didn't improve my mood. A heap of hoard had avalanched into my nose. *A thief. Wonderful.* (To be fair, that's why dragons started acquiring loot in the first place—as an alarm system. Back then our hoard was mostly pebbles and dry leaves. That was when we grew no bigger than rabbits, but were much tastier—our flesh is pre-cooked, after all. Predators would sneak up on us while we slept, knowing the price they'd pay if they tried anything while we were awake.)

These days, intruders have empty pockets, not empty bellies. Ooh, look at the pretty gold in a big pile. *So* tempting. The dragon won't notice. Can a dragon even count? (Note: Yes.) Filching one little coin, what harm will that do?

I don't know, because no thief in history has ever taken "just one little coin", it's always a double handful of hoard. Which caused the coins to collapse on yours truly.

Predictably panicked, the thief tried to flee, only to bump into bricks of bullion. It was dark, after all. One gout of flame lit things up, but my lair now stunk of ash and molten brass. (Royals have no idea how much counterfeiting is going on out there. I ought to charge them a fee to take it out of circulation, but dragons have a strict rule about hoards: all of it has to be stolen.) Under the circumstances, my weary wings would have to take me out to find breakfast farther away than usual.

~ * ~

As far as royals are concerned, even my diet makes me a thief. The king actually thinks every creature anywhere near the castle belongs to him, as if a living thing can be owned. *We beasts have to stick together,* I thought, gulping down a pair of bucks. (The deer should've welcomed my thoughtfulness, but fled when I landed.

~ 219 ~

Ingrates.)

When I figured my lair was sufficiently aired out, I took a return route over the castle courtyard. Mostly I wanted to see if there was anything worth taking in plain sight, which was rare.

But rare ain't never. It pays to check. *My, my, what have we here?* What appeared at first to be a couple of knights in a different shade of armor was actually a pair of bronze statues. Royals don't keep that kind of wealth outside anymore. Sure, some dragons turn their snouts up at that metal, but it makes the ichor flowing through my veins race just as much as gold does. You don't have to be a snob to have a quality hoard, and I appreciated the convenience of not having to break through stone walls for once.

That king's got to be at least half dragon. How else could a single bellowed "Begone!" from a pipsqueak like him make an updraft powerful enough to knock me cloud high? He's got flames down his gullet to match my own, mark my words.

Clearly, it's time that royal gets a reminder of who's the real dragon here. Wings snapped shut, I power dived past two falcons, envy in their eyes. Not that I gloated. *Gotta keep my mind on my work.*

There was no way I'd snag both statues—too awkward and heavy. Time to choose, which was easy enough. One sculpture was of the king himself. Not that it was a *great* resemblance. Too stiff. Too pompous. The royal, that is. In comparison, the statue looked positively noble, even majestic. After that royal opened his mouth to me, it would *have* to be his portrait.

One fiery blast caused the prudent knights to reconsider the wisdom of an impromptu battle with yours truly. None were carrying bows or even lances, for one thing. Have ranged weaponry at hand if you're going up against a dragon, folks.

I'm not counting the bright pink flower that smacked my cheek as ranged weaponry. Surprisingly hard, too, who would've thought petals could pack that much of a punch? It was a royal dressed in pink, maybe one of those "princesses" I've heard about from other dragons. Never met one myself, but they're supposed to be plenty tough and that posy felt like it was launched from a catapult.

With some quick tail, wing, and neck work to reverse position, I made the grab. Snapping my claws around the target, I was pleased to discover it wasn't too heavy to easily lift as I launched myself skyward. *This is the kind of flying real dragons can do, folks. Accept no substitutes.*

In less than a minute, I'd hauled off the latest addition to my humble (ha) hoard. The royal had commanded me to "begone"— well, now I'd "bewent". *Hope that made him happy.* Snickering, I headed for home.

~ * ~

Royals (and peasants, though I don't spend much time around them) like to keep beasts nearby. Most to eat, some to ride, and a few, called pets, to make themselves happy.

Some royals think dragons feel the same way about their hoards, as if it's something we befriend. Nope. It started as a tool, like I said, but now we accumulate gems and precious metals for the same reason they do: we like the shiny stuff.

Including bronze, but I decided I didn't want the king staring at me all night long. *Who needs that kind of face in their nightmares, am I right?* Should I face him toward the cave wall? *Nah.* I seared it smooth and set it to cool just outside the cave entrance. Then I piled another heap of hoard betwixt the cave entrance and myself, lay down on the remainder, and waited for the visitors sure to show up shortly.

~ * ~

"Dragon! Come forth!"

The knight arrived mid-afternoon, as was traditional. Royals always get in a snit after one of my raids. This one was a double-brandisher: sword in his left hand, lance in his right. No shield— not smart—and no grip on the reins, either. His horse, a dapple gray, had to be enchanted—or maybe drunk—to get this close to a dragon.

"I challenge you to a duel, o drag—oof!" Thud. Knights, in my experience, are terrible riders. Just one puff of flame, which didn't come anywhere close to the horse, and the steed decided not to stay. *Guess that sobered him up. Or disenchanted him.*

The knight struggled to stand, yet clung to his sword and lance. Which I could understand, but it's not like he could use them in that position. I yanked both blades from his gauntlets and tossed them into my cave.

"Spare me, kind dragon! Let me go home to my beloved mother." Somehow, he managed to make it sound defiant, even proud. *You have the makings of a royal, my friend.*

Sometimes I wonder what knights say to the royals when they get back to the castle. (If they return at all. Something to ponder some other day.) "Not with that armor, you won't." It was shinier than most. Tilting my head, I admired my glorious crimson scales and glowing amber eyes. I was still blossom-bruised, though.

"I...I know not how to doff it without the aid of my faithful squire."

Which knights always say and which may even be true, for all I know. It's not as if I have any personal experience wearing any armor but what I was born with. Of course, I could claw it off him, but that wouldn't do the armor any good—or his body either.

Not that it mattered. My ears were already twitching in the summer breeze, listening for the inevitably approaching footsteps. "Oh, someone will be along to assist directly."

For a knight is always followed by some kind of trickster. Generally it's a jester, though I've matched wits with my share of smiths and minstrels, along with the odd orphan.

This time it was a minstrel, complete with lute. *Good.* I enjoy their music more than a jester's jokes, and the blacksmiths usually want my help to craft magic swords or armor. Nervy, considering they always show up to trick me out of my hoard. (Orphans always show up hungry, ragged, and entitled, since they've heard stories about how a dragon will befriend someone worthy enough. Do I look like a fairy godmother? Well, not *most* of them.)

"Greetings to you, o dragon! Wouldst care to hear my latest melody?"

"Play away." I settled down to listen. The knight couldn't possibly be more settled down.

The minstrel strummed and sang some ballad about the moon's beauty. Hardly news to me, with all the hours I've spent in darkness with moonlight the only thing illuminating my hoard and me.

When he finished, the minstrel bowed, swooping off his feathered cap. "Not bad," I said. "Do this knight a favor and help him take off his armor. I won it in fair combat, blah, blah. He's got a horse to find, too, and all that metal would only slow him down."

The minstrel didn't look surprised at all. Without a word of protest and no lack of skill, the job was done and the knight went marching off without a glance behind him. I do mean marching, by the way. Usually they trudge.

"Dragon, may I pose a query?"

Here it comes. "You may, but I don't guarantee any answer, still less the answer you'd no doubt prefer."

He grinned. "I understand. What part of your treasure is dearest to your heart?"

"Depends on if I'm lying on my back or side—oh, you said 'dearest' to my heart. I thought you meant 'nearest'. Hmm. That's a good question." And an original one as well. Of course, it was no doubt intended to end with him hoodwinking me out of the entire hoard, or at least whatever I thought was most valuable. That's how tricksters work.

Opening his blue eyes extra wide, he said, "Why then, if you do not cherish one item more than any other, they must be equally dear to you. If so, why have so many things in your possession? Why not own just one stone, if it be worth infinitely more than everything else?"

Gotta admit, he had me curious about that kind of gem. "Which stone?"

The minstrel gestured toward the sky. "The moon."

I slapped my claws on the ground. "Oh, this is a *moon* trick. The version I've heard is trading the hoard for the sun—which is shinier and doesn't change size. Not that it matters. I can't steal either one, and anything unpilfered ain't loot and doesn't count as hoard. Run along, minstrel. Or I'll ask you what *you* value the most."

His fingers unconsciously clutching his lute, he whirled around and made good his escape. That's the key to dealing with tricksters—don't let them talk too much. Too much chance they'll get you to say (or do) the wrong thing.

~ * ~

My third visitor that day was a genuine surprise. (Visitors always come in threes.) Normally it's the local wizard telling me to knock off the raiding for a while, which I would as a courtesy. Thing is, he'd died a year ago and I hadn't heard of any replacement. Since there was apparently a local princess now, I thought it might be her, and was looking forward to it. New experiences are broadening, and I'm centuries old and running out of those.

Instead, it was definitely a male voice, and one that was rather thin and quavery. (From what I've heard, princesses can out sing min-strels.) "You have insulted me, o dragon! I demand satisfaction!"

The sun was setting, so it was a little late for a challenge, but never let it be said I don't hold up my end of this kind of thing. As I've made clear, I can provide any necessary illumination.

Out I went, to where a man past middle age stood half-leaning on a wheeled cart, covered with a stained cloth. He shook a fist at me. He wasn't a royal or wizard, not dressed in that faded brown tunic and leggings. But he couldn't be a peasant, either. He had a farm cart, but serfs don't call me "o dragon", or anything else. They scream and run. That's why there are so many of them—they're sensible.

Not a knight, trickster, or wizard, either. Honestly, I couldn't place this guy at all. "What are you?"

"A sculptor."

Understanding dawned on me just as the sun did the reverse. "You should be honored I took your statue, not insulted. I've swiped plenty of art in my day, and don't do it much anymore."

"But you didn't take *my* statue." Yanking off the cloth, he revealed the other bronze. "You took Gregor's. This is the one I made." He rapped his knuckles against it. "And I had won. The king himself declared my sculpture to be better. He was going to display this, my masterpiece, in his throne room."

It didn't look much like the king to me, but there's no accounting for taste. I blinked. "Then why is it here?"

"The king said…if what I made was truly better, you would have stolen it. He told me to take it away, and laughed."

Well, this is awkward. "You *want* me to have it?" He bit his lip and nodded. "Sorry, but a proper hoard consists of only stolen items."

"You stole my victory. This represents that." Tipping over the cart, he let his work slide onto the ground beside what was left of Gregor's. "Like it or not, in your cave or out, this is *yours* now."

Watching the artist plod back down the mountain, I wondered if the next knight or trickster would remove my unwanted new possession if I acted like I wanted to keep it. *No, that would make me look weak. Besides, they'd need some kind of cart, which they won't think to bring, I bet. I'll have to fly it somewhere and dump it.* I yawned. *Tomorrow.*

As usual, even exhausted after a busy day, I couldn't just nod off on my bumpy bedding. That gave me time to ponder the problem of where to put my "present". *It can't be anywhere near my cave, because my hoard isn't just* in *my home, this miserable mattress is* part *of my home.* My claws twitched, clinking the coins as they had for decades.

Wait.

My hoard is part of my home…yes!

~ * ~

All that happened close to a month ago. I've been traveling ever since, something I've always wanted to do but couldn't due to having to guard my hoard and fatigue from lack of sleep.

But that night I realized that since wherever my hoard is, *is* my home, it can't be stolen! All thieves or tricksters can do is…rearrange it. So I drop a coin in this realm or that wherever I want, for wherever I leave it is part of my lair. I mark my territory with my wealth the way other beasts do with their scent. Bit by bit, the entire world will belong to me, for hoard is where the home is, and vice *very much* versa.

(Although I'd appreciate it if you kept this tale to yourself. I don't want the other dragons to hear about it!)

~ * ~ * ~

Pamela Love was born in New Jersey. After graduating from Bucknell University and working as a teacher and in marketing, she turned to writing. Her speculative fiction has appeared in the anthologies *Havok Season Eight: Vice & Virtue, Happy Holiday Historicals,* and *Wyrms: An Anthology of Dragon Drabbles,* along with *Luna Station Quarterly* and *Tales From the Moonlit Path,* among other publications. Her work is also scheduled to appear in the upcoming anthologies *A Little Fantasy Everywhere* and *Once Upon a Future Time 3*. She now lives in Maryland.

The Investors

Charles Kyffhausen

"Firewind, where's your hoard?" Flame Tongue demanded. Every jewel and piece of gold in the other dragon's hoard was gone. Firewind now lay coiled up in front of a computer monitor with a keyboard in front of it, and he was using his front claws to type on the keyboard.

"I invested it," he explained.

"Does that mean thieves or adventurers stole it?"

"Nobody stole it; I used it to buy stocks and mutual funds. I finally realized after several hundred years traditional hoards don't get any larger on their own; they just sit there with a zero rate of return."

"I am glad I did not listen to those Dutchmen who wanted me to invest in tulip bulbs back in sixteen thirty-four," he continued his tail twitching absently. "They told me the price was going up, and it was a good time to get in. I asked why tulips were so valuable, even for decorative purposes, and they couldn't give me a credible answer. I realized that, when people figured out they had no intrinsic value, the market would crash and it did in sixteen thirty-seven. Then my hoard would have indeed been gone, just as if thieves or adventurers had stolen it."

"What, then, makes a hoard grow?"

"You have to invest it in corporations that actually make things, and have a track record of growth," Firewind explained. "Dot com stocks were valuable only because people thought they were valuable, and they crashed in two thousand. These companies in my portfolio," he indicated some symbols on his computer monitor, "actually make things people want to buy. They have steady income streams, and these increase every year."

"I have heard of something called cryptocurrency," Flame Tongue said. "People are promoting it as a sure way to make money."

"Somebody tried to get me to invest in cryptocurrency a while ago," Firewind said. "It reminded me so much of those tulip bulbs I ate him on the spot. In any event, my investments tend to track the Standard & Poor 500, Dow Jones Industrial Average, and NASDAQ. As you can see from these charts, the indices go up and they go down, but the long-term trend is up. Plus, I have as long as I need to make money."

"Now I understand!" Flame Tongue exclaimed. "John Maynard Keynes wrote, 'In the long run, we are all dead,' but that applies to humans. Dragons are immortal unless something kills us. We have all the time we need!"

"Exactly," Firewind confirmed. "The Dow Jones Industrial Average was below three thousand a hundred years ago, but now it's well upward of thirty thousand. If I'd invested my hoard back then, it would be ten times as large as it is now. Well, it's never too late to start so I am glad I got started."

~ * ~

"What's going on, Firewind?" Cloud Ruler asked several months later. "You look like thieves or adventurers have been after your hoard."

"It's not thieves or adventurers, it's the Internal Revenue Service," Firewind said holding up a Form 1040 and some other documents. "The IRS says we have to report our dividends on Schedule B, and capital gains on Schedule D, and then pay taxes on all our gains."

"Can't we just eat the IRS agents?"

"No, because then they can seize our hoards. The problem with putting a hoard in an investment account is the government can get at it without having to come into a lair to face teeth, fire, and claws. I suppose we'll have to pay up. I looked into it further, and the top bracket is twenty percent."

"Twenty percent of our hoards?"

"No, twenty percent of the gains," Firewind elaborated. "We have to pay only if we make money."

"I suppose it could be worse," Flame Tongue interjected; she also had invested her hoard.

"What is this?" Cloud Ruler asked looking at a document. "It reminds me of an insanity spell a sorcerer tried on me before I ate him."

"It's worse than an insanity spell, it's the Capital Gains Tax Worksheet. Don't get me started on the Form 1040 instructions themselves, but I'm just glad I didn't invest in any of those assets for which there are special rules. I suppose we will have to learn to live with this every year."

Five Years Later

"We are collecting more money than ever," the head of the IRS reported. He indicated some large bays, or more precisely lairs, the agency had installed for the new workers.

"We should have thought of hiring dragons a long time ago," his aide affirmed. "If they can keep track of every last coin in a mountain of treasure, they can track down every last penny of somebody's income and tax that as well."

"Yes, and they can follow the tax code without going totally insane; we lose a lot of good people that way every year. How is it going in there, Flame Tongue?"

"These silly humans think they can hide cryptocurrency trans-actions," she replied. "Every debit has to be matched by a credit and, if I look closely enough, I can find where money went into a crypto account and realize it had to come out somewhere."

"Why do you bother to work for us at all? You have so much money in your hoards you don't have to work."

"As we can't beat you, we decided to join you. We're dragons, and we enjoy counting money. We used to count our hoards penny by penny, but that eventually gets boring. Now we can count other people's money and even tax it; did I mention I recently got my Certified Public Accountant credential?"

"You wouldn't need all this money if the government lived within its means," Firewind added. "I remember what happened to Rome when its Emperors spent more money than they had."

"You remember that?" the IRS Commissioner asked.

"I was there when it happened; they debased the denarius, which differs little from printing money the way the Weimar Republic did. Maybe the Emperors could fool the Roman people, but they couldn't fool the basic laws of economics and they could not fool me. I know when a purportedly silver coin contains base metal, and the denarius contained plenty of base metal. The same can be said, by the way, of the US Dollar which buys less and less every year."

"It seems dragons have more common sense than people."

"One Emperor tried to hire Flame Tongue, Cloud Ruler, and me to fight for Rome, and for ten thousand silver denarii per day," Firewind remembered. "I told him he might as well try to pay us from the Cloaca Maxima, as with what he called money. I was going to eat him but another Roman got to him first with a dagger; they didn't have what you call impeachment in those days."

"We do know one cannot get something for nothing," Flame Tongue added. "A wizard once told me he could double the size of my hoard if I paid him a tenth of what I had. I let him try it on a few hundred silver coins, and he did indeed double them, but the ones he created vanished by the next day. The magic isn't permanent, you see. I went after him and ate him before he could swindle anybody else, and I even got back the money I paid him. They didn't have small claims courts back in the Middle Ages, so that was the fastest way to settle the problem."

"If you went around eating people…" the Commissioner said, "…I'm surprised the King or Duke didn't send his knights to try to slay you."

"The King didn't object because the same wizard swindled him. He said he could turn base metal into gold, and would do so for a substantial fee. The King didn't realize, if the wizard could really do that, and make the transmutation permanent, he wouldn't need anybody to pay him. The magic lasted long enough, though, for the wizard to get well out of town before the gold turned back into lead."

"I think we call the corresponding racket an advance fee fraud today," the Commissioner said.

"Do you mean like the guy in Nigeria who sent me an E-mail that said he had a hoard worth twenty million dollars, and he would share it with me if I paid him fifty thousand in transaction fees?" Firewind interjected. "If he really had twenty million, he wouldn't have needed fifty thousand from me. I thought of flying to Nigeria to eat him, but the problem with Internet scams is that you can rarely find the scammer. It was so much easier when adventurers, thieves, and wizards tried to steal from us in person."

"You dragons seem to be experts on how economics really works," the Commissioner said. "Tax collections go only so far, though, and they don't fix the problem that we're spending more than we have."

"I think we could fix this country's problems, Flame Tongue," Firewind observed.

"I don't think they'll let us burn down Washington DC or eat all three branches of the government."

"That might be the simplest solution but we can do even better; why don't we run for Congress? I think we could give this country the kind of common-sense governance it needs."

~ * ~ * ~

Charles Kyffhausen is the SF/Fantasy pen name of the author of stories published in *Fear and Trembling*, *Weird and Wonderful*, *The Lorelei Signal*, *Dragon Soul Press*, and others.

The Memory Dragon

C.N. Wheaton

I wasn't expecting the cave.

In my line of work, I'd seen just about anything, but a cave was new. Still, I was nothing if not adaptable. There was no door. Walking in unannounced seemed rude, however, so I did the next best thing to knocking. "Hello?" I called into the darkness.

An echo was my only answer.

I looked around nervously. The path up to the cave was winding and deserted. There were stories of monsters in the mountains, not that I'd ever seen any. I nervously patted Dusty, the donkey attached to my cart. He focused on me for a second. Then, when he decided I didn't have any carrots, he nibbled at a nearby clump of grass.

Whatever was waiting for me, Dusty was clearly not going to be much help.

"Oh good, you're here," a tired voice said from behind me. I jumped, my heart suddenly going double-time. Whirling around, I studied the speaker standing in the entrance to the cave. Although she wasn't very tall and didn't appear to be armed, her stance was threatening anyway. Her eyes seemed to shine in the darkness. When she stepped forward into the light, her green eyes appeared almost reptilian as they narrowed. "You *are* from Magi-Clean, right? Because if you're selling something…"

"Yes, I'm from Magi-Clean," I assured her hastily. I had no interest in finding out what she did to traveling salesmen. "I'm Nell. I presume you're Vesta, right?" At that, she nodded. Emboldened, I continued on. "How can I help you? You mentioned it might be a tricky job when you contacted my boss."

Vesta's mouth opened and closed. She stared at Dusty for a second, the donkey staring implacably back. Then she sighed. "I think you'd better come in. It'll be easiest to show you. Bring the donkey."

"C'mon, Dusty," I whispered as I led him into the cave, following Vesta into the dark.

We crossed the entrance cavern and into a wide tunnel. A light appeared at the other end, getting brighter as we went. Our destination was well-lit. And it suddenly became clear why I was there.

We had reached a large cavern. Crystals were embedded in the walls. Hundreds of candles flickered in glass jars throughout the space, all of them clearly enspelled not to go out. I was grateful for them because there was a lot to see.

There were piles everywhere.

It took a moment to spot the narrow pathways, to understand it wasn't just a solid mound of *stuff*. This was somebody's home. I looked over at the woman who'd hired me to help. Vesta stared at the mess as if it was going to grow teeth and bite her. While I tried to think of the best opening gambit, a tactful way to ask the questions on my mind, she laughed ruefully. "This belonged to my grandmother. She was a dragon."

"Ah," I said, trying to absorb that. "So, this was her…hoard?"

"Yes." Vesta turned those reptilian eyes on me again. "I'm a dragon too if you were wondering. Figured my human form would be best for the duration. In my dragon form, I'd be tempted to burn it all down and I promised my mother I wouldn't."

"Ah," I said again. "I thought a dragon's hoard would be—"

"—gold?" Vesta supplied. Her smile was sharp. "That's the classic choice of course. The shine of it calls to something in our blood. But a hoard can be anything. Some dragons collect books, entire libraries full of first editions and single print runs and beautiful hardcovers. In that vein, I once met an old dragon who specialized in love letters, stacks of passionate missives and urgent verse. Another hoarded recipes, the more obscure the better. Others collect art or timepieces, teacups or toys."

"What called to your grandmother?" I asked, taking a surreptitious look at the closest pile. It was composed entirely of old newspapers, near as I could tell. Another nearby section seemed to be cans of paint stacked against the remains of a charred carriage. There was no theme I could see.

"Seraphine was a memory dragon. She kept every memento from everywhere she ever went. She also kept anything that was useful once and could be again as well as things that had never been useful but might be one day." Vesta looked around the space, her shoulders slumping under the weight of it all. "We're all memory dragons in my family. I guess I'd just never considered what that might mean, what all those memories would look like when we're gone."

The cave might have been new, but the rest of it was not. I felt a swell of compassion. Dragon or not, Vesta was an overwhelmed family member and I helped those every day.

"I'm here," I reassured her. Then I looked out over the space. "In fact, it might be best to bring in the rest of my team."

Her voice got very small. "I can't afford it."

While the idea of inheriting a dragon's hoard and pleading poverty sounded ludicrous, I followed her gaze to the piles. If there *was* any treasure in the cavern, it was well-hidden.

"Do you have any family who can help?"

She shook her head. "Nobody else could come," she said softly. "I'm all alone."

"Not anymore," I promised. My clients didn't need judgment or pity. Most of them already felt ashamed of their circumstances without me piling on after all. What they needed was a kind ear and a willing pair of hands. I rolled up my sleeves, unhitched Dusty, and tied his lead to the nearest stalagmite. Then I turned back to Vesta. "Now, if you'd be so kind as to show me around, I'd love to get the lay of the land."

Vesta led me along the narrow paths between the piles. *Labyrinthine* was the word that kept springing to mind as we wandered. We finally made it to a mound of pillows, large enough for a dragon's nest, up at the highest point of the cave. Seraphine could have surveyed her entire hoard from there.

I'm not sure what emotions the older dragon had felt when she'd looked out over the piles, but her granddaughter was easy to read. Anxiety radiated off of her. When she spoke, her voice was practically inaudible. "I don't know where to start."

"Start by starting."

Vesta shot me a look.

"I'm being serious! So often people get hung up on there being a *right* way to start that they don't do it at all. They get paralyzed by indecision. But it doesn't matter where you start, as long as you do. And, if you think about it, you did start already—you hired me."

Vesta laughed. "Well then, since you're the organizing professional, what should we do first?"

I looked out over the crowded cavern. "We're going to make three sections: keep, sell, and toss."

"I can do that."

It was never going to be that simple, of course, but it felt good to have a plan. I could tell Vesta needed one. And, quite frankly, so did I. Even though I'd been working for Magi-Clean for over a year by that point—helping recently bereaved spouses who were about to move in with their children figure out what they needed, organizing estate sales on behalf of relatives, and clearing out people's homes before they set off on a quest—I'd never dealt with anything as big as a dragon's hoard before. To date, the strangest job I'd had was helping a wizard's apprentice clean out his master's tower after an unfortunate potion accident and a whole team of us had worked on that one. The hoard was a much larger undertaking than any of those had been.

Vesta and I slowly made our way back to the entrance of the cavern. "We can do this," I promised her, trying to reassure myself as well.

Together, we tackled the pile closest to Dusty. That one was relatively easy. The newspapers turned out to be recent, from just before Seraphine had died. As I bent down to grab a huge stack of them to shift to the trash pile we'd started, Vesta put a hand on my arm. "We need to check them before you throw them away."

"Why?"

Vesta grimaced. "Dragons tend to be paranoid. It gets worse as we get older and our hoard grows. The more we have, the more afraid we are of losing it. Seraphine was ancient and," Vesta spread her arms wide to illustrate her point, "as you can see, she had a great deal to lose."

I set the newspaper stack back down. We started rifling through the papers. "Is there anything you're hoping to find?" I asked. Before Vesta could answer, I lifted up another newspaper and let out a startled yelp. Vesta appeared by my side with the suddenness of a snake.

We both stared at the little desiccated mouse that had been hidden in the pile. It had obviously been dead for a while.

Vesta raised an eyebrow. "Well, at least it wasn't a person."

I turned to her in horror. "Is that likely?"

"From what I've heard, Seraphine faced several knights when

she was younger. They could still be here."

I'm a professional; I will not run screaming from the cave. After repeating that in my head several times, I felt calm enough to open my eyes. My gaze immediately landed on the dead mouse. I shuddered.

Vesta patted my arm. "I'm joking. Mostly." She sighed. "To answer your question, my mother told me once Seraphine had something of great historical significance to dragons in general and our family in particular. It's an illustrated manuscript. Unfortunately, I don't know the title."

"We'll be extra careful as we check the books," I promised. I gingerly picked up the corners of the newspaper under the mouse and moved it to the trash pile. The dead rodent was quickly joined by the rest of the newspapers from the stack.

The next section was harder. While it was easy to decide to discard the congealed paint, it turned out that the charred carriage—which was thankfully corpse-free—had been used as a makeshift cupboard. "What would you like to do with these?" I asked as we opened a small travel bag to reveal several exquisitely painted wooden birds.

Vesta searched the bag in the hopes of finding more information, but she came up empty. She picked up one of the birds. It was painted in swirls of gold and green, a work of art that could fit in the palm of her hand. It was so lifelike I half-expected it to start singing. Then she let her hand drop down into her lap and slumped back against the carriage seat, releasing a small cloud of dust. She shook her head. "I don't know. All of this, all these memories, and I don't know why they mattered. Everything had a story once. And now Seraphine is gone, and I can't ask."

"I'm sorry." The words felt inadequate.

"My mother would tell me to keep them."

"She isn't here," I gently reminded Vesta. "Do *you* want to keep them?"

The young dragon shook her head. "Right now, I don't want to keep anything." Despite her words, her hands curled protectively around the carved bird in her lap.

"Maybe just this one?"

She met my gaze. "Aren't you supposed to tell me to get rid of everything? Until my 'place is Magi-Clean'?" she asked, quoting the business motto.

"Marketing," I said with a shrug. "My colleagues and I aren't actually magic. I can't wave a wand and make it better. All I can do is help. And part of that is making sure you don't get rid of things you'll miss. For better or worse, Seraphine was your grandmother."

Vesta looked down at the bird sculpture in her lap. "We can put this in the keep pile for now. It's beautiful. I don't know if that makes it easier or harder, knowing there are items like this to find here."

Harder, probably, but I kept that to myself. We kept going, clearing the carriage before starting on another section that contained a porcelain cabinet, a set of silver, broken tools, and numerous dusty blankets. Before I left for the night, we stacked all the trash into Dusty's cart. When I was ready to leave, Vesta spoke up. "I'll escort you home."

"You don't have to," I insisted, thinking of the deserted path. We'd only reach the village by sunset. "Besides, how would you get back?"

She grinned that reptilian grin of hers. "Are you worried about a dragon, Nell? You shouldn't be." As soon as we got outside, Vesta rolled her shoulders back and *changed*. It happened so quickly my brain couldn't make sense of it. One moment, a young woman was standing next to me. The next moment, a dragon three times my size with scales the color of rainclouds was unfurling her wings. Only her eyes looked the same. She smiled again, this time with dagger-like teeth.

I winced. "No, I'm definitely not worried about you," I said even though I had been. Working beside Vesta all day, I hadn't thought of her dragon form; she'd reminded me of so many other clients I hadn't considered how different she really was. I looked at Dusty, who was focused again on the patch of grass, and then considered the full cart. "I don't think we have space for you to ride with us."

Vesta shrugged and leapt off the cliff, soaring up into the sky to land on a peak up ahead on the path. She nodded to me. And so, under the watchful gaze of a predator, I made my way back down the mountain path to my village.

I went back the next morning. In her human form, Vesta greeted me at the entrance to the cave. I still couldn't believe I was working with a dragon. "Are you ready to get started?" I asked brightly, determined to be cheerful despite what I knew was waiting for us inside.

Vesta grimaced. "When I started to fly yesterday, I didn't want to come back."

"But you did. That matters. And it will get easier," I promised as we headed into the hoard.

"Will it?" Vesta asked softly as we took in the scene. Despite hours of work the day before, we'd barely made a dent in all the chaos.

"Yes." My voice was firmer than my conviction.

We didn't find the book that morning, but we found other treasures: beautiful baskets from faraway lands, jewelry, a bronze sculpture depicting Seraphine in her dragon form, and other surprises from Seraphine's youthful adventures. The trouble was, they were buried by all the rest. A sword whose hilt was inlaid with rubies was under a pile of almanacs several decades out of date. And, even when the treasures weren't concealed, it was hard to appreciate them when faced with jars of preserves so old they'd turned black or the dried-out husk of yet another small animal who'd wandered in and never made it back out. The sheer scale of it all was overwhelming.

While Vesta flipped through a series of portraits, she sighed. "I did love her, you know. It's just that the waste of all this makes me somehow both angry and unbearably sad. Even though I've been here many times, I feel like I've never *seen* it before. My family's cave is almost exactly like this one. It got that way so slowly I didn't notice. But they're adding to it every year. As I go through all this, I just keep thinking of how I'm going to have to do it again in a few decades. This is hard enough. When they go, it won't just be someone else's memories I'll have to sort through…it will be my own."

"Maybe," I conceded. "But that hasn't happened yet. Right now, all you have to do is deal with this." I looked down at the small sack of coins I'd found buried behind aging ingredients in the pantry. "Speaking of dealing with all this, can I call in my team now?"

Vesta nodded.

It really did get easier after that. The next day, Dusty and I led the way for three other donkey carts. My colleagues' eyes all widened when they saw the hoard, but they were too professional to say anything. Lola and Adele were on trash duty while Millie and

James set off for the market with the saleable items.

The original week Vesta had contracted Magi-Clean was rene-gotiated for a month, thanks to the sale of a filigreed set of armor Seraphine had taken from a knight she'd fought in her youth…or possibly seduced, it was unclear from the accompanying painting. Vesta looked ill at the thought and quickly agreed to the sale.

It took almost the full month to find the book. I was the one who found it; not that I knew it at first. All I realized was that I'd located an ornate chest at the bottom of a cabinet full of old toys. "Vesta? Can you come here?" I called.

The words had barely left my lips when she appeared at my elbow. She reached past me and broke the lock with one hand. Then it opened. Inside was a book bound in vellum entitled *A History of Dragons*. With shaking hands, Vesta turned to the first page, reveal-ing a vibrantly illuminated manuscript. Dragons soared around the words.

I stepped back to give her privacy when she reached a section with "Concerning Memory Dragons" at the top. She read silently. Then she closed the book.

After a moment, she looked up. "The author says our hoards kill us in the end."

"What do they know? That's not why Seraphine died." While a month before I might have been concerned we'd find a dragon skeleton in the mess, we'd almost completely cleared out the hoard by that point, save for a growing "keep" pile.

"Trouble is, I'm not sure the author was wrong. At a certain point, we stop living because of the hoard. You can't take it with you, but you can't leave it behind. It becomes too much. And, when it's like this, it's almost impossible to stop. Even when something Seraphine kept became useful again, she couldn't find it, so she'd get a new one. Then she'd keep that too. And so, it became a little worse. Eventually, holding onto all these old memories meant it was hard to go out and make any new ones. It feels like such a waste. And I'm a memory dragon too. I'm always going to want to hoard."

"You might. But the hoard doesn't have to win. And, if you ever feel like it is, you can come find me," I promised. Vesta laughed and gave me a hug.

When the month was up, I was standing next to Vesta in the main cavern. Crates with the treasures Vesta had wanted to keep were already on their way to her cave on the other end of the valley. The trash was gone. Everything else had been sold or given away. As I stood there, looking around the empty cavern, the wizard's apprentice I'd helped once upon a time packed up the enchanted candles.

Vesta walked me back out. As I took a step toward my colleagues and our donkey carts, the idea of leaving the cave made me feel surprisingly bereft.

"Could Lola and Adele take Dusty back for you?" Vesta said suddenly.

"Why?"

"I'd like to fly you down to the village as a thank you. I'd never have made it through this if not for you."

It sounded terrifying. I opened my mouth to say no, then closed it again. Seraphine's hoard had reminded me how important it was to live. "As long as you don't let me fall," I said, thinking of the sheer drop off the edge of the path.

Vesta grinned. "You're from Magi-Clean, but *I'm* actually magic. You'll be safe."

And, between one blink and the next, she was in her dragon form next to me. She lowered herself down so I could climb onto her shoulders and hold onto her neck. "I'll see you down in the village," I told my astonished colleagues.

Then Vesta and I soared off over the mountains. The cold wind whipped my hair back over my shoulders. From that height, fields looked like patches of a quilt. Houses resembled toys. She took her time, flying around until the sky was painted gold and red, a sunset prettier than any jewels I'd ever seen. I never wanted the flight to end.

But, as soon as I started to shiver from the cold, Vesta landed next to my village. She turned back into a human and gave me a warm hug. As she drew back, she pulled a silver dragon figurine from the pocket of her coat and pressed it into my hands. "I'd like you to have this."

"It's too much, I couldn't," I said, trying to give it back to her.

"Yes, you can. I couldn't have done this without you," Vesta insisted. Before I could protest again, she shifted back into her dragon form and flew off into the sunset. I looked down at the silver dragon in my hand, knowing I'd keep it forever. I was still thinking of how it had felt to fly as I walked back into the village.

I wasn't a dragon, but I knew I'd treasure that memory until the day I died.

~ * ~ * ~

When she isn't playing around in fictional worlds, **C.N. Wheaton** can often be found teaching science to semi-reluctant teens. Her short stories have recently appeared in the *Beach Shorts* anthology from Speculation Publications, *The Initialization of Briar Rose* anthology from Manawaker Studios, and the *Queens in Wonderland* anthology from No Bad Books Press.

You Are What You Keep

Renee Carter Hall

On the eve of the dragon Quill's hundredth birthday, the Elders paid a visit to his cave. They were dragons who measured their ages in eons, and very few ever saw them anymore. Quill was a little intimidated by all four of them showing up at once, and his first thought was that he must have broken some dragon law. Still, he prided himself on being hospitable, so he invited them in—thankful his cave was large enough to hold everyone—and brought out the nice tea service he'd been given once by a grateful princess.

"What is this?" Aureus asked, tapping the gold-rimmed cup with a claw.

"Tea," Quill replied.

"This is…a potion of some sort?"

"I suppose you could say that," Quill said. "It soothes and strengthens."

Aureus dipped his tongue into the hot liquid and jerked back, snorting through flared nostrils. His golden scales jingled faintly against each other as he moved, like coins tossed in a purse. Aureus' hoard had always been gold, and he had lived long enough now that every bit of him, snout to tail-tip, was gilded. If you looked closely at the round scales along his back, you could see ridged edges on some of them, along with various dates and the profiles of long-dead human rulers.

Another of the Elders, Bryne, had scales of pearl and abalone, and their horns curled like seashells. They ignored their tea and focused their iridescent eyes on Quill. "We are here because we're concerned about you, dragonling."

"About me? But why?"

"You are nearing one hundred," Sidabras, the next Elder, said. He was entirely silver, from shining claws to delicate filigree wings, his scales reflecting each other like mirrors. The other Elders privately thought him a bit foolish to choose a hoard that required so much polishing, but the work gave him a singular sense of accomplishment, and few human villages could keep silver polish in stock.

"It is, as you know, a crucial age for our kind." Aureus intoned. "A hatchling's hoard is…an amusement. A mere collection of curiosities. But we indulge that, for youth is the time to explore the vast and marvelous array of the world's human riches. But as time goes on, one is expected to…naturally gravitate toward a particular focus of worth."

Bryne nodded, their pearls clicking softly against each other as they curled their long, finned tail around their body. "I'm sure you remember our proverb: 'The dragon shapes the hoard; the hoard shapes the dragon.'"

"As true as ever it was," Aureus agreed.

Of course Quill remembered it. He remembered it from the egg. It was one of many proverbs dragon mothers crooned over the clutch, though these days it was usually phrased much more simply:

"You are what you keep," Quill said. "I know that. And I've made my choice already. I can show you."

He led the four Elders into his largest and driest cavern. He had put a great deal of work into the immense space, and this was the first time he had shown it to any of his kind.

The stone walls were lined with bookcases, some made out of elaborately carved wood and given as tribute from nearby kingdoms, others roughly built by villagers happy to hammer together a few planks of wood if it meant keeping their livestock safe for another year. Some shelves had even been carefully chiseled from the stone walls themselves, though these mainly held flickering candles and other magical sources of light.

And on those shelves was Quill's hoard, the human wealth he'd loved best since he first poked his snout from his egg: Books bound in leather, books bound in paper, books that were actually scrolls of intricate calligraphy, books of every shape and size, every subject and era. He had read many of them already, but he looked forward to a dragon's long life in hopes of someday reading them all. To one side, by a massive hearth, was a gift from the High King himself, a kind of low, armless chaise upholstered in crimson velvet with gold braid and tassels, where he could recline to read, and a matching stand of dark wood to hold his book. At the fireplace, a teakettle burbled softly over a low fire, adding a counterpoint to the quiet crackle of the flames.

Quill pulled himself up a little straighter. Surely this was a hoard of which any dragon could be proud.

A deep sigh came from the final Elder, the one who had not yet spoken. Faceta's hoard had been of precious gems, diamonds and rubies especially, and it was actually a little difficult to look directly at her in full sunlight, given how she glittered and sparkled with every breath. In the firelight, though, it was bearable, even if Quill secretly thought she looked like she'd been sea-bathing and gotten crusted with salt.

"Clearly," she said, "you do not understand. Did your clutch-mother not tell you what happens to our kind, when one reaches the end of one's long life?"

"Of course," Quill said. "We become what we've kept."

She nodded gravely. "We become monuments of enduring splendor. Our very bones sing of opulence and grandeur for generations yet unborn."

Quill had seen some of those monuments. Some were still dragon-shaped, though most had been so plundered by humans that little, if anything, of them remained. He wondered if some of Aureus' gold had once been part of another dragon.

Then he thought of all the songs and tales bound in the pages around him, all the characters he'd laughed and cried with and the impossible vistas he'd seen. It didn't seem like a terrible way to end up. "I appreciate your concern," he said finally. "In fact, I'm honored by it. And I'll think about everything you've said, I promise."

The four Elders lowered their heads as one. "That is all we ask," Aureus said, and he led the others out of the cave. When they were gone, Quill sighed with relief, and then he steeped a fresh pot of Darjeeling and settled in to read one of his favorites again.

~ * ~

It started, first, with his scales, how they became paler, smoother, drier, with watery streaks of handwriting and printed text that slowly darkened year by year. His wings grew larger and thinner, the color of parchment held to candlelight, and though he couldn't quite crane his neck enough to see, he thought they might even be watermarked. When he folded his wings, they made a papery rustle he found delightful.

Year by year, his library grew, expanding into a second cave and then a third. He traded gold and jewels from his hatchling days for rare volumes and more shelves, and always he felt he'd gotten the better bargain. The villagers' livestock had never been safer, though city scholars dreaded the plunder of—as they called him—the Bookwyrm, and for a while there were rumors of a bounty on his head at the largest university. Eventually, though, they realized he was actually *reading* the books—well, at least *most* of them—not eating them or setting them aflame, and as time went on, he often hosted visiting scholars who needed access to a particular work.

His claws grew flatter, softer, sharper. He found if he slit them carefully, he could use them as nibs, and it was much easier than trying to handle a pen. Encouraged by this and a little saddened by the lack of dragon-penned scholarship, he began writing himself, first transcribing dragon lore and customs, plus a few traditional egg-songs, and then branching out to a smattering of poetry.

Perhaps this was what attracted the Elders' attention again. They had no real power over him—a dragon was permitted to choose their own hoard, after all—but tradition held a great deal of weight among their kind, and they tried to use it to their advantage. When that had no effect, they reminded him of what awaited him.

"We want you to endure," Faceta explained, in a patient, motherly tone. "So many things of this world do not. All of this" —she swept a dazzling wing across the cavern— "will one day crumble into dust. It will melt away with rain. Touched by flame, it would burn to ash in moments. That is not what we wish for any of us. That is not what we wish for you."

"It's what *I* wish," Quill said firmly. He knew all they could see were the objects around him, stacks of paper, leather, thread, and glue. They knew nothing of what was inside and what those words could mean, what they could do. And though the Elders looked sorrowful—except for Aureus, who just looked annoyed—they accepted his choice, and they never came again.

By the time Aureus had become a magnificent golden statue perched in the snowy mountains, Quill himself had been transformed enough that he could have stood unmoving in a pile of papers and disappeared among the text. His back was the ridged leather spine of a book, complete with decorative gold leaf, and his scales were covered in manuscripts, some written in his own hand. A passage from one of his favorite stories was printed in full on his chest, and sometimes he touched the words and softly recited them from memory. The tea service was only for guests now; he had no need for food or drink anymore, though he found the occasional sip of ink a bracing treat.

He felt the last change coming for many seasons. He had thought the knowledge would make him feel hurried or cheated; there were so many books he still hadn't read, so much of his own perspective he hadn't yet put to paper. Instead, he found himself content to reread his old favorites one last time, and he savored each quiet evening he could spend talking with those who loved them too.

He had no idea what to expect. Faceta, he'd heard, had simply disintegrated into a glittering cascade of gems, with two particularly large rubies left behind that had been her eyes. At least one human had supposedly been killed over them, which he thought probably would have pleased her. Bryne had settled into the depths of the sea, where pirates longed for their riches but whispered of curses and shipwrecks. (Sidabras, it seemed, still lived, with only hints of tarnish in places that were hard to reach.)

In the end, it happened on an ordinary evening. Quill had a sense of a page being turned, a binding loosening, and the rustle of pages like a flock of fluttering wings. There was no pain, only a kind of dissolving, the way a drop of ink blossoms into a watery cloud. His books, at least, would remain, for others to read, to learn from, and to love. There was comfort in that.

But just as books were not merely paper and thread and ink, neither, it seemed, was Quill. A warmth like flame licked at his tail-tip and worked its way along his fading sense of his body, the way paper burns along its edge, and he felt himself laugh because it reminded him of a story. All the tales he'd read were not only part of his memory; they were what he was. The dragon shapes the hoard, and the hoard shapes the dragon, and Quill had become what he truly kept closest to his heart. In all his love of story, he had become Story itself.

He became inspiration. He became image and metaphor, symbol and song. As long as stories endured, so would he, long after the world's coins and gems had been scattered and spent. He became ink on a ribbon and pixels on a screen. Far beyond his caverns, in lands he'd never seen, tellers of stories brightened at their work and found just the right words. And among all those tales and all those tellers, in all the ages to come, there would always be stories of dragons.

~ * ~ * ~

Renee Carter Hall writes fantasy and science fiction for kids, teens, and adults. Her short fiction has appeared in numerous magazines and anthologies, including *Strange Horizons, Podcastle,* and *Androids and Dragons*, and her novels include the Cóyotl Award-winning young adult fantasy *Huntress*.

She lives in West Virginia with her husband, their cat, and more books than she will ever have time to read. Readers can find her online at www.reneecarterhall.com.

More Books from
WolfSinger Publications

The Dragon's Hoard 2 – edited by Carol Hightshoe

Welcome to realms where dragons reign, treasures abound, and every adventure leads to magic. Explore stories that spark the imagination and might just awaken the dragon within. Are you brave enough to face the dragon and claim your prize?

From the unyielding grip of ancient magics to the cunning of those who seek dragons, their treasure or both—each story weaves a rich tapestry of magic and lore.

Whether it's a battle for survival, the forging of an unlikely alliance, or a humorous twist on hoarding habits, our authors invite you to delve into realms where dragons not only hoard gold but also secrets, spells, and sometimes, even friendships. After all, in the world of dragons, not all treasures are silver and gold—some are stories waiting to be told.

The Hounds of Ardagh – Laura J Underwood

Ginny Ni Cooley never desired more than the simple life she had, living in Tamhasg Wood and using her magic to occasionally assist the folk of Conorscroft while putting up with the machinations of the ghost of her former mentor Manus MacGreeley. But her peace is shattered one night with the arrival of a lad who is fleeing a pack of red-gold hounds led by a hound-shaped demon known as Nidubh.

So much for peace and solitude. By rescuing Fafne MacArdagh, Ginny becomes wrapped in the fabric of an intrigue involving a family feud, a traitorous son, and a blood mage named Edain who is determined to keep her soul. It is she who cast a spell on Fafne's family and household and transformed the MacArdaghs into hounds.

Ginny gives Fafne her word to take him to Caer Keltora so they can report the matter to the Council of Mageborn. But Edain is determined to keep her secret and her soul intact and moves to thwart Ginny at every turn.

For Ginny Ni Cooley who has faced many bogies, dealing with

a demon, a bloodmage and the Dark Lord of Annwn will be no easy task. But she will do what she must to undo Edain's spells. If not, Manus' soul will become part of Arawn's Cauldron of Doom. Ginny will become a demon's feast, and poor Fafne will join the Hounds of Ardagh.

Wee Folk and Wise: A Fairies Anthology
– edited by Deby Fredericks

All over the world, fairy tales are told.
There are big fairies and little fairies.
Ugly fairies and pretty fairies.
Wise fairies and silly fairies.
Sweet fairies and scary fairies.

Seventeen authors share their own fantastic fairy tales in this magical collection. What kind of fairy will you meet here?

Infinity – Ted Pennella

In the distant future, when peace between humanity and the artificial intelligences their ancestors created has been settled, Conrad Conner tries to live a quiet and unassuming life in orbit about Jupiter on the city-station Socrates' Odyssey. When Conner's attempt to create a prototypical communication artificial for use by the Sol-Humana Confederation's Stellar Fleet gets derailed by the attempted murder of the very artificial he's created, his life spirals into a mad flight back to Earth to try and save at least his sister's children, if not his sister herself. Past failures and heartaches resurface as seemingly unconnected dots become a plot by the First Admiral to steal not just power over the Confederation, but a secret Conner holds within himself.

A secret not even Conner knows about.

Flatlanders - Mike Sherer

Young theoretical physicist Mickey Haiku has fallen into Eden's trap. She is a much smarter scientist who is intent on saving her own dimension by destroying his. Unbeknownst to either, beings from several yet higher dimensions have their own strategies. This sends the mixed-up pawns off on a wild odyssey through a dozen weird, twisted dimensions. As if this hyper-dimensional odyssey isn't challenging enough for Mickey, he has the additional difficulty of embarking on this whacko tour as a (pregnant!) female. Which means Eden is stuck in Mickey's body. The two are soon forced to cooperate since each holds the other's body hostage.

The strangest relationship this side of the 11th dimension develops between the two.

Fires of Rapiveshta: Book Three: A Familiar's Tale
– Verna Mckinnon

With Obsydia's chaos growing and more kingdoms falling under her control, Runa, Mellypip and their friends scramble to find a way to stop her from discarding her mortal form and claiming their world in the name of her Eternal Father Ahridum and plunging it into a never-ending age of darkness and evil.

The dragons of Rapiveshta are awakened from their long slumber by Obsydia's attempt to steal the egg that holds the unborn dragon who will become the next leader of the dragon clans. The egg is given to Runa's grandfather to protect it. When it hatches, Mellypip finds himself bonded to the baby dragon as her guardian.

As Obsydia reaches the climax of the ritual that will burn away her mortality, Runa, Opaline and Panthara find themselves captured to be used as sacrifices. Will the Gate of Souls claim Runa and Mellypip as the Winged Fey have foreseen? Or will the Fires of Rapiveshta and those chosen to be the Scions of Light be able to save them and their world.

Borne in the Blood – edited by Carol Hightshoe

Delve into the mysterious and powerful world of blood in "Borne in the Blood"

This collection of enthralling stories explores the multifaceted essence of blood—as a symbol of life, a medium of magic, and a bond of kinship. From the chilling tale of a minstrel haunted by a spectral king to the whimsical account of a vampire ice cream vendor, each story weaves a unique narrative around the theme of blood. Encounter a woman whose body bizarrely intertwines with metallic elements, and follow a girl's journey as she confronts her isolation due to her heritage. Feel chills as those who were wronged reach across the years to have their final revenge on the blood descendants of those who oppressed them.

Shifters, Vampires, Witches, and other ordinary and extraordinary folk—all bound together by that which they carry in their blood.

These tales will transport you through a spectrum of emotions, from the depths of fear to the heights of fantasy, as you unravel the mysteries and power that lie within the blood.

Proceeds from sales of Borne in the Blood will be donated to the Multiple Myeloma Research Foundation – themmrf.org/

Winter Emergence – Dana Bell

Kat has lived in the mountain her entire life. Going outside is allowed only to a select few, many of which never return, including her brother Ned. She doesn't want to believe he might be dead and tries every night to contact him via the coms. Silence is the only response.

Desperate to find an answer to his disappearance, Kat steals a snow cat and searches for her brother, putting the safety of everyone in jeopardy. She's joined by a cat who, for some reason, wants to come with her, and leaves once they reach the city, leaving her alone to face unknown challenges and threats for which she's not prepared.

In the city Word Warrior faces a new threat. A Striped One stalks the cats, wolves and snow ghosts killing any unfortunate enough to be caught as if they are rightful prey! He must find a way to stop the predator or all he has worked to accomplish might fail, forcing them to revert to the old laws of challenge and mate.

A new female appears bringing news of two legs, an enemy they all feared, who lived in a strange world where she had been forced to stay until she managed to escape. In fact, one was in the city and close by.

Faced with multiple threats, including worse snowstorms, Word Warrior faces the responsibility to protect their community from all dangers, knowing if he fails - they could all die.

Space Brides, LLC – edited by Dana Bell

Tired of those lonely dark nights? No one in your settlement suitable? We are here to help! We will help you find the bride or husband to keep you company, raise your children, and be your partner building a dream together. Contact us directly and give us your specifications. Success guaranteed.

In this collection of 15 testimonials read about the challenges and triumphs of some of our clients as they found love on the frontier of space.

From aliens to vampires, we brought these couples together and together they found acceptance and love—each in their own way.

A man with three kids finds an unexpected match in the brother of the woman he had contracted to marry when she runs away.

A woman running away from an abusive marriage finds acceptance and respect with a colony group that marries everyone to everyone in order to ensure they know they belong to a family.

A woman constantly rejected because of her skin color and origins finds acceptance and love with a wounded soldier.

Even though we encourage absolute honesty in your profile and correspondence with your potential spouse—many people don't. However, like some of the testimonials you'll read here; they still manage to expand their horizons—together.

Contact or walk into any of our offices 24/7. We are here to help you find that special someone and start a new future!

Other conditions apply.
Please ask for more information before contract is drawn up and signed.

The Dragon's Hoard – edited by Carol Hightshoe

Dragons are well known for their hoards—but not all hoards are created equal.

A young dragon starts his hoard with some very precious gifts.
One dragon shares her complaints about taxes with a friend as they wait for a lunch delivery.
Another dragon defends her most precious treasures against a

group of greedy goblins.

And yet another may hold the solution to saving the Earth after a devastating apocalypse in his collection of bottled treasures.

In addition to the normal gold, silver and jewels here you will find dragons who collect many different treasures. 25 storytellers invite you to enter *The Dragon's Hoard* and share the treasures within.

And more – check out our books at www.wolfsingerpubs.com

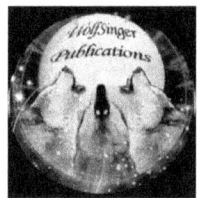

www.ingramcontent.com/pod-product-compliance
Lightning Source LLC
Chambersburg PA
CBHW070749280626
47162CB00018B/2815